11

good wishes at
Christmas time,

JEMIMA
Against the World

A romance in a time of war

by
David Shepherd

MEADOWSIDE PUBLICATIONS
DUNDEE
2014

Meadowside Publications
14 Albany Terrace, Dundee DD3 6HR

© Meadowside Publications 2014

Printed by
Robertson Printers
Forfar

ISBN: 978-0-9574915-1-9

Especially for

PATRICIA

The story is set in Bidworth and London
from September 1939 to August 1941.

1: The Unexpected Guest

(Mary's Story: September - November 1939)

One

For me, the story began on Friday 8th September - just five days after Mr Chamberlain declared war on Germany. It was about 9-00 in the morning and I was pouring the last drops of cream into my breakfast coffee, when the telephone rang.

It was Mrs Williams, a supremely irritating woman, who seemed to be involved in every facet of village life. In a rather breathless voice, she said: "I should like to take you up on your offer."

Not yet being fully awake, I tried to think what offer I could so foolishly have made. Had I promised a dozen jars of marmalade for the autumn fayre? Or to give a talk on 'Life at Cambridge' at the village institute?

I was not left in ignorance for long.

"You promised that if all else failed, you would take in one of these evacuees..."

At this point I woke up extremely quickly - and listened to Mrs Williams' tale of woe with an increasing sense of horror.

"You know, we've had these dreadful children billeted in the village. It's a frightful business. They've got such disgusting habits. They never seem to wash. I think we've got rid of the lice - but there's still the bed-wetting. And you can't understand a word they're saying." She paused in her tirade. "Well, Mrs Taylor's got a perfectly vicious little brute. There's no other word for it. She's always fighting with her two children. She spits. She swears. They're desperate to get rid of her. I believe she's already bitten another child down at the school. It's no use putting her with another family. I'm afraid her reputation's gone before her. No one else will have her. You're my last hope!"

It had been a casual conversation in the village shop about three weeks before. At that time, war had been no more than a cloud on the distant horizon but Mrs Williams was going on and on about the dangers of London being bombed ... hundreds of thousands being killed... and the need to offer the children a safe haven from the rain of fire which would surely descend the moment war was declared. Bidworth would be the ideal place, she said. No one would bomb Bidworth. The government had been sounding out the rural communities around London as to their willingness to take in evacuees; and Mrs Williams had appointed herself as chief spokesman for the village.

I had only been in Bidworth a few weeks and was living in a small rented house. John was away in foreign parts, deeply involved in a chess championship; and I was on my own.

Perhaps I was lonely. Or perhaps I felt a need to show I was not lacking in public spirit. Looking after a child seemed satisfying and vaguely maternal. But, in retrospect, I am sure it was more a way of getting away from Mrs Williams that prompted me to say: "Well, if you have any problems, let me know."

Like most people, I had no idea that war would be upon us so soon; that evacuated children would actually arrive in our village; or that I would be taken up on my rash offer. But in a few hectic days, all the sorrows of war had fallen upon us and I was being asked to take in one of these 'dreadful children'. And not even a nice one - polite and well-behaved; but as Mrs Williams had said: 'a vicious little brute' that spat and swore.

What could one say?

I wanted to say: 'No'. But Mrs Williams was such a

compelling personality that it was difficult to stop her in full flow. The words: 'patriotic duty' seemed to ring in my ears. To refuse would be selfish. What if the child was sent back to London and was killed in some savage air raid? Might one's selfishness end in interminable guilt?

I don't remember saying: 'Yes' but I do remember Mrs Williams thanking me profusely for my kindness; saying what a wonderful woman I was; and that she would be around with the 'wretched creature' at about 11.00am and could I give it lunch?

I drank my coffee very quickly and put away the paper. I looked at my small larder to see if there was anything that could be cooked in a hurry. There seemed to be eggs, sausages and potatoes - but little else. I would have to go to the shops.

I went upstairs to see what state the small bedroom was in at the back of the house. It was full of suitcases and heaps of books, which I had just dumped in there when we first arrived. It had been intended as John's study. What would he say when he got back? I cleared the books out into the passage and hunted through various cardboard boxes to find where the spare sheets and blankets had been packed. I opened the window to let in some fresh air - and made up the bed.

I gave the room a quick once-over, arranged a few ornaments on the mantelpiece and put my favourite teddy on the pillow. Although a bit battered and moth-eaten, he was an old friend. I hoped he would not be torn limb from limb. On second thoughts, I decided not to risk it - and moved him back to my own room.

Dusty, our blue roan cocker spaniel, followed me around wondering why our peaceful morning routine was being so thoroughly disrupted. I couldn't explain to him that we were expecting a guest - but I think he probably knew. He kept trailing me from room to room, getting in the way, till he was accidentally trodden on - and retreated downstairs out of harm's way.

The more I looked at the house, the more I realized what a mess it was in. I remember being terrified that Mrs Williams might come in and discover what sort of home-maker I was. She would then go round the village telling everyone I was a lazy midden and that the wretched 'vac' was getting no more than it deserved.

Up to that moment, I had rejoiced in the cachet of being a recent graduate of Cambridge University, a bit of a blue stocking; certainly a person to be looked up to. I could imagine my public persona taking a rapid plunge - and all because of this wretched child, who was bound to be a nuisance - constantly demanding to be fed and entertained. My life would no longer be my own.

To be sure I cursed as I swept through the house, cleaning out fireplaces, scrubbing the sides of the ancient bath, dusting every flat surface and lugging the vacuum cleaner up and down stairs to scour every threadbare carpet. Eventually the place looked passable.

Only when I was able to draw a breath did I remember to do something about my own personal appearance. I washed my hair and put on a bright and cheerful dress - dark-blue with white spots - with a pair of blue sandals.

Thinking Mrs Williams might want a cup of tea, I put on the kettle - and then realized I had completely run out of milk. That was why I had been using the last of the cream for my coffee.

I sighed.

The doorbell rang.

This was the moment of truth. I took a deep breath and went to the front door. I opened it with what I hoped was a warm and welcoming smile.

Mrs Williams occupied the whole front step. She was a large woman, wearing a thick green coat, a brown silk scarf and a pudding basin hat. Her smile was transparently insincere.

"Oh, Mrs Woodward," she gushed, "I simply can't tell you how good it is of you to help us out - and at such short notice. I can't tell you how grateful I am. Mrs Taylor too. She can't thank you enough. I hope you've had time to get things ready. I know it will be a terrible disruption in your life. But, after all, we are at war... and we all have to make sacrifices, I'm sure. If you need any clothes, the WVS will be able to help out. Don't hesitate to phone them. I'm sure they've got some left-overs from the last jumble sale."

Every word she uttered made me feel more uncomfortable. I could not doubt I was being passed some hideous burden; abandoned to some dreadful fate. But I could not see the object of all this misfortune. All I could see was the massive figure of Mrs Williams.

Eventually she ran out of words, grinned apologetically at my puzzled face and turned round to reveal a small figure who stood about eight feet behind her - completely eclipsed by her bulk.

"And this...," she said, waving a leather-gloved hand. "This is Shaw... Jemima Shaw."

Two

The small figure was wearing a curry-brown coat with a dark-brown velvet collar. On her feet were small blue rubber boots. Her legs seemed very thin. Her hair was lanky and unwashed. She had a look of profound indifference on her face.

As Mrs Williams spoke, she didn't bother to look my way. Instead, very deliberately, she put her finger up her left nostril.

"Don't pick your nose in front of Mrs Woodward!"

Mrs Williams turned back.

"I'm afraid she's got no manners. I did warn you. Of course you can't expect it from those sort of people. They've lived in slums all their lives. No idea how to behave with decent people."

Jemima was once again invisible.

Whether she was still picking her nose was uncertain.

Mrs Williams realized that her mission was now accomplished. She handed over a small cardboard suitcase.

"These are the rest of her things. Couple of pairs of knickers, some socks and a spare dress.... Mrs Taylor was going to put in a nightdress but she tore it up. Said she didn't like the colour! I ask you. A complete savage!"

Mrs Williams thrust the suitcase into my arms and turned to go.

"Now, Jemima! Remember to behave! Do everything that Mrs Woodward tells you and you won't get smacked."

With these few choice words of advice, Mrs Williams bustled down the garden path and out through the gate before I had any chance of changing my mind.

8

"She's gone," I said - mainly to say something.

But the child did not register any reaction. Her mouth was set in a hard thin line that expressed total resistance to any outside involvement.

I put down the suitcase, walked down the steps and reached out a hand to take hers. Very pointedly, she put both hands in her pockets. Not a very good start.

Undeterred, I said: "Would you like to see your room? It's got parrots - blue parrots - on the wallpaper."

Jemima looked at me with a contemptuous stare, as if to say: 'How could any intelligent person be expected to get excited about blue parrots? Or, in fact, any colour of parrot?'

"Well," I said, "you've got to sleep somewhere; and that's the only room we've got."

If I had not realized it before, I realized then how completely out of touch with children I was. For the last three years - in fact, for the last ten years - I had spoken almost continuously to adults - mostly in very high-powered conversations. There were no younger children in my family - nor in John's. I knew nothing about child psychology. But faced with such rigid intransigence, I was determined not to lose my temper. Not to be another Mrs Williams.

"Would you like something to eat?"

She shook her head.

I sat down on my heels so that I was at her level - and put my arm round her waist. I could feel the instant recoil of her small body as she tried to draw away from me. I held on to her, hoping she would not kick or bite.

I said very quietly: "I'm not like Mrs Taylor. There are no other children living here. Just you and me. If you go back to London, you might get bombed. That's what they're frightened of. Lots of people getting killed. They want you to be safe - out here in the country." I paused. "I know it's all very strange round here - but we've just got to make the best of it. I wasn't... expecting... to have anyone living with me, but when Mrs Williams phoned me this morning and asked if I would take you in, I said: 'Yes'."

I tried to catch her eye but she had her eyes firmly fixed on the hedge. (It was a very boring hedge.)

I said: "It would be very nice if we could be friends."

There was no response. But I felt that the little body was not as tense as it had been.

I tried to imagine what she must be thinking.

Stupid, stuck-up woman, trying to get round me. She wants me to talk - but I won't. I'll be as difficult as possible. I'll make her angry so she'll lose her temper. Then I can hate her - just like the rest of them. If I'm really bad, perhaps they'll send me home.

I looked at the turned-away head.

"Would you like to go back to London?"

She nodded slowly.

"I don't suppose this war'll go on for all that long. It's bound to come to an end one day - and then everybody'll be going home."

I felt a small tear drop on to my hand that was holding her. She put up her hand and rubbed her nose vigorously.

I gave her a squeeze.

"I'm feeling lonely too. My boyfriend's in South America. I'm hoping his boat won't be torpedoed on the way home. But if he doesn't come back, we'll just have to look after each other. Do the shopping... Take the dog for a walk..."

Her head turned suddenly.

"Have you a dog?"

It actually sounded like: 'Ha-u-a-dug?'

But I was pleased to get some reaction. She obviously preferred animals to human beings. The Taylors might have been more fortunate if they had had two dogs rather than two sons.

"Yes," I said. "He's called Dusty. He must be in the kitchen. I'll go and get him."

I got to my feet and walked into the house. I picked up her suitcase and carried it into the kitchen. As I opened the door, Dusty bolted down the passage and shot out into the garden - heading straight for Jemima. He gave her a tremendous welcome. He circled her about five times at great speed, then jumped up on her. Then he collapsed at her feet. Licked her knees. His cropped tail wagged furiously.

He was just a bundle of fur and a pair of bright black eyes. It was difficult not to love Dusty.

Within a few moments, the dog seemed to have broken the ice. She was laughing. She was down on her knees. Trying to hold on to him whilst he scampered round the garden. Together they rolled on the small lawn. Dusty kept barking with excitement.

I reflected that whilst John had been away, Dusty had had rather a raw deal. I was always glad to have him around. I took him for walks. But we didn't roll all over the floor together. I discouraged excitement.

But now, with Jemima, he seemed to have found a friend. The garden was full of sound and action. Jemima had taken off her coat and was throwing a canvas package which passed for a rat and Dusty was obligingly returning it - but growling furiously as she tried to take it from his mouth.

Whilst they were busily engaged, I opened the child's suitcase to see what it contained. As Mrs Williams had said, there were several clean pairs of socks and knickers, one yellow smocked dress - with a torn hem, and a pair of shoes. There was also a towel, a toothbrush, a cheap wooden hairbrush and a couple of photographs in a bakelite frame. One was a family portrait of herself with what must be her mother and a younger brother. On the right hand side, there was a more dashing photograph of a fair-haired young man. Her father?

I wondered what human drama lay behind those pictures. Was her father dead? Had he deserted his family? I thought about her mother, stuck in some dreary corner of London, without her children, waiting for the bombs to fall. Would she be worrying about them? Wondering who was looking after them? Perhaps she didn't even know where they were.

I made a mental note to ask Jemima if she could remember her home address. She must write to her mother and ask her to come and see her. That would set her mother's mind at rest. But perhaps she would not be able to afford the train fare? I would have to send her a postal order to cover the cost.

And where was the younger brother?

According to the BBC, brothers and sisters were being sent to the same area. Was he being properly looked after? Or would I eventually have two of them in the house? At the moment, one seemed quite enough - especially if she was as much of a troublemaker as Mrs Williams had said.

But, looking out into the garden, she seemed a different child. She was twirling round in her pink dress, throwing the 'rat' in all directions. She was laughing and shouting. I found it difficult to hear exactly what she was shouting but it seemed perfectly clear to Dusty with whom she had established an immediate rapport. She was his mistress; he was her slave.

I took her belongings up to her room and laid her few possessions in the top drawer of the dressing table. I hung the dress in the wardrobe - one item on a single hanger. (I would have to go and buy her a lot more clothes.) I stood the photograph frame on her bedside table underneath the lamp. Relenting, I went through to my own room and brought back the teddy bear. I tucked him under the top sheet with just his beady eyes and his black nose peeping out. It was an act of faith.

I went downstairs and cut up the potatoes for chips. As I got the plates and glasses out of the cupboard, I gathered that the fun and games on the front lawn had now come to an end. Jemima and Dusty were storming through the hall passage, breathless and barking.

Jemima had at last had the courage to enter the house. She had found her way to the kitchen. Small, resolute, with the most direct and piercing grey eyes, she looked at me.

"Dusty's very thirsty. He wants a drink."

Three

It seemed that Dusty was not the only one who was thirsty. Whilst the dog was busy lapping up water under the attentive eye of his new mistress, I poured out an orange squash for Jemima and a gin and tonic for myself. Somewhat irresponsibly, I added a couple of splashes of gin to the orange squash - just to see what would happen.

Jemima gulped it down - and asked for a second glass. Even more irresponsibly, I added some more gin, hoping it might loosen her tongue.

Rather like the operation on the mute wife in Anatole France's famous short story, the spiking of the orange juice proved almost unbearably successful. The flood gates were opened. Jemima chattered away nineteen to the dozen - her eyes sparkling with great animation.

But as Mrs Williams had said, it was very difficult to understand what the little girl was saying. I heard the words 'Ma', 'Pitch' and 'Josh'. It was a story about someone's dog which had escaped and done great damage, which she found hilariously funny and which she was sure I would find equally amusing. I tried to look as if I was taking it all in - which I suppose I was in part - though the detail escaped me.

As she spoke, she fell over her words and repeated herself. I wondered if it was the gin. I kept asking her to go slower and to speak more clearly. She looked at me very critically: "Ar-u-deff?"

"No," I said, "I'm not 'deff' but we come from different parts of the country where people speak in local accents. You come from London; I come from Hastings. We've got to learn to understand each other.

"Dusty 'stands what I tell 'im!"

"Good for Dusty!" I said. "But he doesn't have to answer back."

By the time, I'd made my explanation for the third time, Jemima seemed to understand that people who were 'deff' didn't need to be shouted at. She proceeded to speak more slowly and precisely, but even then it was still difficult to take it all in.

Suddenly she said: "Where's the bog?"

"Upstairs. Beside your room. The room with the parrots."

I smiled.

She stomped out of the room, closely followed by Dusty.

I plunged the chips into the hot fat and lit up the grill.

The ice had certainly been broken - but it was not going to be easy for either of us. My speech was as much a problem to her as hers was to me. I resolved to let her do most of the talking.

I heard the toilet flush upstairs and hoped that she had not made a mess on the floor. It would be hell coping with someone who was not toilet-trained. I would have to be very strict.

She did not come downstairs for a while. I imagine she was inspecting her room - and the parrots. I hoped she would appreciate my bear. Eventually I heard child and dog pounding down the stairs.

I shovelled a heap of golden chips on to her plate, adding three sausages and an egg. I put it down on the table.

"Don't try and eat it too quickly," I said. "You'll burn your tongue." I sprinkled her chips with salt and vinegar - and smiled. "Have another orange squash?"

This time I didn't put in any gin.

She gave Dusty a chip which he refused. I noticed she

ate her chips with her fingers.

She looked at me.

"Mrs Taylor din' give me chips."

"What did she give you?"

"Mince," She scowled. "And tatters."

I reflected that what she was eating was precisely the same - but served up in a more colourful and tasty fashion. Mashed potatoes could look extremely dull.

I decided not to urge her to use her knife and fork, but tried to lead by example.

Eventually Jemima picked up her fork, speared a sausage and bit into it in a thoughtful fashion.

I wondered if the gin was wearing off.

"Issat your bear?"

I nodded.

"Wasis name?"

"Well, I call him Mr Brown."

She looked at me.

"Why?"

"'Cos he's a brown bear."

"'Ow old isse?"

"About eighty-five years old."

For a moment she took me seriously, then she laughed.

"Garn!" she said, "'e told me 'e was same as me. Eight 'e said 'e was."

I smiled.

"Well, perhaps he is. What else did he tell you?"

She looked even more thoughtful - chewing her second sausage in an absent-minded way.

"'e sez 'e likes this 'ouse..." She looked at me. "And 'e likes parrats. 'e sez the food's OK - and 'e likes Dusty."

She looked at the dog which was now lying in an untidy heap beside the back door. As his name was mentioned, he opened one eye.

"Why did yer put 'im in my bed?"

"Just for company. I thought you might like him."

Jemima nodded slowly.

"I 'ed a bear - once"

"When?"

"When I came 'ere."

"What happened to him?"

Tears came into Jemima's eyes.

"Donny Taylor burnt 'im."

"Burnt your bear?"

"Put 'im on the stove. 'e did it 'liberately. Burnt a girt 'ole in 'is back. Smelt 'orrible." She ate her final sausage. "There was nuffin' I could do. 'e were finished." She sighed. "But I 'it 'im. I 'it 'im 'ard. Just where my Uncle Josh told me to 'it 'em. On 'is nose." She grinned at the pleasant memory. "'e were bleeding... all over 'is new shirt. Mrs Taylor went off ' er ' ed. She 'it 'im - then she 'it me. But I bit 'er tits. She din' like that! She screamed blue murder, she did. But she din' 'it me again." Her voice sounded triumphant. "'e deserved it, din' 'e?"

"I should think so," I said. "I should attack anyone who hurt my bear."

"I'll look after 'im," said Jemima, "'e'll be OK with me." She looked round the kitchen. "Do yer 'ave any hice cream? I like hice cream."

I was apologetic.

"I'm afraid there's no more food in the house. We've eaten the lot. We'll have to go into Aylesbury this afternoon and get some more..."

Jemima nodded understandingly.

It was just like being at home. Her mother standing in front of an empty cupboard and then sending her down the road for a penny's worth of chips and a couple of pickled onions. It seemed that even toffee-nosed folk could have the same problem. It was a great disappointment. One would have expected people like that to organize things better.

I sensed her disappointment.

"... We'll have an ice cream at a cafe in Aylesbury. I want to get you a couple of new dresses..."

"Mrs Williams sed..."

"I know what Mrs Williams said, but I'm not having you wearing somebody else's cast-offs. You're going to have your own clothes."

She didn't look as if she really believed me.

I looked at her with a teasing smile.

"I take it that you don't want a nightdress?"

She shook her head violently.

"I always wear pyjamas."

"You haven't got any in your luggage."

(It sounded better to say: 'luggage'.)

"They got torn. Mrs Taylor threw 'em in the bin."

"And how did they get torn?"

I scarcely needed to ask the question.

"Fightin'," she said. "I do a lot of fightin'."

I'm sure she expected a stern rebuke but, instead, I just shrugged my shoulders.

"When you find yourself at war," I said, "you have to fight. And lots of things get destroyed. Not just pyjamas. People, houses, aeroplanes, ships. Lots of things are going to be destroyed before this war's over. If they were all replaced as easily as a pair of pyjamas, there'd be no problem."

She nodded her head thoughtfully.

I hoped she understood what 1 was saying. But perhaps she was just anxious to get into town and get her 'hice cream.'

Four

After lunch, we set off for Aylesbury.

Dusty had been left behind to look after the house. Jemima was once again in her curry-coloured coat and her blue rubber boots. There was a grim look on her face - and she refused to take my hand. I could understand her feelings. Jemima *contra mundum*.

The bus stop was in the middle of the village. To reach it, we had to pass the Taylors' cottage and the village school. Fortunately, as we passed, there were no Taylors to be seen and all the schoolchildren were in class - as Jemima ought to have been.

As we took our place in the bus queue, a superior-looking woman in a dark-blue dress showed some sign of recognition. She took one look at Jemima and snorted with contempt:

"So you got her, did you? Mrs Williams must have been round half the village trying to palm her off on someone. I wish you luck."

My small companion gave the woman a glacial look - appallingly hostile for a child of that age.

I was so frightened Jemima might attack her that I immediately leapt to her defence.

"There are two sides to every story. I believe Mrs Taylor's sons treated her abominably. She was obliged to defend herself."

"These evacuees are all complete savages," said the woman. "I don't know why they bothered moving them. It wouldn't matter if such riff-raff got killed. Why they have to inflict them on us, I just don't know."

19

"Perhaps if you got to know them personally, you would like them more!"

The woman laughed sarcastically.

"When you've had that creature for a couple of days, you'll be begging Mrs Williams to take her back."

I began to feel my temper rising.

"You're just a stuck-up snob!" I said. "A self-righteous hypocrite! If people knew a bit more about your background, they'd probably find quite a few skeletons lurking around in your cupboards!"

The woman coloured - but said nothing.

I felt I had touched a raw nerve.

There did not seem any likelihood of the conversation being resumed. Fortunately, a few seconds later, the bus arrived. The snobbish woman climbed up the steps closely followed by the despised evacuee. I entered rather more slowly.

We sat near the back of the bus.

My small charge said nothing, but there was a slight smile - a mischevious smile - on her lips. I wondered what was amusing her but she wouldn't say.

The snobbish woman left the bus at the next village. As she got up, I realized that her elegant dress was split in two straight lines down the back and her pink knickers were strikingly visible. She made her way off the bus quite unaware of all she was revealing.

I looked at Jemima to see if she had noticed. She was smiling more broadly - and I realized with a shock that she might have been responsible for the snobbish lady's undoing.

"Did you do that?"

She grinned happily.

"How?"

"Razor blade."

She produced a Gillette blade from her coat pocket.

"Where did you get that?"

"Stole it from Mr Taylor!" she said proudly.

"That's dangerous! You could cut yourself."

Jemima looked unmoved and pocketted the blade.

"You'd better give it to me."

She shook her head.

I could scarcely believe that she had attacked the woman so viciously. It must have been whilst she was climbing the steps on to the bus. She had just slashed at her dress. It would perhaps be several hours before the woman realized what had happened. Would she connect it with the young evacuee? Surely not? The attack had been swift and silent.

I drew my breath at the audacity of her deed and looked at her reprovingly.

"This is a civilized country. You can't go round attacking people with razor blades."

Jemima looked quite unrepentant.

"She were askin' fer it. She were there the night wot we came. 'er an' that Williams woman. They were lookin' down their noses at us. She's a nasty piece of work. I swore as I'd get 'er."

I admired her determination but I couldn't let such behaviour pass.

"If you do things like that to people, you'll get locked up. They'll go to the police - and then we'll all be in trouble."

Jemima looked out of the bus window in a dreamy fashion.

"My Uncle Josh sez the bes' form of defence is attack. 'e sez you gotta 'it 'em back. You gotta 'it 'em 'ard. Jus' to show 'em." She giggled. "Jus1 wait till someone tells 'er she's showin' 'er bloomers. She'll go off 'er 'ed!"

21

It was an experience we sadly missed.

*   *   *

In Aylesbury, we went first of all to the large department store where I intended to kit Jemima out with some new clothes. I had hoped to get hold of the razor blade - but it was no longer in any of her pockets. I suspected that she had hidden it somewhere else.

I bought her two more dresses, a smarter coat, two pairs of pyjamas, a couple of plain jumpers and two skirts.

I let her choose the colour of her pyjamas and dresses - but I was careful to make sure she would be sensibly dressed when she went back to school. Hopefully, we should not have to fight about that.

Shoes were the most expensive item. Everyone was expecting clothes to be rationed - and prices had shot up. I was appalled at the price. I bought her a good pair of sandals to replace the blue rubber boots and then three pairs of shoes - in three different sizes - so that even if shoes were rationed, she would have something to grow into.

She stood in the shop quite mesmerized. First of all by the size of the store and the huge variety of clothes. She had never been in anything bigger than the local corner shop. When people had bought her clothes, they had simply guessed her size, brought the garment home and hoped.that it would fit. Mostly she had worn other people's hand-me-downs. It was a totally new experience for her to see someone buying clothes for her. She looked at me dipping into my purse.

She said rather breathlessly.

"Is it all fer me?"

"Of course," I said, putting my purse back into my handbag - and wondering what John would think of me spending all his money on this unknown and difficult child. "If you're staying with us, we've got to have you properly dressed. Then you'll be able to look down your nose at Mrs Williams!"

I knelt down and looked at her small, pale, elfin face.

"I hope you won't attack your own clothes with razor blades?"

"Coarse not!"

I put out my hand.

"Watcherwant?"

"You know."

There was a long silence.

Then she opened the palm of her left hand. I took the razor blade away.

"Thank you."

Jemima smiled an enigmatic smile.

She knew that I would be less grateful had I known that she had three other blades hidden away at home. She had no intention of facing a hostile world without some defence. But, she reflected, if she was better dressed - people might not be so nasty. Nice clothes might be a defence in themselves.

* * *

We moved on to the food shops - those that were still willing to deliver. I bought all those things that we could not get in the village. I ordered large quantities of things that would last - tinned fruit, tinned meat, large packets of rice and dried vegetables, jams and cereals. I obtained enough to keep us going for the next two months.

Then we made our way to the Kardomah Cafe where we had the long-promised ice creams - chocolate for her, strawberry for me. We returned to the bus station, each of us laden with bags and parcels. We counted the bags carefully to make sure we hadn't left anything behind. I reflected that if Jemima was minded to mount a second attack on some unsuspecting womaan, she would not have a spare hand to do so.

When we reached Bidworth, it was quite a struggle to get all our possessions back home. Arms got sore. Fingers tended to ache.

I noticed that as we passed the Williams' house and the Taylors' cottage, Jemima tended to walk more slowly. But as we drew near to home, she speeded up; anxious to see Dusty and - despite the ice creams - very hungry for tea.

We had macaroni cheese.

It didn't take long to make. The pasta was cooked in about ten minutes and Jemima was profitably occupied grating a large lump of Cheddar cheese. We mixed it all together and put it in the oven to brown. We sliced up a wholemeal loaf and covered it with lashings of farm butter. It was decided that the evening would be spent trying on the new clothes - but first, she must have a bath.

"There's nothing nicer than a hot bath!" I said.

But I could sense that she resented the suggestion. Whether it was because she was shy - unwilling to be seen naked in front of a complete stranger - unhappy to admit she was dirty - or whether it was because of some childhood trauma - I don't know. But the prospect of trying on all the new dresses proved an overpowering inducement to co-operate. She decided that having a bath was a small price to pay.

I filled the bath with hot water and stirred in some liquid shampoo which bubbled up into fleecy clouds of white foam which amazed her.

I helped her off with her clothes and coaxed her into the water. She was a bit frightened and, truth to tell, I was not surprised. She looked quite lost In the large old-fashioned bath. I was conscious of how thin she was - and how dirty. She needed a really good scrub.

I started on her neck and arms. Then I tackled her legs and feet. I don't know how long it had been since she had last had a bath, but her feet were encrusted with grime. I made sure I went between her toes. A nail brush helped. I tried to make a joke of it - claiming that she had lost a couple of toes. They must have fallen off. I asked her if she had left them in her blue rubber boots. I don't think she found my remarks particularly funny.

As I had previously noted, her hair was greasy and unkempt. Several dollops of shampoo were poured over it and I gave it a number of hot rinses. She held a face cloth over her eyes to avoid the soap running into them.

I had never washed a child before so perhaps I was a little rough. But the ingrained dirt certainly took some shifting and, after I had finished, her skin looked red rather than pink. Before she got out of the bath, I did her hair up in a turban and then wrapped her in a thick white bath towel.

"Look at the water!" I said.

Instead of the nice green colour with all the foamy clouds of white, it was now dull and grey.

She looked at the water without comment.

I pulled out the plug.

"Now you're lovely and clean," I said, "let's go and put on some perfume. It'll cheer you up."

I had a bottle of Schiaparelli which John had given me. It was far too sophisticated for a child of eight, but I put a dab behind each ear and on her wrists.

"Gosh," she said, "it don' 'alf pong!"

Whether that was a compliment or not, I don't know.

We went downstairs beside the fire and I took off her

25

turban and dried her hair. It looked so much better now it was washed. A very pale golden brown. I got a pair of scissors and trimmed her hair so it was even.

We tried on the dresses first - with the new shoes. I put up a long mirror against the wall so that she could see what she looked like. If anything, she seemed slightly dazed. She said: "Is it me?"

"Of course it's you. That's what you look like when you're properly dressed."

Even the school outfit - white blouse, grey pullover and skirt looked smart. We tried on the new coat and the pyjamas. She walked up and down the room in her new shoes.

"Not too tight?"

"No. They're O.K."

I sat on my heels and watched her enjoying herself. She never actually said 'thank you' but she put her arms round my shoulders and gave me a big hug. I fancied there were tears in her eyes.

I sent her upstairs to put away all the clothes on hangers and into the drawers. I told her I would bring her up some milky cocoa and a biscuit.

She sat in bed, looking very smart in her pyjamas. I put a towel over them to prevent accidents and gave her the cocoa.

"Bedtime?" she asked.

"Yes," I said, "It's been a long day..."

(I might have added: "... for both of us.")

I read her one of the 'William' stories. I thought he might perhaps be her sort of hero. Certainly she had very little in common with Violet Elizabeth Bott.

I finished the story and waited till she had finished her drink. I took away her mug and made sure she had Mr Brown beside her to keep her company. She looked sleepy and I gave her a small kiss on her forehead.

"G'night," she said.

"Goodnight."

I went downstairs to tidy up, to have a large brandy and lock up for the night. The bath could wait till tomorrow.

Five

I suppose I must have been asleep for about an hour when the bedroom door squeaked open. All the doors in the house squeaked in one way or another. It was impossible to enter or leave any room silently. I had meant to get the hinges oiled.

Normally, whilst John was away, I slept with my bedroom door open - to allow Dusty to come and go. But, tonight, I had shut my door, perhaps subconsciously asserting my desire to be alone after what had been a most demanding day.

I woke with a shock.

There was someone in my room. Like a small ghost, Jemima was standing in the doorway, holding my bear in one hand, the door knob in the other. She looked frightened at the violence of my reaction.

"It's you!" I said - feeling relieved. "What's wrong?"

She spoke in a half whisper.

"Mr Brown was frit. 'e says 'e's not used to sleeping with a strange person."

I smiled.

"He's never complained before."

"'e says 'e allus sleeps with you."

"Most times," I said, "he sleeps on the floor."

But I got the gist of what she was saying. I pulled back the sheet and the cover.

"I think there's room for three of us."

Jemima climbed into my bed in her new pyjamas. At least she seemed dry. That had been my first fear.

"What woke you up?" I asked.

"Some animal.... a wild animal, outside my winder. A wolf, perhaps?"

"There are no wolves in England."

"It kep' makin' an 'orrible noise. I think there were two on 'em."

I listened.

An owl hooted in the distance.

"That were it!"

"It's an owl."

"Wasanowl?"

"It's a bird. Flat face, big eyes, furry body."

"Does it eat people?"

"No, just mice and things. Most people like them. They sit on the branches of a tree and talk to each other."

An owl hooted nearby.

"Thatsim!"

"I see what you mean. We'll have to give them a name. That could be Annabelle...."

We waited for the distant bird to reply.

"... and that were Joey!"

It seemed that the best way to diminish her fears was to personalize the birds. Make them seem like household pets. Suppress the harsh reality of nature red in tooth and claw. "Dusty doesn't seem to worry about them. He hasn't barked."

"Perhaps they's eaten 'im?"

A fourth visitor entered the bedroom.

"No. Here he is, still alive and kicking."

Dusty licked my outstretched hand and lay down on the floor beside my bed.

Jemima snuggled closer to me.

Obviously greater awareness of the owl kingdom was not going to make her return to her own room.

"You'll know who they are in future."

"I'll tell 'em not to be so noisy."

"They've probably been sitting on the same branch on the same tree for years. Didn't realize anyone was sleeping in that room. They're probably a bit lonely as well."

"You don' mind Mr Brown waking you up?"

"Not at all."

"'e was mos' 'sistent."

"I'm sure he was."

I put my arm round the little girl in a protective fashion. What a strange day! To suddenly find oneself lumbered with a slum child - so frightening in prospect; and yet much nicer than one had feared. Unknown in the morning; and yet sleeping curled up in one's bed just a few hours later. To start with, so hostile; and now, apparently, so trusting. I felt a little tearful, realizing just how lonely it must be to be an evacuee dumped amongst strange people. To be unwelcome. To be attacked. To lose one's bear. To be shifted around like an unwanted possession in a real-life game of Pass-the-Parcel. How reassuring it must be to crawl into some warm bed and feel a kind arm enfolding you.

It was strange; because I didn't think of myself as a motherly person. In fact, quite the opposite.

"Do you sleep with your Ma at home?" I asked quietly.

"I used to," she murmured,"but she says I'm a big girl now. I must sleep in my own bed."

I smiled - and squeezed the small, thin body.

"Well," I said, "you're not really a big girl yet." I looked at the teddy bear which she was still holding tight. "And, anyway, it was Mr Brown's idea."

She smiled contentedly.

"All 'is fault."

Two minutes later, she was fast asleep.

Six

Saturday morning, it rained. Not exactly a downpour, but quite enough to keep everyone indoors for the rest of the morning. As I made up breakfast for child and dog, I wondered how I could keep Jemima amused. We had no games - except chess. No cards. No snakes and ladders. No musical instrument. I had no idea whether she was a person who could knit or sew. (I was not particularly good at either.)

Eventually, I decided that some simple arithmetic might be worth trying. I remembered how my own father had taught me the basic arts of multiplication - the sums being multiplied getting larger and larger - both of us competing to see which of us could get the correct answer first. Something of that sort might appeal to Jemima. I would also be able to get some idea of her IQ.

So, after breakfast, I said: "Have you ever done fractions?"

She looked at me blankly.

"At school?" I said. "Halves and quarters?"

From her vacant expression, I gathered that fractions were something of a closed book.

I put a large sheet of paper on the kitchen table, a set of coloured pencils, a knife and a couple of apples.

I picked up one of the apples.

"One apple!" I said. "But if we cut it, we have two bits of apple. Two halves."

I put down the apple and wrote a figure one on the paper and then, underneath, a two.

"One apple - two halves. OK?"

Jemima nodded.

What was all this about?

"Suppose we cut the two bits of apple into two more bits? Four..."

"Quatters."

"Precisely. Four quatters. Which we write down like that one over four."

I cut the apple into four pieces.

I said: "We'll eat it when we've finished." I smiled reassuringly. "So two halves make..."

"One apple."

"And four quarters make..."

"One apple."

"Good. But what happens when you have half an apple and a quarter apple?"

"Three quatters."

"Correct. How do we write it down?"

We laboured over the written sheet till I was sure she had got the idea. Then we ate the apple and I peeled an orange. It had eight segments. I looked at Jemima.

"It gets more complicated."

We explored various combinations of halves, quarters and eighths - she doing most of the work. Then we ate the orange.

Finally, we tackled twelfths and sixteenths. At each success, I rewarded her with a couple of squares of chocolate. It seemed to help her powers of concentration - even if it ruined her teeth. Within a remarkably short space of time, we had mastered fractions.

We moved on to geometry - which seemed to me a logical extension of our efforts.

Using a plate, I drew a large circle.

"No more apples?" she asked.

"You can have another if you want."

"'elps me think."

I cut up another apple.

Then, with a ruler, I divided the circle into four sections with two straight lines meeting at right angles at the centre. She crunched her apple noisily but she seemed interested in what I was doing.

I handed her a plastic protractor.

"Wassat fer?"

"To measure the angles."

I showed her how each angle was 90° at the centre.

"Four nineties?"

With not too much help, she reached 360°.

Then I drew a square linking up the four points where the straight lines met the edge of the circle. Once again, we measured it. Each corner was 90°.

"Four nineties?"

"360°."

No hesitation this time.

Jemima seemed to enjoy discovering new facts.

I then drew her attention to the four triangles which had been created. I got her to measure the angles at the corners. 45°.

"Two 45 degrees?"

"Ninety?"

"So how many degrees in a triangle?"

With a little effort, we reached 180°.

"All triangles add up to 180°!"

Just to prove it, we drew all sorts of peculiar triangles and Jemima measured them. Give or take a degree, they all added up to 180°.

"Magic?"

"No, logic. The laws of mathematics."

I decided to baffle her a little further.

"You measure the width of the plate."

She measured it as ten inches.

"How long d'you think it is round the outside edge?"

"Dunno."

"Guess!"

"Twenty inches?"

I shook my head.

"Fifteen?"

"Miles out!"

"Thirty?"

"Much nearer. It's thirty-one and a half inches."

"'ow d'you know that?"

"Worked it out."

She looked disbelieving.

We got out a long piece of string and measured round the plate. It was exactly $31^1/_2$ inches.

"You measured it before breakfast!"

"I did no such thing!"

"You did! You did!"

I smiled.

"You choose any plate and I'll tell you how big it is. And I'll give you another piece of chocolate if I'm wrong."

Jemima raided the kichen cupboard and came out with a small plate - just six inches in diameter. She didn't want me to measure it. She said it wasn't fair.

"I'll still tell you how big it is."

"Garn!"

"Just under nineteen inches. 18.8."

The plate was laboriously measured.

No chocolate for Jemima.

She had to concede I was right.

I explained the joys of $2\pi r$ where 'r' was half the diameter and 'π' is twenty-two divided by seven.

Jemima seemed to be able to multiply easily enough but dividing a total by seven caused much sucking of the pencil and many false starts.

Plates and saucers of various sizes were got out of the cupboard to prove that the formula really worked. Eventually, she conceded that the laws of mathematics were sound.

"Coarse it's magic!" she said.

"Coarse it is!" I agreed. "But only if you don't know how to do it."

"Bet they don' know that at school!"

"Bet they don't."

We consumed another bar of chocolate between us. By the time we had finished, the sun was shining. It was time for a walk.

Seven

"How d'ja work aht them sums?"

"I do it in my head."

We were walking along the canal bank, squelching through the mud and wet grass. The rubber boots had come into their own. I was glad I had not put them in the bin as I had intended.

Dusty scampered on ahead, looking for rabbits. He had seen one and chased it for half a mile. He kept barking and wagging his tail. He seemed happy.

"But how d'ja do it?"

"I can count in my head without writing it down. You can do it if you try."

Jemima looked doubtful.

"Four times three?"

"Twelve."

"Twelve times seven?"

A bit of a pause. She wasn't good on her sevens.

"Ten times seven?"

"Seventy."

"Add seven - eleven times seven?"

"Seventy-seven."

"Add another seven."

"Eighty-four."

"Yes. Eighty four. You can do it. When you do it a lot, you can do it more quickly. What's nine times eight?"

We seemed to spend the whole afternoon doing sums. Even her seven times table began to improve. We also tried doing fractions. Once she caught me out:

"You're wrong!"

"No, it's eleven sixteenths."

"It's nine!"

"Yes, so it is."

She seemed proud of her victory.

"D'ju do sums all day?"

"I used to - when I was at University."

"Why?"

"Well, someone has to work things out. Lots of people haven't got time to work out the really big sums. Someone has to do it for them." Out of curiosity, I asked: "Who taught you?"

"Miss Baker."

Jemima's face clouded over.

"She does the sums on the blackboard and we write them down in our books."

It was her first sentence spoken in normal English. It took me by surprise.

"Is she still in London?"

"No. She's stayin' 'ere. With the vicar..."

"Oh?"

"... she doesn't like it - any more than us do. She's really unhappy. I think she cries a lot. People are so nasty to 'er."

"Who?"

Jemima's face turned hard.

"That Mrs Williams."

"She's nasty to everyone."

"She were nice to you."

"Well, that was because she wanted something. I don't like her. She's far too bossy."

"She's a right cunt!"

It was strange to hear such a crude Anglo-Saxon expression coming from a mere slip of a child. I wondered if I should rebuke her. Tell her such language was unacceptable in polite society. But who cared? She was right.

"Yes," I said. "She's a right cunt!"

Jemima smiled slyly.

"My Antie Jean told us I shouldn't use that word. She said it were bad."

"Well, sometimes we have to use bad words. They suit the person in a way no other words can do. Mrs Williams is a very nasty woman. It was only because she bullied me that I agreed to take you in. It was the last thing on my mind."

"No one in the village wanted us."

" I know. It's difficult adjusting suddenly to a large crowd of strangers..."

"Same 'ere."

"Yes. It's difficult for all of us."

She took my hand.

"But are you glad you got me?"

"Yes," I said honestly. "It's more fun than I expected. I didn't realize how lonely I was without John."

We continued to hold hands.

There was a long silence.

"Where did yer say he were?"

"Probably in the middle of the Atlantic at this moment," I said gloomily. "Surrounded by German submarines. He may have to swim." I looked at Jemima. "Can you swim?"

She shook her head.

"I tried once at the baths but Sylvie kep' puttin' me 'ed under the watter. She were a right..."

I stopped her.

"Once is enough!"

She laughed mischievously.

"I weren't goin' to say it."

She paused.

"I were too frit to go back."

That was another thing we could do.

"I'll teach you," I said. "Or John will. We'll go to the public baths in Aylesbury and get you started. It's not difficult. Like sums, once you get the idea, it's quite easy. Just like riding a bicycle..."

"I can't do that neither. And I ain't got a kozzi."

"A kozzi?"

"A swimmin' kozzi. I hed to borrow 'un."

"Oh, we can easily get you a kozzi. I'm sure that even with the war, no one'll be rationing kozzis."

"Has John got a kozzi?"

I laughed.

"I don't think he has. Bit nasty if the sharks go for him!"

Jemima laughed. It was the first time I had really seen her let herself go. She thought it was very funny. John swimming in the Atlantic - with no kozzi - pursued by sharks. I smiled. But like all good jokes, it had a bitter tinge. The possibility was all too real. How long would it be before I knew where he was? It must be at least a fortnight since he had left Buenos Aires. What was his ship? The *Alcantara*. I put up a quick prayer that he would get home safely.

But Jemima was still revelling in fantasy.

"D'yer think 'e might come 'ome with no clothes?"

I laughed.

"At least you'd know who it was."

"We'd go up to the station and watch for a man with no clothes!"

"He'd probably get arrested."

"Then we'd 'ave to go and visit 'im in clink?"

"Yes. But they might arrest you too."

"Me?"

"For cutting up a lady's dress with a razor blade."

Jemima quietly glowed. She was proud of her deed. "You gotta show 'em," she said.

"There are other ways."

"Garn!" she said. "You can't attack anyone with sums!"
I smiled thoughtfully.

I was thinking of a phone call I had received two nights before. Jemima's arrival had quite put it out of my mind. If John survived his journey across the Atlantic, there might be quite a lot of things mathematicians could do to hit back against the enemy. Something more subtle than razor blades. But something equally sly. The thought of what we might do cheered me up.

"We seem to have lost Dusty," I said. "I hope he hasn't got stuck down a rabbit hole!"

Eight

On Monday morning, I went to the school at 8.30am so that I might have a few words with Miss Baker before morning assembly.

She was a plain-faced woman in her mid-fifties. At a distance, she might have seemed younger; but close up, one could see all the lines and cracks which no amount of powder could camouflage.

"I wanted to see you about Jemima Shaw."

"What's she done to you?"

Her voice seemed resigned to more trouble.

"Nothing at all. She's staying with me."

"I thought she was staying with the Taylors."

"No. It didn't work out. I've had her since Friday..."

"... And you've had no trouble?"

I thought about the woman on the bus; but decided to say nothing about that.

"I've bought her some new clothes. We've gone for a few walks. And we've been doing some simple mathematics..."

Miss Baker raised her eyebrows.

"... fractions, multiplication and a little geometry."

Miss Baker registered more surprise.

"You are talking about Jemima Shaw?"

"I am."

"You must be a miracle worker! She's the terror of the classroom. I'm surprised you're able to teach her anything. Are you a teacher?"

"No. I've just graduated in applied maths from Cambridge."

A slight look of contempt appeared on Miss Baker's lips.

I knew what she was thinking. A blue stocking. Not someone dwelling in the real world.

"Well, good for you," she said. "You seem to have succeeded where we've failed. I must say I have a long experience of her behaviour and it's always been most disruptive. Both here and in London."

I looked at her.

"I know you haven't got much time. But I would like to know a little more about her background. Why does she have this reputation for violence? And what can I do to help her be more civilized?"

Miss Baker smiled a sad but superior smile.

"It'd take longer than five minutes to answer either of those questions, but I can give you a brief outline. Her mother's a lazy bitch who never bothers about her. She gets fed by various friends and relations. She spends most of her time on the streets. And then she brings the law of the jungle into the classroom.

"Her father is in jail for murder. I'm not sure whether he and her mother are married. Probably not. But I think she gets her bad blood from him. She was told he'd gone to Australia; but other people have told her the truth. I think she glories in it. If you've survived a weekend, I would say you were lucky."

"It was a bit difficult at first. She wouldn't speak. But we have a dog and she seems to get on with him. I got her kitted out with some new clothes on Friday and we've spent the weekend doing sums and going for walks. I just wondered if there were other things we might tackle."

Miss Baker looked as if there were an infinite number of things one could do to improve Jemima Shaw. Manners would be a good start. No more spitting, kicking or biting... Keeping her mouth shut during lessons; listening to what was being said; ceasing to radiate hatred and malice... She had long taken it for granted that the young street urchin would never change. She was going to be trouble wherever she went. If anything, since they had come to Bidworth, things had got worse. There was no restraint whatsoever.

Miss Baker did not know where to start.

"It's her behaviour that's the real problem."

"I've told her to behave."

The teacher looked amazed at my naivety.

"I don't think she'll listen to anyone. I'm sorry to disillusion you, but in my opinion, the child is a complete psychopath. She terrorizes the other children. She tries to terrorize me - but I meet force with force. Whenever I catch her doing anything wrong, I give her the belt. Sometimes it works..."

"She seems to like you."

Miss Baker laughed coldly.

"I very much doubt it. You should see the looks she gives me. My name is certainly on one of her bullets. If she had a knife in her hand, she'd use it without hesitation..."

(Again I thought of the razor blade episode.)

"...I dread to think what she'll be like when she grows up. If you can do anything to civilize her - anything at all - you'd make all our lives much happier. I tell you, it's no joy teaching a child that refuses to learn."

I didn't want to contradict her.

"Well, she's spent most of the weekend learning new things. If she's interested, I think she'll respond. I rewarded her with blocks of chocolate."

"Well, you won't be able to do that much longer. They say chocolate's going to be rationed."

"I'm just asking you to give her a chance. I think she's willing to turn over a new leaf."

The bell rang for morning assembly.

Miss Baker gladly seized the opportunity to turn away.

Her final words were far from encouraging:

"I'll believe it when I see it. But a leopard can't change its spots - not in a weekend - not for anyone."

Her attitude irritated me.

As I walked home from the school, I wondered whether Miss Baker was not herself part of the problem. If she didn't have any faith in her pupil, was that not in itself counter-productive? Conclusions had long since been drawn - on both sides. If she had met force with force, it was not surprising that Jemima should bring the laws of the jungle into the classroom. No doubt, like the lady at the bus stop, Jemima was biding her time and waiting for a chance to get even. Miss Baker's name was certainly written on some bullet.

And yet, when the child had had a chance to learn something, she had responded immediately. She had not listened for two minutes and then shown herself bored and gone off to play. She had entered into the spirit of the game. Stuck the course most of Saturday morning; and then we had gone on talking about it afterwards. We had done a lot more calculations - at Jemima's request. She had not been buttering me up - or doing it just because of the chocolate. (She knew we had eaten up our entire supply.) It had seemed to me that she was genuinely interested in discovering new things.

Like the clothes we had bought in Aylesbury, she was not used to being given new things. She was not used to people taking time to explain things to her - person to person. Her past life had been one long series of confrontations where you had to be tough to survive. It must be a relief not to be facing hostility and constant judgement. Perhaps, quite unconsciously, I had hit the right note - I, who knew absolutely nothing about children.

And yet, one had to remember that Miss Baker had

known her for much longer than I. Perhaps for two or three years. If her father had committed murder and if she was following in his footsteps, no doubt she could be dangerous. I already had proof of what she was capable of doing with a razor blade. I could imagine her still causing immense trouble in the village. The complaints would all come rolling back to me.

What would I say then? Whose side would I take?

Clearly, Miss Baker did not expect any improvement. She had only seen one side of Jemima. But I had seen her playing with Dusty; I had seen her trying on her new clothes; I had seen her laughing in the bath; snuggling into my bed; measuring plates, drawing pictures, washing up dishes, helping me prepare food. I did not doubt she was capable of great wickedness - but I also thought she had all the attributes of a normal child, providing she felt unthreatened and secure. Whether that could extend into the rest of her life remained to be seen.

I went home feeling that there was perhaps some hope. Not in London; but here. How much longer the evacuation would last was anyone's guess. But if she was here for a while, something might be done.

Nine

If I had hoped that the new clothes and the private tuition might have wrought a miraculous change in my evacuee, I was swiftly disillusioned.

She went off to school neat and tidy, but when she returned home, her shoes were badly scuffed, a button was missing from her blouse and there was blood on her skirt.

"I tried to wash it off," she said.

"Is it your blood?" I asked.

"Coarse not!" She looked horrified that I should even suggest such a thing.

I gathered that it belonged to a friend of Donny Taylor who had tried to attack her. She had grabbed his hair and jerked down his head whilst raising her knee. The resultant collision of knee and nose had caused Donny's friend to lose a lot of blood, some of which had found its way on to her skirt.

"But I've still got the button," she said proudly.

I sighed sadly, gave her a needle and thread and showed her how to sew on a button.

I asked her whether Miss Baker had said anything to her.

"No," she said.

Her denial did not ring true.

I waited to see whether she would be honest with me. Eventually, she looked me in the eye.

"She said as how she'd spoken to yer..."

"And?"

"She told the class: 'Hime told Shaw 'as turned over a new leaf. I think we'll believe it when we see it...' They all laughed. She said: 'Take it from me, Shaw, fine clothes do not a laidy make; you may 'ave bin scrubbed up, but you're still a little guttersnipe underneath…'"

I raised my eyebrows.

"Well, it's true, ain't it? When she gave us the belt, she said: 'Just because you're mixing with the hamadictally extinguished, don't think you can escape punishment…'"

I wanted to smile, but I was disappointed with Miss Baker. She had used my best efforts as a weapon against her pupil. I could almost see the sarcasm dripping off her tongue. The 'hamadictally extinguished' indeed! I must remember to tell John that.

Jemima watched my reaction carefully.

"I din' tell 'er us were doin' German."

I smiled then.

Some things were sacred.

"We don't need to tell her anything. We'll just surprise her by getting your sums right and doing your exercises correctly. Did you bring back your English book?"

Jemima nodded.

"I stuffed it up my jumper. Doreen saw me do it but she won't say nothing."

I said: "Well, let's have a bite of tea and then we'll see what you'll be doing next. Forewarned is forearmed!"

Jemima grinned.

"You bet!"

*　　*　　*

We took three steps forward and two steps back. Jemima's classwork improved and for the first time in her life, she began to score high marks. She was quite proud of this.

For a few more days, the battles continued in the playground and different articles of clothing came home torn and soiled. Running repairs were fairly constant. But within a fortnight, things began to improve. I asked her what had happened.

"They're frit!" she said. "Yella. They know we'll dish it out on 'em."

"So they've stopped attacking you?"

She nodded.

"'sides, I've not bin goin' into the playground so much."

"What've you been doing?" I asked suspiciously.

"Lookin' at 'em books. They've got the same 'uns as youse."

She indicated the ten volumes of Arthur Mee.

Books had become Jemima's latest discovery. After tea, she would stretch out on the sitting room floor and turn the pages - looking at flags, ships, butterflies. Things that took her fancy.

I think her interest was aroused that Monday night after Miss Baker had called her a little guttersnipe. We had done half an hour of English and another half hour of sums, and she was wandering round the sitting room, looking at the heaps of books piled in every corner.

"Mary?"

"Mm."

"Why d'you 'ave so many books?"

It was a perfectly understandable question. The place was full of them. We had not yet had time to get bookcases built.

I shrugged my shoulders.

"Well, John and I enjoy reading. We both buy lots of books. But it was only when we came to Bidworth that we realized how many we'd got."

"'ow many 'ave you got?"

"About a thousand."

"'ave you read 'em all?"

"No. Some of them are for reference." Another new word which she didn't understand. "There are some books which you only use when you want to know the facts. Such as how far it is to the moon..."

"'ow far is it?"

"About two hundred and forty thousand miles."

She absorbed the information.

I pointed to a box of books beside the sofa.

"Those are the books John used to read when he was a boy. Biggies. P.C. Westerman..."

Jemima moved over to the box and looked at the highly-coloured covers of the adventure stories. Next to them was a heap of children's encyclopedias.

I picked up one of them and opened it at random. 'Animals of the Empire.' I moved on. 'Electric bells... railway engines.' She enjoyed that. I had to answer numerous questions about how locomotives worked.

"It's like a kettle," I said. "It boils the water. And they use the steam to drive the pistons and make the wheels go round."

Fortunately, there was a superb cutaway drawing of a Great Western 'Hall' class engine.

"D'you see 'em round 'ere?"

"No."

"In Haylesbury?"

"No. All you see is dirty old tank engines. Those are the ones that pull the great expresses from London to Penzance."

"Where's Penzance?"

We turned to a map of England and discovered where Penzance was.

But mention of Aylesbury reminded me of my promise to take Jemima swimming. I was not sure whether the baths would still be open. So many things had been closed down because of the war - but some of them had then re-opened. Even the BBC had shut up shop. Most of its staff had been moved to Bristol and all the regular programmes had gone by the board. Instead, we had constant news bulletins and marathon performances by Sandy Macpherson on the organ. I made a mental note to phone Aylesbury and see if the baths would be open on Saturday morning.

Jemima did not seem all that keen.

"Yer won' duck me?"

"Of course I won't duck you. I want you to swim - not drown!"

But she still looked anxious. I think she was genuinely frightened of water and her previous experiences in London had not helped.

"We'll get you a kozzi," I promised.

The thought of new clothes cheered her up. I bought her a navy-blue costume and a blue rubber cap. But when we reached the poolside, she was less confident and hung back.

"We're going into the shallowest part of the pool," I said. "You can't possibly drown."

We were surrounded by a noisy crowd of children who were leaping into the water, making huge splashes. Others were roaming around wearing goggles. It was not the ideal place to teach a beginner.

I coaxed Jemima into the water.

"Now," I said, "you're going to float on your back. I'm going to put my arm under your neck. Just let yourself fall backwards.

She looked extremely doubtful.

"Just lean back. You won't even get your face wet."

She leant back. I supported her.

"Now let your legs float upwards."

"I'll drown."

"No you won't. Let them go."

Eventually, she had sufficient courage to lift her feet off the bottom. But the moment she felt herself going out of control, she began to thrash her arms.

"Lie still!" I said. "Lie still!"

Realizing that her head was still above the level of the water, she stopped struggling.

I said: "Put your hands down your sides. Float!"

Miraculously, she did. I gently steered her away from the other children to a quieter corner of the pool.

"See! You float. You don't sink. Now put your feet on the ground and stand up."

She was quite surprised to see how far we had come.

We spent another ten minutes getting her used to floating on her back without panicking.

"Now," I said, "the next step is to float the other way round. A little more difficult."

I made her take hold of the ledge with both hands. I held on to the back of her costume.

"Now," I said, "don't let go. But let your legs come up slowly."

It took her some time to lift both feet off the ground. There is always the sickening feeling that your body will sink; but I held her tight and her legs came up. Unfortunately, she let go of the ledge and a small wave washed over her.

"Try again!" I said. "But don't let go of the ledge."
After another four attempts, we had a successful lift-off, the legs floated up and she did not let go.

"Now kick your legs."

I was very pleased with her progress.

"Keep kicking - and hold on."

I let go of her costume and she went on kicking.

"O.K.," I said. "Put your feet down."

I felt that we had won at least two battles; she now had confidence and had discovered her ability to keep afloat. We practised the manoeuvre several more times.

Then I said: "We're going to move away from the ledge. I'm going to hang on to you. Bring your legs up... kick... keep kicking... Now paddle with your hands. Paddle..."

I walked down the pool, gradually releasing my hold on her costume. I didn't let go entirely.

"I think we're almost there."

We practised for another twenty minutes until she seemed able to do it herself. She was a quick learner and she had a look of grim determination on her face.

I said: "Right. You can swim. It's easy when you know how."

As we packed up our towels and our costumes, Jemima asked: "Is John a good swimmer?"

"Yes," I said. "He's a very powerful swimmer. He's won lots of competitions."

I hoped she wouldn't say anything more about ships sinking. I was beginning to feel quite anxious, having heard nothing for almost four weeks.

"When John comes back, will we all go swimming?"

"I expect so. He'll probably want you to jump off the diving board."

From the look on her face, it was clear that there were still some things she was scared of.

"Don't worry," I said. "By the time he comes back, you'll be a really good swimmer. You won't be frightened of anything."

As I combed her hair, she said:

"D'you think John'll like me?"

"I should think so. He likes brave people."

"D'you think I'm brave?"

"The bravest little girl I've ever met."

Jemima was not to know that my experience of children was almost nil. I had hardly spoken to one for years. But I felt she had just the sort of spirit which would appeal to John.

My words pleased her. There was a big smile and a quiet radiance about her. On the bus home, she snuggled close and I put my arm round her.

I heard her whispering to herself.

"What are you saying?"

Her eyes twinkled.

"'The bravest little girl in the world'."

It was probably the first compliment she had received. I smiled.

"Make sure you tell Mister Brown."

Ten

I suppose it was my fault. I should never have mentioned the word 'bicycle.' It opened the floodgates of expectation in Jemima's mind. It was apparently one of her most deep-seated and cherished ambitions 'to ride a bike.' Once I realized the genie I had released from the bottle, it was too late to back-pedal on my suggestion.

I pointed out that we hadn't got a bike. 'No matter,' she said. The Vicar's son had one and he was going away to prep school. He wouldn't be using it. Surely we could borrow it? Just for a week? Once she had learnt to ride, she would be satisfied.

I said that the bike might be too big for her. But no. She had already looked at it. It had a small frame. It would be ideal.

I decided that, unpleasant though it might be to have to approach the Vicar and ask a favour, it would perhaps be easier than enduring the constant demands of an over-eager child. Besides, I didn't think her demands were unreasonable.

I remembered how I had pestered my father to get me my first bike. The challenge of learning to keep one's balance - and the moment I achieved that miraculous state; only to crash into an apple tree a few seconds later, bruising both knees.

Yes, it was an appeal worth making.

On Monday morning, after delivering Jemima to the school, I called in at the vicarage on the way home. His housekeeper showed me into the front sitting room.

"He's across in the church, praying for peace. He does

that every morning at 9.00am. He'll be back in a few minutes.

I thanked her - and thought that his prayers were proving somewhat unsuccessful. Warsaw was now surrounded on all sides and it seemed that the Polish army would not survive much longer. After that, it would be our turn. Still, it was better to do something rather than nothing.

The Vicar bustled in.

He was quite a young man; people spoke well of him in the village.

"Mrs...?"

"Woodward."

"You're new to our little community?"

"I've been here since July."

"And your husband?"

"He's been in Argentina at the World Chess Championships. He's on his way home."

I twisted the gold band on my finger which passed for a wedding ring - and hoped it would not be too long before I wore the real thing.

"I don't think I've seen you in church?"

"Not yet," I said tactfully.

(It seemed better not to say I was a convinced atheist.)

"Now what's the problem?" he asked in a kindly manner.

"I have one of these evacuees..."

It might have been better if he had waited to hear the exact nature of my problem but instead he gave vent to his own feelings.

"Oh, yes. A terrible burden for us all. So uncouth! So uncivilized! So different from our own children. More like savages, some of them. I suppose we should be thankful we haven't got their mothers as well. That would make it completely intolerable." He shook his head sadly. "Let us hope they soon go home."

He looked at me pityingly.

"So you've bitten off more than you can chew? Is that the problem?"

"Not at all," I said defensively, sensing that from his point of view I was on the wrong side of the barricades. "I want to teach my evacuee to ride a bicycle. We haven't got one; but I'm told your son has a model with a small frame. I just wondered if I could borrow the bike for a couple of weeks so that I could teach her to ride?"

Up to this point, the Vicar had appeared quite genial and welcoming; but when he heard my request, he shook his head firmly.

"Quite out of the question," he said. "There's no telling what damage might be done."

"I would pay for any damage."

"No," he said, "it's not a question of money. When you lend things to people, they never come back in the same state. My son would never forgive me if I lent his bike out to some stranger. It was a birthday present from his godfather."

I waited for a few moments in the hope that he might change his mind. But no. He remained with an apologetic look on his face. I stood up.

"I'm sorry you were unable to help me; but thank you for taking the time to listen to me."

"Perhaps we shall see you in church on Sunday?"

I raised my eyebrows.

"I very much doubt it," I said. "And certainly not now. We're all giving up quite a lot to help these children. To make them welcome. To feed them. Entertain them. To stop them being ... 'savages'." I put a strong emphasis on the word: 'savages.' He had annoyed me. "The least you could have done is to have lent me the bike."

He bristled angrily.

"You're not the only one who's helping these people. I'm putting up their teacher, Miss Baker."

I gave him one of my most chilling looks.

"I'm sure you're being well paid for it!"

Though I had no doubt that I had achieved a moral victory in my conversation with the Vicar, it riled me for the rest of the day. When Jemima came home from school, I told her about my lack of success.

"Perhaps Miss Baker told 'im about us?"

"I don't think so. I didn't mention your name. He just didn't want anything to happen to his precious bike. It was a present from his godfather. But by the time he comes back from school, he'll probably have outgrown it. It'll probably lie in an outhouse gathering dust. No use to anyone."

Jemima seemed to take the news quite placidly.

"I'll ask around," I said. "I'll try and get one as soon as I can."

She took Dusty out for his evening's walk. I quite admired her for accepting the bad news so well. From that moment onwards, she never said a word about the bike.

Three days later, I began to see why.

She was back from taking the dog out and seemed a little hot and breathless. I was making the tea and talking to her over my shoulder as I put the chip basket into the fat. However, I was conscious of a certain reserve on her part.

I turned round.

"You've cut your knee."

She nodded.

"And bruised it."

I turned down the chip pan and reached for the red tin of Elastoplast.

"Have you been fighting again?"

She shook her head.

Then I noticed oil on one of her white ankle socks. I immediately realized what she had been up to.

"You've been riding a bike?"

She denied it at first.

"It's no use fooling me," I said. "I can see the oil on your sock."

I got a wet cloth and bathed her knee.

"It's all bruised. You must have had quite a bump."

She nodded.

"And whose bike was it?"

"I found it in a barn."

That seemed plausible.

I pulled the wings off the plaster and put it round her knee.

"Could have been worse," I said. "You might have needed stitches." I looked at her. "You certainly knock yourself about. And what was happening to Dusty whilst you were trying to ride the bike?"

"I tied 'im up. He were all right - he jus' kep' barkin'.'"

I decided that there was perhaps more to these long walks than met the eye.

"When did you find this bike?"

"Tuesday."

"You haven't managed to ride it yet?"

"No."

"I think it'd be better if I came with you. You might have more chance of doing it properly."

She did not look entirely enthusiastic about my involvement. Later that evening, I understood why.

At about eight o' clock, there was a knock at the front door. I opened it. A large, red-faced policeman was standing on my doorstep.

"Constable Bell, Bidworth police station, Ma'am. Are you Mrs Woodward?"

I nodded.

(I wasn't; but who cared?)

"I wonder if I might come in and discuss a certain matter with you?"

I took him into the sitting room.

My first thought was that John's ship had been torpedoed - and he was bringing me the grim news. I tried to appear as calm and brave as possible.

"I'll come straight to the point, Ma'am. You went to see the Vicar, Mr Jones, on Monday morning?"

"I did."

"And you asked him about the possibility of borrowing his son's bicycle?"

"Yes."

"You wanted to borrow it to teach one of these 'ere evacuees?"

I nodded.

I felt so relieved that his visit was not connected with John's death that I was more than willing to face any lesser disaster. By this point, I had already guessed the end of his story and was now feeling light-headed and rather amused.

"Well, I have to tell you, Ma'am, that this 'ere bicycle has been stolen from the said vicarage by person or persons unknown. I wonder if you can shed any light on this serious matter?"

I smiled politely.

"And who suggested to you that I might be your chief suspect? The Vicar? Did he accuse me of being a thief?"

From his obvious embarrassment, it was quite clear who had put the idea into his mind. But he struggled on bravely.

"We have to consider every possibility, Ma'am."

"Well, I can assure you that there is no bicycle hidden in this house. It is a very small house and it has a very small garden - so it won't take long to show you."

I escorted him through the kitchen and out into the back garden. I opened the shed, the coal hole; and I invited him to come upstairs and inspect the bedrooms; but he refused.

At least he had the grace to apologize.

Once he was gone, I immediately went upstairs to Jemima's bedroom. Mr Brown had just been put to bed and she was reading him a bedtime tale - closely watched by Dusty who was having some difficulty following the gist of the story.

I waited till she had stopped reading.

"That was a policeman!" I said ominously.

"Constable Bell?"

"You know him?"

"Everyone knows him. He's going out with Mrs Williams' niece."

"Is he?"

(There was food for thought.)

She looked a trifle shifty.

"What did 'e want?"

"He's searching for a bicycle which was stolen from the vicarage.

Jemima looked at Mr Brown as if he might have an answer. I was amused at her reaction but didn't show it.

"Is it at all possible," I said in the most roundabout way, "that the bicycle you 'found' in the barn was the bicycle that was stolen from the vicarage?"

Her first instinct was to lie.

"Corsit wasn't!"

"Would you like to take me to see this bicycle so that we might know for certain it is not stolen property? That you have not been involved in any criminal activity? Shall we take Dusty for an evening walk? I expect he will know where to go."

Jemima looked at me in a speculative fashion. How much should she admit? Would it pay to be honest? Could I be trusted to help her out of this mess? Or would she be handed over to the police and sent back to London? (A couple of weeks ago, she might have welcomed such an outcome; but now she was beginning to enjoy life in Bidworth. It would be very unpleasant to go home.)

There was a long silence which I did not interrupt. I sat down on the other side of the bed and waited whilst she weighed up the pros and cons of coming clean.

"I wanted to learn to ride," she said at last.

"Of course you did."

My positive reply gave her more confidence.

"I felt very angry about 'im refusin' to give us 'is bike."

"So did I."

"Well, I didn't mean to pinch it. I jus' went to 'ave a look at it. It was in 'is garden shed. Not locked up or anythin'. No one around, like. So I took it down 'is garden and into the wood. But when I came back, 'e were there. So I 'id it in the barn. I was goin' to tek it back."

"And when was this?"

"Tuesday night."

"I see. And where was Dusty?"

"'e were with me. 'e didn't say a wud. 'e didn't bark. 'e was very good." She looked at the dog with proud eyes. The dog thumped his small stub of a tail on the floor - pleased that his good behaviour was being praised.

"So for the last three nights, you've been trying to ride it? But not very successfully?"

"No. I keep fallin' off. One way or t'other."

I shook my head.

"I told you you needed someone to help you. You can't do it on your own. When I first learnt to ride, I hit an apple tree and did myself quite a bit of damage. You need someone to run alongside you and hold your saddle. I did promise that I'd teach you - but not on this bike."

She looked anxious.

"Wadowedo?"

"Well," I said, "the first thing we've got to do is to return the bike to the vicarage. We can't do it in broad daylight or we shall be arrested. We'll have to take it back in the middle of the night when everyone's asleep. About three o' clock, I should think."

"What if we get cort?"

"I don't intend to get 'cort'. We're going to do it very professionally. If you're going to commit a crime, you have to do it so well that no one even knows a crime has been committed."

Jemima looked instantly thoughtful.

I said to myself:

"That wasn't a very sensible thing to say. She'll get ideas."

Aloud, I said:

"And we'll leave them a small red herring just to put them off the scent."

*   *   *

So, at 3.00am on Friday morning, we both got up and dressed in our darkest clothes. We put Dusty on his lead. He seemed a bit surprised to be going out for a night-time stroll, but he didn't complain. We didn't put on any lights in case anyone was watching the house - and we crept out by the back door and escaped across the fields.

Jemima and Dusty showed me the way to the barn. There, by the light of a torch, I inspected the bicycle. It was almost brand-new. I could easily understand why the Vicar had been so reluctant to lend it.

Fortunately, it did not seem to have suffered any bumps or scratches. The handlebars were a little askew and one of the mudguards seemed to have come loose. I put it back into place with the help of a screwdriver and straightened up the handlebars. There were bits of earth and straw clogging the chain. I removed them. But everything else appeared to be in working order.

We went off along a back lane to the wood which abutted on to the vicarage garden. This was the dangerous part. We were out in the open, visibly in control of the bike - and there was nowhere to hide.

I told Dusty to warn us if he heard anyone coming - and he was very attentive. More than once, he stopped, lifted an anxious paw and then moved on. We watched his movements like a couple of hawks.

Then we were into the wood and standing on the edge of the vicarage lawn. A wide expanse of grass separated us from the garden shed. We did not want to rush over it. We waited for a full five minutes to make sure the coast was clear.

There were no lights on in the house - and there were no streetlights in Bidworth. Blackout was complete. There was no moon so it was extremely dark. But we had acquired night vision; however, we still listened for any tell-tale sounds.

"You stay here with Dusty," I whispered.

I moved slowly across the lawn, pushing the small bicycle. I was expecting at every second to be challenged. But, as I had hoped, most people were fast asleep at 3.00am. I opened the shed door, took one final look round the garden, manoeuvred the bike against the wall and was careful not to knock over any spades or forks. I then wiped the main frame to eliminate any finger prints and tied a small brown luggage label to the handlebars. With a sigh of relief, I slipped out of the shed and took off my gloves.

I stood and listened. All was still silent. The deed was done. I walked across the lawn as quietly as possible but I could hear Dusty give a low growl.

"Good dog!" I said. "But you don't need to growl at me."

We went back through the wood.

An owl hooted.

"Joey?"

"Probably waiting for Annabelle."

"He won't eat us?"

"No. He's probably eaten about twenty mice already. Suffering from acute indigestion."

She chuckled.

We returned home by a very circuitous route - completely by-passing the village. We reached home about an hour after the adventure began. We were feeling very pleased with ourselves. We locked the back door and put on the lights.

"Cocoa," I said. "I think we should both have another cup of cocoa. I'm sure all good burglars get a hot drink when they return home to their wives."

Jemima seemed to have enjoyed the outing. But I thought this was the moment to strike a note of authority. Whilst the milk was heating up, I said:

"This must never happen again! You mustn't steal things from people. Even if there is a war on, you must ask for things. If I can get them for you, I will. But if not, you'll just have to learn to be patient. You can't have everything in one go."

I spooned out the last of the week's sugar ration into our cups. For me, it was the only thing which made cocoa drinkable.

Jemima looked up.

"Did you leave 'em the red 'erring?"

I smiled.

"Of course I did."

In very childish writing, I had written a small note of thanks - 'from Donny Taylor.' It was a very irresponsible thing to have done, implicating a totally innocent person.

"But if you hear anything," I said, "and I'm sure you will, you mustn't show any reaction. Keep your mouth shut. Not the flicker of a muscle!" I gave her a conspiratorial hug. "Promise?"

She was happy to promise.

Revenge is sweet!.

*   *   *

Next day, various people were surprised.

First of all, the Vicar, going out to his garden shed for some slug pellets, discovered that he had not lost his son's bicycle after all. There it was - in perfect condition - almost as if it had never moved. The Vicar was tempted to believe he had imagined its disappearance. But there was the thank you note from Donny Taylor.

Constable Bell was also surprised. One of the few cases of theft to come his way had suddenly vanished into thin air. There had been no crime after all! Had he been more of a detective - or a psychologist, he might have noticed the all-too-visible connection between his visit to Mrs Woodward and the return of the bike. But the luggage label pointed him in a different direction (as it was meant to do) and Constable Bell was not one to pass up such an obvious clue.

Donny Taylor was surprised to be summoned to the headmaster's study. He knew nothing about the bicycle or the label, but as he denied it, his face went red and he looked extremely guilty. He was upbraided for stealing other people's property and told not to do it again. During the lunch break, Jemima quietly fed in the story of Donny's guilt - so that by the end of the afternoon, the whole school was talking about it.

When he got home, Donny had his ears boxed by his mother and his father took off his leather belt and gave him four powerful lashes on his bare backside for bringing shame and dishonour to the family.

The final surprise - for me - was a phone call from Lady Rowley at Bidworth Hall. She was an elderly lady in her eighties. It seemed that someone had told her about my need for a small bicycle for one of the evacuees. She had one belonging to her great grand-daughter which I could borrow. Would I like to come up to the Hall and collect it? I fancied that someone - most probably the Vicar - had experienced some guilty feelings and was trying to make amends.

Jemima and I went up to Bidworth Hall on Saturday morning, introduced ourselves to Lady Rowley who was very gracious and very charming. (Her son had been at Cambridge - a third, of course, but then he had been a rowing blue. Tout comprendre, tout s'excuse!)

Within three days, I had taught Jemima to ride.

Eleven

On Tuesday morning, John phoned to say that he had arrived safely in Southampton. He did not have much loose change so the call was a short one. Too short to tell him about the unexpected addition to our family. Before he was cut off, he managed to tell me that he would be arriving at Bidworth station just after 6.00pm.

We walked to the station - Jemima, Dusty and I making sure we arrived in good time. I think we got there about half past five. Jemima was in her pink dress and sandals. Her hair had been washed and with the Alice band, it looked neat and tidy.

Apart from wondering how my fiancé would react to this domestic intrusion, I wondered how Jemima would take to him. Would it be a question of 'two's company, three's a crowd?' Or would she try to play one off against the other? I hoped not. Everything had worked so well up to now; it would be a shame to spoil it.

We sat on the solitary platform seat, waiting for the train to appear. Very few trains stopped at Bidworth so the station was a peaceful spot. Swallows continued to swoop and soar. At least they had not been evacuated! The evening sunshine gave everything a warm, golden glow and there was a pleasant smell of newly-cut grass. It was difficult to imagine the country was at war.

At about six o' clock, things began to happen. The station master arrived on his bicycle. The ticket office was opened for business and a number of interesting brown paper parcels were deposited on the platform. Dusty wanted to go and inspect them, but was restrained. The station master came to ask us if we were travelling on the next train but we had to disappoint him. He stumped off down the platform and closed the level crossing gates. Strong bolts locked them into position. He pulled another lever and an old-fashioned signal moved into the 'down' position. It seemed that our long-expected train was not far away.

It was about ten minutes late - as such things usually are. We could hear it as it set off from the preceding station further down the line. The distant hoot; the slow, laboured chugging as it gathered pace; the uncomfortable screech of wheels as the carriages negotiated a sharp bend; the sudden drumming sound as it crossed an iron bridge; and then the furious pounding as it headed up the slight incline to Bidworth station. It emerged through the bridge in a cloud of smoke and there was a whistle of escaping air as the brakes went on and the little tank engine with its four dull red carriages clanked to a halt.

"Bidworth!" shouted the station master. "Bidworth!"

Five passengers got off the train but there was only one I was interested in. And there he was - waving to us from the third coach. I ran down the platform to give him a big hug. Then I helped him get out his suitcase and knapsack. He slammed the door and then gave me another long hug which swept me completely off my feet. I think I must have cried with relief. I do not normally shed tears but I remember him saying: "There's no need to cry." But those ten weeks had seemed an age especially when we had been used to seeing each other every day in Cambridge and the four weeks when we had been setting up house. I was so thankful to have him safely home.

Whistles sounded and the little train began to move.

The station master came up to take his ticket. He looked at the date stamp.

"Been away, sir?"

(He probably thought John was a spy.)

"South America."

"You'll be glad to get back to the wife."

John smiled.

"Still got the ring?"

"Still waiting!"

He laughed.

"Not for much longer. It's time we made a respectable woman out of you."

He looked past me at the small figure who was standing patiently in the background, holding Dusty tight on his lead.

"And who is this?"

Rather nervously, I said: "This is Jemima. She's an evacuee. She's come to live with us."

It seemed that another introduction was needed.

"Jemima," I said, "this is John, my fiancé."

John put out a brown hand and very seriously shook hands with Jemima. In the process, she let go of the dog lead; but there was no way Dusty was going to run away. Having waited so long, he kept leaping up and down, trying to lick John's face.

"Jemima and Dusty have become great friends."

"So I see."

He stood up.

To Jemima, he seemed tremendously tall. After all, he was well over six feet.

He looked down at the small girl.

"And how long have you and Mary been living together?"

Jemima was tongue-tied.

"About three weeks," I said. "And she's very fond of ice cream."

"Aren't we all? But can you still get it?"

We began to move down the platform.

"And where d'you come from, Jemima?"

"Lime'ouse."

"East London? And d'you like living in the country?"

Jemima shrugged her shoulders.

"It's all right. 'Cept for the people."

"And what's wrong with the people?"

I quickly intervened. "They've not been very nice to the evacuees. Some of the children persecute them. And the people who've taken them in are very quick to judge them. Culture shock on both sides."

As we left the station, Jemima looked up at John.

"And where're you from?"

"Me? I come from Guildford. Just outside London."

"No. Where've you come from today?"

"My boat landed in Southampton this morning. I've been in Argentina, playing chess..." He looked at me apologetically. "We did win most of our matches."

Jemima plodded at his side, flicking the dog lead and dictating to Dusty.

"What's chess?"

"Don't you know? Has Mary not taught you? It's the love of my life."

Jemima looked blank.

"It's a game," I said, "played with wooden pieces. Castles, knights, a couple of bishops, a king and a queen."

"I'll teach you," said John. "Then you can become an expert and beat everyone else."

This sounded a very good idea to Jemima. Perhaps the arrival of this strange man was not going to be so bad after all. She loosened her hold on Dusty's lead and, as he galloped off down the lane, following the scent of some elusive rabbit, she ran after him.

For me, it was wonderful to have John back - safe - just

walking side by side. Such a relief when one thought of what might have been. Now that he was back, the war did not seem to matter all that much.

We exchanged items of information. There was no order to our thoughts. Things just came out higgedly-piggedly. When I had asked him about his journey, about Argentina, about his health, about the rest of the team, he said to me:

"What's she like, this little stranger?"

I smiled.

"When she was first delivered to my door, I was told that she was an absolute terror. That she spat, swore, bit, fought like a tiger - all of which was probably true. But since she moved in, she's been improving. Dusty helped. She spends hours playing with him. When she first arrived, I could hardly understand a word she said - she had a terrible accent. But now, she's beginning to copy me. It's most amusing. Broad cockney - and then, shades of Girton! But she's a tough little creature. Stands up for herself." I told him about the snobbish lady at the bus stop and her pink knickers.

"Good grief! Razor blades!"

"And she bit another woman's breasts."

"Is she making a habit of it?"

"No. She's perfectly behaved with me. But I believe that at school she's regarded as a cross between Lucrezia Borgia and Attila the Hun. The other children are terrified of her. She has an incredibly hostile stare which turns them all to stone. Her reputation's gone before her."

"Is she capable of learning anything?"

"I've taught her to swim; and she's just about mastered the bicycle. We've been doing a lot of schoolwork together. Arithmetic, history, geography - that sort of thing. She seems to take in things quite quickly. If you teach her chess, you'll soon find out. But I have to say she's been quite good company. I didn't realize how lonely it would be without you. The weeks just dragged."

John smiled and hugged me closer.

"Well, it's good to be home. I began to wonder if I'd ever get back. If we'd stayed any longer, we might have been interned."

"Good job you weren't. Gordon's got a job for you. He was on the phone on Friday. Something very hush-hush. He wants you to phone him the moment you get back."

"I wonder what it is?"

"He didn't tell me; but apparently they need lots of mathematicians, chess players, German speakers, logicians... anyone who has a peculiar turn of mind..."

He laughed.

"They should have included you."

"As a matter of fact, they did. I'm part of the deal."

"When do we start?"

"I don't know. Gordon'll tell you. But let's have a few days of peace and quiet together. There's no rush. I've missed you so much."

John nodded.

"Me too. I was so worried about the submarines. We had several alarms. Had to zig-zag all over the place. I was so terrified of being torpedoed at night, I slept on deck."

"On deck?"

"Well, in one of the lifeboats. It seemed the safest place to be. And I've made it back home. I can tell you one thing - you won't catch me going back to sea again. If I'm going to die in this war, I'll die on dry land."

"Nothing's happened so far."

"Phoney war."

"Phoney?"

"That's what they're calling it in America. All that fuss and then nothing happens. I expect that when Adolf's cleaned up in Poland, they'll have another big conference - just like they did at Munich. There's no point in fighting. Everyone's going to suffer. Germans as much as ourselves."

"Did you meet any?"

"Germans? Yes. There were quite a few of them at the championships. Nice blokes. Got on well with them. They'll probably be interned. I don't think there was any boat to take them home."

We took it in turns to carry his suitcase. It was a warm, peaceful evening. I remember dog roses in the hedgerows; butterflies fluttering back and forth. The feeling that we were the only people alive on earth. And that nothing else really mattered.

By now we had caught up with Jemima and Dusty. The dog was completely exhausted and his tongue was hanging out. He was no longer scampering up and down the road. He plodded slowly and painfully down the dusty lane.

"'e needs a drink," said Jemima.

"We all need a drink," said John.

"And a game of chess!"

"Give me a chance!"

Twelve

John's return made an enormous difference to the life of the house. Now there were three of us, we felt like a proper family. After being away for almost three months, John felt a compelling desire to get things done - to dig up the garden; to paint the house; to build a new front gate; to buy us both bicycles so that we could all go on expeditions together.

"No use getting a car," he said. "They'll be cutting down on petrol rations. All inessential transport will have to be laid up for the duration. But if we all have bikes, we can go where we please."

It seemed a sensible idea to me. I was glad to let someone else take the decisions. John always sounded so sure of himself. He had talked me into renting the house in July and I had gone along with him. He had promised that we would be married by Christmas. Even before he had been back a week, he took me into Aylesbury and bought me a beautiful diamond engagement ring.

He was full of plans - full of energy. In the course of one morning, the wooden staircase was completely sanded down. In the afternoon, it received an undercoat. By bedtime, it was finished. He went along to the local builder and persuaded him to sell him a load of planks. Within a couple of days, he had knocked together three strong bookcases and all the untidy heaps of books were soon shelved.

John made it his responsibility to escort Jemima to and from school. He had quickly seen the wisdom of making sure there were no opportunities for fights outside the school gates. She was delivered to the door and collected at

3.30pm. Jemima seemed very much in awe of John. He was so tall, strong and forceful - and good-looking, that she felt quite proud to be seen trotting along at his side. Sometimes, he swung her up on to his broad shoulders and brought her home that way.

In the evenings, they were soon to be seen huddled over the chessboard which was inconveniently placed on the kitchen table. John started off with just the pawns - and there were some short, sharp battles. Then he concentrated on the back line, showing her how each piece moved. Predictably, the knight caused her the most trouble. It was difficult for her to comprehend the many angles of attack of which the knight was capable. Eventually, full scale combat was engaged. I watched Jemima struggling to master the moves and John trying to avoid pouncing on her obvious mistakes and checkmating her king long before she ever knew it was in danger.

I remembered John showing me similar indulgence when he had taught me to play in Cambridge. Like me, Jemima began her game with ruthless zeal, launching her most powerful pieces across the board towards the enemy camp; but whilst she was hammering John's rooks and bishops, he was quietly taking advantage of the gaps she had left in her rear defences - and suddenly her game was lost.

She tried hard. I give her that. She did not give up in the face of defeat. She gave John some nasty looks.. And she began to slow down her attack and pay more attention to her defences. The games became longer. Pots and pans steamed away on the stove waiting till some drawn-out marathon had ended. Sometimes I sat down beside her and suggested what moves to avoid. But John was equal to both of us. Playing chess certainly made Jemima think hard. I could see her weighing the pros and cons of each move. She was well and truly hooked.

John bought her her own wooden chess set. When he was not around, she challenged me to play instead. I was a more equal opponent - not having John's skills. With me, she had at least a chance of winning. But then John would come in and sit down beside her and together they would attempt to demolish me. I think she enjoyed that.

But I had learnt quite a lot over the years - and I was often able to use John's own tactics against him. I had also been reading the chess reports in the daily paper; and there were one or two good moves which I had picked up. So John didn't have it all his own way.

When Jemima wasn't playing chess, she was walking the dog - or reading - or eating. I taught her the rudiments of cooking. I tried to make sure that she didn't dominate our lives; she went to bed at a fixed time and I continued to read her a bedtime story.

Early in October, we went over to Bletchley to see Gordon Welchman who was responsible for cryptanalysis at Bletchley Park and had invited us to join him. Gordon had been my mathematics tutor at Sidney Sussex College in Cambridge. We had lunch at *The Shoulder of Mutton* inn in Old Bletchley and he outlined the problems he was facing.

For almost six years, the Poles had been breaking into the German codes. They had built replica Enigma machines and discovered the elaborate wiring circuits connecting the inner wheels. But as war approached, the Germans had introduced two extra wheels which made deciphering their messages infinitely more difficult. With their own country in danger of invasion, the Poles had shared with us all their secrets and given us a copy of the German machine.

With Poland defeated and divided, we were now on our own. We had various slips of paper containing coded messages - the longest being about two hundred words; but without some key or crib, they were quite incomprehensible.

In addition, we were aware that the Germans changed the settings of the wheels every twenty-four hours; so that, even if we were lucky enough to find the setting, a fresh challenge would face us every day.

Gordon was convinced we could break their codes; but for this purpose he needed mathematicians and people with a good grasp of the German language. In every message, there could be numbers, military titles, addresses, references to items of hardware such as tanks and aircraft, weather reports - even punctuation. If we could work out the presence and frequency of such words, it would greatly assist us in the decoding of the messages.

Fortunately, it was still early days - for the Germans as for us. Most of the military messages were still being sent by landline, but if the field of war expanded, then Enigma would become the primary form of communication for the German forces. Their staff were still learning the ropes - typing out proverbs and nursery rhymes for practice. We were a bit suprised - and deflated - when we discovered what they were doing. They made mistakes quite regularly and these also gave us vital clues.

We began to see what Gordon needed from us. It was challenging, but we should be in very good company. About thirty graduates and undergraduates were being recruited at that time and there would be many familiar faces gathered together in Hut 6. The pay would not be great - not more than five pounds a week - and probably less for a woman.

But it would be a vital job in a time of war. John would be in a reserved occupation and not be called up. We would have a grandstand view of the forthcoming conflict. And we were desperately needed. Gordon wanted us to start the very next day; which we did.

It didn't really seem like work - more like an extension of the common room system we had known in Cambridge.

People discussing problems; going away to work things out; coming back to argue a point; taking on board other people's discoveries.

It was more complicated than any game of chess. But, in this case, we were not trying to beat each other; we had a common enemy. Our aim was to beat the Germans at their own game. With fresh minds and a will to win, Gordon was convinced that we could crack it.

Thirteen

The news that the evacuees would be returning to London came almost as suddenly as the news of their arrival. On Sunday November 5th - a bonfire night without bonfires - the message was suddenly released. The children would be going home on Friday.

Considering the hostility with which the children were received, one would have thought that the village would have breathed a collective sigh of relief, put out the flags and cheered; but, instead, there was genuine regret. Bidworth had begun to feel it was doing something to help the war effort - but now its contribution would come to an end. So would the 8/6 billeting allowances. Bad news for the families and the local shops. The sweet shop, in particular, would suffer.

Mrs Williams proposed a farewell party in the village hall the night before their departure. Jellies and ice cream were still available and there was ample bunting and streamers left over from the Silver Jubilee celebrations.

There would be games, a speech by the Vicar and a packet of biscuits and sweets for every child. A bus would be provided to take them to the station and the Evacuation Committee would be on the platform to see them go.

Jemima came back from the school with a duplicated note in purple ink, thanking those of us who had looked after the children and giving us the times and details of their departure.

Jemima looked at me.

"Do I have to go?"

I looked at the letter again. It had come from the LCC - not a body to be trifled with.

"I don't think they'll let you stay. One class and one teacher were sent to Bidworth; one class and one teacher will return."

She sniffed.

"But I don't want to go back."

"I know."

"They can't make me."

"I'm afraid they can. Miss Baker would go to the police and then they'd come round and collect you."

Jemima changed her approach.

"But you don't want me to go."

"No. We'd be quite happy if you stayed."

"My mother doesn't want me."

I smiled sadly.

"At least you'll be able to see your little brother again."

"Him!"

One word said it all.

"Well," I said, more encouragingly, "you could always come back for the holidays. For Christmas - and in the summer..."

"Could I?"

"Of course. People often go away for holidays. You could come here."

For the first time since I had known her, Jemima was crying. Not in a big way. Solitary drops rolled down her cheeks. Dusty licked her hand.

I gave her a big hug.

There was really nothing one could say. I could imagine fairly exactly what was going through her mind. There was nothing to go back to. No love. No affection. No dog. Poor food. Poor clothes. Back to the slums.

For the past eight weeks, she had had a glimpse of a different world. It had taken her time to adjust to it, but it appealed to her - far more than life in London. To go back was a cruel fate.

I gave her a glass of orange squash.

But her mind was far away.

*   *   *

We went to the party at the village hall. Everyone seemed quite cheerful. There is nothing Londoners enjoy more than a party. The children let themselves go. There were songs. I remember: "Roll out barrel" being sung with great gusto.

I noticed that the Vicar made a bee line for me. My atheism seemed to attract him. He grinned cheerfully.

"Mrs Woodward - and Mr Woodward! I don't think I've met you before."

John smiled politely but did not offer him his hand.

"I hear that you took part in the International Chess championships in Argentina..."

John nodded.

"... I play chess myself..."

Surely he was not expecting John to play with him!

"... but obviously not as well as you."

John smiled a genial smile.

Mr Jones turned to me.

"I'm sure you'll be glad the 'vacs are going home. Be able to get a bit of peace at last."

"Not really," I said "We've quite enjoyed it."

"I hope Lady Rowley's bicycle came in useful?"

"It was a very kind gesture," I said. "It brought Jemima a lot of happiness. She learnt to ride and she's also explored quite a bit of the local countryside."

"You'll make sure it gets back to Lady Rowley?"

"I'm not in the habit of hanging on to other people's property."

It was meant to be a stinging rebuke but it seemed to run like water off a duck's back. He was extraordinarily thick-skinned.

John chose this moment to intervene. In his beautifully modulated voice, he said: "I'm sure it'll be a burden off your conscience."

"My conscience?"

"Accusing defenceless women of theft. Reporting them to the police. Not the sort of thing one expects from a man of the cloth. It was a rotten thing to do."

The Vicar's face went red.

"I thought...»

"You thought?" said John. "I don't think you've got a single intelligent thought in your head. You're just a bundle of prejudices. You hated all these children coming to the village. You never lifted a finger to help them. You wouldn't even lend them a bicycle. Now they're going, you're putting on a big act. Pretending you love them... Pretending you're sad to see them go... What d'you call a man like that?"

"A hypocrite," I said. "A complete hypocrite!"

Mr Jones turned on his heel and walked away.

"Is he always like that?"

"He always manages to say the wrong thing. It makes me so angry. I just wish I could puncture his balloon. Make him see how false he is."

I clenched and unclenched my fists several times.

Jemima emerged from the crowd.

"What were 'e sayin' to yer?"

"He was just causing trouble. John laid into him."

"Mary called him a hypocrite."

Jemima smiled - a secret smile.

"You know that jam they gave us?"

"Plum jam."

"Yea. Nobody liked it."

"Well?"

"I put some in 'is coat pocket. Both pockets!" she said proudly, "'e'll not forget this party."

"He'll be caught red-handed!" said John.

It was the sort of joke Jemima liked.

I turned to John.

"We speak - she acts!"

He laughed.

"It's the jam he'll remember. Poor man! I feel almost sorry for him."

*   *   *

Friday morning arrived - and the short trek to the village hall. Mrs Williams was much in evidence - ordering people around. Miss Baker, once more in full command, was ticking off the children on her list and making sure they all had their suitcases, gas masks and personal labels.

One of the things I noticed was how healthy the children were - and how much cleaner. Their faces, which had been pale and sallow, were now a healthy pink or brown. They were not as subdued as they had been. There was a lot of laughter. They were going home.

All the fears of bombing and destruction had proved groundless. Hitler had been exposed as a coward. There had even been a bomb attack on his life in the Bierkeller in Munich. In eight or nine weeks of war, there had been a few incidents involving submarines - but nothing serious. The Allies were safe behind the Maginot Line and British strength was increasing day by day. We were told so by the BBC. I think we all believed it.

Jemima stayed close to us - as if wishing to postpone the moment of separation for as long as possible.

There was not much to say. All that had to be said, had

been said. Now we were in that uncomfortable no man's land between 'what is' and 'what is to be.' A sort of limbo where one waits for the inevitable to happen. I had noticed that same spirit amongst sheep waiting outside a slaughterhouse. I had felt like shouting: 'Run away - whilst you have a chance!'

There was no point asking whether she had got this or that. She had everything that belonged to her - as well as one or two things I had added at the last minute. A couple of half crowns and a ten shilling note. A sheet of paper with our address printed in large capitals. I had wrapped up Mr Brown and put him into her suitcase. It would give her someone to cuddle at night.

Dusty stood beside us, his tongue lolling out. He could not understand why everyone was hanging around when we could all go and chase rabbits.

Eventually, the bus arrived. There was a strong smell of diesel fumes. There was much waving of arms as Miss Baker endeavoured to get everyone on to the bus in an orderly manner. Quietly, we exchanged hugs. Jemima set off across the road. Dusty wanted to go with her. John pulled him back. Another moment - and she was lost in the crowd.

We could not see her on the bus - but we waved until the ancient vehicle was out of sight. Then we walked home.

Neither of us said much.

We went into the house. John went into the kitchen to make us both a cup of coffee. I went upstairs and had a quiet weep in the bathroom. I washed my face, went into the bedroom to put on some make-up... and stopped.

There - tucked up under the top sheet - was Mr Brown! She had not taken him. She had put him back in my bed just before she left. I was surprised.

I was sure she would have taken him. Treasured him. Talked to him. It was strange that at the last minute she should have had a change of heart. It suggested a depth of feeling I had not expected. Mr Brown was mine! And in Bidworth, he would remain! There were some gifts too precious to be accepted - and my poor bear was one of them. John saw that I had been crying - but he wisely said nothing. We sat drinking our coffee; then got out our bikes and went back to work. It was Friday, November 10th.

My brief excursion into motherhood was over.

2: Unarmed Combat

(Jemima's Story: September - December 1939)

Fourteen

For me, the story started a little earlier.

At the end of the summer term, we were all given a letter to take home to our parents. The letter gave them the first hint that, in the event of war, children from our part of London would be immediately evacuated. The letter contained a list of items we would need to take with us - clothes, shoes, gas mask, etc.

The letter did not make much impact on us. I actually lost mine on the way home. My mother found out about the plans from a neighbour.

The possibility of evacuation seemed remote. Nobody was fighting anyone at that moment. The dictators appeared to be extending their empires without war. Having compromised and conceded territory for the past three years, it seemed unlikely that the Prime Minister would prove any more resilient if confronted again. Besides, it was too beautiful a summer to think about bombs and things like that.

All one cared about was shade - and something to drink.

The dusty streets were a sun trap; in the East End, at midday, the pavements were hot enough to fry an egg. The neighbourhood cat declined to be stalked; intelligent dogs refused to go for walks; hopscotch and skipping had lost their charm; it was too hot even to fight the gang at the other end of the street.

Who would want to attack us? With the constant testing of the ugly barrage balloons and the white con-trails of invisible fighters weaving their way across the city, it was generally felt that in attacking the capital of the great British Empire, even the clever Mr Hitler might be biting off more than he could chew.

But as people gathered round their wireless sets to hear the news, it seemed that war was steadily coming our way. Poland had been invaded. We had delivered an ultimatum. A stand was at last being made. But, as usual, too little, too late. Our ultimatum was ignored and it was feared that the moment war was declared, thousands of German aircraft would fly over and pulverize our great city.

No such excitements came our way but on the Monday morning, with our small suitcases packed, we were assembled in the school playground which was to be our departure point.

Our names were ticked off - several times. Labels were tied to our lapels. Gas masks were checked. Two by two we were lined up and marched off to a waiting bus which would take us to Euston station and destinations unknown. Our teachers went with us but they did not seem to know any more than we did. For all of us, it was a great adventure.

Many parents were weeping bitter tears, not knowing when or if they would ever see their children again. The bombing of Warsaw was fresh in everybody's minds; no one could afford to take any chances. The sight of their parents crying affected many children, but I was quite unmoved. My mother had not come down to the school to see us off. I had delivered my little brother to his teacher and now, freed from all responsibility, I was more than willing to go along with the crowd.

At the station, there was total chaos. Thousands of children were milling around, waiting to be directed to their trains. Teachers were trying to keep their charges together, but some children had to go to the toilets - and by the time they returned, it was by no means certain that their class would be still in the same place. Teachers were left behind to wait for stragglers; others were sent on ahead to find where they were supposed to be; platforms were packed; whistles kept blowing; tempers exploded; there were more tears.

After about an hour of chaos, we were assigned to a train on platform six. Our class was allocated three compartments - twelve to a compartment meant to hold eight. There were no corridors on the train, so no access to a toilet. I think it was the excitement and the novelty which helped us to survive the two hour journey out to Bidworth.

For me, it was a pleasant journey. I had never been out of London before and the sight of fields with cows and horses was a revelation. It was like visiting a foreign country for the first time.

We stopped at every station, depositing its quota of children. They streamed out of their compartments and on to the platform. Soon it was our turn. Bidworth station seemed to be in the middle of nowhere. The village was a mile down the road.

As the train chugged off down the line, we felt rather lonely. We seemed to have lost our last connection with civilization. Once again we were lined up two-by-two and our names ticked off by Miss Baker. She seemed thankful that we were all there.

We were kept waiting at the station for about fifteen minutes, expecting a 'welcome party' to arrive. Telephone calls were made. Apparently there had been some misunderstanding. The 'welcome party' was waiting for us in the village hall. There was no transport from the station. We walked. Clutching our cheap suitcases, we plodded down the road in hot sunshine.

We were hungry. We were thirsty. And we had already gained the impression that we were not wanted. This suspicion was quickly reinforced when we reached the first houses of the village. People came out to look at us - but there was no warmth in their eyes. To them, we were aliens... curiosities... objects of pity or derision. Some of the local children jeered at us. We were too weary to respond. With sinking hearts, we followed Miss Baker to the village hall.

At last we could put down our luggage. But there was no sign of any food or drink. The toilets were primitive. Word spread rapidly that there was no toilet paper. Complaints were made and one middle-aged lady was detailed to tear up sheets of old newspaper.

Mrs Williams was in charge. Supported by two very hostile-looking spinsters, she made it clear that the evacuees were a most unwelcome imposition on the village. Very few families were willing to put us up and before we were allocated to any family, a local nurse would examine us for lice. In the meantime, we must be patient and well-behaved. We must sit quietly and not make a noise. The boys would wait at one end of the hall, the girls at the other. The girls would be examined first.

To make sure she knew who everyone was, Mrs Williams conducted her own roll-call. She seized the list from Miss Baker and shouted out our names. Most of the children felt intimidated and replied in whispers. We were told to speak up. Gratuitous comments, guaranteed to make any child uncomfortable, interspersed her rollcall. "What an ugly child!" "You with the spotty face!" "Must be a Jew with a name like that!" Miss Baker's face reddened with shame that her pupils should be so cruelly treated. She tried to protest but was savagely cut down: "I have no intention of being lectured to by a slum teacher!"

I decided that the time had come to rebel. I was normally considered to be the chief troublemaker in the class. It seemed to be a good moment to live up to my reputation.

"Shaw?"

No reply.

"Shaw? Jemima Shaw? Is there anyone here with that name? A ridiculous name."

All the girls looked in my direction.

I looked in the same direction as them.

The girl at the extreme left of our group was Yvonne Black, who had already said: "Present."

Mrs Williams assumed that she was Shaw.

"Speak up child! Are you Shaw?"

"No, Miss."

"Don't lie to me!"

"I'm not lying. I'm Black."

Mrs Williams looked over the group.

"So where is Shaw?"

Miss Baker came to her rescue.

"The girl in the brown coat is Shaw."

Mrs Williams eyed me coldly.

"You didn't reply. Why not?"

As I shrugged my shoulders, she came forward.

"Causing trouble already, are we?" She sneered at me. "I'll make sure you get a really uncomfortable billet."

I was waiting for her. As she leant forward menacingly, I spat accurately in her face.

The other children cheered.

Mrs Williams wiped the spittle from her'cheek.

"You dirty little bitch! You're not fit to live among civilized people!"

She would have said more but Miss Baker intervened.

"The children have had a long journey. They're tired and hungry. You didn't provide them with transport from the station and you're keeping them away from their meal."

Mrs Williams turned on Miss Baker:

"Don't speak to me, you stuck-up hussy! You're in our

village now. We'll decide what happens to the children."

Miss Baker's cheeks flushed angrily. She did not like being humiliated in front of her class.

Fortunately, at that moment the district nurse arrived and Mrs Williams immediately became more co-operative.

One by one, we were examined for scabies, head lice or impetigo. I decided that there was no need to quarrel with the nurse. She was only doing her job. And the sooner we were inspected, the sooner we should be fed.

After the inspection, we were marched along to the local school where we were given soup, stew and mashed potatoes, jam roly-poly and custard. It was rather tasteless - but filling. After eating it, we all felt much better.

Then it was back to the village hall to meet the people with whom we would be billeted - those who would be collecting their 8/6 allowance at the Post Office each week.

Mrs Williams ignored me.

All the other girls were quickly placed but there was some haggling over the boys. People said they didn't want this one; they preferred that one. If they could have these good-looking children, they would take three; but if they were forced to take that one, they wouldn't have any at all. It was for all the world like a Roman slave market.

I watched the whole process of allocating billets. It struck me then as it does now, sixty years on, as completely disorganized and corrupt.

Eventually everyone had been allocated a place except me.

Miss Baker was still holding her list, ticking off our names. She kept giving me sidelong glances to see how I was coping.

I sat placidly on a bench looking at a picture on a nearby wall. It was a Silver Jubilee portrait of King George V and Queen Mary. I tried to shut my mind to what was going on.

Mrs Williams turned to Miss Baker.

"And you'll be staying with the vicar."

"Yes, I know that. But what's going to happen to Shaw?"

Mrs Williams looked in my direction.

"Well, I suppose we can't leave her out in the street. But she doesn't deserve to live with decent Christian people. Filthy little savage!"

I scowled at her.

"Don't make faces!" said Miss Baker. "Behave!"

I resumed my contemplation of the royal portrait.

"Haven't you got anything for her?"

"Well, there's Mrs Taylor. Normally I wouldn't dream of putting anyone there. She's a hopeless woman. No control over her own children. Her husband drinks - like a fish. They're complete misfits. But I've sent Miss Graham round to see if she could squeeze another in. They have a very small cottage, but I'm sure she'll do anything for the money. It's not really a suitable billet but for this little savage..." she looked at me coldly,"... for her, it's probably better than she deserves."

Mrs Williams fell silent.

Miss Baker said nothing.

I tried to pretend it was nothing to do with me.

Eventually Miss Graham returned. There was a whispered conversation in the corner. All three women looked in my direction. Mrs Taylor was obviously not a push-over.

She needed some persuading.

Mrs Williams left the hall. Mrs Taylor would not resist her!

Half-an-hour later, carrying my suitcase and my gasmask, I was billeted with the Taylors.

Fifteen

The moment I saw Mrs Taylor's two sons, I recognized them as having been the most vocal of the village children who had jeered at us as we entered Bidworth. Donny was the elder - aged ten; his brother, Patrick, was seven. They were united in their opposition to my coming to live at their house.

"We don't want a girl!"

"She smells!"

"Where's she going to sleep?"

"She's not coming into our room!"

They had a point. The Taylors' cottage was quite small. There was one living room, a kitchen and two bedrooms. Mr and Mrs Taylor occupied one room; the boys, the other. It seemed that Mrs Williams had arranged for a camp bed to be delivered later that afternoon - but at first sight, it seemed that I would have to share both the boys' room and their bed.

I was immediately on the defensive.

Mrs Taylor explained the proposed sleeping arrangements, but her sons kept shouting: "We don't want a girl!"

The younger boy pulled my hair.

I kicked him.

"Ma, she kicked me!"

Mrs Taylor looked at me reprovingly.

"If you're going to live here, you'll have to behave."

She took my suitcase and put it down on the kitchen table. The boys gathered round.

"Knickers! Knickers!" they yelled. "She wears knickers!"

"Put them down!" said Mrs Taylor.

But Donny did a dance round the room before he flung my blue knickers back on the table.

Greater torment was in store.

"She's got a bear!" said Patrick.

Donny immediately stuck his nose into my suitcase. He tried to grab Buster. Mrs Taylor pushed him away.

"Behave, you two!"

They ignored her.

At the first opportunity, Donny seized Buster and threw him across the room. I immediately went to his rescue. Donny pushed me sideways and I tripped over the fender and grazed my arm on the stone mantlepiece. I scrambled quickly to my feet. Patrick now had the bear.

"Throw it here!" shouted Donny.

As Patrick tried to throw it, I fell on him. He lifted his arm to protect himself. I bit his forearm hard and drew blood.

Patrick screamed.

I rescued Buster and held on to him.

"Ma, she's bitten me. I'm bleeding!"

Mrs Taylor looked at the wound. The clear evidence of teeth-marks and the trickle of blood. She wanted to rebuke me but it was clear I had been severely provoked. I sat in a corner holding Buster tight in my arms. I wasn't going to let him go.

Mrs Taylor ordered Donny to go out and play in the garden. Patrick was taken to the kitchen sink; there was a strong smell of disinfectant as his wound was bathed and bandaged.

Patrick was then sent out into the garden to join Donny, whilst Mrs Taylor unpacked the rest of my clothes and put them away in a drawer in her room.

"They're very rough," she said. "They take after their father."

I didn't want to part with Buster but she persuaded me that he would be safe on the top shelf of her wardrobe. I didn't have much confidence in her judgement. The two boys were peering through the bedroom window. They saw exactly where the bear had been hidden.

They made rude faces at me.

I put out my tongue.

"They're just showing off," said Mrs Taylor apologetically. "You'll get used to living here. They won't make any real trouble. Mr Taylor'll see to that."

I felt glad to think that there was some authority figure in the house and wondered how long it would be before he returned. Apparently he drove a lorry for the local council. He was normally home by 5.30pm and tea was at six.

Not too long to wait.

Mrs Taylor suggested that I should go for a walk round the village. She obviously wanted me out of the house to avoid any more trouble with the boys. I was happy to oblige. I wandered into the centre of the village. It was quite a small place with about two or three hundred houses. Nothing after London. There were eight shops including the post office: a butcher, a bakery, a wool shop, the village store, a dress shop, a licensed grocer and a sweet shop. I looked at all the colourful bottles of boiled sweets. Sadly, the shop was closed.

The doctor had a surgery with a well-polished brass plaque beside his door. There were two pubs: *The Fox and Hounds* and *The Woodman*. There was a garage with a solitary petrol pump and a blacksmith with a large forge, making some fencing for a local farmer. I stood and watched the blacksmith for quite some time.

The biggest house in the village was the vicarage. It stood beside the church. I did not venture through the lychgate. There seemed to be a lot of stone graves and yew trees. The church clock said five to four. The golden weather vane pointed east. A few clouds scudded across the watery blue sky.

To familiarize myself with Bidworth, I walked round the few streets and wandered out to the end of the village. The road headed out into unknown country. There were lots of trees, empty fields, ditches filled with water. I felt safer within the confines of the village even though I knew there were dangerous folk like Mrs Williams and Miss Graham lurking behind their net curtains.

I met Doreen, who had also been sent on a tour of the village. I didn't particularly like Doreen but for once we were thrown together by circumstances.

"What's yours like?" I asked.

"Seems OK. Huge bedroom. Very dark. She's got a cat. What's yours like?"

"Nasty," I said. "Two boys. They attacked me."

"Attacked you?"

She seemed surprised.

"I bit 'im."

"Quite right," said Doreen. "You stick up fer yerself."

"Don't worry," I said. "I will. They don' know what's comin' to 'em."

We wandered through the village again. I showed her the local blacksmith. She took me down a back lane to the nearest farm. We spent the rest of the afternoon, leaning over the wall of the pig-sty and watched the cows being brought in to be milked.

"It looks like milk," said Doreen.

"Don' be daft!" I said. "Yer get milk in bottles!"

I was reminded of my afternoon visit to the piggery when I had my first meal with the Taylors. It was mince and mashed potatoes, garnished with cabbage. What I noticed was that Mr Taylor and both boys approached their plates in much the same way that the pigs had approached their trough. Heads down, mouth open, shovelling it in. When their plates were empty, they raised their eyes with a greedy look to see if there was more to be had. A second helping was dished out and the human pigs dug in once more.

When I came back to the cottage after my tour of the village, I was careful to avoid Donny and Pat. They were in their bedroom, playing with a toy fort. I went into the kitchen and helped Mrs Taylor wash up the plates and mugs. She asked me a few questions but I didn't say much. I didn't want to get too friendly.

When Mr Taylor came in from work, he looked at me with some surprise.

"What's this then?"

"Mrs Williams has arranged for us to put up an evacuee."

Mr Taylor's brow darkened.

He was about to say: 'We're not putting up any of those damned kids!' But Mrs Taylor anticipated his reaction.

"We're being paid 8/6 a week for her."

At the mention of money, Mr Taylor's mouth loosened into a faint smile.

"Getting paid for it, are we? That'll be a help."

The prospect of a few more pints a week at *The Fox and Hounds* cheered him up.

"Have you got the money yet?"

"Collecting it at the post office tomorrow morning."

He laughed.

"Mind you don't spend it all right away!"

Mrs Taylor shook her head sadly.

"I know what you're thinking."

"I bet you do. Might as well get some benefits from this damned war!" He rolled up his sleeves and washed his dirty hands in the kitchen sink. "Covered all our 'eadlights, they have. Left us a mere slit of light. ' ow we're goin' to drive on a winter's night with that, I just don't know. Bloody dangerous, if you ask me!"

*   *   *

Once the meal was over, Mr Taylor sat for half an hour reading the evening paper. This was obviously a sacred moment which begged of no interruptions. Donny and Pat played quietly at his feet. I again helped Mrs Taylor with the washing up.

"'e's a great one for reading," she said proudly. "I allus said 'e should 'ave been a teacher. But 'is father sent 'im out to work before 'e 'ad a chance."

I looked through the open living room door. It seemed that Mr Taylor was an extremely slow reader - or perhaps he had to read the same paragraph two or three times before he understood what he was reading.

After his meditation was over, he stood up and stretched himself. "I think I'll go out for a breath of fresh air," he said. It appeared that he said exactly the same thing - at the same time - every night.

He looked down at the two boys.

"And don't cause your Ma no trouble. D'you 'ear me?"

He gave each of them a playful kick as he stepped over them; put on his cap and strode out into the night.

Once he was gone, Mrs Taylor took charge again.

"Now," she said, "'oo's 'aving a bath?"

Both boys declared themselves more than ready to do battle in the bathroom. Their eyes lit up with childish mischief.

"Bags she goes first!"

I eyed them coldly.

"Would you like a bath?" asked Mrs Taylor.

I shook my head.

"She's frit!" said Donny. "Frit of showing us 'er minge!"

Mrs Taylor walloped him.

"I told you not to use that word!"

Pat duly echoed his brother's taunt and was also walloped by his mother.

Mrs Taylor realized that there was no point in pursuing the point any further. She went off to fill up the bath. I was left with my two tormentors.

Without warning, Donny punched me in the eye. It was a nasty blow and left me dizzy for about half a minute.

Pat used the opportunity to tug at my hair.

It was not in my nature to take such an attack lying down. I grabbed the younger boy by the throat - my two thumbs thrust down on his gullet. I pressed hard.

He immediately let go of my hair.

Donny tried to pull me off his brother. I heard the ripping sound as he tore my dress. I lashed out with my heel. I think I caught him on the knee.

He screamed.

"Ma! She's killing Pat!"

I let go my victim. He sank to the floor. His eyes were bulging. His cheeks were purple. He could hardly breathe. I stood back and folded my arms.

Mrs Taylor rushed in to protect her son.

"What's goin' on? Leave 'im alone!"

She lashed out at me.

I ducked.

She pulled Pat to his feet.

"What were you doin' to 'er?"

"Nothing!"

Mrs Taylor caught sight of my torn dress.

"Din' I tell you to behave? You leave 'er alone!"

There was no more fight left in Pat. Very meekly, he followed his mother to the bathroom.

Donny turned back to me.

"You little turd!" he said. "You touch my brother again and I'll..."

I was ready for him. I had seen his father's pipe lying on the arm of the chair. I had picked it up in my left hand. As he opened his mouth, I swung my arm fast and rammed the pipe into his mouth - bowl foremost.

He was unable to say much more. All the blackened shreds of tobacco spewed out into his mouth. They must have tasted vile.

He first of all choked several times, spat out the muck on the carpet and went off into the kitchen to wash out his mouth. But it was difficult to get rid of the taste. Even twenty minutes later, he was still trying to spit out the final bits.

His mother noticed him spitting and belted him.

I moved rapidly to the bathroom and stayed in the background whilst the two boys washed themselves.

Mrs Taylor asked me if I would like to get into the dirty water.

I refused.

Mrs Taylor shrugged her shoulders.

"You can allus wash yourself in the kitchen. You've got a toothbrush. You can do your teeth."

Later, I stayed close to Mrs Taylor as she set up my camp bed in the living room - near the window. The boys kept well away. But before we finally went our separate ways, Donny uttered a final threat.

"Jus' wait till you get to school tomorrow. We'll finish you off! I'll get one of my gang to break your leg!"

It seemed that he was too big a coward to do it himself.

I crawled into my camp bed - which was small but cosy. I was not unprotected. I had picked up Mrs Taylor's sewing scissors. If either of them disturbed me, I would stab them.

After all that had happened that day, I was taking no chances.

Sixteen

On Tuesday morning, we met together in one of the smaller classrooms in Bidworth school. Old desks had been drawn out of retirement for our use. Many past pupils had engraved their names in the woodwork and their surfaces were deeply scored. The seats were predictably hard and uncomfortable. We were seated very close together. I sat near the back.

Miss Baker's eyes ranged over her class.

"Good morning, children."

"Good morning, Miss Baker."

She smiled a contented smile. Even though circumstances had dramatically changed, order and decorum were being maintained. She would make sure that the villagers realized that the children from London were as well-behaved and respectable as their own. They all looked clean and tidy.

"Are you all happy in your new homes?"

"Yes, Miss."

The replies were sufficiently thin and patchy to cause Miss Baker some anxiety.

"Are there any complaints?"

Several hands went up.

"Yes, Jane?"

"Please, Miss, the people isn't very friendly."

"In what way?"

"They don' speak to you nice. They shout at us."

"It's probably because they don't understand the London accent. Yes, Doddy?"

"It's very noisy, Miss."

"Noisy? In the country?"

"The animals, Miss. They make a terrible noise."

"What sort of animals, Doddy?"

"The cocks, Miss. They woke me up at five-o-clock. Then the ducks and cows. It were terrible."

"And where are you staying, Doddy?"

"Beside the farm, Miss."

"Well, I think one would expect a farm to be noisy. If it's too bad, Doddy, we will move you. I expect some of the other children would like to live closer to the farm."

Four hands instantly shot up - including mine.

"I thought so." She looked at me. "And you too, Shaw? Are you not happy with your digs?"

I shook my head.

"And why not?"

"They fight, Miss."

"I'm sure you'll find yourself completely at home, Shaw. It sounds just your cup of tea."

Everyone laughed at my expense.

Miss Baker decided that this was not the moment for the class to air all its grievances.

"Well," she said, "I'm sure there'll be quite a few difficulties still to be sorted out. But if there are, you must come to me and I will speak to the Evacuation Committee and try to put things right. Is that understood?"

"Yes, Miss."

Miss Baker turned to the blackboard and picked up a piece of chalk.

"This morning, we are going to start with a little geography. First of all, where is Bidworth? Where exactly are we...?"

*   *   *

After geography, came arithmetic. We were busy adding

up the cost of nine cakes at five pence each and transposing it into shillings and pence. Then it was rolls of linoleum at 4/6 a yard to cover a room nine feet square. It was not a subject I particularly enjoyed.

I made a half-hearted effort to discover the answers. I got the first one right - but before I had finished the second, Miss Baker was writing the answers up on the board. One or two swots in the front row got it right. The rest of us were as dim as a glow-worm's armpit.

Doddy, in particular, was completely out of his depth. He was a little simple and tended to dribble. Miss Baker often directed her sarcasm at Doddy, knowing there was no way he could answer back. Although the class normally joined in the laughter at Doddy's expense, there was nothing hateful or malicious in their laughter. Most of the children liked Doddy. He was a kindly soul, generous in sharing his sweets with others.

At elevenses, Doddy and the rest of the class were out in the playground with the village children. Each side kept very much to themselves and eyed the others with suspicion. But with that unerring accuracy with which a pack of wolves descends on the weakest victim, it was quickly perceived that Doddy was one shilling short of a pound. They shouted abuse at him and then one of the older boys went over and started kicking him.

We looked at each other.

We had been told to behave, not to cause any trouble. But we all felt that it was the locals who were starting it. We looked round to see if there were any teachers in sight. There were none.

Very bravely, Doreen went over to the boy who was kicking him. "You leave Doddy alone!" she said.

I was standing near her.

I glowered menacingly.

The older boy, who must have been about thirteen, laughed.

"You can't stop me!"

He turned and kicked Doddy twice more and then grabbed him round the neck.

This was not to be tolerated.

I threw myself on to his back and violently tore back the neck of his shirt. There was a sound of material ripping. The London children cheered.

The older boy lashed out at me with his elbow. It was a futile gesture. I kicked him in the back of his knee. He immediately lost his balance. Still holding the collar of his shirt, I followed him down to the ground and savagely bit his ear. He screamed loudly. I let his collar go - stood up - and kicked him in the face.

I walked back to my classmates - and folded my arms.

Now that justice had been administered, two teachers came running into the yard.

"What's been happening?" they shouted.

"One of the 'vacuees attacked Paul!"

The teachers looked at the Londoners all grouped together.

"'e 'ttacked Doddy," said Doreen.

The teachers looked at the older boy who had got rather shakily to his feet. His right ear was bright red and blood dribbled from his nose. He looked as if he was about to cry.

"And who attacked you?" they asked.

He pointed at me.

"She kicked me in the face and bit me."

The two teachers looked at me unbelievingly.

The incident was quickly hushed up. We were all ushered back to our classrooms. The teachers were clearly embarrassed that hostilities should have broken out between the locals and the visitors at the first break time. It was not a good omen.

Miss Baker looked grim as she re-entered the classroom.

"So, Shaw, you've begun to cause trouble already?"

I remained unmoved.

The rest of the class came to my defence.

"'e 'ttacked Doddy, Miss."

"Well, I'm sure Doddy can look after himself. He doesn't need Shaw to defend him. Shaw go outside and stand in the corridor. I'll speak to you later."

From the sullen atmosphere, it was clear that in punishing me, Miss Baker was taking an unpopular decision. She was aware of it. Normally, she would have given me three belts with the strap at the end of the morning's lessons; but this time she simply lectured me on not causing any more trouble.

"We're not at home now, Shaw. We're visitors here. We must be very careful to behave properly. As guests should." From the look on my face, she knew she was speaking to a brick wall.

*   *   *

At lunchtime, the rest of the evacuees made it clear that they regarded me as their heroine. La Pasionaria of the playground! It was equally clear that the local children felt their humiliation keenly. Paul had gone home to his mother - but the rest of the boys were looking at us with revenge in their eyes. It was only a matter of time before open warfare was resumed.

The twenty minute break before afternoon classes provided a convenient opportunity. A teacher was sent out into the playground to keep an eye on us - but stones were thrown.

One hit Doreen.

"What do I do?" she asked.

"Tell the teacher."

"She won't do anything..."

"She's on their side..."

We moved over as a body towards the teacher.

"They're throwin' stones at us, Miss."

The teacher was not sympathetic.

"Go away - and stop provoking them," she said.

But it seemed safer to stay close to the enemy. If we went back to the other side of the playground, the stone-throwing would resume.

We were almost within arm's reach. Far too close. It was eyeball to eyeball. Various insults were exchanged. I noticed that Donny was actively stirring up his cronies against us. I saw him pointing at me. I knew what he was saying: 'Get her!'

It didn't particularly worry me. I was so used to fighting that I was willing to take on all comers. Speed, a vicious assault and utter ruthlessness were the secrets of success. I almost willed them to attack us.

They did not need much encouraging.

They continued to sneer at us: "Slummers!... Dirty pigs! ... Filthy Jews!" (I think only one girl in our class was Jewish - but you would have been hard pressed to recognize her as such.) Then they started to shove us away.

We shoved back.

Someone slapped someone's face. There was a general outbreak of kicking. The teacher tried to reason with us:

"Children, behave!"

She was lost in the milling crowd.

Doddy was again attacked. Someone put pebbles down his neck.

I hung back, anxious not to be considered a ringleader. But if there was going to be a full-scale battle I was determined to be part of it. I kept my eye on Donny Taylor.

He was keeping in the background - as were most of the village children. There were about ninety of them, thirty of us. It was really only a handful of older boys who were causing the trouble.

The Londoners stuck together.

Suddenly, two of our boys were attacked. Their arms were locked in half-nelsons. Several of the class tried to rescue them. They were kicked or punched. People got knocked down. One girl was trampled on. Everyone seemed to be screaming.

The teacher ran into the school to get extra help.

I decided I had waited too long.

The two boys who had been given the half-nelsons were now on the ground, still being tormented by the Bidworth thugs. I dived through the crowd and got my teeth into the fore-arm of one of the assailants.

When I bit people, I did not just give them a gentle nip. I used to sink my teeth deep into their flesh - and I have been told that my teeth were particularly sharp. It also had the virtue of surprise. People did not expect to find themselves being eaten alive.

The Bidworth youth immediately released the Londoner and grabbed my hair. I refused to release my piranha-like grip on his arm - and with my spare hand I tore at his flies.

I remembered my Uncle Josh saying that boys were particularly vulnerable down there. I thrust my hand into his groin. Like many of the country lads in those days, he wasn't wearing any underpants. I tugged at his penis and then found what I was hunting for. I seized his small, delicate balls and squeezed them viciously.

The youth screamed blue murder.

I didn't stop. Why should I? I was clearly winning. He had now let go of my hair and was thumping me on my back. I stopped biting his arm; it was clear that it was my grip on his balls which was causing him more pain. I silently thanked my Uncle Josh for his excellent advice.

We both fell on the ground.

He was begging me to let go.

Above me, some figure of authority was trying to drag me away.

"Let him go! Immediately!"

Reluctantly, I loosened my grip and was pulled to my feet. Miss Baker looked down in horror.

"Shaw! What were you doing!"

"I were squeezing 'is balls, Miss. He were 'ttacking Billy. I stopped ' im."

"You don't attack people like that, Shaw! It's disgusting. Dirty. Vile!"

I was not greatly moved by her strictures. So long as it worked, any form of attack was justified. And, quite obviously, the youth would not be in any hurry to attack us again. He was still on the ground, weeping piteously.

I spat on him.

Miss Baker slapped me across the face.

"Shaw! Behave! And you...! Do up your trousers! There are girls present!"

The girls did not seem all that worried by the indecent exposure. On the faces of the Londoners, there was a glow of jubilation that one of their persecutors had suffered so acutely. On the part of the Bidworth children, there was a certain awe that a class of eight year olds should have stood and fought people so much older.

The teachers stood round - shocked by the violence they had witnessed. The headmaster, who was an elderly man in his sixties, kept shaking his head.

"We should never have allowed them to come. It's destroying our school... It'll destroy our community..."

Miss Baker bristled with anger.

"It was your boys who attacked my children. They're only eight. Your boys are twelve... thirteen... fourteen, even. They've been throwing stones at them. Persecuting them. D'you think we wanted to come to this wretched village? We've had nothing but rudeness and vicious behaviour. For God's sake, man, show some guts! Put your own pupils in order before you condemn mine!"

It was a bold speech and we much admired her for it.

She looked at the other teachers.

"I shall hold an enquiry into precisely what happened. And I shall send a report to the Education Authority." She turned to us. "Into class! Immediately!"

*   *   *

She was scrupulously fair. I give her that. She asked us one by one what had happened. Who had done what first. The attack on Doddy had clearly been the spark which caused the explosion. Doreen had tried to stop the boy, Paul. When he had ignored her, I had attacked him.

The humiliation of Paul had clearly irritated the local boys. They had been determined to get even. Doreen showed us the bruise on her forehead where she had been hit by a stone.

The failure of the Bidworth teacher to control her pupils was universally agreed to have made a bad situation worse. Then came the unprovoked attack on the two Londoners. As it happened, Deborah, the Jewish girl, had been punched in the face, she had a bruise around her right eye.

Miss Baker wrote down 'anti-semitism.'

There had been more people engaged in the fight than me. But because I had gone on fighting longer than anyone else - and had done some apparently disgusting things - my behaviour was singled out for attention. Twice in one day, I had bitten someone; I had kicked a boy in the face; I had torn his clothes; I had engaged in unspeakable obscenities which must never be repeated.

"Do you hear me, Shaw?"

"I was just helpin' Billy."

"She was, Miss."

"Be quiet, Smith. I'm speaking to Shaw."

I stood my ground.

For once, I had the support of my fellow pupils. In London, I had been extremely unpopular because I had had fights with most of them. I was the child whom most parents told their children to avoid. 'She's rough! Keep away from her!' But in defending them and defeating such a formidable enemy, I was now very much a Joan of Arc.

I felt the sweet glow of success.

Of course I had my bruises. Some of my hair had been pulled out. My dress had been torn and the sole of my left shoe was now flapping open. But these things did not matter. When it came to the crunch, we had won. My example had given encouragement to the other children. Because I had hit back, they too had had the courage to retaliate. And they felt much the better for it.

Miss Baker realized the strength of support I enjoyed, but she was unwilling to give me too much credit. She was inclined to think I had made things worse.

But she kept her thoughts to herself.

When she was sure she had the complete picture, she went to the headmaster and demanded that he speak to the other three teachers, to make sure such things never happened again. She recommended that the whole school be assembled, the troublemakers named and shamed. Apologies should be made to the evacuees and the school reminded that we were fighting a common enemy - the

Germans - and not each other. Perhaps the vicar should be called in?

The headmaster drew the line at that. Twice a year, the school went to the church. On one day a week, the vicar came into school to give scripture lessons to each class. But he was not to be involved in peace-making. The vicar was believed to be a pacifist - an appeaser - a man of Munich. Not the sort of person to subdue unruly children.

Back in the classroom, speculation was rife. Would they be waiting for us outside the school gates at 3.30pm? Would we have to fight running battles to get home safely? Would this sort of thing be happening every day?

Rather unusually, I found myself cast in the role of Demosthenes.

"Yer gotta win!" I said. "Once yer win, they'll look up to yer. If they think they can do us down, they'll keep at it - every day. Once we've shown 'em we're not frightened on 'em, they'll shut up. But if we show them the yella of our eyes, they'll murder us. Yer gotta be strong!"

(Quite unknown to me, Miss Baker was standing just outside the classroom door and heard me giving my advice in my rather petulant high-pitched voice. She told me later - much later - that, for once, she agreed with me.)

Seventeen

For the first twenty-four hours, Mrs Taylor gave me the benefit of the doubt; but when the stories of what had happened in the playground reached her ears, she reacted in a predictable way. She would 'protect her own.'

Paul's mother had taken her son to the doctor to see if he had broken his nose. She had told the whole story to the receptionist, Miss Hodgson, who had relayed it to Mrs Waring, who worked at the grocer's shop. She passed it on to Mrs Taylor when she dropped in for some sugar and a packet of Typhoo tea.

From information received, she only knew that it was 'one of those disgusting evacuees', but when Donny returned from school, he revealed that the villain of the piece was living under their roof. She might appear small and vulnerable, but she had attacked Paul viciously.

Mrs Taylor sent Donny over to Mrs Williams to demand that her lodger be removed from her house - immediately. Mrs Williams refused.

In fact, she rather insultingly reminded Mrs Taylor that she had received her 8/6 allowance that very morning at the post office. If she were to get rid of her evacuee, that money would have to be repaid. But, the previous night, Mr Taylor had spent a generous proportion of the week's housekeeping at *The Fox and Hounds* - in anticipation of the 8/6 coming his way. If Mrs Taylor had to hand back the money, then there would be a financial crisis at the end of the week and a flaming row between herself and Mr Taylor.

I had wisely kept away from the Taylor's cottage. After school, I went to visit the farm with Doreen. We spent a happy hour watching the pigs. We waited till it was almost teatime before we went home.

When I walked into the house, I was greeted with total silence. The boys looked at me with undisguised hatred. Mrs Taylor looked at me as if I were some vile reptile. She shook her head in disgust. I went to the toilet to think things over. I decided that the best policy was to say nothing. But Mrs Taylor had her own plans.

"There's no tea for you!" she said. "You don't deserve to have any tea! When Mr Taylor comes home, he'll put you across his knee and give you the belt."

I did not doubt that she meant every word.

Four plates were put on the table; four sets of knives and forks. Four chairs were drawn up.

I sat down on one of the chairs to make sure of my place; but Mrs Taylor wasn't in the mood to give way. I was dragged off the chair by the scruff of my neck, frogmarched to the kitchen door and pushed out into the garden. The door was slammed behind me.

Donny and Pat appeared at the window, making vulgar faces and jeering at me.

"No tea! No tea! You dirty evacuee!"

I quietly considered what I should do. The logical decision was that if I was going to be deprived of my tea, then they should be as well. I waited till they had got tired of shouting at me. They went off to their bedroom to play. Mrs Taylor was stoking up the fire.

I went back into the kitchen and calmly emptied the pan of mince on to the floor. It fell like a brown curtain of sludge. I then overturned the heavy saucepan. Yellow, half-cooked potatoes rolled into various dusty corners. It was not a pleasant sight.

Mrs Taylor came back into the kitchen - and screamed.

By the time she screamed a second time, I was back out

in the garden. I climbed two walls and ran away as fast as my legs would carry me. I wasn't sure where I should run to. Doreen's was perhaps the best bet. I knew where she was staying and that her landlady was quite kind. I banged feverishly on her door and then pulled the door handle and let myself in. Her landlady seemed a little surprised to see me but she gave me a cup of tea and a biscuit. We played snap in Doreen's dark bedroom whilst I told her what I had done.

I was told later that Mrs Taylor wept for nearly fifteen minutes after I had left. She felt completely paralyzed. The tea had gone and Mr Taylor was due home at any moment.

The boys were hungry. The kitchen was a foul, slippery mess of mince, hot water and crushed potatoes.

Pat had foolishly tried to get across to the door, slipped and was now covered in grease and mince. He burst into tears. Donny was helpless with anger.

There was a sudden crash as the front door was slammed. Mr Taylor walked into the kitchen. He saw his wife sitting on a kitchen chair, weeping. For a moment, he could hardly take in the scene.

"What the hell!" he said.

"Don't blame me!" she screamed. "It was her!"

"Who's her?"

"The evacuee!"

Mr Taylor could see no evacuee. All he could see was the remains of his supper lying in sloppy lumps all over the kitchen floor. He had had a hard day. He was not in a forgiving mood. He lifted his hand and belted his wife hard, right over her right ear.

The blow was fierce. It partially lifted her off the kitchen chair. She screamed. She kept screaming: "It's not my fault! It's hers!"

He hit her again.

Donny tried to reason with his father. But his father was not listening to any excuses. He picked up his son, shook him and flung him down on the floor. Then everyone started screaming. Mr Taylor turned on his heel and walked out of the house.

He headed rapidly for *The Fox and Hounds*. A couple of pints of heavy and perhaps a bite of Mrs Forrester's steak pie; he at least would not starve.

For another ten minutes or so, Mrs Taylor sat weeping on her chair. Her ear was very sore and she felt dizzy. Inside, she began to feel some faint glimmerings of remorse. If she hadn't deprived the evacuee of her tea, none of this would have happened. On the other hand, it showed what sort of person she was. The boys had said she was violent - now she had seen it for herself.

Both boys were filthy. They were hungry. They were shocked. They had seen their father attack their mother. Home life, never happy at the best of times, was sheer misery.

Eventually, Mrs Taylor recovered her nerve. Both boys were made to strip off their shirts, shorts and shoes and go into the bathroom, wash and put on clean clothes. Meanwhile, she picked up the mop and bucket and started to clean up the mess. It took another fifteen minutes. By that time, the kitchen was once more clean - but there was still no tea.

Mrs Taylor toasted some bread with strips of pink luncheon meat and poured over it tomato ketchup. She didn't keep much in the larder. It was the best she could do. After that, there were some biscuits and several mugs of sweet tea.

And all the time, Donny and Pat kept saying: "Ma, I'm hungry!"

She shrugged her shoulders. There was nothing she

could do.

After supper, she left the house and went to see Mrs Williams. Mrs Williams listened to her tragic tale. Together, they decided that the best thing would be for the two of them to go and see Miss Baker at the vicarage.

Miss Baker had not enjoyed her first day in Bidworth. Quite frankly, it had been disastrous. She doubted whether she could face another week of conflict and strife. She had a headache. She planned an early night.

Mrs Williams had other ideas.

"You've got to do something, Miss Baker. After all, you are her teacher!"

Miss Baker was not in a mood to be bullied.

"I don't think you realize the situation down at the school," she said coldly. "It was the village children who attacked the evacuees. They threw stones at them. They kicked them. Punched them. Tried to break their arms. All the evacuees did was to stand up for themselves.

Mrs Williams tried to interrupt but Miss Baker was angry.

"My class are all eight and nine year olds. The people who attacked them were eleven or twelve. A formal complaint has been made to the Director of Education. The matter will be dealt with first thing tomorrow morning."

Mrs Williams conceded that perhaps the Bidworth children were not entirely blameless. But surely Miss Baker would agree: Shaw was a troublemaker.

The teacher conceded that she had difficulty accepting authority; but all she had done was to defend herself and her fellow pupils.

Mrs Williams shook her head.

"There can be no excuse for her behaviour - for what she did to Paul Watkins. His mother tells me that she kicked him in the face. She could have broken his nose. As it was, she tore his clothes and bit his ear. That's not civilized behaviour."

Miss Baker was privately inclined to agree - but outwardly she maintained a firm line.

"It's been a trying day for everyone," she said. "The evacuees feel they are not wanted in the village. They've been attacked. Quite a few of them were injured. I'm afraid that depriving Shaw of her tea was about the worst thing you could have done. To children of that age, food means a lot. It means 'love'. It means 'home'. I'm not surprised she reacted violently. Sending her out with an empty stomach merely confirmed the sense of rejection she has been feeling all day."

"Are you blaming me?"

Mrs Taylor was close to tears.

"Well, you had no evidence - just hearsay."

"I got it from that woman at the grocer's. She got it from the doctor."

"Well, the doctor should know better than to talk about his patients."

Miss Baker had a sharp manner. She was used to dealing with difficult people. She could stonewall for hours if necessary.

Mrs Williams could see that the conversation was getting nowhere, but Mrs Taylor was still seeking help.

"But aren't you going to do anything about it?"

"I think you have to give her a chance."

"A chance?"

"A chance to settle down. She must apologize to you for what she has done. But you are her hostess - you must feed her; make her welcome."

"I don't want her back in the house!"

Mrs Williams intervened.

"Well, she's got to sleep somewhere. I can't move her at

such short notice. I'll make inquiries tomorrow morning and try to find her a fresh billet. It won't be easy - but I promise I'll do my best."

"And where is Shaw at this moment?"

"I don't know. She ran away."

Miss Baker thought quickly.

"She's probably with Doreen Park. Where's she staying?"

"With Mrs Bailey."

Miss Baker stood up.

"We'll go round there immediately and see if she's there."

The three women left the vicarage.

For the past twenty minutes, Mrs Bailey had been wondering how to get rid of me. I was showing every sign of wanting to stay the night - but she was not having it. The arrival of Miss Baker solved the problem.

"Is Jemima Shaw here?"

I looked round for a way of escape - but there was none.

Miss Baker came into the house, closely followed by Mrs Williams and Mrs Taylor. She did not waste much time.

"Is it true that Mrs Taylor refused to give you any tea?"

I nodded.

"Was there any reason why she sent you out?"

"She said it were 'cos of what 'ad 'appened at the school, 'er boys told on us. She told me as 'ow Mr Taylor would give us the belt when 'e came 'ome."

"Really?"

Miss Baker looked at Mrs Taylor.

"If there's any punishing to be done, Mrs Taylor, I shall do it. Not your husband."

Doreen chimed in.

"'er boys 'ave been 'orrible to 'er. They said she were a dirty 'vacuee!"

"Thank you. Park. When I want information from you,

I shall ask for it."

Miss Baker turned back to me.

"And is it true that you emptied a pan of mince on to the floor? And a pan of potatoes?"

"Good heavens!" said Mrs Bailey. "I had no idea. If I had known..."

"Is it true, Shaw?"

I nodded.

There was no point denying the facts.

"You know that was a wicked thing to do, Shaw. You have deprived Mrs Taylor and her family of food. They are not well off. They can't afford to have food wasted. I want you to apologize immediately to Mrs Taylor."

When Miss Baker was so firm, there was no point in objecting. The only way out was to eat humble pie.

I looked at Mrs Taylor. A very contrite look.

"I am very sorry for what I did in the kitchen."

"And you're sorry for all the mess you made..."

"I'm sorry for the mess."

"...And you won't do anything like that again!"

That was the difficult one. If things got bad, I might be tempted... but, then again, I could always do something else. Miss Baker noticed my hesitation. She knew exactly what was going through my mind. She glared at me.

I said quickly: "I won't do it again."

"Thank you, Shaw."

She turned back to Mrs Taylor.

"Now she's apologized, I think that's all we can do tonight. I shall come back with you to the house to make sure everything's all right."

Mrs Williams made her apologies and slipped away.

The three of us plodded back to the Taylor's cottage. As we came through the gate, Donny and Pat, who had been watching at the front door, promptly slammed it in our faces.

"No tea! No tea!" they chanted "You dirty evacuee!"

Mrs Taylor forced the door open.

"Get to your room. Immediately!"

The boys had no intention of going anywhere. They were primed to fight. For the last hour, they had been making plans. But suddenly, they caught sight of Miss Baker. They realized that here was an authority figure. They immediately went to their room.

Mrs Taylor apologized for her sons.

"They're very difficult. They didn't want any vacs staying in the house."

"It's certainly a very small house," said Miss Baker. "Where does Shaw sleep?"

"We put up a camp bed in the living room - beside the window."

"I'll help you set it up."

The camp bed was soon in place.

Miss Baker inspected the kitchen. Whilst she was there, she opened, her purse and gave Mrs Taylor two shillings.

"I'm very sorry about all the trouble you've been caused. I can see the problem. Do the best you can. And tell your boys to stop provoking her."

Mrs Taylor was pathetically grateful to receive the money. She burst into tears. Miss Baker put an arm round her shoulder and held her till she had pulled herself together.

She came out of the kitchen.

"Go to bed immediately, Shaw! I shall speak to you tomorrow morning!"

After she had gone, Mrs Taylor brought me a glass of milk. I accepted it as a peace-offering. Then she went to have a word with Donny and Pat.

*   *   *

It would be nice to record that the evening ended peacefully. But it didn't. Long after we had all gone to bed, Mr Taylor returned home. He had drunk a lot more than two pints and he was in an aggressive mood.

He staggered into his bedroom.

"Well!" he said. "No tea! What use is that to a man? A hard-working man?"

I couldn't hear what Mrs Taylor said.

"I work all day - and what happens? I come home to find all my food - food which I've paid for - spread all over the fuckin' floor!"

Mrs Taylor told him the matter had been dealt with.

"Dealt with? I'll deal with it!"

"I think you've done more than enough. You had no call to hit me."

"Don't you tell me what I can do in my own home!" He belched loudly. "I'll hit whoever I want... as often as I want. Where's that little bitch who caused all the trouble? I'll beat the livin' daylights out of her!"

I heard him moving towards the door. I clutched the scissors more tightly. Would I be adding murder to my other misdemeanours?

"There's no need to do anything!" shouted Mrs Taylor. "It's all been settled. Her teacher's been here to sort things out. And Mrs Williams is going to find her another billet."

Mr Taylor sounded menacing.

"And what about our money?"

"We won't be getting any more."

Mrs Taylor must have told him that they would be much better off if he spent less on drink. Her husband ranted and raved.

"Be quiet! You'll wake up the children!"

"I don't care if I wake up the dead. I'm not taking this lying down. Coming home to find my food all over the floor! Christ! What do you expect me to do? Get down on my knees and eat it? You're a bloody useless bitch! Can't run a house for fuckin' toffee!"

I think he must have grabbed her because there were several hefty thumps of a body against the headboard. She began to scream: "Let me go!"

I think he must then have punched her in the face. There was a sudden silence and then a wail. "Look what you've done! There's blood everywhere!"

There was a sudden crash as if he'd fallen over a chair. I strained to detect his movements. He seemed to be stumbling round the bedroom. More bumps and bangs - followed by bouts of crying.

He kept saying: "Shut up!"

"You've hurt me."

"You deserve it. So does that little bitch. Where is she?"

"You leave her alone!"

More footsteps coming ominously towards the door.

"Why should I fuckin' leave her alone?"

"Because her teacher said so."

"Her teacher? Who does she think she is?"

"You're not allowed to punish her."

"No one's goin' to stop me!"

"I shall go to the police!"

Mr Taylor laughed coldly.

"Betray your own husband? You cow! You wouldn't dare show your face outside the door."

I decided that I would stab him in the upper part of his thigh. It would hurt him - but it wouldn't kill him I would wait till he bent over me then I would strike. He didn't seem capable of moving all that quickly.

I heard another crash. Had he fallen over another chair? Or perhaps he had just collapsed. There were a series of curses. I hoped he had hurt himself. Certainly, the shouting stopped. There were groans - and the sound of Mrs Taylor weeping.

About ten minutes later, she went through to the bathroom and there was a sound of water running as she washed away the blood.

I got the impression that she helped him into bed. It sounded a long struggle. I waited till the house became silent once more. Then I dropped off to sleep. By the time I got up next morning, Mr Taylor had gone to work. But Mrs Taylor had the makings of a very black eye and there were signs of bruising on both her arms.

I suppose I should have felt sorry for her - but I didn't.

Eighteen

Donny Taylor spent most of Thursday morning, wondering how he could take his revenge. After the disastrous evening meal, his father's anger and his mother's pitiful response, Donny felt it was his own personal responsibility to get rid of the interloper as swiftly as possible.

It did not seem that anything could be done at school. After the prayers at morning assembly, the headmaster threatened tough action if anyone attacked the children from London. Two teachers were now stationed in the playground during breaks. The older boys refused to make a move. Constable Bell was seen outside the school gates at lunchtime and at 3.30pm. No one was frightened of the local policeman but it was a clear sign that the school authorities were taking the matter seriously.

Donny than considered what might be done at home. Like his father, he was a slow thinker so it took him some time to assess all the possibilities.

Jemima - he would never utter her name; she was always "her" - Jemima must be provoked to do something violent which would cause the evacuation committee to remove her immediately. If she broke some windows, set fire to the house, pinched money from his dad... surely that would do the trick?

But what could he do to provoke her? She had so few possessions; there was nothing worth stealing. Both her shoes had split at the seams and been consigned to the dustbin. Now she was reduced to a pair of boots which she wore all the time. She possessed only two dresses and she

128

had already torn the nightdress his mother had given her. He thought of the suitcase on the top shelf of the wardrobe - and a glint of triumph came into his eyes.

The bear! If anything happened to the bear, she would react. The temperature would rise sky-high. The bear must die! A horrible death which would really hurt her.

With a deep sigh of contentment, Donny decided what must be done. Patrick must keep his mother busy in the kitchen whilst he would climb on top of the tallboy to reach the top shelf of the wardrobe, open the suitcase and seize the bear. The animal must be hidden somewhere until an opportunity presented itself.

It would have to be after tea... after his dad had read the newspaper and gone out to the pub... Jemima would also need to be out of the house - and his mother out of the kitchen... then he would perform a simple act of cremation. There was an unexpected calm in the Taylor household that afternoon. I sat in a corner of the sitting room, pretending to read the newspaper: "Nazis bomb Warsaw! Thousands flee city." But I was watchful... waiting for the first sign of hostility.

Whilst Mrs Taylor was making the tea, Miss Graham called. They didn't bother to shut the kitchen door so I heard most of it. Miss Graham reported that Mrs Williams had been unable to find me a new billet. Mrs Taylor must put up with me over the weekend. My hostess was reluctant to keep me. She told Miss Graham that my being there was causing trouble with her husband. He wanted to beat me. She had tried to stop him; but he had beaten her instead. It just could not go on.

"Let him beat her!" said Miss Graham, "it's the only thing that'll stop her."

"I'm frightened about it," said Mrs Taylor. "He doesn't know his own strength. She might end up in hospital."

Miss Graham was quite unsympathetic.

"Best place for her! Get her out of your house. Get her out of the village. It's probably the best thing that could happen."

I made a mental note to steal Mr Taylor's Gillette razor blades. I had noticed four of them in their blue wrapping on the top shelf of the bathroom cupboard. You could do a lot of damage with a razor blade. If he was going to beat me, I would slash his legs.

Whilst Mrs Graham was talking, I noticed Donny going into his parents' bedroom. He came out empty-handed a couple of minutes later. I registered the fact but it didn't have any significance - at least, not till later.

The conversation continued in the kitchen. The word 'vermin' was repeated several times. Miss Graham seemed to think that the more she abused me, the more shame I would feel. Of course, it had the opposite effect. It unleashed the vials of wrath. I hated her social superiority. I hated her accent. But there was no point in saying anything - or doing anything. I would just be deprived of my supper - and I was extremely hungry.

Eventually, the wretched woman left. She glared at me as she walked to the door. I felt like spitting at her, but she was beyond my range and I hoped my silence might prove more intimidating. If we were ever to meet again, the gloves would be off.

Ten minutes later, we sat down to supper. Little was said. Mr Taylor joined us soon after we had started and he cast several disapproving glances in my direction. Donny had a smug smile on his face. Perhaps he was hoping his father would beat me. But the meal passed without incident. Mr Taylor read his paper and went off to the pub. Mrs Taylor decided to do some washing and put the clothes out on the line. To keep me away from her sons, I was ordered to hold the bag of clothes pegs.

Whilst we were in the garden, Donny turned on the smallest electric ring on the cooker. He adjusted it to its lowest heat. Then he went through to his parents bedroom and drew out the bear which he had hidden under the bed. He placed Buster on the electric ring - and retired to the sitting room.

Patrick came out to the drying green - but said nothing.

Mrs Taylor picked up the empty basket and we walked back to the house. We could all smell something burning. Mrs Taylor stopped.

"Somebody's chimney's on fire," she said.

We all looked around.

But, almost immediately, we saw dark smoke coming out through the kichen door.

Mrs Taylor's reaction was that she must have left a towel on top of the cooker. She dropped the basket and ran to the back door.

As we came through the door, all eyes turned to the cooker. There was my bear steadily incinerating. Small flames were eating away at his fur and brown smoke rising to the ceiling.

Mrs Taylor knew immediately who was to blame.

"Donny!" she screamed.

But Donny had fled.

I raced over to the stove and dragged the bear away from the ring. There was a huge black hole where his stomach had been. The stuffing was still smouldering away and burnt pieces of wool floated in the air. His neck was also burnt through. Hot lumps of burning material fell to the floor.

"Don't do that! You'll set the house on fire!"

I didn't care whether the house went on fire - or not. Cold fury raged within me. Where was the rotten little bastard who had murdered my best friend?

Mrs Taylor seized the bear and threw him into a metal bucket. She poured a pan of cold water over him. More steam.

I think that even Patrick was shocked at what his brother had done. I felt like flooring him with a savage blow to his ear but decided to hold my fire for the real culprit who could not be far away. He would want to gloat over my grief.

Sure enough, whilst Mrs Taylor was disposing of the bear in the dustbin, Donny swaggered into the kitchen.

"What's cooking?" he asked.

I didn't hesitate for a second. I was across the kitchen floor like greased lightning. My right fist caught him bang on the nose. My second blow knocked him sideways into the doorpost. Whilst he was reeling from this opening attack, I delivered a sharp uppercut which smashed his teeth together and made him bite his lip. Blood began to dribble down his chin. I hit his nose again and had the pleasure of seeing blood run from both nostrils.

I noticed he was wearing a clean white shirt. His mother had just washed his old one. The effect was quite dramatic. He put up his hands to his nose and soon they too were covered in blood. Large red drops fell on the kitchen lino. Donny did not cry. He howled. He could not run to his mother because I was in the way. Patrick ran out of the kitchen to warn his mother: "The vac's killing Donny!" It certainly looked like it.

Mrs Taylor did not immediately rush to her son's rescue. I expect that, in some strange way, she was glad he was being punished for what he had done.

When she did return to the kitchen, her first concern was for his clothes. She screamed: "Donny! Look at your shirt!"

He blubbered.

"She hit me."

"You burnt my bear!" I screamed. "You killed him!"

Expecting that Mrs Taylor would attack me, I moved to an open space on my right. Donny was now able to run to his mother. As he ran, I stuck out my foot and he slipped on the blood-stained floor. I stamped on the back of his knee. The kitchen was a battlefield.

Mrs Taylor ignored her son. Instead, she lunged out at me, trying to grab my hair. I ducked. But then I slipped on the floor. She took, me by the scruff of the neck, and with her right hand clouted me hard on my left ear.

In those days, the average woman did not wear a bra. Some wore vests - others bodices. Mrs Taylor wore neither. She had large breasts. Close up to my enemy, I bit her several times. As I have said before, I had very sharp teeth. The encounter must have been extremely painful.

In the fracas, Donny had been trodden on by both of us. Now he was clamouring to get into his mother's arms to be comforted. I wriggled out of her clutches and made my escape. She took him into her arms and hugged him - despite the blood.

"Oh, you poor lamb!" she said.

And then she broke into tears.

Everyone wept.

I was crying because I had lost Buster - but I had also suffered from the blow to my left ear. It was still ringing and I couldn't hear properly.

"You little bitch!" screamed Mrs Taylor.

I said: "'e should niver 'ave done that to my bear. It's all 'is fault." I looked at Mrs Taylor. "An' you should niver 'ave 'it me. You 'eard what Miss Baker said. If there is to be any punishment, it's 'er what'll do it. Not yous."

Mrs Taylor said: "You're leaving tomorrow! I don't care who takes you. Even if you have to sleep on the street. I'm not having you here one moment longer."

She took off Donny's shirt and threw it into the sink. She got a towel and wiped his face and hands. The bleeding seemed to have stopped.

Mrs Taylor decided that she could not leave me alone in the house. She said to her oldest son: "Go and put on a clean shirt - and go to Mrs Williams and tell her exactly what has happened. You..." she said to me. "... You go straight to bed. I don't want to have another word out of you tonight! You keep out of my way. But tomorrow - you go!"

I said: "Can I go to the toilet?"

Mrs Taylor sighed.

"If you must - but then go straight to bed."

I went into the bathroom and immediately seized Mr Taylor's razor blades, I flushed the toilet and went straight to my camp bed.

Donny went off on his mission to Mrs Williams. I expected her to come round and read the riot attack - but she didn't. She couldn't stand Mrs Taylor's whining and moaning.

When Donny came back there was a glint of triumph in his eyes. He said: "She'll be around tomorrow morning at 10.30am. She'll find her another billet. The vac's got to stay here till she comes."

Mrs Taylor looked across at me.

"You heard that?"

I nodded.

The hatred was mutual.

Nineteen

Mrs Williams came to collect me on the Friday morning. She looked at me with unfeigned disgust.

"Have you got your suitcase?"

I nodded.

"And your gas mask?"

I nodded again.

"Well! Say goodbye to Mrs Taylor. Thank her for looking after you."

I said nothing.

"Ungrateful wretch!"

"Glad to see the back of her!" said Mrs Taylor. "Right little troublemaker! I hope Mrs Woodward knows what she's getting."

"I've warned her. She'll have no hesitation in punishing her. She was brought up at a girl's boarding school. They're used to spanking bad girls - good and hard - where it hurts." She looked menacing. It was clearly something she would love to do herself. "She'll know what to do with her. If the worst comes to the worst, we'll get Constable Bell to lock her up and send her back to London."

I looked up with interest.

So there was a chance of getting home? But only if I behaved really badly. That was food for thought.

But Mrs Taylor had other matters on her mind. She was trying to hang on to every penny of the billeting allowance. "I know she's only been here four days, but I'm not paying anything back. I've already spent it on food..."

Mrs Williams knew full well where the allowance had gone. For the last two nights, Jim Taylor had been drinking

135

heavily at *The Fox and Hounds*.

"Well," she said coldly. "I don't expect Mrs Woodward will need it. She seems quite well off. But don't think you'll get another evacuee. You're guilty of misappropriating government money. You could end up in court for that."

"I don't want another one!" wailed Mrs Taylor. "This one's been enough to put me off charity for life. A really wicked child. Yes - I'm talking about you! Don't turn away when I'm speaking to you!"

She grabbed my greasy hair and forced me to look at her.

"You've brought nothing but trouble to this house!"

I said nothing. I felt the cause of her misery lay elsewhere. I had heard him beating her up for the past two nights. She probably thought I was fast asleep, but I had heard her crying and whimpering like an animal. It was dreadful.

I wondered whether Mrs Woodward had a husband who beat her.

Mrs Williams clearly found Mrs Taylor as tiresome as - I did. With very little ceremony, the conversation was brought to a close and I was hustled out of the cottage.

"Pathetic creature!" Mrs Williams muttered to herself.

She looked at me plodding along.

"Stop dawdling, Shaw! I promised Mrs Woodward that we'd be there by eleven. We don't want her to be kept waiting."

For the first time, I realized that there was someone whom even Mrs Williams was frightened of. She didn't want to upset this Woodward woman. I immediately assumed that my next hostess would be another ogre.

Mrs Williams seemed determined to reinforce that impression.

"If you misbehave, she'll spank you hard. Black and blue. This is your last chance, Shaw. If you misbehave here, it'll be the police cells."

I smiled to myself.

Perhaps the police cells would be no bad thing. It might be my passport back to the East End. Clearly, Mrs Woodward would have to be endured - and then outwitted. We bustled along.

To speed us up, Mrs Williams grabbed my suitcase and gasmask.

"Do get a move on! We mustn't be late."

We swung through an unpretentious gateway. For a start, there was no gate. The house was a grey semi. I had been expecting something grander. It looked shabby and untidy. There was a scrubby lawn to the left and an untended flower bed on the right.

Mrs Williams climbed the steps and rang the bell.

I tried to switch off. To show no interest whatsoever in proceedings. From all I had heard, Mrs Woodward didn't sound worth meeting. A professional sadist - if not something worse.

I heard Mrs Williams making her apologies.

She did not linger. Once she had handed over my suitcase, she rushed away. I was glad to see the back of her. But I was in no hurry to meet my new hostess. I studiously avoided any eye contact. I would start the way I meant to go on.

She came down the steps and squatted beside me, try to soft-soap me; but I wasn't having any of it.

She sounded quite lah-di-dah. I had met her type before. They seemed all nice and reasonable but it was only a matter of time before they came out in their true colours and started bawling and shouting at you. But Mrs Woodward didn't shout at me. Instead, she started talking about parrots!

I thought she was off her head.

I looked at her. She had a very pretty face. Pale but with large, dark eyes. Her hair was dark and curly. She didn't seem like an ogre. Not the sort of person I was expecting at all. She was also quite young. In fact, if anything, she seemed rather sad and lonely.

But I wasn't being won over that quickly. I was determined to be as difficult as possible. I waited for her to react - to show herself in her true colours.

But, instead, she painted a rather sad little story about being on her own. She hadn't wanted to have any evacuees. She was quite happy on her own; but Mrs Williams had bullied her into it - like everyone else.

I listened to what she was trying to say. I felt a bit sorry for her. We were both on her own. She was wanting to get her fiancé home. I was wanting to get back to London. It didn't seem that it was going to be much fun living with her. There was no one to fight with!

Then she mentioned that she had a dog.

Now that was something! I'd always liked dogs but never had one of my own. Dusty was a mad creature! Just a harum-scarum. You couldn't help loving Dusty. He gave me a wonderful welcome. Barking, leaping, licking, running round in circles, rolling all over the lawn. Dusty was the best thing that happened to me in Bidworth. Forgetting all about Mrs Williams and Mrs Woodward, we tumbled all over the garden together till we both felt quite exhausted.

I didn't really want to go into the house - but eventually we both went in. Mrs Woodward was cooking. I noticed she was making chips. I've always liked chips - so that cheered me up. Then she poured me out some juice.

She told me later that she had laced it with gin to loosen my tongue. Looking back, it seems a most irresponsible thing to have done to an eight year old child, but it didn't do me any harm. It actually tasted quite nice. I had some more.

A little later, I went unpstairs to see my room. There was no doubting which it was. It had blue parrots in ascending and descending order on every wall. When you looked at them closely, all the parrots were the same but the branches and foliage varied from parrot to parrot. My first impression was that it was somewhat excessive - but as the years went by, I became very fond of that room - fond enough to beg Mary not to change the wallpaper, which she once thought of doing.

When I looked at the bed, I immediately noticed the black nose of a very grey and scruffy-looking bear.

Why had she put him in my bed?

Remembering what had happened to my own bear, I felt quite tearful. That would never do! I didn't want Mrs Woodward to think I was a cry-baby.

But the bear was in my bed.

He was a rather battered object. I pulled back the bedspread to look at him... He must be hers... Perhaps Mrs Woodward wasn't going to be so bad after all?

I looked across the bed. She had put up my photograph. And she had put all my clothes away. There weren't many - but it seemed like she wanted me to stay.

I put my head into her bedroom. What a lot of books! It all looked rather untidy. She had a large double bed with a big brass bedstead. Still, it all smelt very clean and fresh. White, sail-like curtains billowed in the breeze. She obviously liked fresh air.

I began to feel more relaxed. I wasn't being watched. I wasn't being pursued. More importantly, I wasn't being shouted at. I was going to have my own room, which had a pleasant view across the fields. There was a meal being made - and there was the delicious smell of chips.

I went downstairs.

This was perhaps the moment of truth. I couldn't hide behind the dog any more. I would have to speak to her and see what she was really like. Would she be sneering and contemptuous? Would she demonstrate that deep hostility towards outsiders which appeared to be the common feeling amongst the village folk? And what about the bear?

I approached the subject cautiously. But it seemed that she had no ulterior motives in putting the creature in my bed. He was just another friend - like Dusty. I found myself telling her what had happened to Buster. She was sympathetic. Even though she spoke in a strange accent, I could see that she was nothing like what Mrs Williams had said. She was quite laid back. Trying to understand me. Trying to be friendly. She spoke to me naturally - just as if I was a neighbour who had popped in for a cup of tea. I began to think we might get on.

After lunch, we had that trip to Aylesbury which made such an impression on me. (I'd completely forgotten about the woman at the bus stop! How one's mind plays tricks! Forgetting the things you want to forget about! Fancy slashing her dress with a razor blade! No wonder Mary was shocked. But she didn't shout at me. Actually, I think she rather enjoyed it; seeing that stuck-up bitch being humiliated.)

It was the shopping expedition that really brought us together. She spent pounds on me. She didn't have to spend a penny, but she wanted me to look smart. Without saying anything, she said it all.

I couldn't believe what was happening. They kept taking dresses off the hangers and trying them on me. Shoes, pyjamas - it was a complete kit-out. I felt like I was in some sort of dream. A Cinderella being got ready for the ball. The lovely smell of new clothes.

I realize now how surprised she must have been at my

few meagre possessions. She was determined to have me looking right - but it was an amazing experience. I couldn't believe that a complete stranger would do all that for me.

We went home laden.

Later, she put me in the bath and scrubbed me all over. It hurt a bit but I expect I was quite grubby. She also went to town on my hair - shampooed it three times and then brushed it till it shone. I was surprised to see how nice it could look. Then we tried on all the dresses and skirts in front of her mirror. It was like looking at a different person. And yet it was still me.

We had some milky cocoa. She put in a lot of sugar which made it taste better. Nowadays, I like plain cocoa but in those days, I had a very sweet tooth.

Then it was time for bed. My first night in that strange house. In my own room. I went to sleep quite quickly - but then that owl woke me up. I remember being terribly frightened. It sounded so close. It wasn't long before I recognized him as a friend. I used to say: "Joey, you shut up because I'm trying to get to sleep!" But he never paid any attention. And so I ended up in bed with Mary. She told me to stop calling her 'Mrs Woodward'. I couldn't pronounce it properly and 'Mary' was easier - more friendly like. I took refuge in her bed - and I was there several times before John came home.

I remember thinking: 'What a day!' Mrs Taylor throwing me out. Mrs Williams threatening me; warning me that I would be beaten. And there I was with a new wardrobe of clothes, Mr Brown in my arms, Dusty on the bedroom floor - and Mary herself, rather lonely and miserable, cuddling up to me. I remember thinking: 'What softies we both are!' And yet, in some strange way, I had fallen on my feet. Been more lucky than I had ever dared to expect. From that day onwards, I began to become a different person.

Twenty

Mary tried to educate me.

I see that clearly. I saw it at the time.

There was nothing she could teach me about hand-to-hand combat, but she taught me that there were other ways of winning my battles; not with fists or teeth, but with my brain. Using my mental powers, I could confront my enemies and beat them. But to do that, I had to have knowledge. Facts and figures at my fingertips. She was prepared to arm me for that battle and I was a willing pupil. She decided to start with the subject she knew best - mathematics. She made it fun. We seemed to be learning new things together and, in the process, we must have eaten several pounds of chocolate and a whole treeful of apples. Once she knew at what level Miss Baker was teaching us, she was able to shoot far ahead and show me what was coming next. For a couple of days, we wallowed in long division. Then we were on to square roots and the square on the hypotenuse. She jumped from one thing to another - but she kept it simple. I responded to her one-to-one teaching.

She taught me history - all the exciting bits - people getting their heads chopped off - Henry VIII's wives, the French revolution. She catered to my most bloodthirsty instincts. As she did at bedtime, when she read to me Richmal Crompton's "William" books. There was no doubt that she despised Violet Elizabeth Bott. We were definitely on the peasants' side of the barricades.

We looked at maps, trying to work out how to get to Paris or Edinburgh. She created blank maps which we proceeded to fill in. Mountains were in purple, rivers in blue, cities in black, national boundaries in red. We drew flags. Swastikas and Union Jacks seemed the most popular. I felt sorry for the poor Russians who couldn't manage anything more exciting than a hammer and sickle. I felt that s skull and crossbones would have been infinitely more exciting - and probably more appropriate!

Mary made a game of it. So much so that I was hardly aware that she was giving me a crash course in all the subjects I was going to be doing at school. We even did a bit of French and German. We wandered along the canal bank shouting: "Ein, zwei, drei..." Spymania was very rife at that time. It's a wonder we weren't arrested.

She made me practise writing in italic script, so that my handwriting would be more readable. She lent me her own fountain pen with its thick black nib and jet black ink. My efforts weren't very successful - but I got the idea. For most of my life, I have written in immaculate italics - and been much admired for the sheer artistry of my letters. It all started with Mary.

Her teaching continued after John's return.

I was a bit frightened about him coming home and destroying our close rapport. We seemed to have reached such a perfect understanding that I was sure a third person would spoil it. But Mary was desperate to get him back. She couldn't live without him. Once he arrived, I realized why. John was so full of energy and drive. The house seemed to pulsate with life.

I think he must have been very disconcerted to find me installed as part of the family; but he never showed any resentment. In fact, he became my best friend; he taught me chess.

I didn't know what chess was; but I learnt very quickly. It was another battlefield. A mere eighteen inches square.

But the massacres that took place there could be devastating. One moment, a full board; the next, one's king hideously exposed and John closing in for the kill. He beat me again and again. I didn't like it but I realized it was quite something to be playing against a world champion. I hoped that some of his brilliance might rub off on me.

I watched his moves. I listened to his advice. I learnt to consider the consequences of moving each piece. The times between moves lengthened as I bit my lip and tried to thwart him. Mary tried to help - but that made things worse because he immediately became more aggressive and we seemed to lose the game more quickly.

Playing chess together channelled my aggression into more acceptable paths. I was still proud to dominate the playground and the classroom, but I realized that there were more subtle and vital battles to be won. Once again, it was something to be fought out in the mind. Glimmerings of psychology began to percolate. I came to understand that John was not just moving his pieces willy-nilly; he was reading my mind, anticipating my moves, challenging me to hit back where I could. It was frustrating - but I knew that if I kept trying, I could do it. I remember the first time I checkmated his king, he was full of admiration. He went out and bought me a watch. I still treasure it - and the chess set he gave me.

Twenty-One

I prefer not to think of my departure from Bidworth. At the time, it was a terrible wrench. The train to London was full of children, noisy, excited, looking forward to going home. There was none of the uncertainty or the anxiety which had marked their previous journey. They had survived life in the countryside; their homes in London had not been bombed; they would be able to pick up the threads of everyday life; to revisit familiar haunts; to look back and laugh at their fears.

I remember being very silent and withdrawn during the journey home. Unlike the others, I was not gaining anything; I was losing a lot. There was nothing for me in London in comparison to what I had left behind in Bidworth. No dog... (interesting that the dog should come first); no nice meals; no games of chess; no swimming; no bicycle; no bear...

I spent part of the journey wondering why I had left Mr Brown behind. Mary had wanted me to take him; but I had stuffed him under her top sheet before I left. Why had I done that? First of all, because he belonged to her. She had had him for twenty years and more. It was terribly kind of her to want me to have him; but I could never have taken him away from his mistress. He had merely been on loan to me. And then, of course, he was a country bear; he wouldn't know his way round London. He might get lost.

So much for the obvious reasons.

But there was a deeper and more personal reason why I had left Mr Brown in Bidworth. He was a symbol of my intention to return. I didn't want to go back to my mother;

I wanted to stay with Mary and John - to live the new life I had discovered. Mr Brown had not been abandoned; he was a harbinger (not a word I would have used at the age of eight) - a harbinger of things to come.

But it was difficult to see how I would ever be able to return. The entire class was being brought back by the LCC. Larger forces were in charge of my destiny. Civil servants issued orders; local authorities were obliged to obey. I was a small cog in a very big machine,

When we got back to London, there were buses ready to take us back to Limehouse. There was none of the confusion which had attended our departure. We were speedily processed and delivered back to the school gates. Parents were waiting - but not mine. I didn't expect her to be there. I didn't even bother to look. I just collected my suitcase and set off down the road - like an actor walking off the stage.

I returned to an empty flat. The key was still hidden in a crack in the wall. I didn't expect my mother to be there.

She spent most of her time sponging on other people. She went for a cuppa and stayed for lunch and tea, coming home only when the pubs closed. Sometimes she stayed out all night. She did not enjoy sitting in the house on her own. Nor did she find my company - or that of my little brother - all that rewarding. She would wash, iron, prepare the odd meal, clean the house; but she never conformed to any recognizable pattern. It would all be done; but one never knew when. Her life was completely erratic.

The kitchen table was filled with dirty cups and glasses. The stove was filthy. I looked inside the kitchen cupboard. There was some hard cheese (which I fancied had been there since September), half a jar of pickled onions, two tins of beans and a packet of custard powder.

I sighed.

Why couldn't she make some effort?

The flat looked dreary and dusty. There were ashes in the grate. The clock had stopped. My bed did not seem to have been made since I had left. The same sheets. The same crushed pillows. My brother's bed also looked untouched.

Had she even been there in the past eight weeks?

Inspired by the cleanliness and tidiness of Mary's kitchen, I moved all the plates and glasses to the kitchen sink, washed them and put them away. I cleaned all flat surfaces with a wet cloth and went over them again with a dry towel,

I opened a tin of beans and cooked them. I grated the hard cheese on top. They didn't taste too bad.

I sat in the silence of the empty flat and thought to myself: "I cannot live like this." If, as seemed likely, my little brother was also sent home, most of my life would be taken up looking after him. It would not be much fun.

No one to talk to. No one to play chess with. No dog to take for a walk. And no use asking for one. I could hear my mother's contemptuous voice: "Wacherwanadugfer? Who's goin'a feed it? Who's goin'a pay the friggin' vet?" There would be no dog. And no books. I had got used to a house full of books. Our flat seemed so empty.

I took out my chess set and played two games against myself. I won both games. It was boring doing it on one's own.

After about two hours of self-pity, I went downstairs to Mrs Barclay and asked her if she knew where my mother was.

"She's been working at the bakery. At least she was when I last saw her. But Mrs Addison will know."

I hid the key and trailed down the street to Mrs Addison at No. 5.

"She's got a new boyfriend," said Mrs Addison. "A

soldier. She's bin havin' a whale of a time. But now 'e's bin posted abroad. To France."

She looked at the resigned look on my face.

"She's probably gone to your Auntie Jean. Gone to weep on 'er shoulder."

It would probably have been better to have gone to Auntie Jean in the first place; but she lived more than a mile down the road. It was a long way to go on a wet night.

Twenty-Two

I heard my mother before I saw her.

As I opened Auntie Jean's front door, I heard her laugh. It sounded rather a hysterical laugh. I thought: "She's been drinking."

As indeed she had. The brandy bottle was standing open on the sideboard - more than half empty. The room was filled with the acrid smell of Woodbines. I felt choked.

My mother was pretty in an artificial sort of way. She looked at her best in the half light of a pub. She had natural, golden-coloured hair, sparkling eyes and a ready smile. She had a great facility for attracting men. She was a good listener but her mind was utterly shallow. Such relationships as she did make, never seemed to last. It was a case of easy come, easy go. She flitted restlessly from one flame to another. To her, pleasure always came first. She would welcome any distraction - even if it totally inconvenienced everyone else.

For instance, if she decided to bring a boyfriend home for the night, we would be sent to our Gran. However late it was - even if we were in bed, we would be made to dress and go round to her mother's house and knock at her door until she let us in. The old lady was far from welcoming and would take us in most unwillingly whilst she volubly cursed 'that cheap tart'. Now even she was gone; she had died a long, slow death from emphysema.

I grew up feeling that my mother did not care about us. Maybe she did in her own way; but she was completely irresponsible and never thought about the impact her selfish behaviour would have on other people.

She registered shock surprise as I walked through the doorway.

"Good Lor'! Look what the cat's brought in."

Auntie Jean turned round to see whom she was talking about. She at least seemed glad to see me.

"Good heavens! It's Jem! What are you doin' back 'ere?"

"They've sent us 'ome."

"Why would they do that?"

My mother sounded suspicious.

Auntie Jean looked at her.

"Well, it's perfectly safe, in'it?" There's no bombs 'ere."

"And where's your brother? Where've you left 'im?"

"'e's still in the country. Nobody said."

My mother brightened up. If it was only me she had to look after, there would be no need to change her lifestyle.

Auntie Jean explained: "Yer mum's feelin' a bit down. Lost 'er latest, 'e's 'ad to go to France. She's not expectin' to see 'im again fer a while."

"Perhaps never!" My mother looked as if she was going to burst into tears. "They'll put 'im in the front line. 'e's an experienced soldier. The Germans'll kill 'im."

I did not share her sorrow.

After all, what was another nameless mug?

My Auntie Jean tried to comfort her.

"They're not killin' anyone at the moment. People do say it'll be peace by Christmas."

"I'll believe that...!"

I watched the two of them comforting each other. Another glass of brandy was poured. I sat down on a stool beside my Auntie Jean and warmed my hands at the fire.

"You're lookin' very smart, Jem! New clothes? New shoes? An' someone's done your 'air nicely. I ain't seen you lookin' so smart for a long time."

This was a reproach directed at my mother.

All she could say was: "She's put on weight."

"Bin feedin' yer, 'ave they, Jem?"

I nodded.

I wasn't going to voice any criticism against my mother.

"Where was yer stayin'?"

I looked at her coldly.

"Bidworth. I sent you a couple of letters."

"So yer did." My mother lit another cigarette and then discovered that the last one was still burning in the ashtray.

"Somethin' about a dug?"

"Dusty."

"Messy things!" said Auntie Jean. "I wouldn't have one in the house. Crap all over the carpet. More trouble than they're worth."

My mother was still perplexed at my sudden return.

"'ave all the other kids come back - or is it just you?"

"The 'ole class - an' Miss Baker."

My mother looked at Auntie Jean.

"I thought as 'ow she might 'ave bin expelled."

"They wouldn't expel our Jem."

I didn't say anything.

"Did you get involved in any fights - with the village kids?"

I nodded.

"But that wasn't why they sent yer back?"

"Oh no. They just didn't like us. They sent us 'ome as soon as they could. They were nasty to Miss Baker as well. Called us slummers and shits."

My mother, unmoved, puffed on her cigarette.

"But the people yer stayed with... they were all right, weren't they?" asked Auntie Jean.

"They were fine. I 'ad a bedroom all to myself. We went for lots of walks and things. They taught me to swim. They got me a bike..."

"... and bought yer new clothes? They must 'ave liked yer."

I thought it diplomatic to say as little as possible. They wouldn't understand. Even now, Bidworth was beginning to seem like a distant dream.

My Auntie Jean smiled.

"Well, yer quite the little laidy now. You'll be... nine... in just a couple of weeks."

"Don't remind me!" said my mother.

The two women continued their conversation. They were talking about Cousin Eddie who had been thrown out by his wife - for interferin' - with whom was not said. It was left to one's imagination. But Cousin Eddie wasn't a very exciting man. He smoked a pipe and drove a delivery van around north London.

"I think 'e's sleepin' down at 'is garage," said Auntie Jean.

"Probably die of pneumonia."

"Serve 'im right!"

The knives were out for Cousin Eddie.

I suddenly remembered to ask after Uncle Josh.

"Back in clink again," said my mother.

"Gravitated burglary," said my aunt, "'e 'it someone."

"'e didn't just 'it 'em. 'e 'alf killed 'im. It were a policeman, weren't it?"

Auntie Jean nodded.

"They gave 'im six months for resisting arrest. But the young constable recognized 'im. Sent a message back to the local copshop. Nicked 'im as soon as 'e got back to 'is 'ouse with the goods. Caught 'im red-handed, so to speak. 'e 'ad to plead guilty."

"And where is 'e now?" I asked.

"Scrubs, in'it?"

"Can I go and see 'im?"

"No," said my mother firmly. "'e's a bad influence on yer."

I had been looking forward to seeing my dad's brother again and telling him about all my battles as an evacuee. He would have been proud of me. But now it seemed that I wouldn't be allowed to go and see him. Perhaps if I worked on my aunt, she would take me. My mother wouldn't.

I was waiting to be asked more questions about my time in Bidworth - but it was not mentioned again. My mother said that she had heard from the people who were looking after my little brother. Auntie Jean said that she should write back to them but my mother declared that she couldn't be bothered. It took her enough effort to send a postcard to France.

"Well," said my Auntie Jean, "now that Jem's home, 'e'll probably be 'ome in the none too distant future."

"Perish the thought! I've got enough on my plate."

I knew how she felt. Children were a burden. Unwanted, demanding. They tied you down. Unlike a dog, you couldn't have them put down. No one would take them off you. You couldn't go for a walk and lose them. Ten minutes of rough pleasure and you were landed with a responsibility for life - whether you wanted it or not.

She didn't really care for either of us.

Which meant there was very little to come home to. No warmth, no interest, no affection. What a contrast with Mary and John! They were complete strangers and yet you knew they cared. They always asked me what I had been doing.

They had tried to make things interesting. Given me hugs and kisses. Fed me at regular intervals. I realized how much I had begun to take that sort of life for granted.

Now I was back to being a burden.

A nuisance.

I felt myself a stranger, sitting beside the fire, looking at the flames chasing each other up the chimney. More than ever, I wondered if there was any way they would let me go back to Bidworth.

*   *   *

I broached the matter with my Auntie Jean the following morning. My mother had gone off to work at the bakery and I was eating my second slab of bread and strawberry jam.

"D'yer think my Ma really wants us?"

My aunt put down her dish-cloth.

"What makes yer ask that?"

"Just that she didn't seem all that pleased to see us."

"She's bin very upset lately, yer Ma 'as."

I shrugged my shoulders.

"She's allus upset about something." I licked some strawberry jam off my thumb. "She didna seem to want Paul back." (Paul was my younger brother.) "Don't yer think she'd be quite 'appy never to see the two on us again?"

Auntie Jean was quite sure that that was precisely what her sister felt - but she knew instinctively that it would be quite the wrong thing to say. I might quote her and then the fat really would be in the fire.

She paused - trying to think of something positive to say. It wasn't easy.

"I don't think she really meant to 'ave any kids," she said at last. "She's not cut out to be a mother."

I took two more bites at my jammy bread before I said what I was really thinking.

"What I mean is... would she mind if I went back to these people in Bidworth?"

Auntie Jean bristled. The suggestion was a reflection on

her just as much as my mother.

"I don't think that'd be a good idea at all," she said firmly. "You've got to know yer station in life, Jem. We're ordinary folk. Them's toffs. They've only just seen the back on yer. If the truth be known, they're probably glad to have done with yer."

I said nothing.

I was remembering the look on Mary's face as she said goodbye to me. It had really hurt her. I could tell. I was sure that she would be glad to have me back - even though she and John were now working. I could help get the meals ready. Peel the spuds. Boil 'em. I could take Dusty for walks at lunchtime. He wouldn't be cooped up all day. He'd be glad to see me again.

To my childish eyes, it seemed the most natural thing in the world. I didn't see them as toffs. Perhaps I had at first. But once I had learnt their ways, they seemed perfectly normal. Of course, they spoke proper. They read lots of books. They talked about University. And they had money.

Yes, they were different.

My aunt was looking at me. I was sure she could guess what was going through my mind. I quickly closed off all thought of Bidworth - and finished my slab of bread.

"Yer gotta know yer place in life, young Jem," she said in a kindly fashion. "We're East End folk. Rough dymons. We speak differen'. We think differen'. Them's not like us. Speaking lah-di-dah. With all their fancy houses. Cucumber sandwiches fer tea. 'Please pass the friggin' salt!'" She smiled. "We're common as muck. We don't belong to their world."

I looked at her thoughtfully.

There was truth in what she said. Certainly, during my first two weeks in Bidworth, I had been conscious of the huge social difference between us and the village people.

They felt themselves infinitely superior to us - hence all the snobbery and the fights. Auntie Jean had a point.

But with all my new clothes; the long conversations with Mary about anything and everything; the battles with John at the chessboard; I had begun to feel part of their world. I had been conscious of losing my Cockney accent. I was beginning to be lah-di-dah myself. I hoped my Auntie Jean hadn't noticed. I had been steadily copying them. I had come to believe I was part of their family. So much so that they had been genuinely upset to see me go.

Either that was true or they were putting on an act. I couldn't believe they were pretending.

I pushed away my plate.

Mary had always cut the bread into neat slices. Sometimes she had even removed the crusts. It was really quite hard work trying to eat Auntie Jean's all-too-solid loaves. One's jaw ached with all the effort involved.

I decided to change the subject.

"Woodja take me to see Uncle Josh?"

"Yer Ma'd never forgive me. Yer know what she thinks about 'im."

"But I love my Uncle Josh."

It was true.

"I know yer do." She picked up a tea towel and dried a couple of mugs. She sniffed. "I could take yer tomorrow afternoon whilst she's working. But mind yer don't say anythin' to 'er or it's orf."

I promised faithfully to keep my mouth shut.

Twenty-Three

We went to the prison the following day. The visit involved a long bus journey to East Acton. That in itself was quite an adventure. I was brimming over with excitement... with all the things I wanted to tell ray Uncle Josh. I hadn't seen him for several months and I was sure he would have missed me as much as I had missed him.

But the act of getting into the prison diminished my ardour. There were lots of heavy doors studded with iron bolts, guards with keys on chains, an oppressive atmosphere not helped by having to sit in a dreary waiting room with some very unpleasant people. They stared at me. I stared at them till they lowered their eyes.

When we finally got in to see Uncle Josh, I was deeply shocked by his appearance. The tall, elegant man of my dreams - and my bedside photograph - was gone. Instead, he seemed to have shrunk and his face had a sort of olive tinge. There was also a wild look in his eyes.

I tried not to show my surprise but I'm sure he noticed.

"Jem wanted to see yer. She's bin missin' yer."

He smiled a sad smile.

"Does 'er Ma know?"

"Coarse not! She wouldn't let 'er come 'ere."

"Too pertickuler."

"Well, yer know what she thinks on yer, Josh Shaw. She don't think yer a good influence on 'er. She's allus sed that." Auntie Jean opened her bag. "Look! 'ere' s some chocolate. They're bound to ration it afore long. Enjoy it whilst yer can."

She put down the chocolate and five packets of

Woodbines. Uncle Josh looked more cheerful at the sight of the chocolates and the cigarettes. He looked at me.

"Bet you'd like a bite of that chocolate, young Jem?"

"It's all for you," I said. "I 'elped to buy it."

"Come into the lolly, 'ave we?"

I coloured a little.

"The people I were with, they gave me a few bob. So me and Auntie Jean clubbed together."

"You're a good kid," he said.

A tear ran down his cheek.

He brushed it away.

Auntie Jean sniffed.

"If 'er mother knew abaht it, she wouldn't 'ave it in 'er pocket fer long, that's fer sure."

"Yer right there," said Josh. "She's a mean bugger. A right mean bugger. Suck every bloody penny out of you, if she got the chance. What's she doin' today?"

"Workin' at the bakery. 'er latest fancy man's gone off to France."

"Probably get shot..."

"Very likely. But she'll allus find another mug."

"Plenty of 'em around."

Uncle Josh looked at me.

"So where'r you bin, Jem?"

"Bidworth."

"And where's Bidworth?"

"Jus' outside the big smoke. I was evacuated."

I was trying to talk naturally but I was suddenly conscious that I had said 'was' rather than 'were.'

Uncle Josh noticed my slip of the tongue.

"Gettin' quite a leidy, our Jem! Learnin' to speak proper. Where was yer stayin'? With the Lord of the friggin' manner?" He laughed.

I shook my head.

"No. Jus' ordinary folk. They were very nice to me. They 'ad a dawg. A spaniel. They called 'im Dusty. I used to tek 'im for walks. They learnt me to swim..."

Uncle Josh looked approving.

"... an' to ride a bike. And to play chess. I can play quite well now."

"There now! What did I tell yer? Mixin' with the nobs!"

Auntie Jean shared his disapproval.

"I've told 'er not to get ideas above 'er station."

Uncle Josh noticed my angry look.

"Seems she enjoyed it, nonetheless?"

"Coarse I did. But not to start with."

"Why not?"

"'Cos the people in the village were really nasty to us. They 'ttacked us." I paused. "So we 'ttacked them back."

"Bet yer made 'em scream?"

I nodded proudly.

"I did all the things yer told me. I 'it 'em 'ard. Where it 'urts. I gave 'em bloody noses. One woman, I bit 'er tits."

"She wouldna thank yer for that."

Auntie Jean looked extremely disapproving.

"And then yer wonder why 'er Ma don't approve on yer? Allus stirrin' 'er up, yer are."

Josh did not apologize for his part in my upbringing.

"She'll never get on in the world if she doesn't stand up for 'erself. It's an 'ard world, wot with people like 'itler around."

Auntie Jean snorted.

"'e's done nuffin' to us yet. Why they bothered to 'vacuate all the kids, I don't know. Not a bomb 'as fallen. Not on London anyroads. The 'ole thing's a complete farce, if yer ask me."

"I volunteered to go and fight 'im."

"Did you?" I asked. The thought of Uncle Josh wielding

a rifle appealed to me. "Would they let you go?"

He shook his head.

"Not they! They said as how my health was not exactly A1."

"You look a bit under the weather," said Auntie Jean.

"Liver's playin' me up again."

"Yer not drinkin', are yer? Not in 'ere?"

"Not really. Now an' again I get a drop of meths."

"I wouldna drink that. It'll really rot yer guts."

"Yer probably right," he conceded, "but I miss my pint at the local. I've even taken to goin' to communion jus' to get a sip." He grinned sheepishly. "That's all yer get; but it's good stuff. I told the Chaplain: 'I could do with a bit more of where that come from...'"

"And what did 'e say?"

"'e said: 'the sooner you get outer 'ere, the sooner yer can buy yer own booze! 'e were right of coarse, damn 'im."

"And when will yer get out?" I asked.

He shrugged his shoulders.

"Two years they gave me."

"Two years an' a 'alf!"

"Well, I've done the 'alf. Probably another eighteen months if I behave meself."

"That's a long time," I said. "I'll be nearly eleven by then."

"So yer will. It's yer birthday soon, ain't it?"

"Next week."

"She's a Scorpio," said Auntie Jean.

"An1 don' we know it!" Uncle Josh laughed. "Real sting in the tail, 'er!"

I smiled.

That was more like the Josh I knew.

"Come on," he said, "tell us a bit more abaht these folk in..."

"... in Bidworth."

"Yer dyin' to tell us."

So I told him about John and Mary. How he was very tall and played chess. About the meals, my bedroom, the parrots, the owls and Dusty. The Taylors and their sons. The bicycle we had stolen from the vicar. He enjoyed that.

"Stole it from right under 'is nose! Then 'e put the police on t'yer! Yer better watch it, kid! Yer'll be endin' up in a place like this."

"That's what 'er Ma's worried abaht!"

"Oh, don't talk soft, Jean! They don't imprison women. Not fer long anyways. Give 'em a rap over the knuckles. Don' do it again. Put 'em on probation fer a few weeks. Bit of a lark usually."

Uncle Josh didn't have much time for the forces of law and order.

I told him about Mrs Williams and Miss Baker. The boy I had attacked in the playground. I related all my battles in loving detail, knowing he would be proud of me.

"I squeezed 'is balls so 'ard, he cried. 'e lay on the ground and jus' 'ollered. Miss Baker was real angry. She said it was disgustin'."

"And so it is," said Auntie Jean. "You've no call doin' that to a person. You should leave 'is privates alone!"

Uncle Josh looked at her quizzically.

"Pity yer didn' tek yer own advice a few years back. Then yer wouldn' 'ave 'ad 'im put you up the spout."

Auntie Jean got extremely angry.

"Don't yer bring that up, yer foul-mouthed git! Yer know what I mean. It's not proper for a girl of 'er age to learn such things."

Josh turned back to me.

"Did yer win all yer battles?"

I nodded.

"All of 'em. They don' fight me any more. They know what's comin' to 'em."

"Time's up!" said the guard.

"So it is," said Auntie Jean. "Don't time pass when yer enjoyin' yerself?"

I felt she was being unnecessarily sarcastic.

"When am I going to see yer again?" I asked.

"Before Christmas?"

"I'll bring yer some more chocolates."

"I'd like that. Yer a good lass, Jem. Not like that..."

"You watch your tongue, Josh Shaw! She'll not be visitin' anywhere if you give me any more of yer lip."

I gave Uncle Josh a big hug. He seemed very thin - just bones really. I think he was crying. Probably because he knew he would never see me again. By the time Christmas came, he had been dead three weeks. Cancer of the liver, they said it was. But that was the end of my Uncle Josh.

Twenty-Four

I decided the time had come to escape.

It was now three weeks since I had left Bidworth. Things were no better - either at home or at school.

My mother was on constant night-shift at the bakery. Once she got me to bed - which was usually about 8.30pm - she went off and had a couple of brandies at the local pub; then clocked in at 10.00pm. She was home by 7.00am, made me some breakfast and sent me off to school. She spent most of the day in bed. When I returned home at 4.00pm, there was usually something for tea; but she did not necessarily cook it. I got into the habit of fending for myself. The sheer emptiness of my existence - the loneliness - got to me very quickly. I had no real friends at school. Most of the children refused to play with me because I was 'rough'. When I tried to pick fights, they would run away. Such relations as we had, lived across the river in Bermondsey. I went round to my Auntie Jean's quite often. At least she had a warm fire in the grate.

But, for the most part, my existence was dull and dreary. I longed for the life I had led at Bidworth.

I decided to use up my final shilling and threepence to pay my way out of London. For good measure, I pinched a two shilling piece from Miss Baker's handbag. I got out my suitcase and packed my best clothes and my chess set.

I looked at the London tube map to see where Euston station was. By following the coloured lines, it seemed that the best way would be to go to Tottenham Court Road on the Central Line and then change to the Northern Line. But first, I had to get to Mile End. That was about a mile

and a half up Burdett Road - straight past the school gates.
That was awkward! Should I take a bus or walk?

That rather depended on what time I chose to escape.
If I left before my mother came home from work - and before
the school assembled, I would have a full day ahead of me.
I would have to set off early so that my mother did not see
me setting off with my suitcase.

My mother would not get worried till about 5.00pm but,
even then, she might think I was at my Auntie Jean's. I
wondered whether I should leave a farewell note but
decided not to send any communication till I had reached
my destination.

I meant to leave on Wednesday - but slept in. Same
thing on Thursday. But, on Thursday night, I banged my
head seven times on the pillow - and it worked! By 7.15am
on Friday morning, I was out on the street, suitcase in hand,
making my great escape.

I walked up to Mile End and spent sixpence on a ticket
to Euston. I negotiated the change of tube lines at
Tottenham Court Road and by 8.45am, I was standing in
the main concourse of Euston station. Although I had been
there before, I felt a bit lost. There were hundreds of people
hurrying past me. I approached an elderly man at the ticket
barrier.

"Where's the train to Bidworth?"

It took him a few minutes to work out where I was going.
"Bidworth, lass? You'll have to chainge at Leighton
Buzzard."

I had never heard of Leighton Buzzard. I had assumed
that the train went directly to Bidworth as our evacuee train
had done.

"Where's Leighton Buzzard?" I asked.

"It's on the main line; but you have to take a local train
when you get to Buzzard. It's the branch what takes you to

Bidworth."

I asked him where I could get a ticket.

He looked at me with some amusement.

"Globe-trotting, are we?"

"No," I said. "My Ma's bin taken into 'ospital and I've got to go and stay with me aunt - on 'er farm."

At least I had my cover story. It sounded plausible. Whether he believed it or not, I don't know. But he was helpful. Later, when I came back to speak to him, he had gone and a fierce man with bushy black eyebrows had taken his place.

I approached the ticket counter.

"Bidworth," I said.

"Single or return?"

I didn't know what he was talking about.

"Are you coming back?"

"No."

He punched the ticket in the machine.

"Three and six."

I looked at the coins in my hand.

"I've only got 2/9."

He looked at me curiously.

I put the coins down on the counter.

"Sorry, love. No cash, no ticket."

I could not think of anything to say. I was conscious that there were several people behind me waiting to get their tickets. I decided not to make a fool of myself. Tearfully, I gathered up my few coins and moved out of the queue.

Furiously, I debated with myself what I should have done to avoid such humiliation. First of all, I should have enquired how much a ticket to Bidworth would cost. With my slender assets, I should have found out exactly how far I could go for 2/9. Then I should have got a ticket to that place - and walked. My chief problem seemed to be that I did not really know where I was going. A train timetable might have helped.

I was feeling cold and hungry. It was December and I had had no breakfast. I decided to go to the station buffet and have a cup of tea and a round of buttered toast.

My reserves shrunk to 2/-.

Certainly, I could not afford to travel to Bidworth - but I was not going to give up.

I roamed round the large station concourse, asking people where I could get a local train to Leighton Buzzard. An amazing number of people did not know. But eventually, I was directed to the correct platform and watched one train leave. I asked when the next one would leave. At 11.25, they said. Would it leave from the same platform? Apparently it would.

Looking back with the benefit of hindsight, I am sure that if I had explained my problem to some sympathetic adult, they would probably have given me the 1/6 I needed. But years of hostility and distrust had led me to regard most adults as 'the enemy' - and that deterred me.

Instead, I loooked for an alternative.

The local train for Bletchley left from platform six. I noticed that there was an empty train parked in platform five. Because it was doing nothing - and platform four was empty, there was no ticket collector at that barrier.

I casually walked through the barrier, waiting for someone to shout at me. But no one stopped me. I walked rapidly down the platform. Those who remember the old Euston station will remember it was a very dark, cavernous building. I hid myself behind a pillar so that no one in the main concourse could see me. I sat on a porter's trolley and considered my next move.

When the local train arrived, it would pull in behind this empty train. All I had to do was climb down on to the track, scramble under the buffers of the carriages on both lines and climb up on to platform six. It was just a matter of timing. I must let all the passengers get off the train; but I must not let people see me emerging from underneath the carriage. Also, I must be careful not to get run over.

I saw the local train coming in. I immediately descended from my platform and hid under the nearest carriage. I moved over to the Bletchley train. I had a worm's eye view of the platform. I watched the feet of passing passengers - and waited till they had gone.

I then crawled under the buffers of the second train and looked up and down platform six. Nothing much seemed to be happening. I put up my suitcase and scrambled after it. Very quickly, I headed into the nearest carriage.

Unlike the evacuee train, the coach had a corridor so I had a choice of compartments. I chose one in the middle, put my suitcase on the floor and sat beside the window.

The train seemed totally empty. No one was going to Bletchley at that time of day.

At 11.30am, whistles blew; the train gave a sudden jolt - and we were off. Slowly at first - then a little quicker; we made our way out of the great station and across a myriad of points and crossovers; there was a steady chugging from the locomotive and clouds of grey smoke.

I could scarcely credit my good fortune. Without any money. I had got on a train - and was now on my way to Bidworth. I exulted in my success.

But, too soon!

Four minutes into the journey, the door of my compartment was wrenched open and a burly man whom I took to be the guard, said: "Ticket!"

There was only me in the compartment. And no means of escape. I looked at him fearfully.

"I 'aven't got a ticket," I said.

"Not got a ticket?" he said. "Where are you goin'?"

"Bidworth," I said, "to see my aunt. I've got to chainge at Leighton Buzzard."

"Not if you 'aven't got a ticket, you don't."

"I've got two shillings," I said, showing him my coin.

But he laughed coldly.

"Travellin' on a trine without a ticket, young lady, is a criminal offence. I 'ave no alternative but to order you off the trine at the next station."

Unfortunately, at that moment, the train was slowing down as it approached Harrow & Wealdstone Junction. My adventure had carried me 4 miles.

He made me pick up my case and, holding me by the collar, he escorted me off the train and into the station-master's office.

"Young lady with no ticket. You sort her aht. We're late."

With that, he hurried back to his train.

The stationmaster looked at me.

"Where've you come from?"

"Lime'ouse . "

"And where're you going?"

"Bidworth. I'm goin' to see my aunt."

"How did you get on the train without a ticket?"

I remained silent.

I had begun to curse myself for my stupidity. If I had at least got a ticket to Watford - which I gathered was the next big station down the line - I would at least have been able to satisfy the guard. Having no ticket at all was stupid.

The stationmaster picked up a phone.

"That you, Bert? I've got a customer for you."

He looked at me.

"How old are you?"

"Ten," I lied.

"She's ten. Comes from Limehouse. No ticket.... OK."

He put down the phone and looked at me in a more friendly fashion.

"That's the local bobby. He'll look after you."

The police had never been my favourite people. I had already been cautioned for stoning someone's house and for several brutal assaults on my fellow pupils. The police must already have marked me down as a future delinquent.

I looked at the door to see if I could escape.

The stationmaster read my mind.

"You won't make it," he said. "It's got a very stiff handle. Anyway, Bert'll be here in a minute. He'll look after you."

I doubted it.

But, when he arrived, Bert seemed quite a cheerful fellow. He had a smiling face, a soft voice and a very comforting manner.

"Well, well, well," he said, "what have we here?"

(I noticed that he had no trouble opening - or shutting - the door. On the other hand, he had large hands - and large feet.)

The stationmaster explained my offence. It seemed to amuse him.

"She's heading for Bidworth. Playing truant, if you ask me."

Bert took charge of my suitcase.

"What's your name, young lady?"

"Jemima," I said reluctantly. "Jemima Shaw."

"Well, Jemima, you come along with me - and we'll have a nice cup of tea and sort things out."

Like the guard on the train, he kept a grip on my collar and escorted me to a small police station situated a hundred yards down the road. Once inside, there was little chance of escape. I was taken to an interview room. It had high walls and barred windows. But Bert kept his promise. I was given a mug of sweet tea and a couple of biscuits.

He examined the contents of my suitcase.

"You play chess?" he said.

I nodded.

He looked at my clothes.

"Planning to stay awhile at Bidworth?"

I nodded again.

"Have you anyone who can vouch for you?"

That was difficult.

Obviously, I could not mention my mother or my Auntie Jean. Nor could I give them the Woodwards' telephone number. There was no point phoning them; they would probably be working.

I shook my head.

He found Mary's letters at the bottom of my suitcase.

"That's where I'm going," I said. "She's my aunt."

He read through the letters.

"Aunt my 'at!" he said. "These are the people you were evacuated with."

"I'm goin' back to 'em."

"Why?"

I gave him a frosty look.

"'Cos I don' like stayin' at 'ome. They're nice people. They've got a dawg. An' they treat us proper like..."

He looked at me pityingly.

I was conscious of being small and thin. A pocket Cinderella. Perhaps he would turn into a fairy godmother? But no.

"Do these 'ere people know you're coming to them?"

"No," I said honestly, "but they'll be glad to see me. They'll pay my ticket. I know they will."

Bert put all my possessions back into the case.

"'e's a champion chess player," I said irrelevantly. "'e plays for Hingland."

Bert clearly thought I was making things up.

"I must go and have a word with the Super."

He was gone for a few minutes; but the judgement he received had clearly gone against me.

"There's a car coming for you." He smiled. "They're going to take you back to Limehouse."

I felt betrayed and angry.

"I don' want to go 'ome!"

Bert shrugged his shoulders.

"It's all we can do. We can't send you to Bidworth without proper authorization. The only thing we can do is send you home." He smiled more kindly. "Next time you decide to run away from home, young lady, make sure you have a ticket."

"I would've 'ad a ticket," I said bitterly, "if my Ma 'adn't pinched all me money. Ten bob, she took. She's a feef!"

"Well, you've still got two bob," said the policeman. "Save up your pocket money - and, next time, you'll get to Bidworth. But, take my advice, let these folks know you're coming. Don't just arrive on their doorstep."

I bit my lip - and reflected that the two shilling piece had been stolen from Miss Baker. I too was a 'feef'. Like mother, like daughter.

*　　　*　　　*

Bert saw me into the police car and asked for my home address. I told him my Auntie Jean's even though I knew it meant more trouble. At least I would get some food. Despite the tea and biscuits, I was starving.

The car swung rapidly through the London streets. It took less than a quarter of an hour to get home. And it had taken me nearly five hours to get to Harrow and Wealdstone.

(I never liked that place. Later, when there was a terrible

rail crash which demolished most of the station, I felt a sense of poetic justice - a wrong avenged. It was just a pity that so many people had to die to satisfy my amour propre!) When I got back, my Auntie Jean gave me a good walloping but she didn't say anything to my mother for which I was deeply grateful.

On the Monday morning, I gave Miss Baker back the two shilling piece I had stolen from her handbag. I had expected another beating; but she looked at me with chilling contempt.

"I thought it was you, Shaw. You're a dirty little thief - just like your uncle! I'm surprised you haven't spent it."

"So am I," I said.

(And wished now that I had.)

I had only returned the money because a bigger and better plan had come into my mind over the weekend. Leaving London in a way that wouldn't cost me a penny! But that plan didn't work out either; so I was left with nothing - not even enough to buy a Christmas card or a stamp. Mary sent me a scarf, some gloves and five shillings; but by that time, it was too late to send her anything.

I spent her money on bags of chips. It was a cold winter.

2: Shadows of War

(Mary's Story: December 1939 - May 1940)

Twenty-Five

I knew that I would miss Jemima when she left. In only eight weeks, she had made herself very much part of the family. John was her hero; Dusty was her slave. I came somewhere in between!

She was the sort of person who made her presence felt. She was always in the kitchen when food was being prepared. With very little encouragement, she would give you a blow-by-blow account of everything that had been happening in the school or in the playground with her own heroic part presented in the most glowing colours.

If one ignored her warlike tendencies, her desire to seek revenge against at least half the members of the village school and the constant need to do running repairs to her clothes (frequent casualties in battle), she was very little trouble.

She had learnt to wash, to eat her meals in a civilized manner and even to speak 'proper English'. She would make her bed, dust her room and always help with the washing up.

She also developed the diplomatic ability to withdraw to her room when John and I wanted to be alone.

This was largely because she had discovered the joy of reading and was ploughing through John's extensive collection of boys' adventure stories. Arthur Mee's ten volume encyclopedia - with 4000 pages - also helped. The price of her withdrawal was usually two games of chess - one with each of us - which meant that she had at least a chance of winning one of them.

The days after her departure were therefore strangely

quiet and rather dull. Dusty did not comprehend what had happened to his mistress. He seemed to think that at any moment she might return. He wandered round the garden like a lost soul and maintained a lengthy vigil at the garden gate. At other times, he went in and out of her room and slept beside her empty bed. He roamed the house with a mornful expression - as near to tears as a dog could be; his tail rarely wagged.

I wrote to Jemima about once a week to give her such news as I thought might interest her - photographs of Dusty; the escape of Lady Rowley's Shetland pony; Mr Taylor crashing his lorry on a dark night; Mrs Williams slipping on the ice and bringing down the Vicar when he tried to help her. (Eventually, five people ended up flat on their backs.) I tried to maintain the easy-going, slightly zany sense of humour which had appealed to her - and expressed the pious hope that, now she was back in London, she would be a reformed character.

It was about ten days before I received my first letter from Jemima:

'Deer Mary and John, I got home last Frydi. The trane was orl rite. Nobuddy was kild. When I got home my Ma was at my Anty jeans so I stay there. On Sunny, my anty jean took us to the jale to see my uncl josh. He did not luk gud. He is ill my anty sez. I told him all abaht yous. He sez he wood like to mit you wen he come aht. My ma were supprisedas how I grode wen I were wiv yous. I am stil playn chess. I am rembring to wash my teef.
lotts of luv,
jemima SHAW'

I smiled as I read it. Her spelling was atrocious but at least she had written. I was sorry to hear that her Uncle Josh was ill. I knew how much she admired him. I was less happy about the thought of Uncle Josh wanting to 'mit' us. The idea of a convicted jailbird sitting down in our living room, eyeing up my silver teapot and the Georgian candlesticks which my grandmother had given me - was a little worrying. Children do not think about such things. I hoped that Uncle Josh might not be liberated for quite some time!

I found myself reading the letter through several times - as one does a love letter. I thought perhaps it was just me. Then I noticed John was doing the same.

She sent us a second letter about a week later:

'Deer Mary and John, I hope yous well. An Dusty. An MR brown. I cood not tek him awy from yous. He is yorn. But I wood very much lik to see him agane. I mis him and yous. thins are bad here, scool is orful. Miss Baker sez as how I was on my own now. I have had the belt 3 times this wek. Fightn of coarse. Wil Smith hit me with a peace of wood. I had a black i. it is much beter now. My Ma is workin a lott. her soja has gone back to France but she pynes for him. my anty jean sez she dos not no y. Plees rite to me. lotts of luv to yous and Dusty and MR brown. I mis him so much, i do reely.
Jem.'

I reflected that nothing much seemed to have changed. Her battles with Miss Baker continued. Her mother obviously had little time for her. Her 'anty jean' seemed to be the one rock in an otherwise disastrous world. My poor opinion of her mother was confirmed in an angry letter I received a couple of days later:

'Deer Mary and John,
I am very angri. My Ma has sode my shoose. The ones

wot you bot me. She sez as how she needs the dosh to pay er bills but she never assed. She also nickd my 10 shillun note. she is a feef. But my anty jean sez there is a war on. it is very dark nyts becos of the blakart. Doddy went aht an fell into a hole, he brok is arm. Serve im rite i say. He is stupit.

all my luv to yous and dusty and MR brown
Jem
PS Can i com and liv wiv yous agane. I wil be gud an no cost yous any dosh.'

This was more alarming. I had given her three half-crowns and a ten shilling note to give her some pocket money. She had obviously been sensible and kept hold of the note - but now that bitch of a mother had pinched it. I shared her anger.

And the shoes! Was it one pair or two? When I thought how I had lashed out money in Aylesbury to buy those shoes - in case they were rationed - so that she would have decent shoes to grow into, my blood boiled.

I wrote back a calm and measured letter, expressing my disappointment at what her mother had done. I could not be sure whether her mother would read my letter so I was careful not to say what I really thought.

I told her to hide the rest of her money - where it would not be found. I asked her how many pairs of shoes had gone. I did not send her any more money at that stage. Christmas was only a month away and, besides, at that moment, I had other things on my mind.

John and I were married early in December. We had been planning to wait till Christmas and make it a family occasion. But what with the war and all the difficulty in getting people together from different parts of the country, we decided to go to the Registry Office in Aylesbury and get it done privately. There was no time to take a honeymoon so, after the ceremony, we just went back to work. Unromantic - I know. But at least we had been able to borrow a car for the occasion.

We went to stay with John's parents for Christmas. His father had just re-joined his old regiment - as an artillery officer, I think. He had served in the last year of the previous war and his experience was needed - if only as an instructor. He had been given forty-eight hours leave. There was talk of him being sent out to Egypt.

He teased John about his 'cushy number' - sitting out the war behind a desk whilst he - twice John's age - would be serving in the front line. John took it in good part. "They need intelligence officers" he said. "In a war with lots of new weapons, you need to know what the other side is doing. Because we both speak German, they need us for translation and interrogation" - which neatly side-stepped the question of ciphers.

His father laughed.

"Wasn't it me who suggested you should do German?"

"It was."

"Well, at least you'll be safe," said his mother.

"Unlike me," said his father. "I might come back with only one leg!"

"Oh, I wouldn't worry about that," said his wife. "I shall probably have gone off with some young officer by then!" She helped herself to another small cup of coffee - and then turned to me: "Did you say you had taken in an evacuee?"

"We did."

"That was very brave of you."

"She was with us for about eight weeks but then they all went home."

"Was she well-behaved?"

Together, both John and I said: "No!"

His mother looked surprised.

"She was all right with us...," I said.

"... but at school, she was a complete terror. Fought, bit, kicked, spat..."

"Good heavens! How dreadful!"

"She was really quite fun..."

"John taught her to play chess. They spent hours battling it out together."

"You must miss her."

Perhaps John's mother had noticed the sadness in my eyes. I did miss Jemima. I had hoped that she would write or send us a Christmas card, but we had heard nothing.

I had sent her a scarf, a pair of gloves and two more half-crowns. I sincerely hoped that she would get to them before her mother. I had told her that we were now married and sent her a small photograph which we had had taken in a studio after the ceremony.

But there had been no response. Perhaps she was jealous of our happiness. Perhaps she had run out of money. Perhaps she was ill - or too busy simply surviving. I thought about her a lot.

We stayed with John's parents for a few days, but the weather was becoming steadily worse - and we were worried about freezing pipes. We need not have worried. There was no thaw till the middle of February. We had a long, slow, miserable journey across country. Bidworth seemed to be under several feet of snow. Beautiful to look at but travelling anywhere was hellish. Some nights, we just stayed in a local pub in Bletchley.

We got our next letter from Jemima early in the New Year:

'Deer mary and John,
I got the scarf an the glovs and the dosh. My Ma dosnt

180

no I got it. I shode her the glovs but she didn as nuffin. I wen to my anty jeans for Chrismus. we ad crakers i ad a stokin but no chox. my Ma is goin wiv anufa soja. he is a smarmi git anty jean sez. he dosn luk at me. I hope yous ad a nice Chrismus - and dusty. It is very cold eer. Lots of sno. we made a snoman at scool. I have lost of your gluvs. It were not my falt.

Jem.

Plees can i come and stay wiv yous. plees say yes.'

I bought her another pair of gloves and sent them off along with some chocolate. About a week later, I sent her a postal order for five shillings. I hoped she would use it to buy food. I was becoming increasingly anxious about her.

Towards the end of January, she wrote:

'It is very cold and my Ma is not eer very offen. She is wiv her soja. They is stayn at anty jeans. Anty jean is in osspittle wiv er ches. She were coffin and weezin. My Ma will not tel me witch osspittl she is in so I cant see er. i hav bin byin chips wiv your dosh so I am orl rite. I hav for blankts at nyt. Ther are eyesiculs in the kitchn...'

When I showed this letter to John, he was very upset.

"She's not being looked after; not eating properly... Living in an empty house..."

"She'd be all right if her aunt was there."

"But she isn't. Her mother's kipping up with her soldier. She's not even bothering about her."

"We've got to do something."

"We've got to rescue her."

I looked at him.

"Do you realize what you are proposing?"

"Yes. Do you mind?"

"No. But I thought you might."

He shook his head.

"I can't bear to think of her being neglected. I'd like to throttle her mother."

It was all very well saying such things but was John really willing to accept all the responsibility of having an evacuee back in the house? I looked at him seriously across the kitchen table.

"But would you be willing to have her living with us long term? Not just a few weeks? Think about our work! Getting her back into that school. Would they take her? If not, can we afford to send her to a private school? Do we want our lives totally disrupted?"

"It's not as bad as that."

John looked at our blue roan spaniel.

"I think I know what Dusty would say."

"It's not what the dog thinks - that matters!" I said angrily. "It's what you and I are willing to put up with."

John was realistic.

"Well, you can't leave her to starve."

"So are you quite willing to have her back?"

"I'm willing, if you are."

"You won't change your mind?"

"Of course not. I'd like to see her again. As I said to Mum, she amuses me." His eyes sparkled. "We'd be able to teach her more chess!"

That was typical!

John was much given to temporary whims and sudden bursts of enthusiasm. He was gifted with dazzling moments of inspiration, but he could easily get bored with routine things. Although he might agree to bringing Jemima out of London, was he prepared to look after her month after month, year after year?

I decided to take him at his word.

"I think I'll go to London and see what's happening. Take her out for lunch. Talk to her mother and her Auntie Jean - if she's out of hospital. Arrange things with them. Then, if they agree, we could both go and collect her."

"That sounds a good idea."

"I'm off on Monday. I'll drop her a letter to say I'm coming. It'll be a nice surprise for her." I looked at John. "Where is Limehouse?"

He shook his head.

"I haven't the vaguest."

Twenty-Six

I met Jemima outside the school gates at lunchtime. It had taken me quite a long time to find the school - but, in the process, I had discovered the nearby ABC cafe. I took her there for lunch.

She looked as if she needed fattening up. Her face was much thinner; her skin looked pale and unhealthy and she had dark rings under her eyes.

She was wearing the coat that I had bought her but the buttons had gone and new buttons had been sewn on. She also had the same shoes but they were badly scuffed and unpolished. Her blouse, skirt and jumper had obviously taken a battering. Cuffs and collar were frayed. The materials appeared to have shrunk, but perhaps she had grown. Her hair, at least, was washed and brushed.

She grinned happily as we sat down at a window table.

"You've lost another tooth," I said.

"Fightin'..."

We said it together.

I handed her a menu.

"Is there anything you'd like? Pie and chips? Fish? Macaroni cheese?"

"Stewed eels?"

She giggled.

"D'you really want eels?"

"Garn," she said. "You don' get eels 'ere."

We settled for fish and chips.

I thanked her for her letters. She thanked me for the money. She had hidden it in a book. Her mother never read any books - so it was quite safe.

184

But she was interested in more important things than money.

"When can I come back with you? I miss you all so much. 'specially Dusty and Mr Brown."

"Not to mention Annabelle and Joey!"

She looked tearful and rubbed her nose with her fist. I passed over a clean handkerchief.

"No one wants me round 'ere," she declared. "They all say I'm a nuisance. Miss Baker 'ates me... I know she does. And my Ma's taken up with another sodja. I'm sure they wouldna mind if I went."

"I'll have to see your mum and your Auntie Jean. If they say 'yes', we'll have you back as soon as we can. But if they say 'no...'"

Jemima had to concede that her Auntie Jean would be the toughest nut to crack. She was bound to be against her going.

"Are you goin' to ask 'em?"

I nodded.

That was why I had come to London. I had decided to tackle them head on. But they were hardly likely to he my sort of people. I had seen the mean little streets around the school. There were many obstacles ahead.

"My Ma's off today. She'll be at my Auntie Jean's. I'll come with yer."

"No," I said quickly. "It'd be much better if I saw them on their own."

Jemima clearly felt that, with her help, I could argue the case more effectively. I resisted her offer.

"Just give me the address."

"But what if they say 'no'?"

"Well, I'll come and tell you. What time do you get out of school?"

"'alf past three."

"Well, I think we shall know by then. Write down your Auntie Jean's address on this envelope and tell me where she lives."

I was instructed no less than five times as to the route I should take.

"And if they say 'yes'?"

"Well, John and I'll come and collect you on Saturday. I'll have to arrange with the local school for you to join their classes. And I suppose I shall have to have a word with Miss Baker."

"I think she's frightened of you."

"No. She despises me. She thinks I'm an idiot."

Jemima looked angry.

"Why?"

"She thinks I'm a frustrated mother. I haven't got a child of my own. And I'm getting a kick out of looking after someone else's child. She thinks I'm sorry for you. A sentimental idiot."

"She's an ijit."

"No. She's just bitter. Cynical. Most teachers are. They've seen too much. She doesn't see any goodness in you. She thinks you're a criminal in the making." I smiled. "Of course, she may be right."

Jemima pronged two large chips into her mouth. She chewed thoughtfully and rather disgustingly.

"Is there any goodness in me?"

"Not when you eat with your mouth wide open."

"Sorry."

She quickly recovered the table manners she had learnt with us at Bidworth.

"Why can't you take me now?"

"These things have to be done properly. Otherwise, they'll put the police on to me - and I shall be accused of abduction. But if they say 'yes' then we can get going."

"Wouldja take me 'ome tonight?"

I looked at her eager face.

Once again there was light in her eyes.

"If it's at all possible."

She smiled.

"I shall pray for you. Very 'ard."

"I shall pray for myself."

*   *   *

I was joking. But later, even though I was in no way a religious person, I found myself putting up a little prayer as I stood outside Auntie Jean's front door.

I knocked - very nervously.

A middle-aged woman opened the door.

"Yes?"

"I'm Mary Woodward."

Auntie Jean tried to remember if she had heard the name before. Was this the new ARP warden?

I explained.

"We're the people who had Jem as an evacuee."

I did not normally call her Jem but I knew they did.

Revelation dawned in the older woman's eyes.

"Oh, that's 'oo you are? Cum in."

I followed her into the living room.

A slim woman with shifty brown eyes was painting her nails. She gave me a quick once-over - then resumed her painting.

"I'm the person Jem writes to."

"Oh, her."

Auntie Jean remembered her duties as a hostess.

"Now, don't be like that, Babs. Mrs Woodward's come all this way to see us. Treat 'er nice. Would you like to tak' yer coat off? Would you like a cup of tea?"

"I should love a cup of tea."

Jemima's mother looked at me more closely.

As I took off my black coat and my red scarf, her eyes ranged over me. She looked at my ring, the cut of my dress, my legs, my shoes. I felt her working her way downwards.

"We very much enjoyed having Jem with us."

"You must be the only ones!"

"We tried to stop her fighting."

She laughed coldly.

"Well, you didn't succeed. She's done nuffin' but fight since she came 'ome. If anything, she's worse. Isn't she, Jean?"

The aunt had put on a clean pinnie and emerged from the kitchen, wiping her hands.

"What's that? Fightin'? Oh, she's a right terror an' no mistake!"

"Gets it from 'er father - not me."

"Is he still in jail?" I asked.

Jemima's mother's eyes narrowed.

"'Oo told you that? Jem don't know."

"Miss Baker told me."

"Oh, 'er?"

"I think some of the other girls have told her. She knows." I changed the subject quickly. "I believe her uncle died?"

"Before Christmas," said Auntie Jean.

"She was very upset about it."

"She were very fond of 'im."

Jemima's mother put down her brush and her paint.

"'e were another rogue. 'e gave 'er bad ideas. She allus listened to 'im. A real bad influence 'e 'ad on 'er."

"Was he her father's brother?"

"Well, 'e certainly weren't mine. That's fer sure! I wouldn't 'ave 'ad 'im in the 'ouse. Jean's more accommodating. She used to go and visit 'im in prison. Scrubs, weren't it?"

Auntie Jean didn't want to say anything nasty. At least, not in front of strangers. Nor did she want to speak ill of the dead. She could see why Jem had liked her Uncle Josh. In fact, to be honest, she had a soft spot for Josh herself. It was no use denying that both she and her niece had been upset by his death.

"Proper spoilt Christmas!" she said.

Cups of tea were passed round.

There was a silence.

"What've yer cum' 'ere fer?"

I was glad Jemima's mother had asked the all-important question - though she had probably already guessed the answer.

"Jem's been writing to me for several weeks asking if she could come back to Bidworth and live with us. She wanted me to come and ask you if you would agree."

Auntie Jean's face wrinkled with disapproval.

"She should stick with 'er own. East End folk don' mix with toffs."

I had been warned that this might be said.

"Well," I said, "I work for a living - and so does my husband. We don't have a large house. We don't have a car. We get around on bicycles. I don't think anyone would describe us as toffs."

Auntie Jean shrugged her shoulders.

"It's the way yer talk... yer can't 'ide it."

Babs eyed me coldly.

"What d'you know abaht kids?"

"Not a great deal," I said. "But I can tell the difference between a child that's well looked after - and one that's neglected." I decided to hit hard. "When Jem came back to London, she was fit and healthy. When I saw her today, she looked thin and ill."

I noticed that Auntie Jean had the grace to look ashamed. But her sister, Babs, was not admitting anything.

"She eats all right. Always piggin' it."

"Well, she told me that she hadn't had a cooked meal for several days. And this is winter."

"She gets a meal at school."

"But not if she misbehaves."

"Well, that's 'er fault."

Auntie Jean sounded apologetic.

"I've been in 'ospital for ten days. I weren't 'ere."

Babs looked at her without a glimmer of compassion.

"Well, I've got my life to lead."

A tear ran down Auntie Jean's face.

"You said as 'ow you'd make an effort."

Jemima's mother turned away. She didn't like being shown up in front of this arty-tarty stranger.

I continued to make my case:

"I have to say, I don't think she's learning much from Miss Baker. All she does is get the belt. At least, in Bidworth, she'd have a chance of learning something."

Babs returned to the fray.

"Are you a teacher?"

"No. I work in a government department."

"Is yer man a teacher?"

"No. He works in the same place as I do."

Babs smiled triumphantly.

"So 'ow do yer perpose to look after Jem if yer both aht all day?"

I was ready for her.

"We both work shifts. There's always someone at home." (It wasn't true; but it sounded convincing.)

I continued:

"We've already taught her a lot. Arithmetic, writing,

geography, chess, reading...

"Readin'?" Babs sneered. "Where d'yer get with readin'? I never read a book in my life. Ain't done me no 'arm!"

I could see that Auntie Jean was getting embarrassed by her sister's philistine behaviour. In her heart of hearts, she knew that Jemima had been neglected. The memory of the shoes came back to her.

"What about them shoes?"

Babs' eyes flashed angrily.

"It were nuffin' to do with you."

There was a great deal more I could have said - but I didn't want to provoke an explosion. Knowing how much money seemed to matter to Jemima's mother, I said:

"It won't cost you anything," I said. "You wouldn't have to pay her billeting allowance."

Babs smiled.

A nasty smile.

"I didn't pay it last time. She did!"

"Well, we didn't take a penny," I said. We bought her clothes. And we paid for it out of our own pockets."

Jemima's mother turned on me.

"Yer a right little goody-two-shoes, ain't yer?"

"Babs! Mind what yer say!"

"Well, it's true. What right 'as she got to cum in 'ere lecturin' us on 'ow to bring up our Jem?"

I was as firm as I could be without being rude.

"I think she'd be happier with us. She'd get properly fed. All the teaching she needs. And she'd be safer."

"Safer?"

"Yes. Safer out in the country. She won't get caught up in the bombing."

"What f-----' bombing? We ain't seen no Jerries over 'ere, 'ave we, Jean? No bombs... no hair raids. I don't know why they sent the kids away. Jus' panic, if yer ask me!"

I took pleasure in puncturing her complacency.

"The Germans will come... when they're ready. You saw what they did to Warsaw - and in Spain. Once the fine weather comes, they'll be over here in their thousands. They'll plaster London. The authorities know what they're doing. When it starts, they'll have to evacuate the kids all over again. This time, perhaps, for good. I think it'd be better if you gave Jem a chance." I paused. "She wants to come..."

"You mustn't believe anythin' she sez."

"Why not?"

"'Why not?' 'Cos she's a rotten little liar!"

Auntie Jean leapt to her niece's defence.

"Now, cum on, Babs! Don't say that! She's a good girl is our Jem."

"She lies to me."

"D'you blame 'er? Arter you pinchin' all that money?"

At last, Babs began to look uncomfortable.

"Well, I gotta pay me bills!" she said sulkily.

"Most of it went on yer boyfriend. Down 'is throat!"

Babs stood up.

"Why don' you shut up! I'm not listenin' to you any more! If you wan' 'er, you can 'ave 'er. And that's my last word!"

She put on her coat and stormed out.

Auntie Jean wept for a few minutes.

"Yer see 'ow it is? She's no 'eart. Never 'ad."

I nodded.

Auntie Jean continued: "I knew she weren't being looked after properly. She were all right whilst I were 'ere. But I were taken into 'ospital with this chest. Pneumonia, they said it were. I put it down to the weather. Summut awful, it were. I was in the 'ospital ten days whilst they sorted us out." She sighed sadly. "I still don't feel all that great."

"I think you've done your best," I said. Then realized I had sounded horribly patronizing. More humbly, I added:

"Her mother doesn't seem to have any time for her."

Auntie Jean wiped her eyes with her pinafore.

"I tell you this. If I were meself, I wouldna let yer tek 'er away. I don't 'old with East End folks mixin' -not wi' the likes of you, anyhow. Gives 'em airs... hairs and grices! Think they're Lord Muck. It don't do 'em any good."

Auntie Jean paused to wheeze.

"But," she said, "I jus' can't look after 'er proper. She's a poor wee thing, right enough. You were right abaht 'er not being fed. Next thin', she'll end up in 'ospital."

"I thought she looked pretty run down. I took her to the ABC for some fish and chips."

"She'd like that."

"I do try to give her things she likes. She also likes our dog."

"She tol' us abaht 'im."

"He's missing her too."

Auntie Jean sighed deeply.

"Well, you better tek 'er afore 'er mother changes 'er mind. Afore Pharoah 'ardens 'is 'eart."

"D'you think she will?"

"No," said Auntie Jean."She don't care a damn abaht 'er kids. Never did! She'll put 'er outta 'er mind as soon as she downs 'er first pint. I know 'er."

I felt there was little more to be said.

"Are her clothes here or at her mother's house?"

Auntie Jean laughed bitterly.

"What there is - is over there. But there ain't much worth 'avin'. You'll 'ave to kit 'er out all over again."

I had already decided to do that.

I said to her aunt: "We'll look after her. Toffs or not! If

you want to come and see her, you'll be most welcome. I'll see that she writes to you."

"A postcard'll do. You better send it to us. That bitch'll never read it. She never reads anything."

"She is your sister!" I said.

Auntie Jean managed a final burst of black humour. "Is she? That's what I'd like to know! My Ma swore blind as 'ow she were our sister. But I reckon it were the milkman! A right cuckoo in the nest! No 'eart! No 'eart at all!"

I left the house with Auntie Jean's blessing.

Now I had to face Miss Baker.

Twenty-Seven

I left Jemima in the playground - radiant with happiness that she was going to come back to Bidworth, whilst I went into the school to meet Miss Baker. I did not relish meeting her. I was sure she despised me.

I met her on a dusty staircase outside the staff room. She looked surprised to see me.

"Mrs... Woodward?"

"Good afternoon, Miss Baker. I wonder if you could spare me a minute?"

She smiled a rather false smile.

"I've come to take Jemima back to Bidworth. I've been to see her mother and her aunt. They've given me their permission. I thought it only right to speak to you as well."

Miss Baker's lips twisted into a sort of sneer.

"It won't do her any good. She's really quite hopeless. Despite all your efforts last autumn, she's reverted to type. Fighting, disruptive, making a nuisance of herself in class, I think she's turned her back on everything - and everybody. She's stolen money, run away from home, boasted about her connections with criminals. I've had to discipline her almost every day. It does no good whatsoever. The only thing one can do is to put her out of the classroom - for the sake of the other children. Those who want to learn should have a chance to do so."

Having read Jemima's letters, Miss Baker's list of complaints did not surprise me.

I said: "Surely you've noticed how thin she's getting? She's not being properly fed. Her mother's sold the shoes I bought her. She even stole the money I gave her."

Miss Baker shrugged her shoulders as if to say: 'What do you expect?'

"I gave her a few months to settle down, but her letters have been getting more and more desperate. I felt I had to do something."

Miss Baker was surprised that Shaw was capable of putting anything on paper.

"Did she tell you that she stole money from my handbag?"

"Yes. But she gave you the money back."

"She had to. The police brought her home. That's when she ran away."

"And where d'you think she was running to?"

Miss Baker made a contemptuous gesture.

"Well, of course, she knows which side her bread's buttered on. You can offer her a higher standard of life. More money; nicer clothes. You have a dog. She loves animals. It's the only lesson she pays any attention to - when I read the children nature stories. Her own mother neglects her. I told you that before - and her father's a murderer. Bad blood runs in the family."

"Her uncle died before Christmas."

"An absolute thug! He assaulted a young policeman. Left him with terrible injuries. It's a wonder he survived. But she admired him..."

"I know. She has his photograph beside her bed."

Miss Baker shook her head.

"Well, there you are! Nothing I say will convince you. You'll have to learn the hard way. She'll turn on you - just as she turns on everyone else. And then what'll you do? Bring her back to London - and dump her on us!"

I said quietly:

"We'll try and make a go of it. I know what you think about her - but I've seen a different side to her. I believe she's quite capable of learning... and behaving. Remember! She was only with us for eight weeks. That wasn't very long. She's devoted to my husband. She was reading all his boys' adventure stories. She'd even begun to tackle Arthur Mee. We intend to carry on where we left off."

"Well, good luck to you! That's all I can say. I think she's one of the nastiest, most dangerous children I've ever met. She radiates hatred. Her eyes are frightening." She paused before delivering her final warning. "Make sure you don't have a baby. She'll probably kill it!"

"That's a terrible thing to say!"

"Don't think I don't know my pupils! I know what she's capable of."

As Miss Baker spoke, I thought of Jemima's reaction when I had mentioned the possibility of my having a child. She had been against it. She wanted me for herself. Perhaps there was some truth in what the teacher had said.

Miss Baker noted my reaction.

"You think about that," she said. "Don't say I didn't warn you!"

"I'll cross that bridge when I come to it," I said. "For the moment, Jemima will be quite enough to' cope with."

"You can say that again!"

She swung her bag over her shoulder.

"I'm afraid I must go."

"She'll be leaving tonight."

"Good."

She walked down the stairs without a backward glance. At the foot of the steps, she stopped and looked sharply to the left.

"Eavesdropping, Shaw? People who listen to other people's conversations hear no good about themselves." She laughed coldly. "Not that there is anything good to be said about you. You're a guttersnipe! And I hope I never see you again!"

Miss Baker moved on.

I could hear her footsteps going down the next flight of steps.

Jemima appeared round the corner.

I came down to her.

"She was right," I said. "People who listen to other people's conversations never hear anything good about themselves."

The thin little ragamuffin took my hand.

"She were wrong..."

"I know she was wrong."

"I'd never 'urt yer baby."

"There's no reason why you should ever hurt anyone." I said firmly. "Once we get you home, I want you to be on your best behaviour. No more fighting. You're getting a fresh start and I want you to make the most of it. You've got to turn your back on all this."

I indicated the school and its silent passages.

"Are we goin' to get me luggage?"

"Yes, we'll go and get your things. There's a train at about half past six. John'll meet us at Bletchley. I think he's borrowing someone's car." I smiled more confidently. "What shall we have for supper... Eels?"

Jemima grinned.

I hoped she would soon grow another front tooth.

"Macaroni cheese?"

That was what she had had on her first night with me.

"If you like. And a nice hot bath?"

"And a game of chess?"

"Anything you like."

She was crying.

I sat on my heels and hugged her. We were like that for several minutes."

I knew what she was feeling. I just wished Miss Baker could have seen her. This was a Jemima Shaw she had never seen. Would never see... because she was blind. This was 'treasure in earthen vessels.'

*   *   *

We managed to catch the 6.25pm train out to Bletchley where John met us with an ancient Morris 8. Even at that time, it looked as if it had come out of the ark.

"D'you think it'll make it?" I asked anxiously.

John shrugged his shoulders.

"Best I could get."

He picked Jemima up and gave her a big hug.

"The wanderer returns," he said. "Is it permament this time?"

"I should think so."

Jemima's mind was set on more immediate needs.

"We're going to have macaroni cheese!"

"Are we?"

"And I want a game of chess."

"Have you been playing?"

"Only against meself."

"Who won?"

"I did. Every time!"

John laughed.

"We'll soon put a stop to that."

We clambered into the ancient car which rattled all the way to Bidworth.

Jemima couldn't stop asking questions. Would she be able to borrow Lady Rowley's bike? Was Mrs Williams still her awful self? When would she be starting school? Had I seen the Taylor's? Was her room the same? And why hadn't John brought Dusty to the station?"

"Because I've just come from work!"

When we arrived at the house, Jemima was impatient to see everything. She was first through the front door. Straight into the kitchen to see Dusty. Lots of hugs. Then the two of them raced upstairs to inspect her room.

It was a little bit different. There was a new bedside light, a bookcase filled with John's adventure stories, some photographs taken during her first visit. And, of course, there was Mr Brown - once again tucked up in her bed. As for the parrots - nothing had changed there.

We left her to explore the house.

Down in the kitchen, John opened a bottle of gin and poured us both some much-needed refreshment.

John shook his head sadly.

"Not in very good shape, is she?"

"Just a bundle of bones."

"She's a bit taller than she was."

"Her clothes will have to be replaced."

"Her mother seems seems to have totally neglected her."

"If you'd met her," I said, "you'd understand why. She's a selfish bitch. Doesn't care about anyone except herself. Her Auntie Jean cares for her - but she's been ill."

"She seems glad to be back."

"Desperate, I would say. She could hardly wait to get to Bletchley."

John listened to the noises from upstairs.

"It's strange having someone in the house again. You forget what it's like."

I sighed.

"There's no disguising the fact that we've got a major job on our hands. It's not just a question of food or clothes. She's got to go back to that school. She's on her own this time. Will they accept her? Or will they gang up on her? Are there going to be more fights? We can't always be there to make sure." I paused. "And, perhaps more importantly, can we leave her on her own in the house whilst we're at work? Can we trust her?"

John was optimistic.

"I think so. She's basically a nice kid. She's bound to make mistakes. But she'll try. She did last time..."

He said no more.

Dog and child were once again pounding down the stairs. Another flood of questions was about to be unleashed. I handed her a lump of cheese and the grater.

"Tea first - then chess!"

Twenty-Eight

We tried to make her homecoming much the same as her first visit the previous September. She had her macaroni cheese. She and John played several games of chess. I went through her clothes and made a list of all we would have to buy in Aylesbury the following day.

I gave her a bath and washed her hair. We sat beside the fire and drank sweet, milky cocoa. John tucked her up in bed whilst I read her a bedtime story. Jemima cuddled Mr Brown close and Dusty lay on the floor beside the bed. Annabelle and Joey provided a mournful welcome - but by that time, she was fast asleep.

This time, there was no midnight visit.

We used the borrowed car to go to Aylesbury. It made things much easier. We went to the same department store and bought much the same clothes - but in a larger size. John bought her shoes. He teased her that she was Cinderella going to the ball. She must have a pair of glass slippers! Once again, we rounded off our visit with ice creams in the Kardomah - and then rushed home to try everything on.

When John went back to work the following day, I resumed our private lessons. It seemed to me that spelling and proper punctuation was an area sorely in need of improvement. We used different colours of pencil for commas, inverted commas and full stops. We wrote letters to Auntie Jean and Miss Baker. We worked out in advance what we were going to say to them - then she tried to write it in simple decent English. There were several rough copies before we tackled the final versions. I thought Miss Baker might get quite a surprise when she saw what Jemima was capable of writing.

After that, we went back to our staple Arithmetic. She didn't seem to have learnt much in the three months whilst she had been away. We ate biscuits instead of apples. We went back through the old favourites - including long division - and then tried our hand at Algebra.

For history, I selected Queen Victoria. I thought that perhaps the accession of a young girl, just a few years older than herself, might help her to discover nineteenth century history. She lapped it up.

I asked her what she had been doing with Miss Baker.

"Cassels," she said. "We 'ad to draw cassels."

"And did you like drawing 'cassels' ?" I asked.

She shook her head.

"When you've seen one cassel, you've seen 'em all."

*   *   *

It took some delicate negotiating to get Jemima back into the village school. The headmaster had breathed a sigh of relief when the evacuees left in November. He did not exactly relish the return of even one of these accursed children. When he realized which particular child it was, he became even more intransigent. He wasn't having her... her of all people! She had been the chief troublemaker.

"You've got to understand," he said. "This is a Church school."

Rather maliciously, I pointed out that this was just the sort of place where one would expect to find love and forgiveness.

When he had calmed down, John pointed out that it was the village children who had attacked the evacuees. The Londoners had been simply defending themselves.

Jemima Shaw would be perfectly well-behaved unless she was attacked. We guaranteed her good behaviour but pointed out the importance of preventing the other children provoking her. She would doubtless fight her corner - if she had to; but it would be one child against ninety.

The headmaster declared that it was too great a responsibility for himself and the school. We said that we would approach the local education authority the following morning and tell them the full story. At this, he began to buckle: "Well, perhaps.... It might be possible... But assurances would have to be given..." We were happy to offer him all the assurances he requested. We promised that we would escort her to and from school. Once things had settled down, the situation would be reviewed. Driven into a corner, he agreed to a two week trial period.

It was interesting to watch the reaction on the Tuesday morning when Jemima returned to the school. People looked at her with curiosity. They felt they knew the face - but could not place it. Then recognition dawned. They looked at her again - this time with undisguised hostility. 'What was she doing here?'

I think her class had been warned that she was coming - but the older boys certainly had not. They looked quite amazed. Her? They thought they had seen the last of her. Paul Merchant, the thirteen year old whom she had assaulted on her first day in Bidworth, was about to say something very cutting - but then caught John's eye. John did not know who Paul was, but when he saw the look, he growled at him: "Leave her alone!"

The Taylors got an unpleasant shock seeing their tormentor once more. Under my eagle eye, Jemima reached out a hand to Donny and Pat. Pat shook it half-heartedly - but Donny turned away.

We had done the best we could. We had spent the

weekend warning Jemima not to over-react; to understand what the other children would feel - seeing her again; not to provoke them in any way. If they threw stones, bullied her or abused her, she was to go to the headmaster and report them. She promised to follow our advice. "Remember your new clothes!" I said. She nodded.

And, quite surprisingly, nothing happened. She was given a desk near the front of the class. She was kept fairly busy. She did well in her arithmetic. Before lunch, they had drawn a Union Jack and read about Horatio Nelson at the Battle of Trafalgar. After lunch, they had done nature study and she had written about her favourite animal. Of course, she had chosen Dusty.

At lunch, she had eaten cottage pie and carrots, jam dumpling and custard. When she had gone out into the playground, her teacher had been on duty. No one had said anything or done anything - but there had been dark looks. She had been very watchful - just in case.

When we collected her, she was still looking clean and tidy and she returned home very pleased with herself.

For three days all went well; but on the Friday, Paul decided that he must have his revenge. He pulled her hair violently and flung her down on the ground. The teacher rushed forward but Jemima was already on her feet and went straight for him. He stupidly put out his hand to ward off her attack - and she promptly bit two of his fingers.

Paul was sent to the headmaster and given a severe talking to. The headmaster would have given him the cane but it was felt that, with two fingers wrapped in Elastoplast, he had already suffered enough. Jemima was also called in and told to control herself. But at least there was no doubt as to who was the guilty party.

Most of the other children had seen the attack and the counter-attack. It did not win her any friends - but it certainly sent a clear message. Even on her own, the evacuee would hit back. They may not have liked her, but they admired her courage.

With a lot of help at home, Jemima began to do better in class. I helped her with her arithmetic; John was now making a valiant effort to improve her spelling and her writing. I think it was in April that she composed her first poem. She got eight out of ten for her nature diary; and she did well in P.T. All in all, she made a considerable effort and we were very proud of her. In fact, I think she was quite proud of herself. As she said: "No more cassels!"

Twenty-Nine

Once Jemima had settled back into family life in Bidworth, I became conscious of a change in her character. There was a brooding thoughtfulness, an unwillingness to say what she was thinking and moments of intense sadness which even Dusty was unable to dispel.

I thought it might be connected with the death of her uncle or perhaps the break with her family in London. But whatever it was, I decided to say nothing. If Jemima wished to tell me, she would no doubt do so in her own good time. But I was curious.

Every now and again, I thought she was about to say something. She seemed to be steeling herself to speak. She would look at me in a speculative fashion as if to see whether I was in a receptive mood - but then turn away and ask some completely irrelevant question. It was infuriating to watch her hovering on the brink - and then drawing back at the last moment. But I was determined not to pry.

One day, early in March, we went up into the woods beside Bidworth Hall. The snowdrops were out in force - together with the wild crocuses. There was a touch of spring. We went on to the Hall farm and fed Lady Rowley's horses with carrots.

Normally, on such an expedition, Jemima would talk away nineteen to the dozen; but that afternoon, she said nothing. Her face was drawn and serious; her lips a grim, straight line. Since there was nothing to be said, I used the time to speculate about Alan's diagonal boards and how we might save ourselves a lot of time using them to penetrate the mysteries of the German Air Force code. I found the silence helpful but, at the same time, I wished the child would spit it out.

Once we got home, she did.

She was sitting at the kitchen table with both hands enveloping a glass of milk - a large pack of chocolate biscuits to hand.

I made myself a nice creamy coffee with two spoonfuls of sugar. I sat down at the other side of the table. We looked at each other. She tried to smile - but it wasn't much of a smile. She ate another biscuit and drank some milk. I drank half my coffee.

Eventually, she looked me in the eye.

"Mary," she said, "would you still love me even though I had done something bad? Something really bad?"

I was amused by her oblique approach. Absolution was being sought in advance of confession. Being ignorant of the offence, it was clearly easier to forgive.

I replied guardedly:

"I don't think you could have done anything so bad that it would change my feelings for you..."

But perhaps she had? Looking at her face, I began to see that some enormous guilt was wracking her.

"You haven't murdered Donny Taylor, have you? Or his brother?"

"Not yet."

She laughed a bitter laugh - as if that would have been a minor peccadillo.

'God!' I thought. 'What's coming?'

"Is it something in Bidworth?" I asked anxiously.

"No. In London."

"Something that happened whilst you were back home?"

She nodded.

I actually thought I could see her teeth chattering. She was deeply upset.

I said: "Let's go through into the sitting room and sit beside the fire."

She didn't bother to pick up her milk. I abandoned my coffee. We sat on the sofa. I put my arm round her and gave her a cuddle. She sat staring at the flames.

"Who's involved?" I asked nervously. "Your Mum? Your little brother? Has something happened to him?"

She shook her head slowly.

"No. It's Cousin Eddie..."

I'd never heard her mention him before. I'd heard a lot about Uncle Josh - and quite a bit about her Auntie Jean; but Cousin Eddie was a closed book.

Despite my determination not to pry, I could not help asking: "Is he ill?"

"No," she said, "he's dead."

"How did he die?"

She burst into tears. A rare sight.

I hugged her closer.

"Were you fond of your Cousin Eddie?"

"No!" she burst out. "I hate him! I hate him!"

I was tempted to say: 'Well, if he's dead, it doesn't really matter, does it?' But obviously, it did matter - in a big way - because the tears kept rolling down her cheeks.

"What did Cousin Eddie do, " I asked, "before he died?"

"'e drove a van. A 'livery van round London. 'e was going to bring me out to Bidworth."

"When?"

"Just afore Christmas. 'e said as 'e would bring me out to stay with you for Christmas... but 'e didn't."

"Why not?"

"'Cos 'e cheated on me."

The tears had stopped. Her voice was bitter and contemptuous.

"He promised to bring you here - but then he didn't?"

She nodded.

"I hadna any money, y'see? My Ma had pinched it. I tried to get on a train but they cort me. The coppers took me 'ome... My Anty Jean, she beat me... but that were all right... I knew she would... she didn't want me to mix with toffs..."

She looked up. "I know you an' John ain't toffs but to 'er you are... Anyone who speaks lah-di-dah."

"I understand," I said.

Jemima sniffed.

"Well, she didna. She gave me it good an' 'ard. So much so, I wet meself. She said I were a dirty lil' pig."

"You probably were."

A faint smile appeared on Jemima's lips - then vanished.

"So I 'ad no lolly. Not even an 'apenny to buy you a stamp. I couldna even send you a card..."

"So you asked Cousin Eddie if - in the course of his travels - he would deliver you to Bidworth?"

"Yes. I packed me case and put it in 'is van. But 'e cheated on me." She took a deep breath. "You see, we 'ad an agreement." She looked at me anxiously - as if expecting disapproval. "... If I did things for 'im, then 'e would 'elp me."

I suddenly began to see what she was trying to say.

"He wanted to have sex with you?"

"'e wanted me to toss 'im off."

"Which you did?"

"That were my side of the agreement." She sounded a little more self-confident. "I did what 'e wanted; but 'e let me down, the dirty beast."

I held her tighter.

"Did it upset you?"

"Lor', no!" she said. "I done it afore. One of Ma's boyfriends? 'e gave us 'alf a crown." She smiled craftily. "You know me. I'd do anything for 'alf a crown!"

I was beginning to wonder if I would ever understand Jemima. She was basically a very amoral person. Civilization was not her natural clothing. She seemed more like a throwback to the days of Queen Boadicea. I could see her driving a chariot bristling with knives, cutting a swathe through Roman lines.

"So, despite you... obliging him, he failed to keep his side of the bargain?"

"'e took me aht with 'im to Watford."

"That's not far away."

"I know. 'e weren't far from 'ere. 'e made me do dirty things to 'im in the van and then 'e said: 'Sorry, Jem, I'm tekin' yer 'ome. Yer Ma'll flay me alive if she knows I've teken you to these 'ere people. I've got to tek yer back!' I begged 'im to let me 'op off. I said as 'ow I'd walk. But 'e wouldna listen, 'e rushed us back 'ome, dumped me and me case; and that were it. I couldna tell me Ma or me Anty Jean what 'e done. I didna want them to know where I'd bin. So I couldna tell them what Cousin Eddie'd been up to. Even if I'd told on 'im, they'd 'ave blamed me for pervoking 'im. I know they would..."

"So what did you do?"

I was not expecting her reply. It hit me like a sudden blow to the heart.

"I killed 'im."

There was no repentance or sorrow in her voice. Her eyes blazed with anger.

"I were so angry!"

I longed to say: 'You don't kill people just because you're angry!' But this was not a moment for moralizing. This was a moment of extreme delicacy. I suddenly realized that our whole relationship was in the melting pot. One false move... I said nothing.

"I did 'im in!" she said. "Good and proper!"

I took a deep breath.

"Does anyone know about this?"

"No."

"You haven't told anyone?"

"No. They all think it were an accident. Even the police said it were an accident... I wouldna've told you - but it's been gettin' to me."

"I know."

"You know?"

She looked surprised.

"I could see there was something troubling you. You've been very quiet for several days. I could see you trying to decide whether you should tell me. I wondered what it was."

"Well, now yer know!"

I thought quickly.

"I shan't tell anyone."

"Not even John?"

"Not unless you want me to."

"He might take me to the police."

"I doubt it. Putting you in jail won't make things any easier. The real trouble's in there." I tapped her on the head. "Isn't it? Everything's just thrashing around - like in a big cement mixer?"

"Summut dreadful."

"It's been weighing on your conscience. Now that you've told me, you'll feel better. We can share the secret."

"You don' mind I killed 'im?"

I took a deep breath.

I was going to say: 'Of course I mind... I mind very much.' I could not justify murder. Not for one minute. But, deep down, I said to myself: 'If there's one less child molester going about, the world's a safer place for everyone.' I hated these people who preyed on defenceless children; who destroyed their innocence; who left them with guilt and shame, leading to breakdowns and broken marriages in later life.

I thought of my own uncle... my own uncle who had tried to do nasty things to me. He had offered me money. He had tried to make it all a secret. So shameful that I would never tell my mother. I had run away; but I had seen enough to frighten me. I remember the memory coming back to me - especially at night when I was trying to get to sleep.

At the time, I wanted to tell my mother, but I wasn't sure that she would believe me. She might have taken his side. Even now - grown up and married - I still could not tell her. To drag up the past would only cause pain - lead to quarrels - and hurt the family. Her brother was now a distinguished lawyer with a silver tongue and a large fortune. He could easily say I was making it up. 'Mary has a vivid imagination.' That was what he used to say. It was his alibi - carefully prepared in advance. It was only since John had come into my life that the unpleasant memory had slipped away.

It seemed that Jemima could cope with dirty old men, but not with people who broke their promises. A deal was a deal. And she had taken her revenge. On balance, it was probably all for the best.

She could see me thinking.

There were once again tears in her eyes.

I could sense that she was frightened of rejection.

"Mary...?"

"It's all right," I said. "I was just thinking..."

But what was I thinking? What should I say? I couldn't say that she had done the right thing - in case she might do it again.

I sighed.

"Lots of terrible things happen when there's a war. People deceive each other. Break promises. People who would never dream of hurting anyone, go out and shoot people. Blow them up; drown them; drop bombs on them... I think that when we see other people being violent, we begin to do the same things ourselves. Things we later regret..."

But just because we were at war, was no excuse for Jemima killing someone.

I couldn't help feeling that she had over-reacted. But unless I showed some understanding of her feelings - of the anger she had felt, then I would be failing her. It would be better to let all her anger and hurt pour out. After all, if everyone thought it was an accident...

"Why did you need to kill him?"

"Because 'e let us down. Don't yer see? 'e promised me as 'e would bring me 'ere. I was lookin' forward to it. I did all 'e asked on me."

"Didn't that upset you?"

She was silent for a while.

I suspected there was a great deal more that she wouldn't dream of telling me.

She sighed.

"It did a bit. But I wouldna've minded if 'e'd brought me 'ere. It would've been a price worth payin'..."

I began to see how much our life and our home meant to her. It was quite frightening - the intensity of her feelings. She had made up her mind to escape from London. To leave her mother and her Auntie Jean. Having tried to escape, she had been caught and taken back to the East End. To return to her 'Garden of Eden' any price was worth paying. Even that. But betrayal had brought all her anger surging to the boil. For a nine year old, it had been too much to contain. She determined on revenge.

I took a deep breath.

"So what happened?"

"I burnt 'im."

I thought I had already got the whole story but her latest words again hit me hard. Burn someone to death! This was an appaling secret to carry round. No wonder she had looked so tormented - and found it so difficult to speak.

I could not help wondering what more she might be capable of doing. It was bad enough battling it out in the playground - biting people, kicking them in the face - and all the other things she had done. But to actually commit murder left me shaken and breathless. But I still hung on to her - and tried to hide my sense of shock.

"Tell me what happened," I said. "Slowly - and from the beginning. Once you got home. When Cousin Eddie dropped you back at your house."

"I said nowt. 'e said nowt. I went into the 'ouse with me suitcase. My Ma was working. Once 'e got me 'ome, 'e was quite cheery-like. 'We mus' try it again, Jem,' 'e said. 'You come down to the garridge and we'll have some more fun.' I smiled at 'im but I'd already decided to do 'im in, the twister."

"I didna say nowt to Anty Jean - 'bout where I'd bin. I waited for a few days to make sure no one knew about me. Then I put my plan into akshern..."

"You planned it?"

"Coarse!" She looked slightly aggrieved to think that she would do anything on impulse. A lot of thought and planning had gone into this.

"'is garridge was under a railway bridge. That's where 'e kept 'is van. 'e locked the place up when 'e was away 'livering; but when 'e comes back on an evening, 'e opens up the garridge - and then 'e goes into 'is office. It's a sort of wooden shed under the bridge.

"Well, my Ma was still workin' nights. She thought I was at my Anty Jean's. I went round there later. First of all, I got some petrol…"

"You bought it?"

"Garn! Don't be soft! You pinch it. Get a tube; stuff it into the petrol tank. Then you suck it out. Pour it into a can. There's allus plenty of cans around. But I sucked it a bit too 'ard. It all went into my mouth. Aargh!"

She looked as if she could still taste it.

Perhaps she could.

"So I got me petrol."

"How much?"

"About a can full. I didn't reckon I needed any more. I went down to Eddie's garridge but 'e wasn't back. So I waited till 'e showed up. Half past five 'e came. Parked 'is van. Went into 'is office. Going for a slash, y'see."

Her eyes sparkled unnaturally as she relived the event. Once again, I found myself wondering if she had psychopathic tendencies. She seemed to enjoy violence.

"'is office 'as bolts on the door, 'e bolts 'em at night. Not that 'e's got much in there. Jus' 'is books and papers - batteries and boxes. A couple of chairs and a table. That's where 'e did things to me…"

She ran a nervous tongue over her lips.

This was the difficult part.

"When 'e comes back, 'e usually goes for a slash. I know 'is 'abits. The bog's at the back of the shed. So whilst 'e were in the bog, I poured petrol all over 'is carpets and' chairs. I'd seen this film about a German pilot who killed ' isself. 'e got covered in petrol. Went up like a bloody torch…"

"And you intended Cousin Eddie to do the same?"

She nodded.

"I emptied the can. Then I went out and bolted the door. I 'eard 'im flushing the bog. So I lit a match and threw it under the door. Whoosh - it went up. You could feel the 'eat. I ran away as fast as I could go. I were lucky not to set meself on fire."

I imagine she was. Lighting a match in a confined space full of petrol fumes was positively suicidal.

"I did burn me fingers..." she admitted, "... and I spilt some petrol on my shoes. They got burnt. So I went 'ome, changed my clothes and put a plaster on me fingers. I told me Anty Jean that someone 'ad bitten me. I don't think she was bothered.

"She told me off for being late for tea but, after that, she did some knittin' and we listened to the wireless. It were a couple of 'ours later that the message came through that Cousin Eddie'd died in a fire at 'is garridge. A man who worked on the railway came in to tell Anty Jean.

"It didn't seem to put 'er up nor down. 'Burnt 'isself to death, 'as 'e?' she said. 'Good riddance to bad rubbish!' She didna like 'im. No one did.

"When my Ma came 'ome and she told 'er, she didn't 'ave any sympathy neither. 'Better dead,' she said. "e deserved all 'e got.' Most people seemed to think the same."

"So no one was particularly upset?"

"No. They all said 'e were a dirty ole man and 'e were better away. No one knew I 'ad bin anywhere near 'im. No one 'ad seen me in 'is van. I kep' my trap shut - till now."

She looked at me.

"You don't mind?"

I couldn't help smiling.

What a question! Being asked to condone a perfectly hideous murder - meticulously planned and carried out.

But what could I say?

I continued to hold her close.

"You can't believe," I said, "... you or anyone... that it's right to kill people. Whatever they've done, it's not right. And the way you killed him was particularly brutal and nasty..."

"It were quick."

"Yes," I said, "it was probably very quick. He was probably dead within a minute. But..." And this was really my point. "... that doesn't make it any better. You don't take the law into your own hands."

"You gotta look after yerself."

"Yes, but there's absolutely no justification for murdering people. If you kill everyone who hurts you, where will you stop? If I upset you - are you going to kill me or John?"

"Coarse not!"

I smiled wanly.

"Well, I hope not. I agree that Cousin Eddie was a bad man. A very evil creature. And the world is probably cleaner and safer without him. No one knows you did it. Everyone thinks it was an accident. Better leave it that way. Never say a word to anyone else."

I paused.

"It won't make any difference to you or me or John. We'll still love you - and look after you. It won't change anything. But you must never, never do anything like that again. If you feel like that about anyone else, you must tell us - and we will deal with it. Otherwise, you'll have a thoroughly bad conscience."

I looked at her.

"You do feel bad about it, don't you?"

"I do now," she said. "It's been going round me all day - every day. I kep' seein' 'im."

"Well, imagine feeling like that for the rest of your life."

She nodded slowly.

"I 'ad to tell yer."

"Of course you had. It was a terrible secret. But you'll feel better now. Now you've got it off your chest."

She stared into the fire.

"My Anty Jean said 'e 'fered with lots of children." She

chuckled. "She said I were lucky 'e'd never gone for me."

"And what did you say?"

"I said 'e wouldna dare."

I gave her a long hug and many kisses. I could sense her feeling of relief as she offloaded her burden on to me. To confess was to experience liberation of the soul. To be accepted - that was all that mattered.

Eventually I said:

"Well, even murderers have to eat! What shall we have for supper?"

"Chips!" she said. "Bangers and chips!"

"And I shall look after the chip pan!" I laughed. "We can't afford any more 'accidents'!"

*   *   *

By the time John came home, Jemima was in bed - and fast asleep. I checked twice.

He had his supper in the kitchen and then stretched himself out on the sofa beside the fire.

I waited till I was sure he was thoroughly relaxed before I told him the latest news.

I was sitting on the floor beside the sofa. I took his hand.

"We have a problem," I said.

"Hundreds," he said pessimistically. "Alan thinks the Germans are going to add another wheel to their machine. Then we shall be absolutely sunk."

"A domestic problem," I said.

"Plumbing broken down again? Chain snapped on the bike?"

"No, it's Jemima."

He groaned.

"What's she done now? Murdered someone?"

He was in a frivolous mood but he wouldn't be for much

longer.

"Actually, yes."

I felt a slight tension in his hand.

He knew that I would not joke about things like that.

"At school?" he said quietly.

"No. In London."

I heard him let out a long sigh.

"Does anybody know about it?"

"No. Just you, me and her. She told me this afternoon. She's been brooding about it for days."

"I noticed she was worried about something."

"A bad conscience. A very bad conscience. And now it's caught up with her. It had to come out."

John sighed deeply.

"So who's she murdered?"

"A lorry driver. Everyone thinks it was an accident - but she did it. He had promised to bring her out to Bidworth before Christmas - but he... chickened out. Said he was frightened of what her mother and her aunt might say. She was highly disappointed."

John turned on his side to look at me rather than the ceiling.

"And she murdered him?"

"Yep. Just like that."

John shook his head in disbelief.

"She's a raving little psychopath."

"Probably. But what you don't know is that this lorry driver had been doing nasty things to her - in return for helping her to escape."

"I see."

"Very nasty things. And he'd been doing it to other children..."

"Go on."

"So she felt very cheated. He failed to keep his side of

the bargain, so she retaliated *maxima forte*. Not on the spur of the moment, please note. But a carefully planned attack four days later. And she followed my advice..."

"Your advice?"

"Yes. After the bicycle episode, I told her that the great thing about committing a crime was not to let anyone know a crime had been committed."

"Did you say that?"

"I did. But I wasn't expecting to be taken quite so literally."

"So what did she do to the poor bloke?"

"Set him on fire!"

"Set him on fire?"

"Petrol. He had a garage under a railway bridge, with a little office built of wood. She knew his movements. So once he was tucked into his office, she shot the bolts, poured in a gallon of petrol - and whoosh!"

I looked at John.

His mouth was hanging open in amazement. I had never seen him look quite so shocked... quite so lost for words.

"So now we have a murderer sleeping in our upstairs bedroom! We can't hand her over to the police. We can't punish her - that would be counter-productive. We can't throw her out. She's deeply upset by what she's done. She wants our love and forgiveness... What do we do?"

I imagine that there are few husbands who come home after a day's work and face such a dilemma.

John was deeply upset.

I could see him crying.

All he said was: "Bloody hell!"

He rolled on his back, put his hands behind his head and stared at the ceiling.

"Would you like a glass of whisky?" I asked.

He shook his head.

I could imagine all the thoughts that were rushing through his head. They had been going through mine for the past four hours - but I had come to terms with it. I couldn't justify her action - but I could understand the way her mind had worked. It was an extreme reaction to a highly damaging series of events.

Although she said that what Cousin Eddie had done to her was nothing new, I could not believe that she had come through the incident totally unscarred. I knew from my own experience the fears, the bitterness, the deep resentment one could feel for such a person. Outwardly, she appeared to cope; but she had felt so humiliated... so cheated... that she was determined to hit back. Even in the playground, her reaction to any insult or attack was immediate and vicious. This was no exception.

Cousin Eddie was obviously a vile creature. Instinctively, she knew that. No one would listen to her. No one would show any sympathy for her. How natural then that she should decide to be his own judge and executioner. This time, he had chosen the wrong child. The child had hit back.

But what worried me was that she always took the law into her own hands. She had done it more than once. And my fear was that she would do it again.

I watched John wrestling with the problem.

He could cope with a game of chess where the rules were well established. But this was a human issue for which there were few clear guidelines. It concerned a human being whom he cared for... whom he loved. Yes, I knew he loved our little evacuee. But how to come to terms with it? How indeed?

He had no answer.

Eventually, he said:

"What did you say to her?"

"I said that terrible things often happen in wartime. Things that nobody would normally do. She had done something very bad - but once she had admitted it... once she had had the courage to tell me what she had done... that was the first step to putting things right. We talked it out - for two hours we talked about it - then had supper. But I had to forgive her - and say that we still loved her. There wasn't any alternative. Condemning her... throwing her out... wouldn't solve anything."

I looked at John.

"But never let her near the chip pan!"

"Don't worry," he said. "I won't even let her near a box of matches. Bloody hell! What a mess! What'll she do next? Murder Mrs Williams? First, it was razor blades - now it's arson."

"It's the law of the jungle," I said. "Cross her - and you're dead!"

"That's no joke."

"No. It's a fact."

John continued to think the thing through. I knew he wouldn't be able to come up with any solution. I had myself considered every option.

"What do we do with a child like that?" he said at last. "How do we even begin to civilize her? To make her a normal person? It defeats me. It really does."

I let him agonize for another ten minutes; then I delivered my verdict:

"I don't see any other way than what we are doing. She wants to live with us. She wants to be with us. For her, it's the most important thing in the world. She was prepared to bear any amount of unpleasantness to get here. She was prepared to kill when she didn't.,

"It means more to her than we realize. For someone brought up in the East End, this must seem like heaven.

Having been to her home - having met her mother - I can see precisely why she wanted to get out. Nothing was going to stop her. So, presumably, if it matters so much to her, in due course she'll adopt our values and outlook."

"In due course..."

"She's not there yet."

"You can say that again."

"It'll take a long time. We'll probably have a few more disasters to cope with. We must expect them. But at least she's honest. She does have a conscience. She told me what she had done. There's no one else in the world she trusts. Remember! Her own father killed someone. It runs in her blood. If we don't help her... if we turn against her... there's no telling what she might do - even to us. You have to think of that."

"I am thinking about it. It's terrifying. That bloody Williams woman has a lot to answer for."

I patted his thigh.

"Well, I still love her - whatever she's done. I admire her spirit. I don't think what she's done is right - I won't excuse her - but I think she's a very brave little girl. And now I know the worst, I think I can live with it."

John nodded.

"It won't change my feelings for her either. I still think she's a poppet. But she never ceases to amaze me. I just wouldn't think she was capable of doing a thing like that. It's inhuman - brutal."

"I think she's capable of anything!" I said quietly.

John shook his head sadly.

"I think you're probably right."

He paused.

"I think I'll have that whisky," he said. "A double. And neat."

Thirty

During April, things began to get more exciting at work and I often found myself doing twelve hour shifts. John, whose talents as a translator were less in demand, stayed at home and looked after Jemima during the Easter holidays. Once again, he was able to scrounge a car and took her across country to Stratford-on-Avon and Oxford, so that she could see a little more of England.

I think that what she enjoyed most was the food. She relished having meals in 'toff cafs' (I think that was her description of *The Mitre* in Oxford.) John also hired a boat and took her on the river. He told her about the Parsons' Pleasure but there were no parsons to be seen. I expect they were all training to be Army chaplains.

Jemima was always bursting to tell me what she had seen and done - and did so at great length. But, sadly, my mind was on other things. I was almost entirely absorbed in abstruse mathematical calculations as we struggled to unravel the mysteries of 'Red' - the Luftwaffe's cipher system. I fear I was not as appreciative an audience as I should have been.

Some nights, we all stayed in a pub in Bletchley. It was not a particularly peaceful place. On Friday and Saturday nights, there was a prolonged knees-up in the public bar - the locals roaring out their favourite songs. 'Roll out the barrel' was the song of the moment. Jemima said it 'were jus' like Lime'ouse.'

Most of the winter, they'd been singing: 'We're hanging out our washing on the Siegfried Line' but now Hitler had launched his surprise attack on Norway. Those of us in the know were painfully aware that an attack on France and Belgium could not be long delayed.

Quite a lot of people asked John when he was going to join up. His standard reply was 'reserved occupation'. But that didn't cut much ice because all that people saw him doing was riding his bicycle on the Bletchley Road at all hours of day and night.

As a village, Bidworth seemed remarkably untouched by the war. The sense of unreality was compounded by the complacency of our leaders. Mr Chamberlain talked about Hitler 'missing the bus'; the papers were full of articles about the BEF assembling in Northern France - all ten divisions of them - fully mobilized - and ready to advance into Belgium should the need arise.

Of course we had our Navy to protect us and we rejoiced at the amazing number of ships the Germans had lost in their Norwegian campaign. Ten destroyers in one fjord! No wonder we felt safe.

So Jemima got her Easter egg full of chocolates; we ate hot-cross buns; we went out on our bicycles and came back from Lady Rowley's wood with our baskets filled with wild daffodils. As a family, we had a day out in Cambridge - going by train. A few more dresses were bought. Dusty had to have a small operation at the vet's which worried all of us, but he came through with flying colours.

On occasions, we had to leave Jemima on her own in the house - but she caused us no trouble. The very fact that she had no close friends in the village, helped. She didn't belong to any gang and so was unlikely to bring anyone back to the house. She was quite used to being on her own and spent hours taking Dusty for walks or playing chess against herself. She was also beginning to 'gobble up' books at an alarming rate.

When the Germans launched their long-expected

attack in the west, she became quite excited about the war. A map was put up on the kitchen wall and we marked the places where fighting was reported. The British and French positions were marked out in blue; the Germans in red. What started off as a few harmless arrows soon became fast-moving columns of tanks moving in dangerous directions. Even to a child's eyes, things did not seem to be going our way.

Outside, in the garden or on her cycling expeditions, Jemima was always on the watch for aeroplanes. John got her an aircraft identification booklet and lent her his binoculars. She claimed to have seen every make of British or German machine passing overhead; but it was still only May and the Luftwaffe was busy elsewhere.

However, whole flights of Hurricanes took off from Debden and Hornchurch and came our way. Training flights from Halton also proved interesting. Small chocolate-coloured planes with tiny clockwork engines purred back and forth across the skies. Magisters and Tiger Moths mostly - plus the occasional Anson. Once again, we felt pleasantly secure.

But it was all an illusion. The British did advance - but the Germans cut round behind them like a scarlet sickle, separating them from their bases and their vital supplies. Soon, the panzers were in Amiens - then in Abbeville. Before long, they were in Boulogne and pressing on to Calais There was talk of the British army falling back on Dunkirk.

All of us stood staring at the map in the kitchen, watching the red plague slowly engulfing our divisions.

"Will they escape?" Jemima asked John.

"Some of them," he replied.

"I wish I could go an' fight 'em!" she said.

John laughed.

"You may have to!"

He looked at her small anxious face.

"Come on," he said. "We've got another half hour before bed time. Let's have another game of chess."

Thirty-One

"Were you married in Cambridge, Mrs Woodward? In King's College Chapel, perhaps?"

"No," I said, "we were married in the Registry Office at Aylesbury."

We were waiting outside the village hall. The children were rehearsing for a concert. As usual with such events, they were running late. The Vicar had decided to use this opportunity to bestow a little pastoral care on one of his lost sheep.

"You didn't choose to get married in church?"

"No," I replied. "I'm not a hypocrite."

My reply was a bit of a conversation-stopper but the poor man persevered.

"I see you got your evacuee back."

"I went to London and brought her out. She was being neglected by her own mother. Not being properly fed. The shoes I had bought her, had been sold. I felt she would be better off with us. Her mother agreed." I looked at Mr Jones coldly. "She's also making very good progress at school."

"So I hear."

It might have been better if the conversation had stopped there; but the Vicar had an incurable habit of needling me. Now he proceeded to do so in a big way.

He asked about John's health.

"He's fine," I said.

"Such a strong, handsome man," he said. "I'm surprised he hasn't joined the armed forces yet."

I took this as an imputation of cowardice.

"He's in a reserved occupation."

"What does he do?"

There was no way I was going to break the Official Secrets Act - but I thought that even to dissemble might be dangerous. As with Jemima, it seemed that attack might be the best form of defence.

"I don't think I could disclose that to a member of the Fifth Column."

There had been much in the papers about Hitler's secret sympathizers. They were supposed to be everywhere - just waiting their chance to emerge.

Mr Jones looked surprised.

"I beg your pardon?"

"I gather you were a member of the Peace Pledge Union?"

"I still am."

I raised my eyebrows critically.

"Well, It was precisely people like you who got us into this mess. If we had stood up to Hitler earlier, we wouldn't be fighting this war. You were the ones that wittered on about peace - and a fat lot of good it did us. You undermined the will of our people. You were the ones who led us astray. You thought that if you kept shouting about peace, Hitler would go away. Now he's on our very doorstep."

Mr Jones was not in the least intimidated.

"Mrs Woodward, I believe you are by profession a mathematician - not a historian. You have a very warped view of history."

"If you had your way, we wouldn't be at war?"

"That's right. We believe that, with God's help, peace will triumph over war."

I looked at him coldly.

"So what about the Czechs and the Poles? Your peace pledge didn't do them much good, did it? And what about Denmark and Norway? They didn't do anything to provoke him. Holland and Belgium bent over backwards to avoid causing offence. That didn't stop him! D'you think we should just lie down and let him walk all over us? At what point do we say: 'No'? It seems to me that you pacifists are playing right into his hands. We might all be murdered - and then what?"

Mr Jones had a pained look on his face as if his cat had brought a dead bird into his front room.

"Mrs Woodward, what are you trying to say?"

"I should think it's perfectly obvious. You and your Peace Pledge cronies are undermining the spirit and freedom of this country. You are cowards... you are traitors. You are still praying for peace when you know it is time for war. You are doing Hitler's dirty work for him."

The Vicar clearly did not share my point of view. Indeed, he was blind to any philosophy but his own. He believed that his suggestion that John should join the armed forces had touched a raw nerve. I could see that he despised me. I was at best an agnostic - at worst, an atheist. A woman with no principles - someone to be pitied.

I felt the need to be more vicious.

"I've already reported you to the authorities under Section 18B."

(That was the regulation concerning the internment of subversives. Only the previous day, a right-wing MP had been arrested. The papers were demanding more drastic action.)

"I expect they'll come and arrest you in the next few days," I added.

The superior look vanished from his face.

"You reported me?"

"Naturally. It's my duty as a citizen to report those who are underminding the war effort."

"Mrs Woodward," he said patronizingly. "You are being

231

highly offensive."

"Deliberately," I said. "Quite deliberately. We've got to get rid of people like you."

He shook his head.

"I think it would be better if you went back to Cambridge and did something useful like teaching - rather than fomenting trouble in our quiet little village. And you can take that wretched 'vac with you. She's caused enough trouble already."

He was beginning to lose his temper.

I decided to deliver one final blow.

I was quite calm.

"Don't think you'll escape," I said. "If the Germans land in our country - and you're still at large - I shall personally come up to the church and murder you. I shall make sure that you do not benefit from the fruits of your treachery."

The Vicar looked at me in disbelief. He could hardly believe that he was standing outside his village hall on a beautiful spring afternoon, being threatened with violence by a young woman in a pink dress. It was clear that he regarded me as highly strung... unbalanced... possibly mad. What he would have said in reply, I do not know. Fortunately for him, at that moment, the doors of the hall opened - and the children poured out.

Mrs Jones, who had been inside, emerged with her youngest child. She looked surprised to see me standing so close to her husband. It must have looked an unholy combination.

"You've been speaking to my husband?"

I smiled sweetly.

"He was trying to persuade me to have an affair with him; but I refused."

Because of the noise of the children, I don't think Mr Jones heard what I said; but his wife certainly did.

Her eyes blazed with anger.

"You keep away from my husband!"

I imagine that tea at the vicarage must have been a singularly unpleasant meal. Now they would both hate me. I felt a small hand enter mine.

"What were you sayin' to 'im?" she asked.

I laughed.

"I was telling him that if the Germans landed, I would personally come and murder him. He didn't like it."

Jemima was nothing if not loyal.

"We'll do it together," she said.

I might have been joking - but she wasn't. The cool, blue light of hatred still burned bright.

Thirty-Two

Defeatism amongst the clergy was perhaps to be expected; but not in one's own family. During June, my mother began to panic. The Germans were now across the Channel; Hastings was no longer a pleasant holiday resort. It was the front line. My mother was sure that paratroops would be dropped in Kent - just as they had been in Holland. Overnight, they would find themselves prisoners... hostages... What horrors would then follow?

She decided that my father could fend for himself. My little brother was in a boarding school in Derbyshire. My two older sisters were married and settled in York and Chester. They would provide suitable boltholes in the event of invasion. I expect she came to see if I could provide a halfway house. If so, she was disappointed.

She booked herself into a country house hotel near Aylesbury, from whence she invited herself to lunch on the first Saturday in July. John and I both took the weekend off and I remember buying a duck.

We made sure the house was clean and tidy. Jemima, who was given a new dress, laid the table and polished the glasses. We had to eat in the kitchen because the house consisted of two rooms upstairs and two rooms downstairs. I made sure the duck was cooked in good time so that there were no unpleasant fumes filling the kitchen..

She arrived in a taxi - a great indulgence in wartime. She expressed herself surprised that we did not have a car - but only a couple of bicycles. She pronounced the house to be impossibly small. She said she was surprised I didn't suffer from claustrophobia. Looking pointedly at John, she reminded him that I had been brought up in a house with six bedrooms and a large garden. That was the standard to which I was accustomed. Both her other daughters had fine homes. The implication was that John was failing me as a husband.

I think that she was annoyed that there had been no 'proper' wedding; just a hole-in-the-corner affair at the register office. If they had known about our plans, they could have laid on a decent reception. We had been secretive and selfish. December was a stupid time to get married. The family had been offended. Uncle Stephen had been looking forward to his favourite niece getting married. (I took that with a hefty pinch of salt.) My mother was sure that he would have given us a very generous wedding gift. Five hundred pounds at least.

And who was this child? She turned her attention to Jemima... An evacuee? From the East End? How long would she be staying with us, occupying the spare bedroom? Indefinitely? She raised her eyebrows at that. Had she got no family to go back to? My mother may have had ideas about occupying the parrot room, but once she had seen it, she declared that it was far too small.

In fact, from her point of view, the whole house was a disaster. How much was it costing us? No wonder it was so cheap - in a village so far from civilization - at least, civilization as understood in the stockbroker belt or along the south coast. Only three trains a day? And an irregular bus service to Aylesbury? It was positively neanderthal!

John kept control of his tongue and was incredibly polite. Jemima took her cue from John and said very little. But I could see her hard, grey eyes taking in every *faux pas*. It was highly embarrassing. This was my mother. They had expected better. So had I. I imagine that had Jemima been billeted with my mother, there would have been battle royal.

She attempted to quiz both of us about our jobs. 'Working for the government' was not in her eyes a proper answer. What sort of work? John mentioned the Official Secrets' Act. She retaliated by asking how much we were paid. She imagined that would not be an official secret! When I told her what I was getting, she said that, at that rate, it was obviously not a proper job. She suggested that there was something shameful about what we were doing.

Like the Reverend Jones, she said it was high time John obtained a commission in one of the armed forces. She thought the Royal Navy would suit him. Uncle Stephen could pull the necessary strings. Remembering John's fears on board the *Alcantara*, I knew that the Navy was the last place he would want to be.

John reminded her that as a civil servant, he was already in a reserved occupation, doing valuable work for the country; but she dismissed his words with contempt. Pen-pushing was no fit job for a healthy young male. I suspect that, in a very unsubtle way, she was trying to break us up. It was all so different to the cheerful camaderie of John's parents.

We managed to survive till the coffee. After that, I felt that I could impose on the others no longer. I asked her if she would like to see the village. She accepted immediately. Jemima uttered an audible sigh of relief. John said: "We'll do the washing-up." I knew that both of them would be glad to see the back of her.

Once outside the house, my mother came out in her true colours. She described John as 'quite frankly, a waster!' As for Jemima - shades of Miss Baker - she was just a 'common little guttersnipe.' She could not imagine why we were wasting our time and substance on her.

I asked my mother provocatively whether she had been

asked to take in any evacuees? Of course she had been asked - everyone had; but the answer was entirely predictable. They didn't need the money. They didn't want other people's children running wild in their house or garden. China would be broken; the parquet floors damaged; holes would be dug in the lawn. There would be noise.

"And you know how your father hates noise!"

But as we walked up the main street, she revealed the full extent of her treachery. There was, she said, still time to get out of the country. Uncle Stephen could get me a ticket on the Pan American clipper. He was willing to offer his niece a job in his New York office. He hoped to join her there shortly. There was no point waiting for the Germans to turn up in Chancery Lane. At best, they might be shot; but there was always the prospect of being sent off to a concentration camp in Silesia.

She looked at me in a meaningful way.

"They say they're even planning to castrate every male."

"What about Daddy?"

She laughed coldly.

"It wouldn't make any difference to him," she said. "He's past it."

"If he is," I thought, "it's your fault."

Since she had hurt me, I decided to hurt her. I was tired of hearing about her ever-obliging brother. There had already been too much mention of him for one afternoon.

"I wouldn't accept any favours from Uncle Stephen," I said firmly.

"Why ever not? He's always been very fond of you."

"Has he? Is that why he used to offer me sweets and money when I was a child?"

"He's a very generous man."

"Not entirely disinterested, I would say."

"What d'you mean by that?"

I stopped and stared at her. I hoped this was a moment she would remember. A moment that would pierce her pride and cause her to feel a lasting guilt.

"He wasn't giving me money for nothing, was he?" I said. "He wanted to touch me. And what was worse, he wanted me to touch him! Why d'you think he kept coming to our house?"

My mother was speechless.

"He only gave me money to shut me up. So that I wouldn't talk to you or Daddy. That's why he paid for me to go to boarding school. To keep me out of the way. I know he paid for it. He told me." I was being cruel, but I didn't care. "A fine brother to have! Corrupting his nephew and nieces! Perhaps he did it to all of us? That's probably why Daddy moved us to Hastings. To get away from him!"

My mother exploded.

"How dare you say that about Stephen! He's a brilliant man. A K.C. One of the youngest K.C.s in the country. He's done so much to help us."

I shrugged my shoulders.

"He buys silence - most effectively. I was too frightened to speak to you about it; but now I'm happily married, I'm not afraid any more."

"Happily married!" she said. "To him!"

"At least he doesn't molest children!"

"And neither does Stephen!"

Suppressed memories flashed unbidden into my mind. "So I'm just imagining it, am I? Didn't he do the same thing to Diana?" Diana was one of my sisters. "Isn't that why she ran away from home? Oh, yes, he did disgusting things to me. He told me that if I said anything, I would be sent away to an approved school and have all my hair shaved off. You've no idea the misery he caused me. And if I go to New York, it'll start all over again. He can't keep his hands off me. If he'd come to our wedding, God knows what he'd have said or done. I paused to let the message sink in. It was not a message I wanted anyone else to hear. Certainly not John. I added brutally: "He's a rat! He's always been a rat! Now he's ratting on his country. Running away. God, I despise him! I hope the Germans do get to him. I hope they castrate him! I hope he dies a long, slow, lingering death!"

What my mother would have said in reply, I do not know. I imagine she would have described me as spiteful and ungrateful - probably a liar. But, mercifully, as I concluded my tirade, who should come out of a nearby gate but Mr Jones himself?

He raised his hat.

(Whatever our differences, proprieties had to be observed.)

"Mrs Woodward! And...?"

"My mother," I said rather gracelessly.

"Are you staying in the village?"

"No. I'm just paying a short visit."

The shorter, the better, I thought.

But Mr Jones had other ideas.

"Have you seen the church yet?"

"No."

It didn't sound as if my mother thought a visit to the church would improve her opinion of Bidworth. But Mr Jones was persuasive.

"There's a very fine view from the tower."

"Of paratroops?" I asked sarcastically.

Mr Jones winced. The thought of the enemy landing in his graveyard and fighting it out round his church must have been very distressing to a pacifist. But, perhaps like the Vicar of Bray, he was already changing his tune?

"The Local Defence Volunteers have established a look-out post in the tower," he said confidently. "I'm sure they'll give us adequate warning. If any Germans do land in the vicinity, you can be sure the bells will be rung loudly."

"And what do we attack them with? Kitchen knives?"

Mr Jones smiled warily. This was the woman who had threatened to kill him if the Germans arrived. It was probably an idle threat, but it was not something he was likely to forget.

"I'm sure we'll think of something."

My mother was not impressed.

"You should get a job in the regular army. A fine young man like you. You'd make an excellent padre. You're wasted round here."

My mother dismissed the rural ministry in a single, contemptuous gesture.

"Mr Jones is a pacifist," I explained. "He's a signed-up member of the Peace Pledge Union. We have to respect his views."

"Respect his views? What stuff and nonsense!" My mother almost exploded. "You should be down in Kent, young man, manning a machine gun, defending innocent women and children. You should be ashamed of yourself, sitting here in idleness, whilst British people are cowering in terror before the invader!"

I was amused by the violence of her words. I imagined that Mr Jones would recognize where my war-like sentiments hailed from. Like mother, like daughter.

The vicar looked at me nervously, twisting his hat.

"Well, actually... only last week... I sent in my resignation... From the Peace Pledge Union," he added quickly, in case I happened to think he had made some greater personal sacrifice.

"Well done!" I said sarcastically.

"I've applied to join the Defence Volunteers. They're a fine body of men." He grinned sheepishly. "I hope to do my bit with them."

I was not impressed.

"All you're doing is protecting your own interests! You'll still sleep comfortably in your own bed. Not much sacrifice there! But I daresay your little wife'll be proud of you."

My mother thought I was being too hard on him.

"Mary! Remember whom you're speaking to. Mr Jones is your vicar. He may be a coward but you never know... one day, he may be called upon to save your life!"

Mr Jones smiled.

I couldn't help smiling too.

The thought of the local vicar rushing to save my life seemed utterly bizarre. My mother had no idea of the deep antipathy between us.

"Is there any role for women in your local organization?" I asked politely. "I'm sure I could handle a Bren gun as well as the next person."

I didn't say that we had already spent an hour or two on a firing range - just in case German paratroops made a sudden descent on Bletchley Park. We had been shown how to load a Bren gun but had attacked targets with rifle and pistol. I had achieved eleven hits; John, four.

Mr Jones smiled his superior smile.

"I'm afraid not..." The last thing he wanted was for this unbalanced woman to get her hands on an offensive weapon. There could be a nasty accident. "... I think you'd be better looking after that wretched child. Try to make something of her. That would be enough for most people!"

My mother nodded.

"I quite agree with you. Dreadful child! Can't even speak English properly."

I reflected that Jemima had hardly spoken since my mother arrived. She had been unusually silent. She was being judged simply *sui generis* evacuee.

Drawing strength from the support he had received from my mother over Jemima, Mr Jones went one step further. A dangerous step...

"And perhaps you would encourage your son-in-law to go down to Kent himself and protect the women and children there. I'm sure he'd do much more good down there than he's doing up here... cycling aimlessly round the countryside!"

As he looked at my mother, I lashed out with my fist. I was standing quite close to him and my blow caught him between his ear and his left eye. He staggered sideways and fell down on the road. His hat rolled into the gutter, I stamped hard on his knee.

My mother was horrified.

"Mary!"

I took her arm.

"Let's go, mother. We have to find your taxi man. I expect he's in *The Fox and Hounds*"

But the taxi man was standing on the steps of the pub, holding an almost empty pint glass. He was full of praise.

"That were a beautiful shot, Miss! 'e went down like a sack o' potatoes, 'e did. 'e weren't expecting that. Good job the local bobby didn't see you. You might 'ave been arrested!" He smiled at my mother. "You should be proud of 'er. If the Jerries come, she'll give 'em 'ell! Brave lass!"

My mother looked daggers at me.

"I've never been so shocked in my life. Hitting a defenceless man. And stamping on him! You should be ashamed of yourself!"

"Goodbye, mother!" I said firmly. "I hope you have a safe journey - back to Kent!"

I turned on my heel and walked home. Down a side lane, I saw the vicar limping away. I smiled maliciously. "Let him explain that to his wife!"

When I returned home - alone - John said: "What happened to your mother? Have you lost her?"

I sighed deeply.

"The vicar wanted to show her over the church; but she said it was time she went home."

Jemima clapped her hands.

John looked suspicious.

"You've got blood on your knuckles. Did you hit her?"

"No," I said. "That was the vicar. He deserved it."

John raised his eyebrows.

"What was he doing?"

"Casting aspersions. Foul aspersions! About you. Saying it was about time you got a proper job and stopped cycling aimlessly around the countryside. He suggested that you should go down to Kent and protect my mother!"

"She lives in Sussex!"

"I don't think geography's his strong point. About as poor as his theology, if you ask me."

"And you hit him?"

"Hard. On the face. I've been longing to do it for a long time. He went down like a ninepin. Then I stamped on his knee. Constable Bell may be calling..."

John looked at Jemima.

"I think we can deal with him."

I smiled.

"Perhaps you would prefer to deal with my mother?"

John shook his head.

"No," he said. "I think we'll leave her to the Germans!"

*   *   *

But, for various good reasons, my mother was spared that fate. I discovered quite quickly that she had not returned to Hastings. She had spent a further two days in the country hotel near Aylesbury. From there, she had gone to my sisters in Chester and York. Doubtless, she had described all my failings in graphic detail. I received worried letters from both of them – which did not merit a reply.

After that, I am told, she moved into a large hotel in Harrogate where she remained till the Battle of Britain was over. When she did return to Hastings, she discovered that my father had dug up the lawns and planted rows of vegetables. A gun crew had been established at the bottom of the garden and were vigorously manning a Bofors. But soon they were moved to Birmingham. Things were much worse up there.

My mother spent the rest of the war in Hastings – posing as Lady Bountiful and even being elected to the local Council as an Independent. After the war, she managed to produce a book about her experiences: *Hastings In Wartime*. A few copies can still be found in secondhand bookshops on the south coast.

I noticed that it contained no reference to her youngest daughter, her visit to Bidworth or her bolthole in Harrogate. Like Uncle Stephen, some things are too painful to be recalled. They are better buried; the ground raked over; flowers planted. The individuals concerned are not likely to forget what lies beneath; but, fortunately, the violence of war was able to conceal many sordid and shameful secrets. My own included.

4: The Heroine

(Jemima's Story: June - November 1940)

4. The Heroine

Hermia's Story, June - November 1940

Thirty-Three

When I first came to Bidworth, in September 1939, I was frightened to set foot outside the village. For me, the countryside was alien territory - as unknown and as dangerous as the Amazon jungle. But in the space of two to three weeks, I began to discover the quiet country lanes and the sleepy corners of rural Buckinghamshire. My expeditions on Lady Rowley's bicycle extended my knowledge and reduced my fears.

In April 1940, John bought me a slightly larger bike and during that spring, I roamed far and wide, often covering ten or fifteen miles in an afternoon.

I imagined myself in various roles. I was a policeman, a spy, sometimes an Army commander - as I explored what the countryside had to offer.

As Mary has said, I took John's binoculars with me and surveyed my surroundings as if I were conducting a military campaign. Unfortunately, there were very few people to be seen; only the occasional car or lorry. More frequent were the small training aircraft which droned overhead.

The chief attraction were the horses who came over to the gate and nuzzled me. Mary had warned me to be careful of their teeth; but I usually carried a few carrots in my basket which established a quick bond of friendship between us. One or two of the farms had donkeys. I tried to climb on their backs, but they were shy and unco-operative.

I tended to stop in villages where there was a shop - or a church. I had discovered that churches were often left open and could be explored at will.

I remember pushing open the door of the first church I

entered. The squeak of the heavy oak door, the slightly musty smell, rows of polished pews, stained glass windows and brass crosses. In several of them, there were large wooden eagles and lots of old books. There were organs with yellowing keys, candles, bell ropes and twisting stone staircases that led upwards to belltowers or downwards to boiler rooms.

No one seemed to occupy these treasure houses. I was all on my own. I was a bit nervous to start with, but gradually I became bolder. I opened cupboards and doors. I discovered where keys were hidden and tried the keys in locks. All I seemed to discover were more rooms, more books, heavy pieces of embroidery and bottles of wine. Of course I took a swig. It was strong stuff. Not as sweet as Tizer! A bit overpowering. Fortunately, I did not drink all that much.

I began to find myself very familiar with the churches in the area. I felt it incumbent on me to inspect them at irregular intervals. In one church, I was able to make my way to the top of the tower and survey the surrounding countryside with my binoculars.

We had heard quite a bit about German paratroops landing in Holland. Who knew? They might soon be landing in England. I might be the only person who would see them. What would I do? Ring the church bells! That was what Mr Churchill had told us to do. At the first sign of invasion, the church bells would be rung. I examined the red, white and blue woollen holders on the bell ropes and imagined myself tugging them for dear life. Perhaps it would be more sensible to get on my bike and ride away quickly to get help.

On one of my expeditions, I was already well on my way home when I discovered I had left John's binoculars behind. Even though I was already late for tea, I had to ride back two miles and climb eighty steps to find where I had left them. Thereafter, I was much more careful.

The exploration of churches swiftly drew my attention to the existence of offertory boxes - 'For the Church Fabric Fund' or 'For Mission Work'. I didn't know what fabric was - or mission. But there was always the fascinating possibility that heaps of silver coins were hidden within.

I poked sticks through the slots and moved them about. Most of the boxes were empty; but I came upon one church where my stirrings and scratchings produced encouraging sounds of loose coins.

I looked at the lock - and the hinges. They looked quite strong. I looked at the under side of the offertory box. It was held in position with four screws. I had seen a screwdriver in a drawer in the Vestry. I went to get it.

It was rather difficult to hold the screwdriver vertically and engage the screw heads. I opted for the easier alternative of prizing the bottom loose and letting all the coins slide out. I was disappointed to see how many of the coins were coppers. Most of them were half-pennies - but some were farthings. There was just one silver sixpence. I gathered up the coins and carefully wedged the base of the offertory box back into position - so that the theft would not be all that obvious. I put all the smallest coins back in the box and counted what was left. 1/3d. A poor haul.

Clutching my slender gains, I headed out into the sunshine, forgetting that I had left behind the tell-tale screwdriver. I had left my bicycle some distance away. I now drove to a neighbouring village and treated myself to some boiled sweets and a bottle of Tizer.

At that time, I was getting a small amount of pocket money from Mary and John - so I was not desperate for cash. But it was nice to know that there was an extra source of funds waiting to be tapped.

I did not return to that particular church for about three weeks. Once again, funds were low. In fact, they were non-existent.

I parked my bike a good distance from the church and approached the building through a small wood. It was a beautifully warm summer's day. The church was cool and full of light. I wandered round, as was my custom, and looked at the brass stair rods, the four angels guarding the altar, the blue velvet curtains in the side chapel and the untidy heaps of music lying round the organ. There was a box of matches lying on a pew. Automatically, I put it in my pocket.

I found the hidden key to the vestry and retrieved the screwdriver from the top right hand drawer of the desk. Perhaps at that moment, I remembered subconsciously that, on my last visit, I had not returned the screwdriver. It was a foolish mistake. (Mary had always said that if you were going to commit a crime, you should be careful to leave no evidence - so that no one would even know a crime had been committed.)

Anyway, I returned to the offertory box which was near the door - and poked around. There was certainly something in there. I hoped it was not the dross I had put back on my last visit. I attacked the under side of the box and once again a flood of half-pennies and farthings showered on to the floor. How disappointing!

I gathered the half-pennies together. Eightpence. Enough to buy a bottle of pop. I was so busy counting my money that I failed to hear the sound of footsteps in the church porch. Suddenly the door was flung open and a shaft of sunshine lit me up kneeling on the floor. A dark shadow loomed over me.

"So you're the little thief!"

I didn't know who the man was - a church warden, the

organist or a bell-ringer - but I was well and truly caught in the act.

I jumped to my feet.

He shut the door.

I grabbed the screwdriver and stuffed it up my sleeve. When he turned back to face me, I was prepared.

"So it was you who broke into the offertory box. Mrs Briggs was right. She thought she saw you coming out of the church."

I didn't remember seeing anyone on my last visit but country people could hide behind a cowpat.

"We've been waiting for you to come back."

I said nothing.

"What's your name? You're not a local, are you?"

He looked at me menacingly.

"Think you can steal from a church without getting punished for it? Well, you're wrong. When my daughters misbehave, I put them over my knee and give them a real thrashing..."

No one was going to give me a thrashing.

"Come here!"

I didn't move.

"Come here!"

I shook my head.

He lurched forward and tried to grab my pink cardigan. I ducked.

He slipped on the farthings but did not lose his balance. I tried to trip him up.

He pulled back and laughed.

"You little hell-cat!"

His eyes lit up in a rather frightening way.

This time, he rushed forward.

He chased me down the main aisle of the church. I was small enough to dive in between the pews but I was unable to get away from him. He kept to the main aisles and tried to box me in.

I realized that I needed to be fifteen seconds ahead of him to lift the heavy metal catch on the door and pull it open. But there was no way I could avoid him for fifteen seconds.

I led him a fair old dance around the church. He kept trying to corner me. He would edge nearer and nearer and then I would run.

I thought of the vestry door. Could I lock myself in? No, that was dangerous. I might be caught like a rat in a trap. What about the bell-tower? The steep steps? Was there anything I could throw down at him? But he might strangle me with the ropes in the bell chamber or throw me off the roof. No. I would have to outwit him at ground level. But how?

I flung a book or two him - but missed. Finding myself near a vase of flowers, I tore out the flowers and emptied the water on the floor. I held the glass in both hands, assessing its weight.

"Don't you touch what doesn't belong to you!"

I glared at him.

He probably thought I was frightened of him. And he was right. I was frightened that I would miss. I intended to hit him in the face. But instead I hit the end of a pew and the glass shattered. Several shards stuck in his hand.

"You little beast!"

He licked the blood off his fingers.

I knew that I could now expect no mercy. I flung more books, kneelers and a picture at him. But he still bore down on me.

Near the door, I decided to stand my ground. As he closed on me, I drew the screwdriver out of my sleeve. He grabbed my hair roughly. I drove the screwdriver hard into his fleshy thigh.

He leapt back.

I Looked down at my screwdriver. There was blood on it. I looked at the man. He was obviously in pain. Blood dripped down on to the stone floor.

I turned to open the door - but, as I turned, it crashed open and there was a tall man in a flowing black cassock standing in front of me.

This was a difficult moment.

Two of them. I was outnumbered.

But the newcomer did not look at me. He looked at my pursuer. I tucked the screwdriver back into my sleeve. There was blood on my fingers.

"Tom!" he said. "What the hell are you doing?"

"She attacked me!"

The vicar - I presumed it was the vicar - looked at me. He saw the blood on my fingers.

"She's the thief!" Tom said.

I shook my head.

I think the situation was so bizarre that the vicar did not know what to do. Tom's hand was covered in blood and a small puddle was gathering on the floor. I knew this was my moment to escape.

I was a fast mover. As I rushed forward, I tore at the edge of his cassock. Buttons flew.

"Stop her!" shouted Tom.

But I was out through the porch like greased lightning. I raced in the opposite direction to my bike - clearly heading north. I covered three hundred yards and then looked back. No one was following me. I climbed a wall and using it as cover, I raced southwards towards my bike. Fields are awkward things. Hedges get in the way. I had to climb back over the wall and fight my way through gorse bushes. I grabbed my bike and accelerated down the road.

I put a couple of miles between myself and the church and then took a back lane which led me down to the canal towpath. Under a bridge, I washed my hands and my skirt. I dropped the screwdriver into the water and tried to get blood off my cardigan. In the process, it got very wet.

After that, I drove along the towpath, heading towards Bidworth. I was hot and angry. All that for eightpence! And I hadn't even taken the money!

It taught me one lesson. Never return to the scene of past crimes. The victims may be waiting for you.

I did not feel any guilt about attacking the man. He had been out to punish me. He might have handed me over to the police. Questions would have been asked. I was anxious not to embarrass Mary or John. They would have been very angry. I might have been sent back to London. I had to avoid that at all costs!

But I heard nothing more about the incident. The defeat of our army in France and the prospect of imminent invasion occupied every mind. I would imagine that the sight of Tom dripping blood must have shocked the vicar.

For me, it was a lucky escape. It also did me a lot of good. It taught me not to steal. It also put me off visiting churches for a long time. But I never forgot that little church. About twenty years later, I returned there on a Sunday morning. A different vicar. No sign of Tom. I looked at the offertory box as I collected my books.

Nothing seemed to have changed. The four angels were still there, as was the eagle lectern and the blue velvet curtain. I even thought there might still be the odd drop of blood on the floor - but I didn't dare to stop and look.

I put a five pound note into the collection plate as a small penance. Five years later, I sent a larger cheque to the Church treasurer and asked what had happened to the vicar who had been there in 1940 - and one of his helpers called

'Tom'.

After all that time, I didn't expect much of an answer, but the treasurer, no doubt stimulated by the size of the cheque, gave me a very full reply.

Father Kelly had been with them until early 1942 when he became an Army Chaplain. He had served in North Africa with the First Army but had drowned in Sicily whilst trying to rescue a paratrooper who had been dropped offshore by mistake. He had been buried in an Allied war cemetery in Italy.

'Tom' - she presumed I meant Tom Crawford - had been the caretaker of the church. He had been jailed for molesting children - members of his own family - and other children in the village. It was even rumoured that he had attacked a child in the church. Soon after he returned from prison, he had been run over by a tractor. It was generally believed that his death had not been an accident.

Thirty-Four

I was cycling along a country lane about two miles west of Bidworth when I saw a parachute descending slowly from the sky. There was a man hanging beneath it - a very wooden, toy-like figure. The two objects disappeared behind a hedge about four hundred yards away.

Although I was already late for tea, I immediately rode my bike to the nearest gate and climbed into the field. I could see the untidy, brown heap of the parachute rising and falling in the light breeze.

I walked across the field cautiously. I could see the man lying on the ground. He was wearing a pair of blue overalls, a mustard-coloured jacket and large black flying boots. The parachute tugged gently at the straps around his chest. My first impression was that he was pretending to be asleep.

I did not go too close.

"Hello!" I said

He did not open his eyes.

'Perhaps he's dead?' I thought. I rather wished I had had Dusty with me. He would have gone straight over and licked his face. Then we'd have known where we were.

"Hello!" I said again.

But there was no reply.

I decide to go in closer and see if he was still breathing. He was. A sort of moaning, constricted noise was coming from his throat.

'Knocked 'isself out,' I thought. 'Konkushion.'

I reached out for his hand and sought his pulse. It seemed erratic but it was still beating. So he was alive.

I sat on my heels and wondered what I should do.

He was obviously a German. I could see the strange markings on his sleeve. He had a white silk scarf round his neck and the Luftwaffe eagle on his breast pocket. There was no doubt about his identity. The question was whether to dash off and get help or conduct my own private investigation.

I reached out for the buttoned pocket on his thigh. There seemed to be something there. Maps!

I pulled them out. They didn't mean much to me but the printing on the side looked black, menacing and foreign. I stuffed them back into his pocket.

There was still little sign of life.

Perhaps I should go and get a doctor?

But that might spoil it.

With a pleasant tingle of excitement, I realized that he was now my prisoner. I would hand him over to Constable Bell - and he would be sent to a POW camp. I could imagine all the excitement it would cause. My prisoner! I hoped no one else had noticed the parachute descending.

I fiddled with the metal fastener on his chest and loosened his parachute straps. I then opened his breast pocket and pulled out his wallet and personal effects. Two pens, a plastic protractor, a couple of letters, a 'flugbuch' and a pair of sunglasses. I looked inside his wallet and counted his money. One hundred and ninety marks. I looked at the name on the envelopes. Erich Roch.

So he was called Eric.

I unzipped his overalls to see what else he had hidden away. The first thing that caught my eye was a broad leather belt with a pistol holder. My eyes lit up. So the man was armed! This would not do. He might shoot himself. Even worse, he might shoot me! Better that I should have his weapon.

I undid the buckle and slowly pulled the belt from under

him. I examined the contents of the holster. It was a small black pistol. I weighed it in my hands. It was quite heavy. Obviously loaded. I longed to try it out but realized that a sudden shot might bring other people running.

I carried the pistol and his other personal effects over to my bicycle and stuffed them into the basket underneath my jumper.

I returned to my prisoner who was now showing some signs of life. He was twitching and groaning. Eventually, he opened his eyes.

He registered surprise - seeing a young girl watching him with such intensity.

"Who are you?" he asked. Then his face contorted with pain. "Mein schulter!" He bit his lower lip to stop himself crying out.

"Have you broken it?"

He did not understand what I was saying.

"Brechen!"

He tried to sit up. I went round behind him and helped him ease off his parachute straps. I bundled up the silken chute and sat on it.

Every movement caused him pain. I imagined that his shoulder must have been broken in several places. He kept groaning and cursing.

He looked at me again - sorrowfully.

"Gefangener."

I thought he was trying to tell me his name; but if he was, he had got it wrong. I didn't realize that he was ruefully admitting that he was now a prisoner of war.

"Eric," I said reprovingly. "That's your name."

He laughed.

"Gescheit kind!"

The laughter turned to pain. He groaned miserably.

"Scheisse!"

I recognized that word. All Germans were reported as saying: 'Scheisse!' or 'Gott in Himmel!' This one was no exception.

He pointed at me.

"Name?"

Fortunately it was the same word in both languages.

"Me? I'm Jemima. Jemima Shaw."

He had a bit of trouble with Jemima.

"Englisch?"

I nodded.

He pointed to his shoulder.

"Doktor!"

"I'll get you to one," I said, "But you'll have to walk. I made a motion of walking with my fingers.

"Ach so! That will be difficult."

I offered him a hand and he rose slowly and painfully to his feet. He swayed slightly.

"Schwinndelig."

I nodded encouragingly.

Now I had got him on his feet, I pointed towards the gate where I had left my bicycle. We moved over the field slowly - me clutching his parachute with one hand and holding his arm with the other.

He seemed quite a nice sort of German. Gentle.. considerate...

I had to open the gate for him. He couldn't possibly climb over anything. I shut the gate and picked up my bike. I wrapped the parachute round the handlebars. I suggested that he might like to sit on the seat but he implied that he would rather walk.

So we set out for Bidworth. A tall, dark-haired German and a small fair-haired Londoner. We must have looked a right pair!

To start with, he walked very slowly.

"Wie weit?"

He pointed ahead.

"Two miles," I said - raising two fingers.

"Zwei kilometre? Nein! Zwei meile? Scheisse!"

I echoed his feelings: "Scheisse!"

He laughed to hear me swear so dramatically - and was once again convulsed with pain.

"Zer brechen!" he said grimly.

"Broken?"

"Ja. Broken." He paused. "I did Englisch - at schule. Nicht gut."

It didn't seem that we should have much of a conversation on the way back to Bidworth. He kept saying: "Jayminah!" I kept correcting him till he got it right.

Then he tried to sing me a little song. I think it was 'Lili Marlene' - but it was constantly interrupted by moans and gasps. I wanted to tell him: 'Save your breath.'

Eventually we could see Bidworth's church tower, so he knew we were getting somewhere.

We walked slowly down the road.

I was miles late for tea.

The first person we met was Mary. I think she was coming to look for me. She was on her bike and she looked pale and anxious.

She saw the tall man in strange clothes moving slowly down the road and immediately realized what I had found.

"Du bis ein pilot?" she asked.

"Wireless operator."

He was glad to meet someone who could speak his language.

"I found 'im in a field," I said, "'e came down in a parachute. I think 'e's broken 'is shoulder. He keeps groanin' and cryin'."

Mary examined his hand, his arm and gently

manipulated his shoulder.

He cried out.

"Das schulder?"

"Ja, ja. I caught it as I fell out of the plane."

"And where is your plane?"

He looked up at the sky.

"I don't know. It was on fire."

"And what about the pilot?"

"He had been shot. He told us to bale out. And now I am gefangener."

Mary turned to me.

"He says he's a prisoner."

"His name's Eric."

"How d'you know that?"

"It's in his book."

I reached for the flugbuch.

"It says: Erich Roch."

"She has taken charge of me."

Mary smiled.

"Very ably, it seems."

She looked at Erich.

"Anyway, you're safe. It may not be much fun being a prisoner but at least you're alive. We must get you a doctor."

"You speak very good German."

"I had a holiday there some years ago. Marburg?"

"Ja, I know Marburg."

We progressed slowly towards the house. Mary was asking him questions. He seemed glad to have someone to talk to.

I pushed the bike - planning how I might secrete the pistol without anyone noticing.

I put the bicycle away in the garden shed and hid the pistol and its holster under an old tea chest. I regarded it as a very welcome addition to my armoury. Something a little more potent than razor blades or teeth. I brought the parachute and other personal items into the kitchen.

Mary had made Erich take off his overalls, scarf and shirt and she was examining his shoulder carefully. She had already phoned the doctor and given the airman two painkillers and a cup of coffee.

The recent incident was beginning to get to him. He started shaking and crying. Dusty began to whine and had to be put out in the garden.

Dr Hill came within a quarter of an hour. Although he had been in the middle of his tea, the prospect of meeting one of Hitler's dreaded Luftwaffe was quite exciting. But Erich was no ogre. I imagine that Dr Hill was quite disappointed to find someone so ordinary.

He tested his arm movements, ran his fingers over his shoulder and upper arm. He listened to his heart and measured his blood pressure; he rigged up a neat sling and recommended that he be taken immediately to a hospital.

"Have you phoned the police yet?"

"No. I thought he needed medical help first."

"They'll arrange with the military police to collect him. They'll take him to a hospital."

"Krancke?"

"Yes, krancke. Mrs Woodward will phone the police - and they'll arrange for you to be collected."

"The politzei?"

"'Fraid so. A bit more sociable than your Gestapo! Better manners!"

Mary did not translate.

I washed up his mug.

Mary saw the doctor out to the door - and phoned Constable Bell. She came into the kitchen and explained to Erich what she had done.

At which point, our visitor blotted his copybook.

"Danke," he said. "Danke. You have been very kind. When the Fuhrer comes, I will see that you are rewarded for your kindness."

Mary raised her eyebrows.

"I don't think your Fuhrer will ever set foot in England."

Erich looked surprised at her naivety.

"But even now - the invasion - it is being prepared."

"I know. We all know. But you won't get further than the beaches. You'll be mown down; everyone who comes ashore will die. The British are ready and waiting."

It was Erich's turn to look surprised,

"Ach, so?"

"Spitfires and Hurricanes - they'll deal with you!"

"Ach, spitfuren..."

"Yes," said Mary boldly, "Spitfires! It was probably one of them that shot you down this afternoon." Erich smiled sadly.

"You may be right."

There was a knock at the front door.

Constable Bell had also been in the middle of his tea but he came round hotfoot to arrest the German airman. He looked at the injured man with a certain savage glee. He said: "We know what to do with people like you."

I felt sorry for Erich.

Even though he did not know what Constable Bell was saying, there was no masking the greedy sense of triumph... the gallumphing hostility ... of a petty bureaucrat.

The policeman took out his black notebook.

"Name?"

"Roch, Erich."

"Spell it."

Constable Bell was a slow writer.

"Age?"

"25."

"Home address?"

Erich had told Mary that he came from Bremen; that he had two brothers and a sister; that his father worked in the Focke-Wulf factory as a fitter. He now became very tight-lipped.

"I must only give you my rank and number. You are not entitled to ask for any other information."

Mary translated his reply to Constable Bell who looked annoyed. He was being denied the wholehearted co-operation of the accused. British justice was being flouted. He started shouting insults at Erich. Mary did not attempt to translate them. We were all embarrassed.

I decided to intervene.

"You don't have to speak to Eric like that! Even though 'e's a Jerry, 'e's bin in a burnin' plane. 'e's bin injured; 'e's in great pain. 'e don't deserve to be treated like that."

Constable Bell seemed taken aback.

"... Everyone knows you're a bully!"

Erich smiled.

"She is brave, the little one."

"What did he say?"

Mary smiled.

"He says that Jemima has great courage. She rescued him and brought him back to Bidworth."

"Where did his plane crash?"

"We don't know. Jemima found him in a field about two miles away."

"Was he alone?"

I nodded.

"'e'd knocked 'isself out."

Constable Bell mellowed. After all, if this child had brought him home - and if these two women were looking after him, the German couldn't be all that dangerous. Perhaps the Herrenvolk weren't so 'herren' after all.

"Well, Mr Rossch," he said ponderously. "For you, the war is over. You'll be locked away - behind bars, I hope. By the time you see Germany again, you'll have learnt your lesson. Not to trifle with us English folk. We don't like Narzees. You're lucky we don't shoot people like you."

I could see Mary looking extremely angry. I knew that she probably hated the Germans just as much as Constable Bell, but it seemed to her intolerable that a wounded prisoner should be insulted in her kitchen.

She changed the subject.

"And when will the military police be here?"

"Any moment. I phoned them before I left the station."

There was an uncomfortable silence.

No one felt like saying anything. Erich was not prepared to give more than his name, rank and number. Mary was not prepared to translate anything more for Constable Bell. Erich was offered a sandwich and another cup of coffee which he accepted. Constable Bell was offered nothing. Mary had not forgotten the bicycle episode when she had been accused of being a thief. She had no intention of showing him any hospitality. To her, the policeman represented officialdom at its inefficient worst. She felt intensely irritated at the impression this might make on the airman.

The RAF police arrived twenty minutes later. They were more relaxed and cheerful.

"Hello, Fritz," they said. "You'll be meeting quite a few of your chums. We've bagged about a dozen of your blokes today."

"Kameraden?"

"Yes. One or two charred and grilled. You were lucky to get down safely... Oh, you've got a broken shoulder? We'll soon sort that out. Aylesbury hospital for a week and you'll be as right as rain..."

Mary intervened.

"I think he's anxious about his friends. His pilot had been shot. He told the others to bale out."

"Crashed near Bletchley. Some of the other chaps are dealing with it."

Mary translated.

"Is he dead?"

"I expect so. Came down near the railway line. Like a ruddy fireball."

Mary did not translate that bit.

"So who brought him in?"

"This girl did."

The RAF police looked amazed.

"'e's my prisoner," I said.

"Very brave of you, tackling this Nazi. He might have killed you." The RAF man looked at Constable Bell. "Is he armed?"

"I never looked."

"You never looked! He could've shot all of us." They ordered Erich to his feet and searched him. Erich said nothing. He was beginning to look sick and grey.

"I think," said Mary, "that you'd better get him to a hospital before he collapses."

"You may be right there. Have you got all his things?"

I handed over the wallet, the sunglasses, the flugbuch and the parachute.

"Thanks, young lady. You've done a good job. Not many girls of your age would think of arresting a German pilot on their own. You deserve a medal!"

I looked at Constable Bell.

He had a sour look on his face.

He was jealous.

I said goodbye to Erich. I shook his hand.

"I 'ope they'll treat you nicely."

"Thank you for being so kind."

The RAF police and Constable Bell escorted him down the garden path. Erich was locked into a van. Constable Bell mounted his bicycle. The drama was over.

Mary shut the front door and we went into the kitchen where she tried to resurrect the evening meal.

"John'll be surprised, won't 'e?"

"Very surprised. He'll be sorry he missed it. He'd have put that stupid policeman in his place."

"Does 'e speak German? Would 'e 've been able to speak to Eric?"

"He speaks better German than I do. He'd have enjoyed talking to him. Probably have got a lot more information out of him than those idiots." She had a very poor opinion of the police - military or otherwise. "Now his guard's up, he'll tell them nothing. They've missed a golden opportunity."

"D'you think 'is pilot will've been killed?"

"Probably. If you're injured, it's very difficult to move quickly. He'll have gone down with his plane."

"A fireball?"

"Yes. Let's hope it was quick."

She served the meal on to two plates. It looked a bit dried up and unappetizing; but it was food and I was extremely hungry.

"I'm sorry 'e's gone," I said, "'e was a very nice prisoner."

"Most Germans are nice people. They're very like us. It's just those Nazis. They're bred to be bullies."

I ate my potato pie with a fork. Mary was always telling me to use a knife and a fork. I picked up the knife.

Mary was sitting at the other side of the table. She looked at me thoughtfully. I always reckoned she could understand me better than most. That evening, she proved it.

Very quietly, she said: "And where is his gun?"

"'is gun?"

"He would've been armed. All these Germans carry guns."

I kept eating.

If my mouth was full, I wouldn't be able to answer her question. It required some careful thought. Should I lie? Or should I admit the weapon was now in my possession? I had always wanted a pistol; almost as much as I had wanted a bicycle. It would be very useful for killing Germans - and others.

I remained silent.

It seemed the sensible option.

"You've hidden it. Where? In the field?"

I smiled sadly.

Mary was too clever for me.

"It's in the shed," I said. "Under the tea-chest.'"

"Thank you," she said. "I hope you weren't proposing to use it?"

I smiled wryly.

"I thought I might use it on the Germans - if they come. If not, I could use it on Mrs Williams. I did tell 'er as 'ow I'd get even with 'er."

Mary had to smile.

"I think that's a little bit drastic - even for her."

Thirty-Five

I don't know what strings John managed to pull but, three days later, we found ourselves visiting a prison hospital to see Erich.

The fact that the Army provided us with a chauffeur-driven car suggested that the visit was not exactly personal. It had the backing of the authorities. One could easily imagine what they were after. Information.

For me, prison presented no problem? but I think the atmosphere intimidated Mary and John. I had already been inside Wormwood Scrubs to see my Uncle Josh. I recognized the familiar smells of bleach and disinfectant; the crash of iron gates and bolts; men with heavy chains of keys who opened each door with such gravity that one might have imagined the inner sanctum to contain nothing less than bars of gold or the Holy Grail.

We were led to the hospital wing where Erich was being kept. Obviously he had had no warning that we were coming.

His eyes lit up.

"Jayminah!"

"Jemima," I corrected him.

"Mein befreiunger!"

Although he was still heavily bandaged and had a sling enfolding his left arm, he managed to give me a big hug and a kiss. His shoulder did not seem to be giving him quite as much pain.

I introduced John.

They shook hands in a friendly fashion.

"Jemima wanted to see how you were getting on."

Erich smiled.

"I am much better, danke. Even my English is improving."

Mary continued the conversation in German.

"You were on the verge of collapse when you left our house. We wondered what had happened to you."

"I fainted on the way. I don't remember the journey at all."

"You had a lucky escape," said John. "I believe your pilot died when the plane crashed."

He produced the local paper which had been delivered that morning. On the front page, there was a grim picture of a heap of twisted metal lying in the middle of a field. The picture was clear enough to show the official markings near the tail.

Tears came to Erich's eyes.

John translated the article into German.

He looked at Erich.

"Was he an old friend of yours?"

"Yes, we have flown together for many months. He was a very experienced pilot. He was with the Legion..."

"... In Spain?"

"Ja. Ja."

Now that they were talking in German, I did not understand a word they were saying. Mary told me later how the conversation developed.

"And what about your front gunner?"

"Johann? Yes, I have known Johann a long time. We were in Poland together. And Norway."

"And you were the wireless operator on the plane?"

"Yes. I was lucky to escape."

"What exactly happened?"

Erich paused. Clearly he was wondering whether he

might be disclosing any secrets to the enemy. But there was nothing to hide.

"We had lost our fighter escort. They had been intercepted south of London. We pressed on. We were heading for Luton - the Vauxhall factory. You know it?"

John had no knowledge whatsoever of the Vauxhall factory but the look on his face suggested that he had been born and bred in Luton.

"You were a little off course?"

"About ten miles. Not much. The navigator had just redirected us. But then we were hit."

"Flak?"

"No, a fighter. We did not see it. It pumped bullets into our engines. One of them went on fire. Hans was trying to control it - but the enemy came round again. This time, he hit the cockpit. Shattered the glass. Hans was injured. He had many splinters of glass in his face - and a bullet tore into his hand. He could not use it. He was screaming with pain. There was a lot of blood. I could see his bones."

Erich's eyes looked wild and frightened as he related the experience.

"I crawled through to the cockpit but there was nothing I could do. Hans told me to get out. He couldn't control the plane. We were going down. I went out through the hatch, but I think I must have hit the tail. I do not remember."

He put a hand to his shoulder.

"Is it still painful?"

Erich nodded.

"Without the painkillers, it is very bad." He looked at one of the medical orderlies who was tending another patient. "But they are very kind in here."

I decided it was time I re-entered the conversation.

"Was it a Heinkel?" I asked. "Or a Junkers?"

Erich smiled at my pronunciation.

"You know a lot about aircraft," he said. "It is no secret. It was a Heinkel. You can see the remains in the picture."

"You were shot down by a Spitfire!" I said proudly.

"Perhaps." He shrugged his shoulders - and winced. "Who knows?"

He turned to Mary.

"She is a very brave little girl. She was not frightened of arresting me - an enemy officer. She took charge."

He laughed.

"She pinched your pistol!" said Mary.

"My pistol? You have stolen my pistol? And who were you going to shoot? Germans?"

I nodded.

"I thought so. She had a very determined look on her face. Perhaps if I had not broken my shoulder, I could have escaped back to France. I might have found a boat - or even better, a plane."

John looked doubtful.

"I don't think you'd have got very far. People have become very suspicious. Anyone who hasn't got the proper papers has had it. There are road blocks everywhere. The police..."

"Ah, yes. The police?"

Erich looked at John.

"You are not in the police?"

"No. I'm a translator. I've just come down from university."

"You speak excellent German."

"I spent a year in Kitzbuhel. In Austria."

"Yes? I noticed the accent. And your wife? She also speaks the language."

"I did it as part of my school certificate. But I find it easier to read than to speak."

By now, the ice seemed to have been broken. A warder

brought us a pot of tea and four mugs. There were also four digestive biscuits.

"V.I.P. treatment!" said John.

"Is the food good?" I asked.

Erich made a face.

"I do not like your English bread. I miss the coffee, the beer, the wurst..."

"Sausages," John explained.

"We have sausages too," I said defensively.

"German sausages are very spicy. They have lots of different varieties."

John turned back to Erich.

"I was in Argentina when the war broke out last year. The world chess championships. Some of your people were taking part. Even though the meat was good, they too missed their wurst."

"You play chess?"

John nodded.

He mentioned one or two of the famous German players who had taken part. Not that Erich seemed to have heard of them. But John sounded as if he had been mixing with Germans all his life. He had stories from Bavaria. An amusing incident in Berlin. Erich told them the story of his life. I put up with it for five minutes; then I broke into their conversation;

"Do you have a girlfriend?" I asked.

Erich smiled.

"I have many girlfriends in Germany. And one or two in France."

"Won't they be missing you?"

"Perhaps they will shed a tear or two."

"You won't be seeing them for a long time!"

Erich laughed sadly.

"It may be that the war will soon be over. We shall make

the peace. After that, we shall all go home..." He looked at Mary's face. "... You do not believe that?"

Mary shook her head.

"Not after all that has happened. I think the war will go on for a long time. If America comes in... or if the Russians invade Romania... things could be very different."

But Erich still believed his country's propaganda - and with some justification:

"The new Germany is...how do you say it? ... invincible. She cannot be beaten. I think we shall have the peace very soon. It is the Fuhrer's wish. We do not want to fight England."

"You want to fight the Communists?"

Erich's eyes sparkled.

"How did you guess? Always we fight the Bolsheviks!"

John decided to move the conversation away from politics....

"Have you sent a message to anyone? To tell them that you are alive? Have you written a note to your parents? Or your girlfriends?"

Erich again put his hand to his shoulder.

"At the moment, I do not write to anyone. But you are right. I should tell them."

Mary produced a notebook from her handbag. John lent her his pen.

"If you give us their addresses, we'll make sure they're notified."

Erich looked surprised.

"You have contacts with people in Germany?"

"No. The Red Gross. They'll help."

"Ach, so. Die Schweizer?"

Instantly, he became much more co-operative. He gave Mary a list of five people whom he wished to contact. He told her about each of them in great detail. Mary wrote down their addresses. Once he had done that, he seemed much happier. More relaxed. But only for a few minutes.

John asked him:

"What about your comrades in France?"

Erich looked shocked.

"I cannot give you their addresses. That would be a breach of military security."

This time, it was John who laughed.

"I don't think there's much the British don't know about you people. You're based at Montdidier. You're part of the second group of the Kampfgeschwader 'Hindenburg'. We've seen your photographs in the *Adler* magazine. We know when you take off. We know exactly how many fighters are escorting you. We know the names of the men in your staffel. Even the names of your pets!"

He reeled off a list of names.

Erich looked at him in amazement.

He almost whispered:

"Are you in intelligence?"

"No. I just deal with your radio signals..."

(Another lie - but because it was said in German, I did not pick it up.)

John smiled.

"You people are incredibly indiscreet. You test out your radios before you start off. Then, when you get in the air, you chat about where you're going. Who's escorting you. Then you're surprised to find twenty, forty, sixty Spitfires waiting for you across the Channel. You tell us all we need to know."

Erich looked thunder-struck.

John continued to speak in a kindly fashion as if he was addressing a patient who was terminally ill:

"That's why we go for the bombers. Your factories are only turning out two hundred a month. There's very few replacements. Everything's in the shop window. Nothing in reserve. The more bombers we shoot down, the less likely an invasion. We've still got over 900 fighters - with more than four hundred coming out of the factories each month. You can work out the result for yourself."

Erich was silent.

He could indeed work it out for himself. John's words rang true. They explained so many things - why every attack encountered its quota of Hurricanes or Spitfires. The Hurricanes went for the bombers whilst the Spitfires engaged the fighters. Twenty or thirty bombers were being lost every day. You could see them being shot out of the skies. The Junkers Ju 87s had been particularly hard hit. Reichsmarschall Goering had withdrawn them from cross-channel raids.

And John was right - replacements were a mere trickle. At the same time, there was no sign of the enemy weakening.

In fact, the previous week, they had met a complete fighter wing over North London. It had given his leader a terrible shock.

John watched his discomfiture.

"And that's not all," he added. "We know all about your Knickebein beams. The beacons at Kleve and Bredstedt. We know you're trying to use these beams to blind-bomb us. We're busy bending them... to make sure you drop your bombs in the wrong places. Your people haven't a clue!"

Erich was white-faced. These were secrets no one should know. Least of all the enemy.

John looked apologetic at being the bearer of such bad news.

"In a few weeks' time, we're expecting you to be using the X-gerat. Beamed from Cherbourg, I'm told... I presume you weren't using that to find your way to Luton?"

Erich shook his head.

"No. It's only for night bombing."

John was glad to hear him admit that such an apparatus even existed. There had been a lot of argument about what the Germans were up to in that direction. Now they had a prisoner who had been briefed about the X-gerat. It would not take a professional interrogator long to coax the information out of him. Erich would hate himself afterwards - but he would never dare to admit that he had spilt the beans. It was important - after their visit was over - that Erich be kept isolated from other prisoners.

Outwardly, John registered no surprise.

"Makes your task doubly-difficult when you realize the enemy are looking over your shoulder, knowing what you're doing day-by-day.

Erich's mind was in turmoil.

He was sure his leaders were unaware of all this. They didn't know the enemy were listening and watching. That they themselves were betraying all their darkest secrets. The Fat Man had assured them that the RAF were down to their last few squadrons. That was untrue. But was there any way he could let his colleagues know? Warn other pilots of the danger?

He looked at the faces of his three visitors. They were kindly - but resolute. There was no panic or fear in them. They knew what they were doing. Their self-assurance unnerved him.

He put his head in his hands.

Now, of course, I didn't know a word of what John had been saying; but it was clearly something which had distressed Erich. There had been talk of Spitfires and Hurricanes. I guessed that John had been telling him the Germans had no hope of winning.

It occurred to me that I had been watching a game of

chess unfolding before my very eyes. John had steadily eliminated all Erich's pawns. He had done it nicely - as he always did. One by one, they had been wiped off the board. Suddenly, Erich had found himself in check. John had moved one or two pieces and Erich was helpless.

This was always the distressing moment when you realized there was nothing you could do; nowhere you could go. In chess, you could always start another game. But Erich was a prisoner of war. For him, the battle was over. John was simply waiting for him to concede.

I decided to add my tuppenceworth:

"At least you're safe, Eric! No one's goin' to kill yer. You'll be well-looked after. You can trust John. 'e'll do his best for yer."

Mary smiled.

Even Erich looked up and smiled.

How could one resist the simple honesty of these ordinary people? What the little one said was true. Even if the Germans did invade, he would still be OK.

"It's very hard to accept," he said to Mary. "When you've believed so much in victory; it's hard to think that the other side might win. I mean... you've got no army to speak of. Your Navy's frightened to show its face in the Channel. We're gathering all the barges and boats to bring our men across..."

"But we have a strong air force," said John quietly. "You've seen what it can do - personally. Given time, we shall do the same to Germany - and much more."

"It's just like chess!" I said triumphantly - with all the self-opiniated confidence of a total amateur. "It's not 'ow many pieces you have on the board; it's 'ow you use 'em!

Erich looked blank.

John translated my words.

My prisoner laughed.

"Your Queen has checked my King! Perhaps in our next game, I shall have better luck?"

Shortly afterwards, we said goodbye to Erich. Mary gave him our address. We promised to send letters to his friends and family. John told him to use his name if he was ever in any difficulty. I gave him a big hug - and he kissed me. We promised to keep in touch.

John gave him a final word of warning.

"Remember!" he said. "From now on, it'll be German bombs raining down on your head! Anything you can tell our people about these new bombing techniques could save your neck as well as ours!"

We were escorted out through barred gates and heavy doors, but John hardly seemed to notice.

"Your prisoner is a very useful man," he said. "He knows all about the latest German plans."

"But do you think he'll talk?" asked Mary.

"I've tried to make sure that he will. I'll have a word with Denys Felkin and tell him what Erich knows. Another friendly chat should do the trick."

It seemed that the chauffeur-driven car had not been wasted.

As we returned to Bidworth, I revelled in Erich's kiss. Even though he was a German, that kiss had touched me. I hoped Mary and John would let me go and see Erich again. Not that I would tell them my secret!

Life was not all chess!

Thirty-Six

So I became famous...

Even though I had had to surrender my gun, the fact that I had captured a German airman attracted enormous attention. Or so it seemed at the time.

The people at school looked at me with new-found respect. It was comforting to think I was turning my aggression on the Germans - doing my bit for the war effort. The headmaster, who had been one of my severest critics, invited me into his study and shook my hand warmly.

John gave me a pound note and promised me a five pound note if I should capture another. The episode was written up in the *Aylesbury Gazette* and a small piece appeared in the national press. Just in case Miss Baker had not seen it, I sent her a cutting. I reckoned it would make her sick as a parrot.

The people of Bidworth basked in my reflected glory. Even Mrs Williams stopped me and said: "Well, done, Shaw!" but was too embarrassed to say any more. Going down the village street, people pointed at me. I could hear them whispering: "It was her..." We were even invited to tea by Lady Rowley.

John teased me that now I was such a well-known figure, I should have to behave. No more stealing apples or bicycles. No more attacks on unsuspecting victims. (I expect he was thinking of Cousin Eddie.) I must live up to my reputation. Mary said that she did not think that I could change, which made me doubly determined to do so.

The battle continued fiercely in the skies above us. It

was an historic moment. I am just sorry that Mary didn't write anything about it herself. What a story she could have told! But after that spat with her mother, she wrote nothing more for a couple of months.

Neither she nor John said anything about their work. I knew they worked in Bletchley and I assumed it was just an ordinary Government department. They talked about Dilly and Alan and Gordon - but I never met any of these people, so I never knew who they were.

Whatever their work was, it seemed very tiring. They would both work long hours and come home exhausted. They would collapse on the sofa and expect the other one to prepare the evening meal. Sometimes, John would be gone before Mary came back. It seemed a very hectic existence.

But what a story she could have told! The two of them were at the very heart of everything that was happening. She was in the hut decoding German messages; he in translation. Once their work was done, the messages were rushed to the Chief of the Air Staff, the Prime Minister and Air Chief Marshal Dowding at Fighter Command headquarters in Stanmore - just a few miles away. It was all very hush-hush, but neither of them ever said a word in my presence. It was many years later before I discovered what they were up to.

However, Mary did write one little piece in September - and I include it here:

Thirty-Seven

On September 13th, I received a letter from Miss Baker. I did not recognize the handwriting but I noticed that the postmark was London. The envelope was addressed to: Mrs Woodward, Bidworth, Bucks. It was enough to find me. I wondered why on earth she should be writing to me.

Dear Mrs Woodward,

You will not be expecting to hear from me but I am writing to tell you that Shaw's mother was killed last Saturday night. She had just left her sister's home and was going to work.

The bomb destroyed most of the houses in the street and eight of our children were killed - two in my class - Peter Mills and Billy Smith.

Mrs Shaw's sister was taken to hospital suffering from shock and several minor injuries. But the ARP warden tells me that she had a heart attack yesterday morning and is also dead.

They were looking for Shaw but I told them she was with you. Perhaps you could tell her what has happened.

If the raids continue, we may have to return to Bidworth. I have notified the family who are looking after Shaw's younger brother.

Yours sincerely,
Helen Baker.

I read the letter through twice. I decided not to tell Jemima until she came back from school.

I had read in the paper about the raid on Saturday night when three hundred tons of high explosive and incendiaries had been dropped in and around the capital. We had seen the red glow over London and heard the distant thud of bombs even though we were nearly forty miles away.

The papers had not said how many people had died but it was clear that quite a lot of property had been destroyed. But London was a big place and even the East End covered about twenty-five square miles. I had not thought much about Jemima's family. I had assumed that most people would have been in the shelters.

It was difficult to know exactly how Jemima would react. She had hardly spoken about her mother or her aunt. One or two cards had been exchanged - but that was all. It could be that she would feel some sentimental attachment to her Auntie Jean.

I waited till she had had her tea.

"I got a letter from Miss Baker this morning."

She looked up.

"What she want?"

I said: "There's been a bad air raid. One or two of the pupils in your old school have been killed."

"Who?"

"Billy Smith... and Peter Mills."

She twisted a teaspoon between her fingers.

"You know them?"

She nodded.

I think she could guess there was more to come.

I sat down at the table across from her.

"It was quite a bad raid. Your street was destroyed. Your mum and your Auntie Jean have both been killed..."

"Both of 'em?"

I nodded.

There was a long silence. She didn't cry. She continued

to twist the teaspoon back and forward. There was a distant look in her grey eyes.

Eventually I said: "Would you like to read her letter?"

She shrugged her shoulders.

I passed it over.

She put down her teaspoon and read the letter. I waited to see how she would react. She read the letter slowly and the only moment when she registered surprise was when Miss Baker suggested that her class might return to Bidworth.

Otherwise, she seemed to accept it as a *fait accompli*. She had already decided there was no going back. She had made her home with us. She had tried hard to put London behind her. The Germans had made sure there was no past to return to.

The only thing she said was: "Where's Dusty?"

"In the shed."

"Can I take him for a walk?"

"Of course."

The two of them went out whilst I was doing the washing-up. When John came back, I told him what had happened.

"Burnt her boats," he said.

"And ours."

"We'll have to look after her now."

"There's no one else."

It was the simple truth.

When Jemima came back, John gave her a big hug. I made them both a milky drink. When I took the mugs into the sitting room, she was staring into middle distance.

"Are you very upset?" I asked.

She sighed.

"I were jus' thinkin' if I'd been there, I might've been dead an' all."

I nodded.

"Most of your aunt's street seems to have gone."

"Good job Mary came and rescued you," said John.

She nodded slowly.

John tried to be helpful.

"D'you want to go back to London and see what's happened?"

"I don't think that's a good idea at all!" I said sharply.

Jemima looked at the two of us. It was rare for us to disagree in public.

She shook her head.

"I don' think I wanna go."

"There'd be nothing to see," I said. "Just rubble."

John climbed down.

"I just thought she ought to have the chance."

Jemima seemed to be glad I had taken a strong line.

"Will they bury 'em?"

"Probably done it already," said John.

"Probably not much left to bury," I said to myself.

"If we wen' to London, we might get bombed!"

"Yes. They seem to have it in for them."

"You're safer in Bidworth," I said firmly.

The longer the conversation continued, the more artificial it seemed. I felt that Jemima deserved some proper assurance about her future. John and I had discussed it briefly.

"We're thinking of adopting you," I said.

It was a new word to her.

I explained: "It'll make you our daughter."

"Part of the family," said John.

Jemima's face brightened.

"Would I be Jemima Woodward?"

"Yes, I suppose you would."

"Don't you like 'Shaw'?"

She smiled.

"I think Wood'ard sounds more toff."

I raised my eyebrows.

"You want to be a toff?"

Jemima cast a long, hard look at Dusty.

"Well, it won' upset Auntie Jean now, will it?"

Only then did she burst into tears.

Thirty-Eight

Yes, I broke into tears. It was an emotional moment. But the process of adoption took quite some time. I remained 'Shaw' for another seven or eight months. At school, there seemed no point in changing my name. Everyone knew who I was and where I had come from. Changing to 'Woodward' would merely invite ridicule. I didn't tell my classmates about the death of my mother and my aunt.

However, the facts slipped out early in October when my fellow-Londoners were once again evacuated to Bidworth.

It was a nasty surprise seeing them all again. I thought I had completely severed my roots; but there they were - and Miss Baker. It is perhaps pleasing to record that they received a much warmer welcome from the villagers on their second visit. This time a bus was sent to the station; a party was held in the village hall. The death of Billy Smith and Peter Mills evoked genuine sympathy. People realized that these children had been in the thick of it.

Newsreel pictures of the King and Queen treading through the rubble of what had been their streets and homes did much to improve the understanding of the Bidworth people. The Cockney spirit suddenly became an inspiration to all. "Business as usual..." "Give it 'em back!" They wouldn't be beaten and neither would we.

But the return of the Londoners immediately raised questions about my future education. Should I return to my old class or stay with the Bidworth children? Mary made up her mind very quickly. I think her last encounter with Miss Baker had convinced her that I would never get anywhere with her as my teacher. So there was a further visit to the headmaster and agreement was reached that I should stay in my present class.

I was quite happy with this decision but the Londoners, I think, regarded it as an act of treachery. I had gone over to the enemy. I had deserted them for a cushy number. I had escaped the blitz and the rain of bombs and hot shrapnel which had descended on their streets. I was cold-shouldered for several days, but that did not bother me. I was a natural loner.

It was then that it came out about my mother and my aunt. For a day or two, even the Bidworth children felt sorry for me. But, very quickly, such feelings were lost in the daily exposure to war. Bombers seemed to be flying over us every night. Coventry, Birmingham, Liverpool and Glasgow were smashed to smithereens. Personal tragedies counted for very little.

For the second year running, the Bidworth bonfire was cancelled. In its place, the school organized a Hallowe'en party for all the children between eight and ten. This was the first major social event held after the evacuees' return and it was hoped that the party would break down the barriers between the village children and the evacuees. And I suppose it did.

When we came into the hall, there were about twenty turnip lanterns burning with a rich orange glow. I had never seen a turnip lantern before. I thought they were quite beautiful, despite their hollow eyes and gaping mouths.

We were all given masks and black pointed hats which were held on with elastic bands which were a bit too tight. Most of us dispensed with the hats after about five minutes. The masks were also rather a nuisance and after the first excitement, they too were ditched.

The meal was as good as one could expect in wartime.

Sandwiches and biscuits, cake and jelly - with watered-down squash. In the course of the meal, some of the cakes and sandwiches were thrown around and trampled on. To prevent open warfare, the teachers quickly organized games. Dunking for apples was quite exciting and many people got soaked. I avoided the dunking, being quite convinced that some enemy would regard this an an ideal opportunity to hold my head under the water that little bit longer - and drown me. I had seen a woman drowning three kittens - and it had not taken long. So I kept my distance.

After the games, a conjuror was supposed to round off the evening's entertainment - but he seemed to be a little slow in arriving. I could see the teachers exchanging anxious words. Someone was sent off to the phone; but the result was more head-shaking. I could guess what they were planning - more games.

I decided that I had had enough. I had no real friends and I thought that I would much rather be back at home reading a book or playing with Dusty. So I went to the toilet and did not return.

Instead, I went out into the cold, crisp night. The stars were shining brightly and the moon was just rising over the eastern horizon.

It was a magical night - so quiet. No one about. No cars. No aeroplanes. Every house a little black box - silent and self-contained. There was not even a cat in sight. I walked down the centre of the road, eating an apple I had pinched from one of the tubs. It wasn't particularly sweet. I threw it away and wiped my hands on my coat.

I turned through the gateway to our house and walked up the steps. To my surprise, the door was wide open. I was not expecting it to be locked; but I could not believe that Mary would have left it wide open. That was the first thing that alerted me that perhaps all was not well.

Secondly, there was no sign of Dusty. Normally, he would hear me coming and rush to the door and welcome me with lots of licks and cuddles.

I paused inside the door.

People were fighting in the sitting room. There was quite a rough house going on. I could hear people bumping into tables and chairs. Sounds of heavy breathing. Gasps and moans.

I had been mistaken once before in this situation, so I proceeded cautiously and looked round the corner of the door. The first thing I saw was the back of a large man wrestling with someone... I presumed Mary. I could see her legs trying to kick him.

My first thought was that she had surprised a burglar and now he was attacking her. He seemed to have her by the throat.

Suddenly, he spoke: "Shut up you bitch; or I'll kill you!"

I did not wait to see any more. Instinctively, I turned to the hatstand behind the front door.

I had noticed that John had placed Erich's pistol in the locked drawer beneath the mirror. The thing that caught my eye was the missing key. Foolish man! I immediately realized there must be something special in the drawer. I hunted for the key. And there it was, on a hook, higher up on the wooden frame, behind the mirror. If I stood on the shoe box, I could easily reach it.

I had taken down the key and put it into the lock. Yes, I was right. I took out the pistol and weighed it in my hand. I couldn't believe it. He had left the bullets inside. I counted them to make sure they were all there. I took them out and pulled the trigger. No luck. But then I realized I had forgotten to release the safety catch. I pulled the trigger again. It was not too stiff. I then put on the safety catch and re-loaded all the bullets. I hid the pistol back in its drawer and put the key back on its hook.

So, tonight, I knew what to do. I jumped up on the shoe box, grabbed the key and unlocked the drawer. I pulled out the pistol and released the safety catch. It took only seconds.

I moved quickly to the doorway of the sitting room with my pistol at the ready.

The sight that met my eyes was terrifying. The man had a thin rope round Mary's neck and was swinging her round like a rag doll. She was trying to tear off the ligature but he was pulling it tighter and tighter. Her efforts were hopeless. He was a big, strong man and he was quite intent on killing her. I could see the look on his face. Totally without emotion. Cold, dead eyes...

As I appeared in the doorway, those chilling eyes turned on me. He looked surprised. As well he might! Who was this child brandishing a pistol? Was it a toy? It most certainly wasn't - as he would soon find out.

I did not hesitate. I pointed the gun at him as I had seen done so often in the gangster films - and fired at point-blank range.

Thirty-Nine

I aimed for his heart. (This was probably a mistake, because I doubt whether he had one...)

Anyway, I reckoned without the recoil. As I pulled the trigger, the power of the shot flung me backwards and the bullet sped upwards, catching him in the forehead, just above his right eye. At such short distance, the impact was fatal.

As I dropped the pistol, I noted the look of surprise on his face. Then there was blood bubbling out of the wound. He put a hand to his face - but as he did so, his body crumpled.

I scrabbled for the pistol but a second shot was unnecessary.

As he fell, so did Mary. Her face was blue; he had almost choked her to death. She was too far gone even to tear the ligature away from her neck. She fell back on to a small table which shattered under her dead weight.

I rushed forward, screaming.

I tore the rope away. There was a savage red line around her throat. Another few seconds and she would have been dead.

Her eyes were closed. She was hardly breathing. I shook her violently.

"Mary! Mary! It's me!"

A small breath escaped her lips.

She inhaled - but with obvious difficulty.

I kept shaking her.

Her eyes opened - but they were peculiar - looking upwards. It was rather as if she had had an epileptic fit.

She put a hand to her throat.

"I've taken it away," I said. "You're all right."

Her eyes focussed on my face.

To start with, there was a look of horror - but it changed into puzzlement as if she was wondering if she was dreaming.

"Him?" she said - with difficulty. "Him?"

I looked to my left.

He was still lying in an ugly heap.

"Dead," I said. "I shot 'im."

She shut her eyes then.

Tears rolled down her cheeks.

I stopped shaking her and went for a cushion to put under her head. I removed the remains of the table so that she could lie flat.

She did not seem to be wearing any knickers. I pulled down her dress.

She began to cry. Then she turned sideways and was sick over the carpet. I wanted to go and get a wet cloth but she held on to my hand. I knelt awkwardly - not knowing exactly what to do.

The man was still lying there. He seemed to have stopped bleeding. There was a trail of blood down his face and his eyes seemed to be staring at his knees. Logic told me that he was dead - but I was still frightened that he might do something unexpected. It seemed strange that life could be extinguished so totally - and so quickly.

I turned back to Mary.

She was twisting her neck and her adam's apple was moving up and down. Her breathing was still laboured and her eyes were shut.

"Yer all right," I said. "I caught 'im in time. I shot 'im with Eric's pistol. He's dead."

She sighed deeply.

More tears.

I wiped them away with my dirty fingers.

Eventually, she tried to sit up. I let go.

As she sat up, she saw the man's body. I think she would have screamed if she could have. Instead, she bunched her knees together - put her head down on them - and rocked back and forward in silent misery.

I went off to get a glass of water and a wet cloth.

I tried to make her lift her head - so that she could sip the water. But she wouldn't look up. She kept saying: "No! No! No!"

I was out of my depth.

"Shall I phone John?" I asked.

She continued to moan.

"Mary," I said, "keep your eyes shut - but let me wipe yer face."

At length, she did as I asked. I wiped her forehead and her cheeks. I got her to drink the water.

Of course, she opened her eyes. And once again, she began to moan: "Him! Him!"

I put my arm round her and shielded her so that she couldn't see the body. But I have to confess I didn't like having my back to him. It made me jumpy.

I kept wiping her forehead.

Eventually, she put her arms round me and hugged me.

"You saved my life," she whispered.

"Good job I knew where the pistol was!"

She smiled a faint smile.

"I'd ' ave done it better if I'd 'ad some practice."

She looked over my shoulder.

"You seem to have done it well enough."

Her voice was still a faint whisper.

Then she went back to her weeping and moaning. I endured this for another five minutes. Then I said firmly: "You need a cup of tea."

"Tea?"

She shook her head.

"Come on," I said, "you've got to get up. Come into the kitchen and I'll put the kettle on."

She put a hand to her throat and massaged her neck. She still seemed dazed.

I pulled her to her feet.

She got up slowly. She was shaking.

She was shaking even more by the time she reached the kitchen. She put her arms on the table and buried her head between them. She kept saying: "What are we going to do?"

Not being able to do anything to help her, I concentrated on making her a cup of tea. Once or twice, I went back into the sitting room to see if the man had moved. I did not touch him - but he lay there slumped against the wall with that fixed stare. I knew he would have to be moved but I was reluctant to do it myself. Quite clearly, Mary would be unable to help me.

I put the mug of tea in front of her. I had used two and a half spoonfuls of sugar so it was very sweet.

"You mus' drink it," I said, "while I phone John."

She looked at me with a look of despair in her eyes. I could not understand the look - although today I understand exactly what she was feeling.

I went out into the hallway and picked up the phone. I dialled the number that went directly to his hut.

"Can I speak to Mr John Woodward?" I said in my poshest voice.

He wasn't far away.

I said: "Gould you come 'ome now?"

I could sense a certain reluctance.

"Dreadful things 'ave 'appened 'ere."

"What sort of things?"

"A man 'as tried to murder Mary."

"Murder Mary?"

"She's all right. I've given 'er a cup of tea - but she's cryin' and shakin'. I think you oughta come 'ome now."

The news about Mary seemed to shake him.

"Can I speak to her?"

"No. She's weeping in the kitchen."

"I'll be back right away."

I went into the kitchen and sat beside her.

"'e's on 'is way."

I put my hand on her arm and encouraged her to drink her tea.

I'd never known her like this. I put it down to shock. It was supposed to do things to people. Shell-shocked, they called it, when people had been bombed. I supposed that being garrotted had a similar effect.

It was only when I sat down at the table and had time to think, that I began to realize I had actually killed someone. His dead body was lying in the sitting room. This was my second murder. Even though it had been done in a good cause, there would inevitably be consequences. The police would come round. There would be questions - perhaps even a trial? It was going to be very unpleasant. Perhaps that was what Mary was so upset about?

At least, none of the neighbours had appeared. One would have thought the sound of the pistol would have attracted attention - but there was no response. Perhaps they were out?

It occurred to me that the best solution would be for us to get rid of the body ourselves. There was no need for the police to become involved. If we said nothing, no one need ever know. But would John agree? Surely he would not want me to be branded a murderer?

I looked at Mary.

She was quiet now.

Her face looked haunted and sad.

"It's all right," I said. "You've got nothing to worry about. He's dead - and John's on the way."

She looked at me - and shook her head.

"You don't know who that man was?"

"No. "

She sighed deeply.

"That was your father!" she said.

I looked at her with amazement.

"My father? 'im?"

She nodded angrily.

"He came here to find you. At least, that's what he said he came for." A bitter tone came into her voice. "He pinched all my jewellery. He raped me. Then he tried to murder me."

I couldn't quite take it in.

"I've shot my father?"

"Yes."

There was little to be said. I had no regrets - or remorse. Father or not, I had had to stop him killing Mary. I had done so very effectively. But for me she would certainly have died. But the fact that the man was my father raised lots of questions.

I had thought he was in jail. Had he escaped - or had he been released? Why had he come to Bidworth? Who had told him that I was here?

I had never seen any picture of him so I hadn't recognized him. He looked nothing like Uncle Josh. He was a complete stranger. I felt no feelings for him whatsoever.

I was amazed at how calm and sensible I had been. Poor Mary, she had gone completely to pieces.

John arrived home more quickly than I had expected. He had borrowed someone's car. I heard the sound of the car pulling up outside the gate and the slam of its door. I rushed to the front door and threw it open.

"Where's Mary?" he shouted.

"In the kitchen."

He dashed into the kitchen and took her into his arms.

"What's happened?"

He didn't really need to ask. The mark on her neck was painfully obvious. Her eyes were red with tears. She was still shaking - and she began to shake and cry even more now that John was here.

I left them for a few quiet moments together. I went into the sitting room and looked at the body.

My father...

It was a sobering thought.

Certainly, I felt no guilt about the killing. Never before or since in my life have I ever felt so justified in my actions.

I went back into the kitchen.

Mary was trying to explain.

"He attacked me... I came back from Aylesbury... And he was there... He put a knife to my throat... forced me to hand over all my jewellery... even the rings on my hand." She waved her ringless hands.

"Who is *he*?" John was angry.

I could hardly hear her reply.

"Jem's father."

John looked as if he could not really understand what she was saying.

"'e's in the sitting room!" I said.

"He's dead!" Mary managed to scream.

"Dead?"

John looked at both of us with disbelief.

He let go of Mary and followed me into the sitting room. He stopped in the doorway. The sight of the body hit him very hard. He stared at the figure for several moments. Then he went over, sat on his haunches and looked at the corpse more carefully.

"He's been shot."

"I shot 'im."

He looked at me.

"'e were killin' Mary. I had to stop 'im."

He breathed deeply.

"Is that Erich's pistol?"

I nodded.

"I saw where you put it. I found the key."

He breathed again.

"Well," he said, "I suppose I should congratulate you. It looks an excellent shot."

This was not a moment for modesty; but for quiet pride. "'e were stranglin' 'er with that rope." I pointed to the length of cord.

John picked it up and ran it through his fingers.

"She were blue."

John nodded silently.

He stood up and led me out of the sitting room, putting off the light and shutting the door.

"Does anyone else know about this? The neighbours?"

"No one."

He returned to the kitchen.

Mary seemed to have pulled herself together. She was resting her head on her arm. She still looked pale but she had stopped shaking. John's presence seemed to have calmed her.

"You've seen him?"

"Yes."

"He is dead?"

"Very much so. It was a good shot."

"He was garrotting me."

She put her hand to her throat.

"Let me look at that."

John looked at her wound. He touched her gently.

"Does it still hurt?"

She nodded.

"I passed out. I thought my last moment had come. Perhaps it might have been better if it had."

She put her head on his shoulder and cried again.

I decided to make a fresh cup of tea for both of them.

John kept his arm round her.

I heard her say: "He forced me..."

And John: "You're alive. That's what matters."

"He was vile... He hurt me terribly... I tried to stop him.'.'

"I still love you... Nothing's changed..."

"It has. I've been polluted."

"You're still mine."

John seemed to be saying the right things.

But I felt the less I said the better. I put two more mugs on the table and sat looking at them.

"And where's the dog?"

"Locked up in the shed. I thought he was going to lock me up in the shed - but he had other ideas - the bastard!" Mary looked at John. "What did you tell them at work?"

"I didn't stop to tell anyone. I just said there was a crisis at home. Graham lent me his car. I'll have to get it back but there's no hurry."

I thought that perhaps John was missing the point.

I looked at him.

Forty

"But where are we going to put it?" I asked.

"Put what?"

"'im. "

John looked at me.

"You can't let 'im sit there!" I said. "He's gotta go."

John continued to look at me thoughtfully.

Eventually, he said: "If we call in the police... there's going to be a lot of questions..."

"I can't bear the thought of the police," said Mary. "That'd be the last straw. Constable Bell! It'd be all over the village in a matter of hours. Mrs Williams! Think what she'd make of it! I couldn't face them. We'd have to move."

Her reaction showed that she was recovering fast. I was glad to see her becoming more herself again.

I had already decided that it would be much better if we disposed of the body ourselves. Mary clearly felt the same. But it had taken John some time to realize the full extent of the problem.

"Does anyone know he was here?"

"I doubt it."

"He's bound to have asked someone where we live."

"So what? If anyone says: "Did he come to see you?' we just say 'Yes'. They'll only start asking questions if his body is found. Otherwise, they'll presume he went back to London - or wherever he came from."

"Would anyone know who he was?"

"Jemima didn't even know who he was. I wouldn't have known unless he'd told me."

She shuddered.

"I'm going to have a bath. As Jemima says, just get rid of it."

John seemed to have made up his mind.

"Well, if no one knew who he was - or that he was here... If no one heard the shot - and no one sees us removing the body... it should be possible."

I said helpfully: "We could move him into the garden shed."

Mary went upstairs and turned on the bath.

John followed her with his eyes. He was very worried for her.

"Gome on," I said, "we've got to get him aht."

"You're not doing anything. Leave it to me."

"He's my dad," I said.

John laughed.

"Well, if you put it like that!"

We went into the sitting room. Although I would never have admitted it to John, the corpse was beginning to give me the heebie-jeebies. The quicker he was removed, the better.

John looked at the mat in front of the fireplace.

"I think that's probably the right size. It's about time we got a new one." He looked at me. "D'you want to take his feet?"

We moved the body face down on to the right-hand side of the mat. John pulled off the man's jacket, shirt, trousers, pants, socks and shoes. He looked at me.

"Removing the evidence."

The clothes were piled up separately.

Then we rolled up the mat and John sent me off to get some scissors. He used the rope my father had used to try and kill Mary. He managed to get two lengths out of it. I was then sent to get more window cord from the garden shed.

In the process, Dusty was released.

He gave me a tremendous welcome - tail-wagging, licking, leaping up and down. But he swiftly noticed that I was engaged in more serious business. When I took him into the kitchen and said: 'Basket!' he was unusually obedient and went straight to his basket.

I took in the cord and John finished tying up the mat. It looked quite a neat package. Together, we manhandled the heavy object to the back door.

John went out to reconnoitre. He noticed that next door's house was still unlit. We had been very lucky. There was the beginning of a new moon but that was on the eastern side of the house. He came back in.

"We must be quick," he said, "but very quiet."

Within a minute, with scarcely a sound, the body was lying on the floor of the garden shed. John covered it with sacks, spades and tins of creosote. One would hardly have known...

He looked around.

"I'll get a padlock for this," he said. "I think we've got one at work."

We walked back into the house. He filled a bucket with hot water and got hold of an old towel. He scrubbed the sitting room floor and carpet no less than three times.

"It's wet," he said, "but it'll soon dry. We'll light the fire. Make the place look as normal as possible."

He looked around.

"I'll take the table with me - and his clothes. I'll put them in a waste bin somewhere on the way to Bletchley. No one'll know whose they were."

He proceeded to empty my father's pockets. There were all Mary's rings, the contents of her purse, a newspaper cutting and a very sharp knife.

John held out the newspaper cutting. It was all about

my capturing Erich. 'Bidworth girl captures Nazi'. "That's what brought him here," said John. "He knew where to find you."

I lit the fire.

John examined everything. He looked at me.

"Are you likely to need this knife?"

I smiled.

"You never know."

"You better bring in that pistol. I'll remove your fingerprints. If we're going to do this, we've got to do it properly."

The fire was soon roaring up the chimney.

John threw my father's possessions into the fire one by one and watched them burn. Then he fed in his clothes. They had a funny smell. Finally, he broke up the remains of the small table and fed them into the flames.

"On reflection," he said, "it's probably better getting rid of them right away."

"When are we going to get rid of the body?" I asked.

John took a deep breath.

"As soon as I get home. I shall take the car back right away. I'll explain that Mary's a bit upset. They'll all be very understanding. Then I'll come straight back. Perhaps, by the time I return, we'll have some bright ideas."

I already had one or two.

But, of course, I was now a professional murderess. Not many people of my age could claim to have killed two people.

I watched John clean the pistol and put it away in the locked drawer. He put the key back in its place. He made no effort to hide it. I took this as a sign of trust.

"I'm going to spend a few moments with Mary," he said. "You get Dusty his supper."

Whilst I was getting Dusty his supper, there was a knock

at the door.

I went to the door.

"Who is it?"

"Constable Bell."

John came pounding down the stairs.

"Who is it?" he whispered.

"Constable Bell."

"Hell's teeth!"

He opened the door.

I stood in the background with a bag of dog food in my hand - rather like Madame Defarge with her knitting...

"Evenin' sir. Is this 'ere your car?"

"Yes."

"Are you aware, sir, that you've left your lights on?"

"No, I hadn't. I'm very sorry."

They walked down the garden path together. I heard John say: "I'm just about to drive back to the office. I had some special papers to collect..."

I walked up the stairs and into the bathroom. Mary was up to her neck in soap suds, reeking of bath oil. It smelt overpoweringly of cleanliness.

"Who was that at the door?" she asked.

"Constable Bell."

She shut her eyes in despair.

"John's left the lights on in 'is car."

"Is that all?"

I nodded.

"Are you feelin' better?" I asked.

Mary was honest.

"I still feel shaky. I keep crying. Every time I shut my eyes, I see him."

"Is your neck sore?"

She put up a hand.

"It feels like a cut.'"

"John's got all your rings and things."

"Good," she said. "And the rest?"

I shut the bathroom door.

"'e's wrapped 'im up in the sitting room mat. We've put 'im out in the shed. When John comes back, we're goin' to take 'im somewhere. We 'aven't decided where yet, but I've got a few ideas."

Mary looked at me.

The look said: "What a child!"

"John's been very good," I said. "'e's scrubbed the carpet, 'e's burnt all his clothes. And 'e's burnt that table what you broke, 'e's kept 'is knife."

"Tell John to get rid of everything! I couldn't bear to see anything belonging to that man still in my house."

"It's nice and cosy down there," I said. "You'd never know anything 'ad 'appened."

Mary shut her eyes.

"It's in the mind," she said. "You can't get away from it."

John entered the bathroom.

"I got rid of him," he said. "What a shock! The police arriving at your door when you've just moved a body."

"Guilty as hell," said Mary.

"It's as well it was only my lights he was bothered about. Are you all right now?"

Mary smiled bravely.

"I'll pull through. I'll help you get rid of the body. Revenge will do me a power of good. It's not every day that a woman gets a chance of hitting back at a person who's abused her."

John still looked anxious.

"Will you be all right if I leave you. I'll return the car and come straight back."

"Be careful what you say to them. A minor burglary. Keep it simple. Remember! I've got to confirm your story tomorrow morning."

John gave both of us a big kiss and got soap suds all over his jacket. Then he bounded down the stairs and out through the front door. I noticed he was clutching a file of papers - just in case Constable Bell was lurking nearby.

I locked the front door and the back door. I finished giving Dusty his supper. I went into the sitting room and looked at the fire blazing in the hearth. It all seemed so normal.

I moved the tapestry firescreen into the space where the body had been lying. I put a pile of books where the table had been. I felt the carpet. It was still wet. I went and got another towel and rubbed the carpet hard. Then I put the towel on the fire. As John had said, it was vital to remove all the evidence.

I made Mary a nice milky coffee with lots of sugar and took it up to her. She was now in her dressing gown - tightly wrapped up. She was rubbing some cream into the mark around her neck.

"It's going to be purple tomorrow. I'm going to have to wear a very large sweater to hide it."

"Are you really going to go to work tomorrow?"

She shrugged her shoulders.

"I don't know. Probably better to keep busy. No time to think."

I sat beside her in bed whilst she drank her coffee.

"Is Dusty all right?"

"Fine."

"We'll take him with us. We shall need a good watchdog."

She smiled bravely.

"Now what are we going to do with the body?"

Forty-One

"We could put 'im in the canal."

"With a bullet hole in his head?"

"Or bury 'im in a ditch?"

"That's more sensible."

"'Ow are we goin' to carry 'im?"

"On a bicycle, I should think. If we put him in a wheelbarrow, he'd keep falling out."

I thought for a moment that Mary was being funny. But she wasn't. She was just being practical.

"Why don' we bury 'im at the church? There's lots of bodies there?"

Mary considered the possibilities.

"If there was a grave just opened, it might be an idea. But if we dug up the ground, someone would notice. That's the way people get caught. They'd say: 'Who's this man with a bullet in his head?' They'd check his fingerprints. Shaw? Father of Jemima Shaw? They'd be round at our door in five minutes."

"We could burn ' im!"

"Yes. But what about the black-out? People would see the flames. Besides, we haven't got any petrol."

I opened my mouth to speak.

"No," said Mary. "We're not siphoning off any petrol. You've done that once. Think of something different."

I ran my mind over other possibilities.

"The boiler at the church 'all?" I smiled. "Or the boiler at the church?"

Mary shook her head.

"What about the bones? When they rake out the ashes

- and they find all the bones. Someone would be bound to ask questions."

"We could take away the bones and bury 'em."

"It'd take several hours for the boiler to cool down. We'd have to go back - and that's dangerous."

"Would we get all 'is body in? Would we 'ave to chop 'im up?"

Mary winced at the suggestion.

Another bright idea flashed into my mind.

"What about Mrs Williams?"

"What about her?"

"She's in hospital."

"So she is... stomach trouble... probably ulcers..."

"We could bury 'im be'ind those bushes near 'er green'ouse."

Mary looked at me suspiciously.

"How do you know so much about Mrs Williams' garden?"

I was silent. Mary laughed.

"Come on," she said, "spit it out. If we can cope with two murders, we can cope with anything."

I smiled a faint smile.

"Well, you know she likes plants and things..."

"I didn't know..."

"... Well, she does. She 'ad quite a nice selection in 'er green'ouse."

Mary caught the nuance immediately. "Had?"

I nodded.

"I went and put salt in 'em."

"And where did you get the salt?"

"School dinners."

"I see. And you killed off all her plants?"

"Most of 'em."

"You went back to check?"

I nodded slowly.

Surely Mary would not think I was the sort of person to do things by halves?

"And does she have a big garden?"

"Not very big. But she 'as these big bushes be'ind 'er green'ouse. No one'd ever think of lookin' there... And she's got a back gate. On to that lane..."

It seemed a sensible proposal. It was not far away. It was approached by a quiet lane. A locked gate would present no problems. The lady of the house was away. But was the garden overlooked?

We put these points to John when he came back from his work.

After we had had a small meal (I was starving), the three of us took Dusty for a walk. When we reached Mrs Williams' back gate, John helped me over the wall and I undid the lock.

We let Dusty off his lead, so that if we were seen, we could say that we had gone into the garden to fetch the dog. So we did a brief survey of the proposed grave. John nodded his head. It seemed all right to him. We put Dusty back on his leash and left the garden. The gate remained unlocked, waiting for our return. We said nothing till we were back at the house.

John organized our plan of campaign.

At 2.00am, the digging party would set out. Whilst John dug the grave, Mary and I would keep watch. One of us near the back gate; the other near the front of the house. If anyone should approach, we should immediately return to John and leave rapidly in the opposite direction. But no one disturbed us and, by 3.00am, there was a fairly deep grave and a huge heap of earth.

We withdrew as silently as possible and returned to the house for meat pies and baked beans.

We gave John an hour to recover from his exertions and then set out on the most dangerous part of the plan.

The body in the carpet was tied to a plank and the plank was strapped on to the front handlebars and the seat of the bike. It was not easy to steer and it was heavy to push. There was no way we could run away in a hurry - and no way the body could be abandoned. It was important that the advance party should give the earliest possible warning of danger.

Mary and Dusty were the advance party. The dog would hear an approaching stranger long before any human being. John and I guided the handlebars and John provided most of the traction. Fortunately, we had only to travel about two hundred and fifty yards and once we got to the narrow lane, we were almost there.

The advance party guarded the far end of the lane whilst we manoeuvred our load through the back gate. This was the point of no return. If Constable Bell chose to appear on the scene, we should be caught red-handed. But we hoped he'd be in bed asleep.

We undid the straps and lowered the plank on to the ground. Mary took away the bicycle. I looked after Dusty, standing beside the back gate. John untied the carpet from the plank and rolled the package sideways into the grave. He then picked up the spade and with steady, even strokes, he replaced the soil. Having half-filled the grave, he stamped hard on the earth to compact it as firmly as possible. Then he finished filling up the trench, stamping it down a bit more - and finally spread the remaining soil across the flower-bed so that it all looked the same. He then went to a nearby tree and gathered up armfuls of leaves and scattered them over the ground. I helped him.

Mary took my place at the gate.

It had only taken another twenty-five minutes and the

garden looked much to same as we had found it.

"I must come and check it in daylight," said John, "and make sure we haven't left any evidence." He said it in a whisper.

Mary seemed thankful that the job was finally done. John pulled the gate to but he did not lock it. We returned down the lane, Mary carrying the spade and John the plank. It looked suspicious but, at 4.30am, there was no one around to ask any questions. Only when we got near to our house did we hear the distant clink of milk bottles which told us the milkman was already doing his early morning round. We slipped into our front garden like ghosts.

I was immediately put to bed - and all too soon was woken up and taken to school. Mary took the day off work and John was not on duty till 2.00pm so he had a chance to sleep.

For the next two or three days, I called into Mrs Williams' garden - always with Dusty as my excuse. I walked round the greenhouse and its bushes and checked that everything looked normal. I think John went in to sweep the path. It rained quite a lot that week and the garden was full of fallen leaves.

John said that in due course the earth above the grave would sink a little - so we knew there was more to be done. But, for the moment, my father's body was effectively disposed of and he had a better burial than he deserved. We felt well-pleased that no one in Bidworth had the slightest idea of the drama enacted in their midst. When I next saw Constable Bell, I felt an immense sense of superiority. He had been completely outwitted.

I also think our midnight burial helped Mary. She did not say much but, within a few days, the ugly wound began to heal and colour came back into her cheeks. Obviously, she would never forget the horror of that night. But,

together, we had made the best of a bad job.
And, if I am to be honest, I quite enjoyed it!

5: A Victim of War

(Mary's Story: December 1940 - May 1941)

Forty-Two

Psychiatrists tell us that one of the best ways of overcoming trauma is to talk about it. But there was no one I could talk to - except John. And kind and caring though he was, I could not imagine that he would want to engage in endless discussions about that dreadful night. He would want to put it behind him and he would expect me to do the same.

And yet, that was something I could not do. Every time I shut my eyes, I could still see him. I could still feel him. That choking feeling. That sense of falling deeper and deeper into the darkness. Losing everything. Losing everybody. Crying for no reason. Crying for every reason... It was no comfort to know that, throughout history, millions of women have been raped - particularly in times of war. For men, it is the event of a moment - a moment of lust, hatred or revenge. But for a woman, it represents a total destruction of everything she is - everything she feels about herself; so inextricably is a woman's mind and body bound together.

Outwardly, one remains a functioning human being but, inwardly, it is just broken glass - thousands of little pieces which can never be put together. Jemima's father may have failed to destroy my body but he had most effectively shattered my soul... my spirit - whatever you care to call it - the inner me.

Uncle Stephen was nothing by comparison. And yet his predatory behaviour had troubled me for years. I had not been able to get him out of my mind, because I could not externalize my feelings. This time I must. It was a

317

question of survival.

Very rapidly, I came to the conclusion that I must write down my experience on paper. Not to brood on it - or to re-read it. God forbid! But through absolutely ruthless honesty to try and exorcize the experience... the nightmare. I would write down every detail I could remember - from the beginning to the end. The words spoken - there weren't many of them! The rough actions. The horror. The fear. The expectation of death. The suddenness of the shot. Had I even heard it? Perhaps not. The disposal of the body. My burning hatred. If I could, I would have stabbed his body again and again with a large kitchen knife.

No, I had not lost my capacity to feel. If anything, I felt too much. But my feelings had switched to irrational violence. If I didn't focus it all on him, I would turn it on myself. Equally irrationally, I could easily understand why so many people, in similar circumstances, would commit suicide. It was easier than enduring the constant pain, the shame, the guilt, the filthiness of the abuser. It was a pardonable escape.

At the first opportunity, I put pen to paper. I did not use my usual notebook. I did not expect my narrative to be entirely coherent. There would be stops and starts... I might wish to stab the paper viciously... I might want to draw knives dripping with blood... I expected to shed tears in vast quantities.

My usual notebooks were very neat and tidy. They recorded happy events... pleasurable moments I wished to remember. I did not think this hideous episode should rub shoulders with the golden hours of memory.

Once I had committed those moments of shame and brokenness to paper, I might tear the whole thing into little pieces... I might burn it.

So where should I start?

The knock on the door?

I had been writing letters - to John's mother and to my sister - and I had gone along to the post office to put them in the box.

Because Jemima was at the Hallowe'en party, I took Dusty with me for his evening walk. We did a leisurely tour of the village, stopping and sniffing at all his favourite haunts.

I remember thinking what a beautiful night it was - all the stars shining so brightly; and the moon - a bomber's moon - rising slowly in the east, about to expose us completely to the enemy.

We got home and I poured some fresh water into Dusty's bowl. I was thinking that the kitchen floor needed a quick mop-over, when there was a knock at the door.

In a place like Bidworth, one didn't get many visitors - at least not after dark. I went to the front door and opened it.

There was a tall man standing quietly at the foot of the steps, smoking a Woodbine. It had a distinctively cheap smell.

He nodded his head in a sort of greeting.

"Is this where Jem Shaw is living?"

"Yes," I said, "it is. But she's at a party."

He stubbed out his cigarette.

"I'm her dad."

He gave me a vague smile.

"Well, you'd better come in. I'm Mary Woodward. We're looking after her; especially now her mother and her aunt have died in the Blitz."

I led him through to the kitchen.

Dusty did not welcome our visitor. He growled.

"Would you like a cup of tea?"

The man nodded. I filled the kettle and put it on the stove.

"How did you know she was living here?"

"Someone told me." He paused. "I read the story in the paper." He pulled a cutting out of his pocket. It was the story about Jemima and Erich.

"Was it in the London papers?"

He nodded.

"We were all very proud of her. My husband promised her five pounds if she captures another."

The mention of money seemed to interest him.

But again Dusty growled.

He said, "That dog annoys me."

"Well," I said, "he certainly doesn't seem to like you."

"Can you put him somewhere else?"

"I can put him in the shed."

I went over to Dusty who started barking. I took him by the collar and dragged him towards the back door. His claws scratched the lino. He didn't want to go.

The man said: "Can I use your toilet?"

"Certainly," I said. "It's upstairs on the right."

I didn't like the idea of him wandering round the house on his own. I remembered Jemima's Uncle Josh and how worried I had been that he might pay us a visit and steal my silver teapot.

I had quite a tussle getting Dusty into the shed and locking the door. As I did it, I knew I was doing the wrong thing. I was on my own. By all accounts, Jem's father was a violent man... a murderer. He was supposed to be in jail. How was it that he had managed to get to Bidworth? I decided that I would ask him when he came downstairs.

The trouble was that he didn't come downstairs - and there was no sound of a lavatory flushing. The front door was slightly ajar. Had he gone?

I stood at the foot of the steps.

"Hello?"

There was no reply.

I felt a sense of relief. He had gone.

But just in case he hadn't, I left the front door open as a line of retreat.

Rather nervously, I went upstairs. There was a light on in the bathroom but the door was shut. Was he all right? I advanced towards the bathroom.

"Are you all right?"

Suddenly, someone grabbed my hair and yanked my head backwards. I felt a sharp blade close to my neck.

I was too shocked to scream.

"Don't make a sound," he said, "or I'll kill you."

I said nothing. I couldn't think of anything to say.

"Put the bedroom light on."

I reached out shakily and put it on.

"Now," he said, "what about giving me that five pounds? I need it more than Jem does. You can always give her another."

"I haven't got five pounds," I said more boldly. "We don't have that sort of money in the house."

"Where d'you keep your money?"

I was silent.

He jerked my head again. I felt like a rag doll.

"Downstairs," I said sulkily. "In my purse."

"We'll collect it later."

He pushed me into the bedroom and put away his knife.

"I daresay there's a few goodies up 'ere."

I looked at him coldly.

"I invited you into this house because you said you were Jem's father."

He laughed.

He had bad teeth.

"A great mistake!"

I felt my temper rising.

"Aren't you supposed to be in jail?"

He smiled a crooked smile.

"Aren't the police looking for you?"

"Probably. But I might as well make the most of it." He looked round the room. "Where d'you keep yer jools?"

"I don't have any jewels."

He raised his eyebrows.

"I'm not giving them to you!"

He produced his knife again.

"Think again, Miss."

He shut the bedroom door.

"I'm not giving you a thing!"

He smiled again.

"Do we 'ave to do this the 'ard way, Miss?"

He moved closer, holding me with his eyes. Suddenly, he punched me hard in the stomach. I doubled up in pain. I was immediately conscious of him grabbing my left hand and tearing off my engagement ring and my wedding ring.

When I began to breathe again, I began to weep. This was a nightmare - happening in my own bedroom. John was on duty all night. It would be another hour before Jemima came home. I was completely at this man's mercy. And he was a murderer.

I looked at him.

"It doesn't pay to fight me," he said. "It just makes the 'ole thin' more painful." He waited till I had fully recovered.

"Now," he said, "what about the other jools?"

Very shakily, I went over to top drawer of the dressing table and took out a blue velvet box.

"Empty it on the bed!"

I emptied it out. He was getting quite a good haul. There were several more rings, brooches with diamonds, good quality costume jewellery, an expensive pearl necklace, a gold bangle... Most of it had belonged to my grandmother.

I would never see it again.

He scooped up the most expensive items and put them in his pockets. He left the costume jewellery, the gold bangle and the pearls.

"Don't you want the necklace?"

I was surprised he hadn't taken it.

His voice was ice cold - and I mean that:

"You'll need something for the funeral. Pearls are bad luck, Miss. And that bangle's got someone's name on it. It could be hidentified..."

I put the remaining jewellery back in the blue velvet box and put it in the top drawer. I straightened up. Was that it?

No.

Mr Shaw had been admiring the bed with its fine brass bedhead. He had also been admiring my figure. He hadn't been alone with a woman for several years. The opportunity was too good to miss.

He took off his jacket.

"Would you mind lying on the bed, Miss?"

I knew exactly what he was thinking.

"No," I said. "You've got my jewellery. I'll give you every penny in my purse. But you're not going to touch me!"

He smiled sadly.

Then, once again he hit me. A savage blow which hit me on the side of my head. I didn't see it coming. It literally knocked me senseless. I crashed to the floor.

When I came round, I was on the bed and my hands were tied to the brass bedstead. He had cut the window cords and he was now putting a noose round my neck and tying it to the top metal rail. If I lay still, I should be all right. But if I moved my head, I would throttle myself. He finished his work with a quiet smile on his face.

I stared at him. I couldn't believe this was all happening - and I was powerless to stop him.

He repeated his words: "it doesn't pay to fight. It just makes it more painful for both of us."

He pulled up my dress and looked at me.

"It's a long time since I 'ad a woman," he said. "A very long time."

He tore off my knickers.

I tried to kick him - but the cord tightened alarmingly round my neck.

He smiled.

"I told you it were no use fightin'. Just lie back and enjoy it."

I shook my head. I wasn't going to make it that easy for him. As he put his hand between my legs, I lashed out with my feet. In the process, I nearly choked myself.

Once again he took out his knife.

"Any more of that, Miss, and I'll split you from arse to tit! A nice liddle present for your boyfriend when 'e comes 'ome."

"It's my husband!"

It didn't matter to him who it was. He shrugged his shoulders - and took off his clothes.He smelt horrible. Dirt, sweat, animal lust rendered him repulsive.

I shut my eyes.

(I have described the next bit - but I have torn the page out of my notebook. I cannot bear to look at the words I have written. They have been written - I had the courage to do that. But they were better destroyed. I have burnt the torn bits of paper....)

What good would it do to remember the vicious details? He just flung himself at me - like an animal. My body rejected him. He forced his way in. He crushed me. He tore at me. He thrust again and again with a demonic energy. His hunger for a woman was almost insatiable. He went at me again and again. I lost count. Every thrust made the noose round my neck tighten. I could not cry out. Feeling bruised and red raw, I was suddenly conscious that he had stopped. He had rolled off the bed and was getting dressed. It was over. A surge of relief went through my body. The worst was over.

He smiled.

"That was nice." He paused. "You could have made it nicer; but you didn't.

He untied my hands and loosened the cord round my neck

"What did you expect?" I said angrily.

"Respect!" he said. "In my profession, a little respect is appreciated." He jerked the cord. "Get up!"

I slowly moved off the bed. My legs felt like water. I was frightened that when my feet touched the floor, I might collapse.

I looked down at the bed.

It looked white and untouched. No one would believe what had happened.

"My shoes?"

"You won't need them."

"What's happening now?"

He made a double loop of cord around my neck.

"We're going downstairs and you're going to pay me for the pleasure of my company. At least five pounds..." he chuckled. "But I think I'm worth more than that."

I was about to say exactly what I thought of him - but it seemed pointless. He ushered me out of the bedroom and out on to the landing. I was afraid he might push me down the staircase. I hung on to the bannister.

We moved slowly down the stairs. I noticed that the front door was still open. Could I run? As I thought - so did he. He jerked the noose backwards.

"No funny tricks."

We paused in the hallway.

"Where's yer money?"

"In the sitting room."

He kicked the door open and put the light on.

"Where's yer purse?"

"On the sofa."

"Pick it up."

With difficulty, I bent down and picked it up.

"How much have yer got?"

I counted out three ten shilling notes, two half crowns, a florin and some coppers.

Holding me tight, he reached out and took the notes, the silver and the coppers - every penny. He stuffed it into his pocket. I could hear the notes crunching and the coins tinkling against the jewellery.

His eyes lighted upon the silver kettle - as I knew they would.

"There's a nice bit of work. Must be worth a few bob."

He laughed.

"Just take it!" I said. "Take it and go!"

He laughed again.

"I shall certainly take it," he said, "but I think we have a little bit of unfinished business!"

I couldn't think what more he could do to me. He had taken all my treasured possessions - my rings. He had raped me. I felt I was dripping blood on the floor. The cord was still biting into my neck.

There was a mirror above the mantelpiece. He held me there so that he could see my face and I could see his.

He said menacingly: "I did warn you not to fight. You don't fight people like me..." He paused. "You show respect. If you don't show respect... Well, in London, you go straight into the river - in a pair of concrete boots - if you're lucky." He paused again. "I could slit your throat; but it's a bit messy.

I don't want blood all over my clothes. I think that this..."
He tugged at the cord round my windpipe. "I think this is
the best way... for both of us. Don't you?"

So he was going to kill me! And no one would ever
know what had happened - or who had done it. I should be
found lifeless, slumped on the floor in my front sitting room.
Jemima would soon be home. It was she who would find me.
But she wouldn't know who had done it. A burglar, it would
be thought; not her dad. He would go back to London, sell
off my jewellery for a few quid, enjoy a few weeks freedom
and then be re-arrested and taken back to jail. And my life
would just be snuffed out - everything destroyed....

I just couldn't let it happen.

I was feeling a little stronger.

I drew a deep breath and then lashed out with my feet.
I think I may have caught him by surprise. I tore at the cord
round my neck. It came loose.

Freed for a moment, I turned on him - with blazing
anger. I punched him in the face. I tried to knee him in the
groin - but failed. He hit me again - but not quite so hard.
Then he grabbed my hair. I was trying to stab my fingers
into his eyes.

I could see him smiling.

He knew my resistance was pointless. He could beat me
down any time he wanted. Perhaps he was even enjoying
this?

He dodged my fingers and did a bit of fancy footwork to
avoid my kicks.

"Temper! Temper!" he said.

He was still holding the cord.

I tried to run towards the door - but he had a firm grip
on my hair. He was able to pull me back and once more
whip the cord around my throat. I thrashed out with my
arms but he pulled it tighter. I still lashed out with my

elbows and feet. His grip was getting tighter. My breath was getting shorter. I felt things getting blurred. There was a ringing in my ears.

I heard him laugh as he slung me from side to side like a rag doll. I knew this was the end.

I never heard the shot. But I was aware of falling, crashing to the ground. This was death. It was the end. Nothing else could happen. The unfinished business - was finished.

Forty-Three

And that was it.

That is what happened.

I died - or at least I thought I had died. I was lying in a heap on the living room carpet. And someone was shouting at me. Their voice seemed a long way away - as if they were down a deep tunnel. I couldn't see who it was.

Was it some devilish figure on the other side of death? Only gradually did I recognize a familiar voice.

It was Jemima shaking me. Shouting at me.

But what had happened? And where was the man?

She was in acute danger. He might kill her as well.

She was tugging at me. Releasing the cord around my neck. I couldn't speak. I couldn't think what was happening. My eyes didn't seem to be working properly. But gradually, a message began to come through:

"I shot 'im!"

How had she shot 'im?

I kept going in and out of consciousness, I was aware that Jemima was forcing a glass of water between my lips. She was wiping my face with her fingers.

"It's orl right," she said. "'e's dead!"

I realized that I was not dead. I was not going to die. Something incredible had happened. A rescue had been achieved at the last minute. A wave of relief swept through me.

When I could at last open my eyes and see properly, I saw 'Him' slumped against the wall, with a trickle of dried blood running down his face.

Jemima had saved me.

But for what? For what?

I was polluted. I had been torn to pieces. Not just outside - but within. I was no longer 'me'. Even if I had survived, I was worthless. I was...

(At this point, words failed. I couldn't express the utter hopelessness of my position. Savagely, I dug my fountain pen into the paper - time after time. I broke the nib. Once I had taken the trouble to replace it - why bother? Force of habit? - I drew line after line on the paper. Tears poured down my cheeks.

I realised that whilst I had been recording the attack, my anger had been contained. Now the floodgates were open and the grief, the helplessness, the shame and the fear all poured out. I couldn't write any more. I put the sheets of paper away in a drawer where no one would find them. I made myself a cup of tea. I paced the floor. A couple of hours later, I took them out of the drawer and tried to write a little more. But the fire had gone out of me. I felt like a limp rag. Perhaps it would have been better to have died?

I looked at all the pages I had written. I couldn't - wouldn't - read it again. But it had helped. I had re-lived the experience and the writing had helped me to control my feelings. I had been as accurate as I possibly could be. I had put down every word I remembered. I could still hear his quiet laugh. I could see his face. Now it was all written down. It had taken several dreadful hours. No one must see this document. No one must know the horror. The way I had been smashed to pieces.

Perhaps I had taken the first step - I hoped it was the first step - back to sanity. It had already helped me a little. I would not burn the sheets of paper. I would not tear them up. The record was there. If I did not fight the memory, I wouldn't be able to live with myself. I had to fight a battle for my own survival. I couldn't let him destroy me - again.

Why should he win? I must climb out of the deep well. It was the only way to escape. I could only live as a shell. But I would live.)

Those were my feelings in the weeks after the attack. I did write a little more - but the rest of that awful night seemed like a dream. John came home - only for a few minutes - and then he was gone. Those few minutes were comforting. He said the right things. Did the right things. He and Jemima moved the body. I went for a bath. I wanted to wash everything away - and for a time, I seemed to succeed. But it was terrifying, standing once again on that top landing. The light was still on in the bathroom - which he had put on to trick me. I hardly dared to take a step forward. I flung open Jemima's bedroom door and turned on the light. I pushed open our bedroom door - frightened he might still be there with the cord in his hand - but I knew he couldn't be.

I turned on the light. The room was empty. I checked that no one was hiding behind or underneath the bed. I found my knickers. I would burn them. I flung them into a dark corner.

I then took a deep breath and approached the bathroom door. I kicked it open. It was innocent - empty of his presence. But as I turned on the bath taps - believe me - my eyes were constantly on the door.

Once I was in the bath, I think I switched on to autopilot. I went through the motions of normalcy, talking sensibly to Jemima, washing away the filth, wrapping myself in a comfortable white dressing gown, putting cream on that savage wound. Later, I found myself dressing up - to go and bury his body!

Walking through the village sometime after midnight - with a body rolled up in a carpet on top of a bicycle - was a surreal experience. I had very little to do. I tried to work up

331

a frenzy of hate; but it wouldn't come. I was utterly drained of emotion. I walked through the whole experience feeling nothing at all. I drank endless cups of tea. I went to bed and fell into a deep, deep sleep.

When I woke up, it hit me hard. It was in this room - on this bed - that everything had happened. Even secure in a warm bed, I couldn't escape. How could I ever make John understand what I was feeling? The huge cracks opening up inside me - like two mirrors colliding in a confined space. He would never understand.

I looked at his peaceful, sleeping face lying on the pillow beside me. To him, it would just be a horrible experience. He would be thankful that I was alive. I could hear him saying: "That's all that matters. You're alive." He would expect me to snap back into everyday life as if nothing had happened. And I would have to pretend that everything was all right - when it wasn't. We would be living a lie. But he wouldn't see it.

I took a few days off work. John spun some suitable tale about the burglary. When Jemima went off to school, I cried and cried. I hammered the bed. I hammered the wall. I sat in the kitchen, staring out of the window. Dusty whined - he stared at me in horror. I couldn't take him for walks. I couldn't face coming back into an empty house. He had to use the garden.

On the third day, I sat down to write. The tears stopped. I concentrated on what I was writing. I re-traced every step of that hideous experience. When I had finished, I put the whole thing into an envelope and sealed it. It would remain my secret. Perhaps one day I would have the courage to open it - read the contents once more - and burn it. But I think not. For better or worse, that moment was part of my life. My shame. My downfall. As long as that envelope remained, I would remember.... everything!

Forty-Four

A few days later, my troubles were compounded. Miss Baker asked to see me. Although she had been in the village for the past four weeks, I had not seen her since my visit to her school in London in January. Quite frankly, I had no desire to see her again.

I imagined that the call related to some misdemeanour which Jemima had committed against one of her former classmates. She could not think of anything she had done; but I was prepared for the worst.

I turned up at the school at 3-30pm on a Friday afternoon. I was pleased to see that she looked apologetic.

"I'm sorry to have to disturb you, Mrs Woodward; but the police in London have been in touch with me..."

Immediately, I thought of Cousin Eddie. Someone had seen Jemima at his garage and reported her. It had taken them almost a year to track her down. Everything was going to fall to bits. She would be taken away to an approved school. I braced myself for bad news.

"Shaw's father has escaped. He was given permission to attend his wife's funeral but he managed to give his escort the slip and did a runner."

A wave of relief swept over me.

Miss Baker noticed - and smiled a sad smile.

"You thought it was something worse?"

"I thought perhaps Jemima had attacked one of your pupils."

Miss Baker shook her head.

"No. She seems to have become much better behaved. The village teachers say she is doing very well."

I nodded.

(This was not the moment to mention a second murder - even if it had been in a good cause.)

Miss Baker returned to the problems raised by the escape of Mr Shaw.

"It could be quite dangerous," she said. "He is a violent man. He should have been hung. Why they gave him life imprisonment, I just don't know. Apparently, when they told him his wife had been killed in the blitz, he asked for compassionate leave to attend her funeral. I didn't know whether they were married or not... apparently, they were... The funeral was delayed - whilst arrangements were made. I'm told he put on a convincing display of grief and lulled his escorts' suspicions - so much so that they took off his handcuffs!" Miss Baker shook her head. "After the interment, he threw a handful of earth into the grave and then ran off as fast as he could go. They were rather a long way from a telephone box and both the prison warders were elderly men - not exactly in the first flush of youth. By the time they raised the alarm, he'd gone to ground."

Miss Baker looked at me anxiously.

"The police fear he may turn up in Bidworth - possibly on your doorstep. He knows his daughter is an evacuee here. He may not know where Bidworth is, but if he does decide to find her, there could be real trouble. I've spoken to Constable Bell..."

"But why should he want to see her?"

"Reflected glory! Someone showed him that piece in the paper about her capturing the German airman. I'm told he went round the prison showing it to people. He was quite proud of her."

I realized that I had to go along with this farce - if only to prevent suspicion falling on us.

"Could Constable Bell get us a picture of the man so that

we might recognize him..." I paused. "... even before he arrives on our doorstep?"

Miss Baker thought that was a good idea; but I don't think she had much faith in the local police.

"I'll ask him. But I advise you to keep a weapon handy. I'm carrying a knife in my handbag."

I thought: "She'll be carrying it for a long time." Aloud, I said: "I'll tell Jemima to be careful not to talk to strangers." I paused again. "D'you think she has any idea what her father looks like?"

"I shouldn't think so. She would only have been three or four when he was convicted. She may remember some feature - a nose, his eyes, the sound of his voice..."

I nodded helpfully, knowing full well that Jemima had not recognized her father. I would have to get her to do her bit of play-acting and ask the headmaster what she should do if a strange man came up to her.

I thanked Miss Baker for alerting me to the danger. It might have been some help if I had been given the information a fortnight earlier. A lot of grief could have been avoided.

But I must say that the news lifted my spirits. If they had only got this far, our secret was safe - providing we made no mistake under questioning.

I felt I could rely on Jemima's natural animal cunning. She didn't care for authority figures and she would instinctively be non-co-operative. She already disliked Constable Bell. He would get nothing out of her.

But John might try to be clever - and let something slip. And I was aware that my face could show my deeper feelings. Miss Baker had immediately noticed my sense of relief when I had realized that Jemima was not the problem. I worked out the basic line we could take.

Miss Baker had warned us about Mr Shaw's escape. We

had taken precautions. But *since we'd been told,* we had seen nothing. No one had appeared on our doorstep. We were still anxious - but we hoped the police would catch him.

All that was at least true - even if it was not the complete truth. My real worry was if some top-notch detective from Scotland Yard came down to Bidworth and questioned us. He would almost certainly realize that we were lying. However, I hoped that being in the middle of a world war - with death raining down on our cities every night, nobody would worry about the fate of Mr Shaw.

When I returned home, I made sure that we had all our alibis prepared. Jemima had been at the Hallowe'en Party. It was probable that no one had noticed her early departure. I would say that I was working. John could doctor the duty roster at work. He, of course, had brought me home.

That was when he had left the car with its lights on at the front gate. He had been heading back to work. Constable Bell, having been at our front door that night, would probably put two and two together and make four. Certainly, when he called, there had been no sign of any escaped convict. It was nice to think that he would be our principal alibi.

But I still felt sure there must be someone in the village who had directed Mr Shaw to our door. They might not remember exactly what night they had seen him - so our carefully constructed alibis for Hallowe'en could prove completely useless.

Had we known who it was that brought Jemima's father into Bidworth, we might have been even more distressed. Because it was Mr Taylor, the lorry driver, who picked him up at a crossroads outside Aylesbury.

Mr Taylor found lorry driving a lonely business. Whenever he could, he relieved that loneliness by picking up servicemen, students and even the odd tramp. He liked to hear their chit-chat - at least as much as could be heard above the roaring engine and the crashing gears.

During the dark winter nights, there was little traffic on the roads; so his kindness in stopping was much appreciated He regarded himself as a sort of rural bus service.

But not many people were heading for Bidworth. It was well off the beaten track. The man he had picked up outside Aylesbury was a surly cove - a hard man - who kept himself to himself. He didn't seem to be in the habit of indulging in idle conversation.

However, after he had offered him the rest of his thermos flask of tea, he managed to get him talking.

"Why are you going to Bidworth?"

Over the noise of the engine, he thought he heard the word: 'evacuee'.

"You're going to see an evacuee?"

"My daughter's an evacuee."

"From London?"

The man nodded.

"Staying in our village? Aye, we've got quite a few of them staying in our village. We had one in our house but she was nothing but trouble. We soon got rid of her."

A few more crashes on the gears to negotiate a bridge.

"Is she missin' her mother?"

"Her mother's dead."

"Dead? In the bombing?"

The man nodded again and poured the rest of the tea down his throat.

"Poor kid! I don't know what the world's comin' to. Those bloody Germans.... they've got a lot to answer for. Does she know 'er mum's dead?"

"I think so."

The man stared ahead.

There was a silence; then he spoke:

"D'you know Bidworth well?"

"Should do! Born and bred there. Two kids and a wife."

The man seemed to cheer up.

"D'you know Bridge Road?"

"Course I do. It's beside the canal. Just along from the doctor's. What number were you looking for?"

"Number 16."

"Name?"

"Woodward."

"Can't say it rings a bell."

"They're looking after her."

"What's her name?"

"Jemima... Jemima Shaw."

Mr Taylor didn't hear properly. He was not really listening. He was concentrating on the road. The dark nights and the reduced headlights made every mile treacherous.

"What did you say?"

"Shaw. Jemima Shaw."

This time Mr Taylor did hear. In the process, he took his eyes off the road and almost crashed into a telegraph pole.

"Her?"

If there was one evacuee whose name he knew, it was Jemima Shaw. She had caused his family untold misery in the three days she had lived with them. She had attacked his boys; destroyed their meals; caused terrible trouble between himself and his wife. He had hit her. She had gone to the police.

He had been cautioned. All because of that little bitch. He knew his boys hated her.

"You know her?"

"I'd say I do. We Had her in our house just three days. She was a right little terror."

The stranger laughed.

"She probably takes after me."

Mr Taylor was silent.

It was perhaps better to say nothing. He wouldn't be able to express his feelings over the noise of the engine. And anyway, they were almost on the outskirts of the village. Better just to drop the chap in Bridge Road.

He pulled up outside the doctor's.

"Good luck, mate."

"Thank you."

A crash of gears and he was on his way. He knew that his wife would not want to hear any more about that wretched 'vac. It would only upset her. So when he got home, he said nothing about the man. He read his paper and then made his way to *The Fox and Hounds* to drown his sorrows in drink.

Thank God they hadn't rationed the beer! But he suspected that they had watered it down. It didn't taste the way it used to... Bloody Germans!

So Mr Taylor said nothing about Jemima's dad visiting Bidworth. And no one thought to ask him. He was not a very approachable man at the best of times and he would certainly do nothing to help Constable Bell.

So our secret was safer than we realized. Miss Baker continued to carry round her knife and we lived on the edge of the abyss for several months. So long as the body did not surface, we were safe. Both John and Jemima paid regular visits to Mrs Williams' garden to see if all was well. I was sure the police were still looking for Mr Shaw but I hoped they would confine their investigations to London. As the war progressed, they would surely have bigger and more important things to think about.

Forty-Five

I was sick - two mornings running; and I knew it wasn't the food. At that time, we were living quite simply. Rationing was strictly enforced - and the portions were being steadily reduced. Our main diet consisted of bread, cereals and vegetables - garnished with a little meat. So we were eating nothing fancy or exotic.

Without any warning, I felt a surge of nausea rising up inside me. The sickness was soon gone; but a horrible acidity stayed with me for the rest of the day. I brushed my teeth several times to take away the bad taste. I drank a lot of water to clear my stomach of any bugs. But I had a nasty feeling the cause was still there.

I then had two days when nothing happened. I was working those two days, cycling to Bletchley, getting plenty of fresh air. But the sickness returned. I went to the doctor's surgery in Bletchley to see if he could give me anything to take away the nausea.

"I don't think so," he said. "I think your body is trying to tell you something."

"Stress? Over-work? Anxiety?"

He shook his head.

"I think you're pregnant."

My heart stood still. Impossible! We had taken all precautions. We had no desire to have a child at that moment. Our work was far too important. There was nothing else on our minds.

The doctor gave me a full examination which was as unpleasant as it was unexpected. I could feel my pulse racing and my mind reaching out for answers.

He returned to his desk. "Six to eight weeks, I would say." He made a few notes on my record card. "Have you not noticed your breasts feeling more tender?"

"Not really."

"No period?"

"I thought it was late. It is a bit erratic."

"Well, now you know what's happening. You should be having a baby in July or August."

In those days, they didn't prescribe anti-sickness pills. The doctor told me to eat more frequently. To take several small meals throughout the day. Not to drink coffee. (It was rationed anyway.) Not to smoke. Not to drink too much alcohol. To take plenty of exercise.

He gave me a final smile.

"Come back if you need any help."

I staggered out of his consulting room in a daze. I couldn't adjust to the terrible news which would mean a complete disruption of our daily lives. How on earth had it happened?

Before I had passed the security gates of Bletchley Park - let alone returning to the hut where I was working - I had the answer. The only time I had had unprotected sex was with Jemima's father. That hideous moment which I had been trying so hard to block out of my mind.

It could not be John's child.

It must be his.

This realization hit me hard.

I stopped on the road up the hill.

"Have you lost something?" asked one of the despatch riders as he was getting back on his motor-cycle.

"No. I've just had some bad news."

"It happens to all of us."

He drove away with his exhaust roaring.

I moved on - slowly.

It would be his baby. Conceived in a moment of violence - as a prelude to death. If I had died, it wouldn't have mattered. But I had survived - and so had this creature. I must say that my first reaction was to turn round, to go back to the doctor and see if I could have an abortion. Get rid of the bloody thing before it totally disrupted our lives - and our work.

I was angry - not tearful.

But I decided I needed time to think about the consequences. John and I were on almost alternating shifts. He had been told about my sickness; but he had probably forgotten about it by now. He didn't know I'd been to the doctor. Perhaps an abortion could be arranged without him knowing anything about it? Afterwards, I would probably be off work for a few days. I might have to go into hospital.

Then he could be told what I had done.

But once I had settled at my desk and started work, decoding the latest cribs, I suddenly realized that if I started to talk to anyone about rape, the information would surely be passed back to the police. They would want to find the man - but Jem had killed him - and we had buried his body! Far worse things might happen to us if I opened my mouth. But if I went to a back-street abortionist - no questions asked - I might die.

I thought about it.

Pregnancy was a natural thing. Unpleasant. Uncomfortable. But it had an ending. A baby would be born; but it could easily be adopted. Better still, I might have a miscarriage - and that would solve the problem.

John would have to be told - but not yet.

There was no immediate need to tell anyone. The sickness - though horrible - would become more bearable as time went on. Anything would be better than seeing Jemma being arrested or myself bleeding to death... And, of course, if Jemma was arrested, we too would be arrested - for not reporting a murder, for perverting the course of justice - so there would be no mercy for us.

Pregnancy certainly seemed to be the better option.

"Have you found any connections?"

Gordon passed by.

"Not yet."

I forced myself to concentrate on the cribs for the German Army cipher. It was four days old and was proving very unyielding. I spent the rest of the afternoon working on it - but without success. A new message was brought in from North Africa. The Italians were trying to escape from Benghazi; but the British had cut across their line of retreat and blocked the only road to Agedabia. A fantastic traffic jam was building up south of Benghazi. The Italian Army was like a rat in a trap. The text of the message was very badly enciphered. Some of it was en clair. It was read extremely quickly. It didn't tell us anything we didn't know. But it was nice to know that one Axis army was tasting the bitter dregs of defeat.

The work of decoding took my mind off sickness and pregnancy for a couple of hours. Then it was time to head home. Eight miles of country road with only a small lamp to light my way.

I resolved that when I got home, I would say nothing to John. This was a secret. I must bear it alone. I needed time to think - and adjust.

His baby! Bloody hell!

*   *   *

Although there was nothing I could actually feel, I was conscious that, day-by-day, this blob of humanity was slowly taking shape. I focussed my hatred on this unknown creature in the hope that the message might get through. "You are not wanted. Please go!" I tried to encourage it to miscarry of its own accord.

This did not seem to work!

But anger certainly helped me to cope with my sickness. I felt that with a little more effort, I might drive the creature out.

My knowledge of gynaecology was rather vague at that time; but I began to hunt through John's books to see if he had anything on the human body. I found one of his mother's books, written by Marie Stopes. I read it through and realized how stupid I had been.

I considered the likely progress of the foetus. What might be expected at different stages of the pregnancy. Nothing would show for two or three months; but, after that, everyone would notice. I had about four weeks to go before I had to acknowledge my condition. I decided to continue working for as long as possible. If neccessary, we would have to buy a car.

A week or two later, I began to look at things more positively. I had stopped beaming messages of hate to my unwanted guest. I began to think that, although the father was a murderer, the child might be more like me. It might be a very gifted child. Perhaps he or she might inherit my talent for mathematics. It would be very immoral to kill such a child.

I also reflected that although Jemima was also Mr Shaw's daughter, she still had some lovable qualities. There would of course be a tendency towards violence; but that perhaps could be curbed. I decided that the child should be given a chance to live. Not to be adopted - but treated as ours.

It took me about three weeks to reach this conclusion. How long would it take John?

Forty-Six

Choosing a suitable time was my first problem. I did not want to burden him when he was setting off for work; nor when he came home dog-tired and collapsed on the sofa. I needed a moment when we were both relaxed; had time to listen and consider all the difficulties which lay ahead.

I chose a Sunday afternoon when John had finished painting the kitchen and Jemima had taken Dusty for a long walk. I poured him a large gin and tonic.

"That looks ominous!" he said.

"Very," I agreed. "We have something to discuss."

"Not about Jem, I hope."

"No. She's fine. I'm afraid the problem is me."

He looked me over.

"You look perfectly healthy."

"I believe that's one of the few advantages of being pregnant."

There! I had uttered the fatal word. There was no going back.

John raised his eyebrows.

"Pregnant?"

I nodded.

"I thought we had agreed not to have a child. At least not till the war is over."

"We did agree." I watched him trying to work out where we had slipped up. "Unfortunately, *Force majeure...*"

He got the point.

"Mr Shaw?"

There was a long silence which neither of us wished to break.

Eventually, John said: "He didn't take any precautions?"

"Obviously not! He intended to kill me."

John put his arm around me and held me tightly.

He said softly: "When's it due?"

"The doctor thinks July or August."

John looked alarmed.

"Have you spoken to the local doctor?"

"No. I went to see one in Bletchley."

John breathed a sigh of relief.

"He doesn't know the circumstances?"

"No."

John proceeded to think about the implications. After a couple of minutes, I decided to move the process forward. "I did think about an abortion.... But too many questions might be asked. If I told them about the attack, they might feel it was their duty to tell the police..."

"No, we can't do that!"

"No. We would be arrested ... All three of us... Guilty of murder, accessories to murder and perverting the course of justice. We would all end up behind bars. Then we'd be no use to anyone."

There was another long silence whilst John followed the same train of thought as I had done.

"When did you find out?"

"About three weeks ago. You may remember I was sick..."

"Yes, I remember that. It did cross my mind that you might be pregnant; but you said nothing more about it."

"That's when I went to see the doctor. I felt such an idiot when he told me I was pregnant. I was absolutely shattered."

"Why didn't you tell me then?"

A note of resentment had crept into John's voice.

"Both of us were just too busy. I didn't intend it to interfere with our work. And it hasn't. I shall go on working as long as I can. But we may have to buy a small car."

"So you're going to keep it?"

"I don't see any alternative. We could get it adopted; but..." I ventured a smile. "... the child may turn out to be extremely clever. A second mathematician in the family. I think we should give the wretched thing a chance to live."

"But think of the father! A murderer!"

It was my turn to be annoyed.

" I have been thinking about it! Every hour! Every day! For the last three weeks! He's Jem's father as well. And, despite all the violence, she's a lovable person."

I knew that John loved Jemima - so that was a good card to play. A Queen of Hearts to trump the King of Clubs.

John nodded.

"But..." I continued, "... if the child has no redeeming features - if he turns out to be a little thug, then we shall certainly get him adopted. We could always say that we didn't have time to look after him - which is true. But I don't think we should say anything to anybody until after the baby is born."

John looked at me.

"You've worked all this out?"

"I have considered every aspect... every angle. Anything would be better than going to some back-street abortionist. That could cause endless problems - even death! People usually recover quite quickly after a pregnancy."

I smiled.

John did not smile. He was still grappling with the consequences of that terrible night. He was perhaps afraid that in some unbalanced moment, I might commit suicide. I had considered it briefly. But a normal pregnancy seemed to be the safest course.

John was still looking for a way out. There wasn't one. It was just a question of time until he came round to my way of thinking.

"What about Jemima?" he asked. "What do we say to her?"

"We leave it as long as possible. We treat it as a great surprise. She won't connect it with her father. If she still remembers the incident..."

"Of course she does! She's already had several nightmares. Remember her screaming one night just before Christmas. And she's always asking me to make sure we lock all the doors at night. And to ask who it is before we open the door."

I shrugged my shoulders.

"If we have to say anything, we could just say that after the horrors of that night, we wanted something good to happen. And this is it."

"You'll have to look convincing when you say that. Otherwise, she'll notice."

"I suppose it will be difficult lying to her. After all, we've always told her to be honest with us. Cousin Eddie and all that... But I still don't think she understands what really happened. She knows that her father tried to kill me. She knows he stole my rings and jewellery. But I don't think she'd connect a baby with all that violence."

John looked thoughtful.

"She would be a step-sister."

"She would. And she would probably look after it quite well - despite what Miss Baker said. I don't think she would attack it - not now."

John looked doubtful.

"It could be her third murder!"

"I'll cross that bridge when we come to it."

John sighed.

"We're always having to re-act to the things other people say or do. Why can't we be the people who decide?"

I said brutally: "It's the war."

I felt that the conversation had returned to normal. And John's next question showed the way his mind was moving.

"But you will continue with your job?"

"Of course. I know where I'm needed. I may have to take a month or two off work, but I can't let Gordon down... or Alan.

"I'm sure we'll be able to find someone in the village to look after the child. Even your mother might give us a hand. I think she might enjoy the challenge."

At long last, John smiled.

"Not your mother!"

"Certainly not! And not Mrs Taylor. Perhaps some mother who already has a child of her own. Someone who would like to earn a little extra cash." I paused. "Are we due for a pay rise?"

John shook his head.

"No. I was talking to Alan a couple of weeks ago. He feels that we need at least another hundred people working on the project. Commander Travis disagrees. He doesn't want to give us any more people - or spend any more money. Alan's getting quite angry. He's thinking of writing to the Prime Minister and explaining the whole situation."

"That would certainly put the cat among the pigeons!"

"Not half. But you know as well as I do; we've got all this marvellous stuff coming in. And we can't work it out without a lot more bombes. The more machines we get, the more people we need to run them."

I smiled bravely.

"I won't let this creature stand in my way."

John held me tight in his arms.

I burst into tears.

Forty-Seven

I don't know who told Mr Jones that I was pregnant but, to my horror, he called at the house whilst John was working and Jemima at school.

I opened the door - feeling large and ungainly.

"Mr Jones?" I said.

"Mrs Woodward, I thought I would come and have a few words with you about the new addition to your family."

Stupidly, I let him into the house.

He sat down on the sofa and grinned at me in his usual sheepish manner. He was wearing his Home Guard uniform.

"Is it a boy or a girl?" he asked.

"I've no idea."

"Some mothers get a feeling..."

"Well, I haven't."

He smiled indulgently.

"And when is the little fellow due?"

"Probably at the beginning of August."

He took out his diary.

"And when were you thinking of having the baptism? I could manage September 7th - or the 14th."

I found his suggestion impertinent.

"I wasn't intending to have the baby baptized. I don't see the point."

"Oh, come, Mrs Woodward! Just because you have extreme views, you surely don't want the baby to suffer."

I looked at Mr Jones with a certain malicious curiosity.

"Suffer?" I said. "In what way?"

The vicar radiated confidence.

"Baptism is our passport to heaven. I'm sure you

wouldn't want to deprive the child of the blessed hope of eternal life. You know what the Church teaches. Unbaptized babies go to hell."

"Charming!" I said.

"We try to prevent such disasters happening."

"I'm glad to hear it."

Mr Jones looked at me sadly.

"It doesn't seem to worry you."

"It seems so drastic. The poor little thing being consigned to the flames... Never having committed a sin in its short life. Not exactly what you'd expect from a loving God!"

Mr Jones ignored my sarcasm.

"You mustn't forget the reality of original sin," he warned. "The child's parents... you've got to think what he's inheriting from them."

I smiled wryly.

Quite unconsciously, Mr Jones had scored a bulls-eye. If he had known that one of the parents was a convicted murderer - who had almost completed a second murder shortly after the conception! At least fifty per cent of the genes were hopelessly flawed. Perhaps he had a point?

"I don't think I'd want to rush into it," I said cautiously. "We can make a final decision once the baby is born,"

"Of course," said the vicar, "of course. But you mustn't leave it too long. We don't want any little heathens wandering round the village."

I took offence at that.

"Heathens?" I said. "I think you've already got some very heathen people wandering round the village. Miss Graham - she's positively evil. Constable Bell - making false accusations. Mrs Williams - with a tongue like a viper. Someone who breaks the ninth commandment several hundred times a day! I should think she's ripe for hell..."

Mr Jones looked pained.

I piled on the agony.

"It doesn't seem to work with your children either! They seem a thoroughly obnoxious lot. Paul Merchant... the Taylor children... all those jeering savages who attacked the evacuees when they came to Bidworth. Surely you can't defend their behaviour? I'm sure they've all been properly baptized. Didn't do them much good, did it?"

"You mustn't judge them too harshly."

"I judge them as I find them. I think there's a lot of evil in this village. And a lot of it stems from you!"

"Me?"

"Yes. Your hypocrisy... your insincerity... your cold, selfish heart... You're not much of an example, are you?"

"Mrs Woodward! Please!"

I shrugged my shoulders.

"What have we had from you in the time we've been in Bidworth? You accused me of being a thief. You accused my husband of cowardice. You've shown nothing but hostility to our adopted daughter... As my husband says, you're riddled with prejudice. You take a joy in persecuting other people. I'm sure that if Jesus were here now, you'd be one of the first to have him crucified!"

Mr Jones winced - visibly.

"That's a terrible thing to say!"

"No worse than what you're proposing for my baby. Hell fire! Did you hear what you were saying? You said that if I didn't have the child baptized, it was doomed! What sort of Gospel is that?" I intensified my attack. "Didn't your leader say: 'Suffer the little children to come unto me?' But what d'you do? You repel them. You condemn them..."

Mr Jones had gone white.

"... Just think how you have treated Jemima. She's an orphan. An orphan! All her family have been killed. Her mother, her aunt - she's no one left. Has she received a single word of comfort from you? Not a word! You despise her!"

"Mrs Woodward..."

"Don't try to excuse yourself!" My blood was up. "Your attitude has been painfully clear. We're not going to be another notch on your statistical cane. I think we can spare the baby any superstitious mumbo-jumbo - especially from you. If we decide to have the child baptized, we'll do it ourselves!"

Mr Jones fell straight into my trap.

"You can't do that!"

"Of course we can. It's the one sacrament that can be performed by a lay person."

"But only in an emergency!"

"I think having you as a vicar constitutes a dire emergency! I think that if we chose to do it, it would be perfectly valid."

Mr Jones shook his head.

"You don't know what you're talking about," he said dismissively.

"I looked at him with scorn.

"Have you never read Anselm? *Cur Deus Homo?*"

Mr Jones looked perplexed. The name, Anselm, rang a bell. He seemed to remember him being mentioned at the theological college.

I watched his discomfiture.

"The classic exposition on the Atonement."

The vicar looked amazed.

"You've read that?"

"Only in translation. Not in the original. I am an educated woman, Mr Jones! Even if I am an atheist, it is only after considerable thought and reflection." I looked at him coldly. "I daresay I know more about the matter than you. At least, I don't suffer from blind prejudice."

Mr Jones picked up his hat.

"Mrs Woodward, you are always extremely offensive."

"You threatened my unborn child!" I said. "I find that quite unforgivable."

I stood up.

"I think you should go now - before your wife gets any nasty ideas. Just leave us in peace. I'm sure we'll manage."

I sounded hard and intolerant but once I had shut the door behind him, I burst into tears.

Why? Why?

Because I had my own fears and anxieties about the baby. Would the child be evil like its father? Would it also be a murderer - and destroy someone else's life? Would I come to hate it? Would I decide to get it adopted?

I desperately needed comfort and help from someone. But all Mr Jones could offer was hell-fire. Perhaps, at the end of the day, that was all one could expect. That would be the child's ultimate destiny. All this - and for what? A monster?

6: A Way of Escape

(Jemima's Story: March - July 1941)

Forty-Eight

It was March 1941. Still the nights were dark and the German bombers continued to pass over us on their way to the Midlands. One grew to recognize the sound of their engines - so different to our own. One could never be sure that they would not drop their bombs over rural Buckinghamshire and turn for home. Survival was often a matter of luck rather than geography.

But, Germans or no, Dusty had to be taken for his evening walk - and there was no one else to do it. John and Mary were working long hours at Bletchley and, most evenings, I had to make my own supper and do the household chores. At least they now had the benefit of a secondhand car and a modest ration of petrol coupons; so their journeys on those winter nights were less hazardous and exposed.

Dusty was not all that demanding. He was very much a creature of habit, stopping and sniffing at the same posts and pillars every night and relieving himself on the same patch of grass. He did not hurry. Twenty-five minutes were all he asked for. Then he was back to the house for a large bowl of water, the remains of his tea and into his basket.

I think Dusty also recognized the sounds of the passing aircraft. With our own, he just raised an ear, lifted a paw and then moved on. But with the German bombers, he became restless and tugged on his lead. Of course, he could hear the engines long before I could; so he acted as our own private branch of the Air Observation Corps.

On one particular night, we had no sooner left the house

and gone down what we called 'The Cinder Path' than he stopped.

I thought: "Oh dear, here we go again. I wonder who'll be getting it tonight? Birmingham? Rugby? Derby?"

But perhaps the danger was closer to hand? I tried to drag him along but he kept looking at some dark bushes that lined the path. What was he hearing? A rabbit? A fox? (We had recently seen our first fox. It seemed quite a friendly creature.)

However, I did not venture into the bushes. And when I let him off his lead, he did not move. So we both stood there, rather stupidly, on the path, waiting for something to happen.

Suddenly, I heard a low voice.

"Jayminah!"

There was only one person who called me that.

"Eric?" I said uncertainly.

Wasn't he supposed to be in a prisoner-of-war camp?

"Erich Roch," said the voice.

It must be him.

Dusty and I moved closer to the bushes.

"Is it safe?"

I looked up and down the path. One very rarely met anyone there at night.

"Yes."

There was a sound of swishing branches and a figure emerged from the darkness.

Dusty growled.

I put him back on his lead.

Yes, it was Erich. I gave him a big hug. He smelt earthy - and rather sweaty. He also had a rough beard.

"What are you doing in Bidworth?" I whispered.

"I have escaped," he said proudly. "I am trying to get back to Germany. I *have* to get back to Germany."

"Why?" I asked.

"Because they are sending us to Canada. Across the sea. I am frightened of the sea. Perhaps I will be drowned? Sunk by one of our own U-boats..."

I could understand his fears.

"Your English is better," I said.

"I have been studying - very hard."

I felt that his situation was hopeless.

"But won't they be looking for you? Won't they arrest you?"

He laughed.

"They will not look for me here. I have a bicycle. I have come a long way. Zwei hundert kilometres. But I need your help..."

"My help?"

"I need some food. And my bicycle is... brechen... broken... It has the flat."

"A flat tyre?"

"Yes."

I didn't know what to do. Even though I believed Erich was a good man, he was still 'the enemy'. He was a prisoner of war - and he had escaped. It was my duty to report him to the police and get him re-captured as quickly as possible. And yet I couldn't leave him out in the cold night - hungry and helpless.

We did not have a lot of food in the house - we never did - but we had plenty of bread and potatoes. No one would notice if we were a couple of potatoes short or if he had some bread and jam. We could certainly rise to a cup of tea but not to coffee or sugar.

Mary and John would not be back till about 11.00pm so perhaps I could feed him and send him on his way. I also knew we had a puncture outfit in the garden shed. He could use that to get his bike mended.

I said: "Bring your bicycle. Follow me." Dusty and I walked back up the path. I waited till Erich caught up. I looked left and right. The road was deserted. We quickly went through our gate and round to the back of the house.

"You are alone?" he whispered.

"Till 10.00pm," I lied. "Three hours till John and Mary come home."

"That is good."

"Would you like a wash?" I asked.

"Very much. I am very dirty. I smell horrible."

He made a face.

I smiled.

Whilst he washed himself in the kitchen sink, I went for the puncture outfit. It seemed to have quite a selection of patches and plenty of rubber solution. John wouldn't be needing it so much now that he had a car. I picked up a couple of tyre levers and my bicycle pump. I was well-acquainted with punctures.

By the time I returned to the house, he had given himself a good wash. He was standing in bare feet, with a bare chest. He was looking much happier.

"You are very kind," he said.

I looked at him.

"You are still my prisoner."

He laughed.

"So I am! I remember so well my first visit to this house. You were both very kind. But the police..."

"Were they nasty to you?"

"They did their job.... but they did not like Germans."

I was about to say: "None of us like Germans!" But I thought better of it. Instead, I opened the bread bin and put a loaf on the bread board and gave him a knife. I got down a jar of damson jam which none of us liked. He devoured the bread and jam as if he had never seen food for a week.

I put on the kettle and peeled some potatoes. When the kettle boiled, I made him a mug of tea and poured the rest of the hot water into a pan and put in six potatoes.

Whilst the potatoes were cooking, he got down to mending his tyre. It was not too bad. Two small holes. He blew up the inner tube and placed it in a bowl of cold water. We watched the bubbles pouring out. Within five minutes, he had mended the tyre.

We sat looking at each other across the kitchen table.

"Where are you going?" I asked.

"I am going to an airfield. You have many round here. I want to find a machine and fly back to Germany. I must go home."

I didn't know where the airfields were; but he did. He patted his top pocket. "I have a map."

"Are you hoping to get there tonight?"

"No. I am too tired. I must rest. And then I must prepare my escape - very carefully. I shall need the drahtzuschneiderin...."

I looked at him blankly. That was a long word.

He imitated a pair of scissors.

"To cut ze wire. There will be a fence. Perhaps more than one. I shall have to avoid the guards - and the dogs. I shall need the pfeffer." He pretended to sneeze. "The pepper?" I understood what he meant.

I looked at Dusty.

I could see that he was not happy with our visitor. His evening walk had been aborted. He had not been able to sniff his way round his favourite places. He sat with his back to us facing the back door. Occasionally, he gave us a reproachful look over his shoulder.

I turned to Erich.

"Can you fly an aeroplane?"

"I have a pilot... lizenz... But I have not flown for two

years."

"You may kill yourself," I said. "Or our fighters may shoot you down."

Erich shook his head.

"At night, your pilots are blind."

"But d'you know which way Germany is?"

"I shall fly to France. It is nearer. Only about one hundred miles. I know the stars. I shall follow them."

I couldn't help admiring his courage. Perhaps if I was a German, I would do the same.

But, of course, I wasn't a German. It was my duty to hand him over to the authorities. But here I was - feeding him. 'Assisting the enemy to escape.' I was sure Mary and John would not approve. I would have to get him out of the house as soon as possible.

He seemed to follow my thoughts.

"Is there anywhere I can hide?"

"Not here," I said emphatically.

"Of course not here. But is there a place in the village? An old barn? An empty house?"

I was going to say: "No" but then a delicious thought came into my mind. How perfect!

I smiled.

"As a matter of fact, there is."

Once again, Mrs Williams provided a solution to our problems. She had gone away to stay with her sister. Her house would be empty. Only the day before, I had been checking the ground behind her greenhouse and I noticed that the place was shut up. I made a few inquiries. It seemed that she would be away for a few days. A week at the most.

What better place for Erich to hide? She would have food in her house - and a bed. Here he could recover before he made his bid to escape.

Erich ate his potatoes - and had more bread and tea

whilst I explained my plan. We would take his bike and hide it behind the greenhouse. (The significance of the location would be lost on him.)

I also knew a way to open her dining room window. You stood on a windowsill and poked a wire through the small top window. Once opened, you put your arm through that window, holding a looped piece of wire which lifted the window catch. I had already been into Mrs Williams' house once or twice - but had been careful not to leave any sign of my presence. I had made a point of not moving anything and had carefully wiped away the tell-tale footsteps on the windowsill.

"You can stay there," I said. "She has plenty of food. And she's away for at least a week."

He looked at me with tears in his eyes. I expect it was the first act of kindness he had received in many months.

As soon as he had eaten, I washed up his mug and plate. There must be no sign of our visitor. I put the puncture outfit back in the shed with the tyre levers. I put Dusty on his lead and we set off on our short journey to Mrs Williams house.

Dusty seemed happy again. He had not been deprived of his evening walk. Once we reached the cinder path, I let him off his lead. He would soon warn us if other people were around.

Erich pushed his bike.

I was ready to run if we met Constable Bell. But, as usual, after dark, Bidworth was deserted.

We went through the, by now familiar, garden gate and up to the greenhouse. The bike was hidden behind the bushes. I climbed on to the windowsill and poked the wire through the small window. It flipped loose almost immediately.

I then lowered the wire with its loop, caught the catch

and tugged it upwards. The larger window was opened. I then stepped through the window, shut the catch - but not the small window - and went to the back door and opened it for Erich.

"This is wunderbar!" he said. "Du bis ein Zauberer! You wave your..."

"... magic wand," I said. "Come inside, quickly. And don't put any lights on."

On the way to Mrs Williams' house, I had been wondering what advice I should give him.

"You must not contact me at my house. Not at all! Not even in an emergency. You understand? And you must not leave any dirty plates - or cups - or sheets. Everything must stay as it is. No one must know you are here."

I thought carefully.

"It is possible that she has a daily - a cleaner - someone who will come to the house each day - early. She must not see you." I thought a bit more. "Perhaps it would be better if you do not sleep in a bed - but in the attic." I pointed upwards.

"Der Dachstube."

I misunderstood him.

"No, she has no dog."

(Perhaps, later in life, I might have distinguished the difference between a dachshund and a dachstube...)

"You must take a clock with you. The cleaner may come at 9.00am. You must not leave anything in the bathroom. And you must be very quiet. Do not move till she goes. You understand?"

I think he did.

I opened the larder door.

"You will not starve!"

I had already explored Mrs Williams' cupboards so I knew she was well-equipped with black market goods. Ham, fish, jams, flour, tea, wine, bottled fruit, tins of pineapple, vegetables, dried milk and coffee.

"Do not use the tins at the front," I said knowledgeably. "Use the ones at the back."

I opened a kitchen drawer.

"A tin opener," I said. "But clean it and put it back in the drawer. And hide the empty tins upstairs. I will take them away when you go."

I led the way upstairs. There were three good-sized bedrooms. She had plenty of space but she had never taken in any evacuee. I was determined she should pay for it. (To be honest, I had already pinched two tins of peaches and a can of red salmon. I had described them to myself as 'the spoils of war'.)

We found our way up to the attic and then explored the cupboards to find extra blankets and pillows. I had to use the lights once or twice but only for a few seconds. One had to be so careful during the blackout. The sight of a lighted window would bring round Constable Bell in a matter of minutes.

When I had warned Erich of all the dangers, I told him that I would come round and see him on my evening walks. That would be between six and seven. I would whistle to let him know I was there. If his bicycle had gone, I would assume that he was on his way. I would then tidy up.

But I told him to conserve his strength. To get plenty of rest - before he came to the most difficult part of his journey. He gave me a big hug and several kisses which gave me great pleasure. But, I said:

"You must get rid of your beard. You look like a tramp. If people see you looking like that, they'll report you." I hoped he understood what I was saying. "If you cut it off," I added, "you could dress up in Mrs Williams' clothes. No one would stop a woman riding a bicycle. But if you look like a tramp, they'll stop you immediately."

I felt he had probably had enough advice for one night.

"You are a wise girl," he said. "I wish you were coming with me. You would be the good company."

I looked at him quizzically.

"Why should I want to go to Germany?" I asked. "They do nothing but kill people there."

The air-raid siren had already sounded. It was time to go home.

I went out through the back door and gave Dusty a low whistle. He was at my side in seconds. We went back through the garden gate. Just a few yards short of our front door, Constable Bell pounced.

"What are you doing on the roads at this hour of night, you little varmint! You heard the siren going, ten minutes ago."

I put on my most sullen face.

"Dusty 'as to 'ave 'is walk, bombs or no bombs!"

"Get inside immediately! And take your wretched dawg with yer!"

I was back in the house by 9.00pm - and breathed a sigh of relief. No one had seen Erich. And no one would know what I had been doing - aiding and abetting the enemy. It was better that way.

I gave Dusty his water, checked that our visitor had left no signs of his presence - and went to bed with a copy of *Swallows and Amazons*.

I had enjoyed the first ten chapters of Arthur Ransome's classic; but I soon put it down. Real life was far more exciting. I wracked my brains. "Where could I find a pair of wirecutters?"

Forty-Nine

The wire-cutters presented no problem.

I had already taken note of the janitor's cubby hole. In his absence, I had inspected his collection of tools in case I needed some offensive weapon to protect me on my way home. I had already "borrowed" a couple of screwdrivers - but returned them when the attacks died down.

During the course of the dinner-break, I slipped into his room and rifled through his box of tricks. Erich had described something with long handles and sharp claws. When you know what you are looking for, it is easy to find it. I found an old pair which seemed sharp enough. I slipped them up the sleeve of my jumper - with the claws neatly tucked under my armpit. If I kept my arm tight, no one would notice.

I emerged from the Janitor's room and made my way to the playground just as the whistle was about to go. I ran over to the far wall and then, as everyone streamed indoors, I pulled the cutters out of my sleeve and threw them over the wall. They would be hidden in the long grass.

After school was over, I went home and collected Dusty and a large carrier bag. Once we got to the long grass beside the wall, I let him off his lead. As he bounded around, I hunted through the grass, found the cutters and popped them into my carrier bag. After that, we went home.

I waited till it was dark and then went down the back lane to Mrs Williams' house. I let Dusty run on ahead. I tapped on the downstairs window six times - it sounded terribly loud. A shadow moved into the room and waved. I made my way to the back door and Erich pulled back the

367

bolts and Dusty and I marched in. The door was once again bolted. I handed over the wire-cutters.

"Are these the right things?"

"Durchaus!"

He ran his hands over the claws.

"Sehr scharf!"

I was glad I had got the right things.

"Have you had a good day?" I asked.

Erich smiled.

"Sehr gut. I have eaten well. For fruhstuck, I had fruit and schinken. Later, I have lechs with tinned erbsen. Heute abend, I shall have the tinned beef with perhaps some pfirsichen and the rahm." (Ham, salmon, peas; peaches and cream.)

It sounded as if he was having better food than I was.

I dug deeper into my carrier bag and produced a razor, some shaving cream and a shaving brush - all belonging to John.

Erich's eyes grew wider.

"You think of everything!"

I smiled.

"I don't like you with a beard. Go and scrape it off immediately."

Erich was a very obedient soul. He vanished upstairs and, within about fifteen minutes, the offending hair had been removed. I made sure that I recovered John's shaving kit. The razor blade had probably been seriously blunted but I had taken the precaution of using one of Mr Taylor's blades. It was nice to think they were at last of some practical use.

I gave Erich a big hug and kiss. He felt so smooth and smelt so nice.

I dug again into my bag and produced a map of rural Buckinghamshire. I think John and Mary must have bought it when they first moved to Bidworth. It had hardly been used. There was no name on the cover. I handed it over to Erich.

"I don't know where the airfields are, but this might help. I wouldn't take it with you, but if you copy out the details, it would certainly help. " I looked at him. "What are your plans?"

"Ah, my planen."

There was a distant look in Erich's eyes.

"First, I have to find the right airfield. A busy airfield with lots of planes. I have some names. I will look them up on your map. I must then go and see which is best."

To my way of thinking, one airfield was very much like another. I said so.

"Nein!" said Erich, "There must be planes that fly by night. Training planes with many different pilots. They will not notice another pilot getting into a plane. I shall creep into the cockpit and open up the throttles."

Many of Erich's words were in German - which made his plan completely incomprehensible to me. But I gathered that he did have a plan. In the morning, he would set off early and identify as many airfields as possible. He would find which ones were most accessible. He would examine the approaches and find a fence which was not too far away from the hangars. He would need to find a place in the perimeter fence where he could use the wirecutters. He might need to see the airfields again after dark to see which ones were being used at night.

Once he had found the right place, he would cut through the fence, approach the concrete apron and chance his luck. He would leave his bicycle hidden near the airfield so that, if neccessary, he could come back through the fence and cycle home.

Erich had arrived in the village on Monday night. He

had needed the past twenty four hours to recover. But he hoped to be away by Friday at the latest. Tomorrow - Wednesday - he would pay his first visit to the airfields. He would be back in Bidworth by 6.00pm and I would again let him into the house.

I would take Dusty for a walk after tea. John and Mary would be at home on Wednesday; but on Thursday and Friday, they would both be on long twelve hour shifts. That suited me perfectly since I intended to go with Erich - at least as far as the fence.

I plucked one final item from my carrier bag. John's pair of binoculars. They were very precious. I didn't dare lose them. Erich would have to be very careful using them.

His eyes lit up as he saw them.

"Fernglas!"

I gave him a stern warning to hide the binoculars whilst he was cycling along the road. He must hide himself behind bushes or trees whilst using them. He must remember that the flash of glass could give his position away. I impressed upon him that the binoculars represented a tremendous act of trust on my part - and he should not lose them; nor - if he was arrested - say who they belonged to. I think I made my message quite clear.

I warned him: "If you are captured with a map and binoculars near an airfield, you will be treated as a spy." I had noticed in the paper that several spies had already been hung.

Erich promised faithfully to guard them with his life. But all these things greatly enhanced his chances of success. He was over the moon. He gave me several hugs and kisses. He told me I was a 'wunderkind'. But I already knew that!

More humbly, I collected all his empty tins and bottles plus the corks. I looked at him suspiciously. Was he a secret drinker? One needs to know these things...

He said he had been celebrating his luck in finding such a well-equipped home.

"There are bottles everywhere!" he said. "This is a treasure house."

I felt pleased that Mrs Williams would be unwittingly involved as a collaborator in Erich's escape. She would not want to admit that she was hoarding food and drink. She could be blackmailed into silence. If word got out that she was a black-marketeer, she would go to prison. It was a pleasing thought.

I examined all the rooms - including the bathroom and kitchen - to make sure there was no sign of Erich's presence. I had discovered that Mrs Williams had a cleaning woman coming in on Mondays and Thursdays. We should have to be extra careful on Wednesday night.

I picked up all the waste and headed to the door. "How are you going to spend the evening?" I asked.

"I have found an old newspaper. I must see what is happening in my country."

I sighed.

"You have just invaded Bulgaria. Next week, John says, it will be Greece. They are beating the hell out of the I-tyes. We are sending 'urricanes to protect the Greeks..."

Erich looked amazed at my knowledge of current affairs.

"You read the newspapers?"

"No. John tells us what is 'appening. We have a map on the kitchen wall. We watch what 'appens. We colour in the maps. John says it is only a matter of time before 'itler goes for the Ruskies. So long as 'e keeps away from us."

Once Jemima had gone, Erich looked through the newspaper. But he had an even better idea. He went into the sitting room and pulled the black-out curtains. Then he turned on Mrs Williams' radio. The valves slowly warmed up. He turned the tuner to the Hamburg station. Reception was poor but, once again, he heard people speaking in his own language and talking about what was happening in Germany.

He hoped that, in a few days time, he would be back amongst his own people. Visiting his family. Perhaps getting a medal from the Reichsmarshall. There were many things he would like to tell him. Particularly about the way the British interrogated their German prisoners. They were devilishly clever. He believed that every aircrew should be specially briefed before they flew over England. The Germans were too trusting. A little kindness - and a good cup of coffee - a friendly chat - and you fell into their trap. He had been one of those who blabbed. He still cursed himself for being so stupid. Of course, when he got home, he would not say anything about that. He would be hailed as a hero - the one that got away.

Fifty

Wednesday morning brought a bright, clear day with just a touch of frost. Erich set off early in the morning to identify all the airfields within fifteen miles of Bidworth. There were three to be seen. As he passed by them, he did not stop; but cycled on for another quarter of a mile before finding a suitable place to hide his bike. Then he would work his way back through the trees and rough ground till he could see what was happening.

Two of the airfields seemed quite busy. At Deepdene, there was a constant succession of Magisters and Tiger Moths taking off and landing. They flew so close to the ground, that he could identify them quite easily.

Using John's binoculars, he surveyed the airfield. There would be no difficulty getting close to the planes; but he doubted whether such small machines would be capable of getting him back to France. The one thing which really worried him was running out of fuel and having to ditch in the Channel. At night, there would be no hope of rescue.

Stourton was little more than a field. There were about a dozen gliders, but no sign of any aircraft to tow them. He moved on to East Marston, which looked more promising. There were Airspeed Oxfords and Avro Ansons - both twin-engined machines which were used for training navigators, wireless operators and for coastal reconnaissance.

The Ansons had a range of about 600 miles and a cruising speed of 150mph. They would take about two hours to reach France. Erich reckoned that he would need a clear night with plenty of stars. He would steer to the west of London to avoid the anti-aircraft guns and would then veer to the east so that he could cross the Channel somewhere to the north of Boulogne. He hoped his own colleagues would not shoot him down.

Erich felt he had a good chance of making an escape, but this airfield was surrounded by a strong wire fence. It was about eight feet high with rolls of barbed wire strung between concrete posts topping the wire. It would be impossible to climb over. The wirecutters would be extremely useful.

Remembering Jemima's advice, he carried the binoculars and the map in a dark green bag which could be dropped amongst the ferns if he saw anyone approaching. He was also attentive to the sounds of dogs barking. But, as Jemima had already discovered, the countryside seemed to be deserted.

He spent a lot of the day working his way through the woods which surrounded East Marston. It was a cold job and he wished he had brought with him a flask of coffee. However, he had some sandwiches and they filled him up. But, eventuallly, the cold got to him and he made his way back to his bicycle. Before he ventured on to the road, he stood listening and waiting - but very few cars passed along that road. There were a number of lorries and vans - and a few RAF vehicles heading into East Marston. He was very conscious that he would look conspicuous as a solitary cyclist.

However, by early afternoon a light drizzle was falling. He took refuge in a church porch three miles from the airfield. By four o'clock, it was getting dark and he made his way back to Bidworth by a roundabout route. He had no lights; so when he heard a vehicle approaching, he quickly got off the bicycle and walked. By 5.30pm he reached Mrs Williams' back gate. He was feeling wet and tired. He hid his bike and took shelter in the greenhouse. Within fifteen minutes, I was there to let him into the house.

* * *

Erich was very pleased with his achievements. He now knew which airfield he would be using. He knew the road. He had found a good place where he could hide his bicycle. And he made careful note of the section of wire where he could snip away without being seen or heard.

He returned the map and the binoculars. The map was quite damp but John's binoculars were undamaged. I was glad to get them back.

Because Mary and John were both at home, this visit was of necessity a short one. I reminded Erich that the cleaner would be arriving early the following morning. I checked through the kitchen cupboards, waste bin, the larder, the drawers, the pots and pans. I looked through each room - upstairs and downstairs - to make sure there was no evidence of Erich's presence. He had been remarkably careful to cover his tracks.

"Where are you sleeping?" I asked.

"In the attic. Last night, I slept in one of the beds. But I shall be careful not to make a sound."

"You must do all the washing up. Hide the tins in the attic. If you're going to have a bath, wash the bath."

Erich promised faithfully to do everything I had ordered. What a wonderful man he was!

I departed rapidly with Dusty.

* * *

We had decided that Thursday was to be the great day. I remember the sun was shining and the temperature was much warmer.

I spent most of the morning thinking about Erich. He would be leaving that night; and I would be going with him - at least as far as the security fence. I ran his plan through my mind again and again. My silence was noticed. The teacher asked if I was well.

"Perfectly well," I said - in my poshest accent.

But even nature study failed to capture my imagination. So many things could still go wrong. We might be seen setting out together. We might be stopped on the road. In the darkness, we might crash into something. (At that time, we were only allowed the smallest slit of light on our bikes. As if the Germans would ever see us!) We might have a puncture on the way - that was far more likely. Would I have to let him take my bike? That would raise questions. Could I pretend it had been stolen? No, if he had a puncture, he would have to walk.

Even when we reached the airfield, there might be guards hiding in the woods. We might both be captured. It was possible that I might be stopped on the way home, taken into custody and questioned. I must say nothing. Nothing until Erich had had a fair chance to get away. And even then, I couldn't tell anyone the truth. Certainly not Mary or John. The best thing I could do was to invent a cover story.

I could say I had seen a man acting suspiciously in Bidworth. I had seen him get on a bike and drive west in the direction of East Marston. I could say that I had followed him. I could describe his bicycle fairly accurately. But I had tried to capture him. That would tie in with John's challenge to catch another German and earn five pounds.

If Erich was captured then my suspicions would have a foundation in fact. I would be praised for my powers of observation. For my bravery. But Erich would have to keep his mouth shut. I was a little bit worried about that.. . He had broken down the last time he was captured.

He must escape! I was sure about that. He would not be happy being a caged animal. And if he was re-captured, he would be put back in that cage. He might be shot on sight running around the airfield. Even before his escape, there had been talk about sending him to Canada. On the high seas, he might be torpedoed by one of his own U-boats.

Of course, he might be shot down in the stolen plane. But, as he had said, it was difficult to see an aeroplane at night unless you were caught in the searchlights. He planned to fly low. He must be careful not to switch on any lights.

I sighed loudly.

The teacher looked in my direction.

"Yes, Jemima?"

"I'm sorry. I was just thinkin'."

"Thinking about what?"

Damn the man!

I scowled.

"I were thinkin' 'bout the moon."

Everyone laughed.

"Well, you may be thinking about the moon, but we're thinking about the snow leopard."

I smiled knowingly.

"There are no snow leopards in Bidworth."

"We are thinking about snow leopards in Russia!"

Ah!

I asked: "Will there be a full moon tonight?"

The teacher was clearly annoyed by my irrelevant question but he answered it.

"No, there will not. There will be a half moon rising about five o'clock. Does that satisfy your curiosity?"

I nodded.

We should need a little light. A half moon would be

sufficient for both of us.

The teacher gave me a cautionary glare.

"Now, back to the snow leopards..."

Fifty-One

The house was empty when I returned home.

I had been worrying that one or other of them might have taken ill - or come home early. But everything seemed to be in order. My evening meal was in the oven - just waiting to be heated up. Dusty had been fed and watered. He needed his evening walk. I would deal with that right away. Then I would have my tea. At 6.00pm, I would go round to Mrs Williams' house and collect Erich.

I noticed that I was very nervous and jumpy. This was the final and most difficult part - helping a prisoner to escape. If we were caught, the consequences would be terrible - more for me than for him. I would be classed as a traitor. They couldn't hang me but I knew it was a stigma I would bear for the rest of my life. If anything could cause a rift between me, John and Mary, this was it.

Nothing must go wrong.

I dealt with Dusty. I ate my sausage stew with mashed potato. I drank a glass of milk. I gave Dusty one or two pieces of stew and filled up his bowl of water. I checked my bicycle tyres, my brakes and my lights. Everything was in working order - except me.

Dusty knew what I was feeling. He looked at me with sorrowing eyes. His ears drooped - even more than usual. He made small whining noises. I spoke to him firmly. I told him what I was going to do to help Erich get back to his family. Once that was done, I would be back home and he would have a small portion of biscuits with a dollop of gravy from the stew. He had to be brave - and not say a word to anyone. I think he understood.

At half past five, I went round to Mrs Williams' house. I parked my bike inside the back gate and went up to her back door. Erich was watching out for me. He waved from the darkened dining room window, and then opened the door.

"You are early!"

"I couldna wait any longer."

He gave me a big hug. We clung together for several minutes, then he let me go.

"Are you ready?" I asked.

He nodded.

"Have you eaten?"

"Very well."

I told him I wanted to check the house one last time. Once he had gone, I didn't want to come back to this place. It would be tempting fate.

Together, we worked our way from the attic down to the scullery, making sure everything was as it should be; every key in place; the contents of the larder neatly arranged; all the rubbish collected. It would be disposed of *en route*.

Satisfied that we had left nothing to chance, I breathed a sigh of relief.

"We go," I said.

"We go," said Erich.

He took all the rubbish out through the back door. I went into the dining room to make sure all the window catches were locked in place. Then I followed him out through the back door. It had a Yale lock. I closed it one last time.

Erich collected his bicycle from behind the greenhouse.

"Is it all right?"

"I checked it one hour ago."

We got our bikes out into the back lane. I pulled the gate to. We set off fifty yards apart, with me leading the way.

There was no one around. Unseen, we reached the open road.

Erich said goodbye.

"Danke, Bidworth,"

I set off - still fifty yards ahead. I pulled up at the canal bridge. One by one, we sank the tins in the water. Packets became waterlogged and sank into the depths. Cloths and towels we stuffed in an old litter bin.

Then back on to the road west. The moon was not giving us a great deal of light; but by now we had acquired night vision. The hedges and walls were dark patches to our left and right. The road was a lighter grey. We set off in convoy. Fifteen miles to go.

I think we chose our time well. People were having their tea and the black-out discouraged people from going out in the dark. One man on a motor cycle passed us and one lorry sped by the other way.

By 7.15pm, we were close to East Marston. It too seemed quite dead. Perhaps they were having their tea as well.

We left our bikes about a quarter of a mile away from the fence. We laid them flat in the grass behind a hedge that bordered on to a field. I took the wirecutters and Erich led the way. We used the public road for two hundred yards and then cut through the wood on a path that would lead us to the fence which surrounded the airfield. Beyond us were the back walls of the hangars. No window overlooked this part of the fence.

I handed over the wirecutters - and then mounted guard. Erich made the first clip. Fortunately, there was a light wind which caused the branches of the trees to rise and fall, making various creaking noises.

I nodded and Erich cut through a few more pieces working upwards through the fence. He then bent both sides back and clipped more until he could be sure of wriggling through.

I kept looking at him. And then back to the dark buildings. We were being very lucky. At any moment, I expected someone to appear.

But soon the job was done.

Erich handed back the wirecutters. I laid them beside the nearest tree. When I turned back, I realized that he was crying. He picked me up in his arms - kissed me - and hugged me again.

"Jayminah," he whispered. "I love you."

"And I love you, Erich."

"You have done so much.... I could not escape without you...,. You have been so brave."

We must have clung to each other for nearly five minutes. But we both knew he would have to go.

"I will write when I can," he said.

"I will pray for you," I said.

Though I was not exactly blessed with holiness, I meant it. Quite a few of the things I had prayed for had already come to pass.

Erich got down on his knees to crawl through the fence. I gave him a few more passionate kisses. Then I stood back.

"Off you go."

He slipped easily through the fence and ran rapidly across the grass towards the hangars. I waited anxiously for the sound of a shot or the barking of dogs but there was not a sound. I could no longer see him. At least he was on the airfield. I could do no more.

I walked slowly back through the wood and had reached the road when I realized that I had left the wirecutters beside the tree. Overwhelmed by passion, I had made my first mistake. I walked slowly back to the fence. I tried to bend back the wire flaps; then I picked up the wirecutters and returned to the road.

All the time I was listening. Watching. There was no one in sight. But, behind me, I heard the rough clatter of an aircraft engine. The noise was very clear. But there were no shots. The roar of the engine increased. My hopes soared. I ran back up the road to where we had hidden the bicycles. I could hear the engines revving up. I willed it to move - as quickly as it could. But at least no one was stopping him.

I had been listening to the engine for about five minutes when I realized that there was another aircraft approaching. Was it a German plane? I could see it flying in from the west. Erich must be waiting for it to land. I could see its landing lights as it got closer. One of ours.

Because of the trees, I couldn't see it land. But I imagined it - blocking the runway and then moving on to the taxiway and coming back to its hangar. That would distract the attention of the ground staff. Whilst the new arrival was shutting down its engines, Erich would take off. And, sure enough, there was a distant roar which got louder and louder. A dark object rose above the trees to my right, slowly gaining height. A small two-engined plane with its RAF roundel just visible.

The plane was about two hundred yards away and a hundred feet above the ground. I couldn't expect a wave. Erich would be concentrating on all those knobs and switches. He knew how to fly; but this was an enemy aircraft. All the controls would be different.

But I waved. And I cried. I was so proud that he had got away. I watched the small plane vanish into the darkness.

I cried because I knew I would never see Erich again. He was returning home - to his family; to his girlfriends; to his dog. (He had told me that he had a dog called Ludwig. He hoped that one of the other pilots in his geschwader would have been looking after him. When Erich had last seen him,

Ludwig was just a puppy. Would he still remember him?)

But his dangers were by no means over. Erich still had to get past London and over the Channel. Then he would look for 'Boo-loin'. From there, he knew the route to his home airfield. He would fly in low - and surprise them. Before they had time to shoot him down, he would have landed. He was sure he would receive a great welcome. And possibly even a medal!

I picked up my bike.

There was nothing more to do but go home. I put the wirecutters in my basket. I decided to cover up Erich's bicycle with branches and leaves. No one would find it. It only took a few minutes. Then I returned to the road - still deserted - and made my way back to Bidworth.

I had travelled a long way. Thirty miles there and back. My legs were very sore and so was my bottom.

The half moon was now casting a helpful light on the road. I pedalled slowly. There was no need to rush. I found myself saying: "There are no snow leopards in Bidworth." And no German prisoners either! He had escaped and the whole thing had been managed perfectly from beginning to end.

Of course, when I got close to Bidworth, I began to worry about P.C. Bell. I was doing nothing illegal. There had been no air raid warning. You could hear the siren for miles. My bike was properly lit. People might wonder where I had been - but no one would know. The only thing I would have to do was hide the wirecutters.

Just over the canal bridge, there was a large bush - holly, I think. Prickly anyway. I decided to hide them there. Very painfully, I got off the bike and pushed them deep under the bush. Then back on the bike for the final quarter of a mile. The most painful part of the journey.

I put the bike back in the shed and slipped through the

kitchen door. Dusty gave me a fabulous welcome. I gave him a generous helping of dog biscuits, drenched in gravy, with two more pieces of cold sausage. He loved it.

I went upstairs and changed into my pyjamas. It was better that John and Mary should find me peacefully tucked up and asleep when they returned. It was now almost half past nine. They should be back within the next hour.

But, before I went to bed, I had a promise to keep. I knelt down beside my bed and prayed for Erich. I prayed that God would protect him on his dangerous journey; that no one would shoot him down; that he would reach his home airfield and be given a warm welcome by his friends.

What more was there to say? I said my prayer twice to make sure the message had been understood.

But then I cried. I cried for myself because I had lost someone precious. Someone who had loved me, kissed me, hugged me. It was only then that I realized how much I cared for him. But he was a grown-up; I was only a child. He had his own life to lead.

But I had saved him! He would never forget that. I had helped him to escape. To do so, I had broken the laws of England - and betrayed my country. I knew I had done the right thing. But no one must know.

There were no snow leopards in Bidworth!

Fifty-Two

Mrs Williams returned home on the Monday night. The train had been terribly late - and terribly slow. Part of the main line had been damaged in the previous night's bombing and all the trains had been diverted. So they had lengthy delays in many strange stations.

She wished she had never left home; but her elder sister had been in hospital. When she herself had been in hospital, her sister had come to look after her for a fortnight when she returned home. She could do nothing less for her. She had hoped to get home early in the afternoon but she missed the connection to Bidworth, so it was shortly after 6.00pm before she stepped down on the platform. Fortunately, Constable Bell had arranged a taxi to collect her. So she was home by 6.30pm.

She opened the front door - thankful to be home. She put on the hall light and quickly drew the blackout curtains. Then she put all the lights on.

She was desperately hungry. She felt that she deserved something special. This was the moment to raid her emergency stores. Her sister had been living on her 1/2d meat ration - which didn't go all that far - certainly not for two people. They had eked out their meals with bread and potatoes.

Mrs Williams decided that a tin of Canadian red salmon would be nice - plus a glass of red wine. Perhaps two. She opened her larder door and reached towards the back of the cupboard.

She paused.

She could have sworn that she had six tins of salmon.

Now there were only four. Had there been five tins, she might have admitted that she was wrong; but she knew that she had more than four. It was good pre-war stuff bought two months before war was declared. She had more hidden in a locked dining room cupboard.

No. Two tins had definitely gone.

She looked at the shelves more closely. The three front rows were unchanged, but the number of tins of ham, corned beef and fruit seemed to have diminished.

No one had been in the house except Irene. Surely she wouldn't have stolen them?

Mrs Williams took the salmon into the kitchen and reached into the drawer for the tin opener. Because she was not in the habit of using tinned food except as an emergency, the tin opener was normally buried under a heap of knives, graters, serving spoons. Tonight, the tin opener was on top.

Once again, she wondered if anyone had been in her house. Remembering the childhood story of Goldilocks and the three bears, she wondered if they might still be there.

She picked up a carving knife and went into each of the downstairs rooms. Everything seemed normal. She went upstairs - slightly fearful - and examined each bedroom. Everything was in its place but perhaps the patchwork quilt in the spare bedroom was the wrong way round. There had always been a little tear in the top left-hand corner. Now it was in the bottom right.

She went into the bathroom. No, everything was in its place.

She checked all the windows and pulled the blackout curtains.

It was odd.

She must ask Irene.

She went downstairs and cooked some potatoes and

made a white sauce to go over the salmon. But the absence of certain items in her store cupboard niggled. There were several tins of vegetables missing. She was sure she had had more than one tin of French beans.

Whilst the potatoes were cooking, she checked all her supplies. The tea was untouched but the tin of coffee was half empty - not that she drank much coffee. It was just for visitors.

The sugar... Yes, the sugar had definitely been raided. Half a box of sugar lumps had gone.

It was when she went to get a glass of wine that she became really shocked. The dozen bottles that she had bought under the counter at the grocer's had been reduced to eight! She examined the dustbin but there were no empty bottles.

She wondered whether there had been children in the house - but they would have made more mess. They would not have been so careful about taking tins from the back row.

She examined the bolts on the back door. There was a large key in the lock. All was as it should be. She had another look at the front door but there was no sign of damage. She bolted the front door in case the sneak thief should return.

It was a mystery.

Had she not decided upon the salmon, she would not have noticed anything for several weeks. She did not use the sugar - or the wine - except on special occasions.

She wanted to phone Constable Bell and tell him of her suspicions; but she did not want him rooting round her house. He might discover that she had been dealing in black market goods. She could get herself into trouble. Perhaps it would be better to say nothing. Certainly until she had talked to Irene in the morning.

*   *   *

Irene had been Mrs Williams' charwoman for the past three years. The fact that she had lasted so long suggested that she was not just thick-skinned, but must have the hide of an elephant. Could it be that she actually enjoyed all the slander and gossip which poured from Mrs Williams' putrid lips?

No! Not at all. The only thing that kept Irene working for this wretched woman was money. Her husband was in the Merchant Navy and she had an elderly mother and three small children to maintain. Every penny mattered; and she was prepared to put up with any amount of vitriol for four hours a week for the sake of the ten shilling note which came her way.

However, this Tuesday morning, she wasn't expecting any complaint. She had washed and polished the house to perfection whilst Mrs Williams had been away. She knew the place was immaculate.

So she took off her headscarf and hung up her coat.

"Mornin', Ma'am," she said. "Did you have a good holiday?"

Mrs Williams was standing in the kitchen, wiping her hands on a tea towel.

"The trains were very tiresome. There were delays all the way back."

"And how's your sister?"

"Much better. I think she'll pull through. She's got some excellent neighbours. I spoke to them before I came away."

"That'll set your mind at rest."

Irene put on her overall.

She was conscious of 'an atmosphere'. Something was troubling the lady of the house.

Mrs Williams eyed up her charwoman.

"Irene...," she said, "... I'm afraid there are a few questions that I shall have to ask you..."

"Fire away, Ma'am."

Mrs Williams hesitated.

"Has anyone been in this house whilst I've been away?"

"Not a soul, Ma'am."

"No children hanging around?"

"Not as I've seen. Been too cold. Most of them'll be huddling round the fire." She looked at Mrs Williams' grim face. "What's troubling you, Ma'am?"

The lady of the house was reluctant to speak.

Eventually, she said: "Whilst I've been away, one or two of my cans of food have been used..." She indicated the store cupboard.

Irene shook her head vigorously.

"I'd never touch your reserves, Ma'am! Wouldn't dream of it. If you think anyone's been doing that, you'd best be phoning Constable Bell."

Irene put both her hands on her hips. It was a gesture of defiance. She wouldn't be accused of stealing - not her! She knew Mrs Williams had a formidable supply of black market goods, but she wouldn't think of touching them. Now and again, she was given a tin of fruit cocktail for the children - or some rather fusty chocolates for her mother. But she knew her catechism. It had been drummed into her at the village school - especially her duty towards her neighbour: "To hurt nobody by word or deed; To be true and just in all my dealing; To keep my hands from picking and stealing; Not to covet nor desire other men's goods; But to learn and labour truly to get my own living, and to do my duty in that state of life, unto which it shall please God to call me." She had been well brought up, she had!

"You're not accusing me, are you Ma'am?"

Faced with such resolute determination, Mrs Williams

quickly gave way.

"No. Of course not. It's just that I can't understand what's been happening... Quite a few cans of salmon and ham have gone..." She looked again at the cupboard. ".. and almost all the vegetables. The sugar... the coffee... The tin opener was at the top of the drawer. Usually I have to hunt to find it." She looked again at Irene who still looked angry - there were patches of high colour on her cheeks.

"... And there's four bottles of wine missing from the cupboard in the dining room.'"

"Four?"

"Yes. I had a dozen on the bottom shelf. Now there's only eight!"

Irene was stunned. She knew how particular Mrs Williams was about her stocks of wine. She had announced that she would be keeping them till the light of victory dawned. Then she would celebrate.

"Well, I certainly haven't touched them!"

"You haven't heard of anyone trying to sell them in the village?"

Irene shook her head.

"There's been nothing happening in the village since you went away."

"No suspicious people hanging about?"

"No. Constable Bell would have seen them. He's often out of an evening, checking up on the blackout. Why don't you speak to him?"

There was a long silence.

Both women knew why. Mrs Williams didn't want anyone poking round her house. Once he saw what she had stocked away, he would know she was dealing with the black market. He might feel obliged to report her. Then all her goods would be confiscated. She would lose the lot.

Irene understood her silence.

"Could be awkward?" she said.

"Very."

"What about the vicar? You could speak to him."

"I'd rather he didn't know."

Mrs Williams realized that she was in a very difficult position. Perhaps she should not have said anything to Irene? She sighed.

"I just can't understand how anyone could have got in. There are only two keys. You have one; I have the other."

"I haven't lent mine to anyone." Irene brushed back a lock of dark hair. "And there's been no sign of a break-in. If there had been, I'd have seen it immediately."

Slowly, the two women worked their way round the house, checking every cupboard, looking under every bed. Irene went up into the attic, but since she very rarely visited that part of the house, she had little idea whether there had been any sign of an intruder.

"This bedcover," said Mrs Williams. "It's the wrong way round."

Irene looked at it.

"I never touched it."

Mrs Williams moved on to the bathroom.

"And the toilet paper... That's a new roll..."

Irene was silent.

"The roll was nearly finished when I left."

"I don't remember replacing it."

Mrs Williams opened the bathroom cupboard. There was only one roll left on the shelf.

"I know there were three left. Now there's only one. Someone's taken one away..."

Irene was beginning to share Mrs Williams' anxiety.

"It looks as if someone's been living here."

Mrs Williams nodded glumly.

"And what if they come back?" she asked.

Both women looked at each other.

"Get an extra lock on the door, I would..." said Irene.

"You don't think it could be children?"

Irene shook her head.

"You'd have known. They wouldn't have cleaned away all the rubbish. Left everything so neat and tidy." She looked at the new toilet roll. "Even took away the old cardboard tube!" She shook her head again. "You'll have to tell the police!"

"I'm not having that man in my house. Within half an hour, it would be all around the village."

"Someone must know..."

It was a mystery.

It would remain a mystery - rather like the body buried behind her greenhouse which might one day be discovered. Mrs Williams was frightened. How had the man got in? (She supposed it must be a man...) She changed the locks on her doors and added two extra bolts. She even put a new lock on the back gate which Jemima promptly discovered on one of her evening visits of inspection.

Erich's presence had been discovered - but nothing was said. There were no public inquiries. The matter was kept very hush-hush. Jemima was pleased that she had taken Mary's advice: "If you're going to commit a crime, you have to do it so well that no one even knows a crime has been committed." The whole plan had worked perfectly.

Fifty-Three

Having helped Erich to escape, I did not secretly rejoice. In fact, I suffered from a very bad conscience. And for a very good reason. During April 1941, the number of bombing raids over Britain increased - reaching their climax on May 10th when a large part of central London went up in flames. It seemed a miracle that St Paul's Cathedral escaped. In fact, a huge unexploded bomb buried itself under one of the western towers and, but for the incredible bravery of the bomb disposal team, it would also have been lost.

I could not help feeling that I had betrayed my country. Erich would have returned to the Luftwaffe and would be in some bomber guiding the pilot to his target. Obviously, he had to do his duty; but I wondered how he felt actually doing it. Did he think about me? About the ordinary people he had met in England? Was he as sick of war as we were? When the Luftwaffe moved to the Eastern Front and attacked Russia on June 22nd, I imagined him heading out over the Russian plains, bombing other people's homes. Perhaps he would die in Russia. His luck couldn't last for ever.

The trouble was that I couldn't talk to anyone. Couldn't tell them what I had done. I was supposed to be the local hero - the one who had captured a German airman. How differently I would be treated if they discovered that I had helped him to escape.

And why had I helped him? Was it love? The excitement of a cloak and dagger operation? Having a secret? Was I just plain wicked?

I think it must have been because I cared for Erich. I

knew that he hated being a prisoner. He was first and foremost a man of action. He had served with the Luftwaffe in Poland and Norway. As a prisoner of war, his spirit was broken.

I admired him for trying to escape; cycling two hundred kilometres; facing danger; depending on me to help him. He had come to Bidworth to find me; I couldn't let him down. I was glad to help him; to share his adventure. To help him get back to his own country - to his family. But I might also be sending him to his death.

So I had a double dose of guilt.

He might have crashed in the Channel. His own people might have shot him down. There was no news about his escape.

There was a great deal of news about Rudolf Hess - all about him flying to England in his Messerschmitt 110; how he had been shot down in Scotland. A peace mission, it was called. But there was no news about that other flight.

I imagined him dying in Crete, shot down at Maleme aerodrome - or later over Moscow. Life was cheap and radio operators were probably two a penny. By now, he was probably dead. Would he think of me as he died? But why should he think of me?

All these thoughts kept pounding through my mind - day after day. For the first time in my life, I went through the newspapers, hoping to learn about his survival before the questions began to rain down - and blame fell on me.

I longed to tell Mary - to share my secret with her. But I didn't. I thought she had suffered quite enough from my vicious behaviour. Murder might have been forgiven but 'assisting the enemy to escape' would be quite unforgivable. I knew it. And, believe me, I suffered - silently - for almost four months.

Fortunately, in early July, John received a letter from

Canada. It meant nothing to me. It came in an official brown envelope - and looked exceedingly dull and boring. Mary didn't bother to open it - but John eventually picked it up and read it.

He whistled with surprise. "This'll interest you..."

"My friends, I write to you from Canada. You will see that I have safely crossed the Atlantic. We did not see any U boats. I am now working on the land. The weather is good. I would like to thank you for your kindness when I was with you in Bidworth and when you came to see me in hospital.

Earlier this year, I tried to escape back to France, but I was caught on the airfield before I could take off. I was very sorry to be captured - but perhaps it was for the best.

For me, the war is over. I am very happy in Canada.

I have asked a friend to write this letter for me.

I have told him what to say. But his English is better than mine.

Once again, my thanks to you all - especially Jayminah. I hope to see you again when the war is over.

Good wishes,

Erich Roch."

I sat open-mouthed.

So he hadn't escaped! He hadn't died. It hadn't been his plane I had seen taking off. I had not betrayed my country.

What a relief!

I wanted to grab the letter out of John's hands - but I knew that I would get hold of it later.

"I'm glad he's safe," said Mary. "He was a good man. He deserves to survive."

John looked through the letter several times to see if there was any hidden message contained in the text. He was naturally suspicious.

"There are one or two sentences which have been censored. I can't read them. They're most effectively blacked out."

I breathed again.

There was no evidence of my treachery. Erich was alive - that was what mattered. He hadn't been shot down over the Channel. He hadn't been part of the bombing of London. He hadn't died in Russia. He would survive the war. We should meet again.

A feeling of great joy surged within me. I could not explain why. It seemed that I could now hold my head up high. I had stood by Erich in his hour of need. I had fed him - and sheltered him. But, through no cause of mine, he had been re-captured. As he had said himself: "it was all for the best."

It was perhaps as well that he did survive, because he became the father of my three children. Despite the great difference in our ages - he was fourteen years older than me -we were married for thirty-two years. And he always called me 'Jayminah'.

Two years after the war, he told me the story of what had happened after he had gone through the wire fence:

Fifty-Four

Erich ran across the grass heading for the nearest building. It was about one hundred yards away. He followed the back wall as far as it went and then ventured up its west side towards the concrete apron on which several planes were standing.

To his left, in front of the large hangar, there was an Airspeed Oxford surrounded by five or six people about to go on a night training exercise. They were laughing and joking, smoking their final cigarettes - in no hurry to get going.

To his right, there were two Ansons also facing the taxiway leading out to the runway. There was no one near them. Rather than venture out on to the apron, he returned to the back of the next building and worked his way round to the west side of the Ansons.

By the time he had done this, he noticed that the young men were climbing into their plane - and the pilot had switched on the first engine. It coughed and spluttered into life and the propellcer began to turn. Erich was pleased to note that the planes did not seem to need a starting trolley.

He peered round the corner, looking in all directions, before he made a dash for the most distant Anson. The noise of the Oxford firing up both engines drowned all other noises. Erich reached the door of the plane and ducked down beneath the wing to see if he had been noticed. There was no sign of anyone keeping watch.

He tugged at the handle and the door flew open. He climbed in and shut the door behind him. He waited in the darkness for the sound of running footsteps or the bark of a guard dog.

No. No one had seen him.

He was tremendously excited to have got this far. He was actually in an enemy plane. In a few moments, he would be sitting in the pilot's seat and, once the Oxford moved off, he would follow it out on to the runway.

He walked up the aisle to the cockpit and sat down. In front of him were all the instruments. The lay-out was unfamiliar but one set of controls was much the same as another. A joystick; levers to raise and lower the undercarriage; controls for the elevator and the flaps. An altimeter and a speedometer. There were many switches. Which one would light up the instrument panel? Which one would start the engines? In the dim light of the cockpit, he tried to get the feel of the aeroplane.

He had learnt to fly in a Bucker Jungman, which was more like a Tiger Moth - a single-engined trainer with an open cockpit. Since then, he had flown in many bigger aircraft - like the Heinkel 111 and the Junkers 86. He had also been chosen to join a Junkers 88 geschwader. If he had not been shot down, he would have been flying in them by Christmas.

Over the years, he had watched many pilots handling their controls.

The "Annie" was quite primitive by comparison. But a single mistake would expose him. He could not take off on one engine. There would be a delay in getting the second one going.

Erich watched the Oxford moving off the apron and turning right. Then it stopped. It seemed to be waiting for something. Another plane was coming in. It came in on his right and glided down in a perfect landing. The pilot of the Oxford put on his wing lights. Once the runway was clear, he would be off.

Erich had now adjusted himself to the darkness in his plane and he began to try the switches one by one. Almost the first one he touched lit up the instrument panel. Success! The controls were neatly labelled for the young pilots; but they were all in English. There were warnings which he. could understand: "Do not pull up the undercarriage whilst you are still on the ground." He smiled. It must have happened many a time. Easily done.

He found himself gaining in confidence. He could now see the switches which controlled the engines. He would start with the one on the right - the one furthest away from the buildings. He looked at the fuel gauge; it was three-quarters full. That should get him across to France.

He looked out at the Oxford. She was now revving up at the end of the runway. The other plane was on its way back to the hangars. The noise of the two planes should cover him. He pressed the switch for the right-hand engine. The propeller slowly began to turn.

In all his excitement to get going, Eric had not noticed the control tower; but the control tower had noticed him. Whilst the Oxford was slowly setting off down the runway, one of the staff noticed a dim light in the cockpit of the Anson.

He turned to his colleague.

"Is the Anson due to go out?"

"No."

"There's someone in the cockpit."

The other officer looked across at the plane."

"Yes. You're right."

They watched as the flaps rose and fell and the elevator swung from side to side.

"Strange?"

"Very."

The senior officer said: "Phone the MP and get them to

take a dekko - as quickly as possible."

They had no sooner phoned than the right-hand engine burst into life and the propeller began to turn.

"An illegal?"

"Someone's trying to pinch one of our planes!"

"Put through another call. It's urgent!"

The arrival of the newly-landed plane proved a major distraction. But the senior officer pulled open a window and took his pistol out of its holster. Whether he could hit the Anson at this distance was problematic; but he would aim to hit one of its tyres.

However, the call to the Military Police had brought a swift response. He could see a dark figure running over to the Anson.

The left-hand engine had begun to turn. In less than a minute, it would be moving on to the taxiway.

The dark figure got into the plane just as the Anson began to move. Two other dark figures were running in the same direction but they were too late.

The Anson headed for the taxiway quite quickly - but it started to veer to left and right. There was a struggle for the controls.

The senior officer hit the alarm button. The siren blasted into life. The aerodrome lights were switched on. The men playing poker beside the fire engine sprang into action.

Like everyone else, Erich had been watching the arrival of the new aeroplane. As it stopped, he pulled on the throttle to get the Anson moving. She moved off quite quickly.

Erich felt the rush of air as the door behind him opened and shut. He was so busy with his controls that he did not notice the sound of feet running through to the cockpit. But he felt the heavy hand of the military policeman descend on his neck. And a rough voice saying: "Where the fuck do you think you're going?"

Eric tried to escape from the man's clutches but he was even more determined to keep the plane moving. He pulled harder on the throttle; but the man grabbed his hair and yanked his head backwards.

"Switch off the bloody plane or I'll shoot you!"

Erich couldn't move his head. He couldn't see where he was going. The plane was now off the taxiway and rolling over the grass. A pistol was pressing against his ear.

Erich realized that he would have to stop the plane. He turned off the fuel switches and cut out the engines.

The pressure of the pistol against his right ear did not diminish.

"Put your hands up!"

The plane came to a sudden halt.

There was a crash of boots. Two men in dark jackets arrived in the cockpit.

"Have you got him?"

"Yep."

"Who is he?"

"I don't know. We haven't had time to be introduced."

Erich sat with his hands in the air. He realized that he must keep silent for as long as possible. Jemima might still be in the vicinity of the airfield. If he said anything, they might go out looking for her. Every extra minute could be precious. He must give her time to get away.

He said: "I shall come quietly."

His accent gave him away.

"He's a bloody German!"

Erich nodded.

"Have you got the handcuffs?"

"Yeh."

It was difficult to fix the handcuffs in the semi-darkness of the cockpit - even though Erich was trying to co-operate.

Once they were on, the pistol was removed from his ear.

"O.K. Fritz. Get up - but move slowly. No funny tricks."

Erich stood up and looked at his captors. They were small thick-set figures with hard faces and thin lips. They would probably enjoy beating him up. He knew what rough soldiers could do.

He moved slowly down the aisle to the door. He was conscious of the man with the pistol. It was now in the middle of his back. He emerged from the door of the plane and jumped down on to the ground.

The alarm was still blaring. The fire engine was now close to the Anson. The firemen surrounded him. Two of them were holding axes. With all the lights on, he felt very conspicuous. The pistol nudged him in the direction of the main building. He walked slowly over the tarmac.

The senior officer was waiting for him.

"What have we got here?"

"A Kraut. Trying to nick an Annie."

"Bring him through to my office."

"Yes, sir."

The full weight of defeat fell upon Erich. He would never get back to Germany. Once again he was a 'gefangener'. He would receive severe punishment. He would be sent to the slammer. He would be in solitary for at least two months. He would receive very little food. But it could be worse. They might kill him - no one would know. It would be said: "He was shot trying to escape...".

For the last week, he had been so full of hope and excitement that capture was doubly humiliating. All Jemima's efforts had been in vain. Whatever he said or did, he must protect her. He wondered where she was at that moment. He did not want to see her brought in. He did not want to involve Mary or John. They had been kind to him. They had to be protected too.

He followed the senior officer into his room. The three military police stood behind him. One had a pistol. The others now had rifles. He noticed that they also had bayonets attached.

The senior officer looked at him.

"You were trying to escape?"

"I was."

"How did you get on to the airfield?"

This was a dangerous question. He could not mention the fence. Wherever she was, Jemima would still have the wirecutters

"Through the main gate."

The senior officer raised his eyebrows.

"I had been hiding in the woods till it was dark. Once it was really dark, I crept in."

"The guards didn't stop you?"

"No."

"You speak very good English."

"I learnt it at school... sir."

The senior officer smiled in a friendly fashion. At least the man was speaking.

"And what is your name?"

"Erich Roch, sir."

"And are you a pilot in the Luftwaffe?"

"No sir, I am a wireless operator."

"But you know how to fly an aeroplane."

"Yes. But only training aircraft. I was better as a radio operator."

"Have you any means of identification?"

One of the military policemen tore open his shirt.

"I think you'll find the tag on his wrist."

The military policeman read out the number. He got it wrong. But Erich said nothing. A little confusion would do no harm.

"And when did you land in England?"

"In August, last year."

The officer looked up with some surprise.

"And have you been wandering round the country since then?"

"No, sir. When I landed I broke my shoulder. I was taken to a krancke."

"So you are a P.O.W?"

"Erich did not recognize the abbreviation.

"A prisoner of war?"

"Yes."

"And you have escaped from your camp?"

Erich nodded.

"You could be a spy."

Erich shook his head.

"You are wearing civilian clothes."

"I stole them."

"That is your story. You know that we hang spies."

The senior officer intended to inject an element of fear into the interrogation. He might get a few more useful answers to his questions.

"What is the name of your camp?"

Erich told him.

The senior officer told one of the military policemen to get on the blower and find out if that camp had lost a prisoner.

Erich relaxed.

He would get his answer soon enough.

The senior officer sounded more friendly.

"How long have you been in the Luftwaffe?"

"Since 1935, sir."

"You are quite an experienced officer?"

Erich stood up straighter.

"I have served in Spain, in Poland, in Norway and

France."

"And then your luck ran out?"

Erich nodded.

"And why did you want to escape?"

"To get back to my country..."

"To return to your squadron? Your... geschwader...?"

"Of course! I am sure you would do the same."

The senior officer nodded. He was glad the man was willing to speak. It made things so much easier. He would be able to write a full report on the incident.

He looked at Erich. He must be be a very brave and resourceful man to have escaped from his prisoner of war camp and attempt to fly home in a stolen aircraft. He had nearly succeeded in his attempt.

He said: "You have come a long way from your camp. How did you get to this airfield?"

"Zwelrad."

The senior officer did not speak German.

"A bike..."

"You cycled all that way?"

Erich nodded.

"And no one stoppped you?"

"No."

"And where is your zwelrad now?"

"It is in the woods."

Erich gestured vaguely to his left. It was hidden near the road to Bidworth - in the opposite direction. They would never find it in the dark. But when they did find it, it would provide no clues. Someone near his camp would probably have reported it stolen.

The man sounded honest. But the senior officer was still suspicious. He could not believe that he could have got all that way without being apprehended. He must have had some help.

Erich knew what he was thinking.

He did not volunteer any more information.

There was a lengthy silence in the room.

Then the military policeman rushed back in.

"There is prisoner missing, sir. But with a different identification number! It may not be him!"

He examined Erich's identity tag.

"No, it is him. They want to speak to you."

The senior officer smiled.

"Mr Roch, you will not be shot. But you will have some very serious questions to answer. I thank you for being honest with me."

He turned to the military polcemen.

"Put him in a cell. Make sure he is carefully guarded. We don't want him escaping again." He looked at Erich. "We shall hand you over to the authorities as soon as possible. I imagine they will come for you quite quickly."

Erich breathed a quiet sigh of relief.

At least they were not going to kill him - or beat him up. There would be more questioning; but nothing more would happen that night. The longer he was in the cell, the more time there would be for Jemima to get home. He was sure she would say nothing to the authorities. She would not dare to say anything to Mary or John.

But he would have to explain how he had managed to feed himself during his journey south and where he had stayed. Before he came to Bidworth, he had stolen many bottles of milk from people's doorsteps. He had broken into one or two houses and stolen bread and biscuits. He had once joined a queue at a soup kitchen. He was a bit hazy about his geography. He would not mention Bidworth.

All of a sudden, he realized that in his top pocket he had his original map - drawn on paper - with the name of the towns and villages he needed to pass through on his way south. Bidworth was on that list!

No one had searched him. But they would. And they would find the map and the list of airfields which he and his friends had put together.

Whilst he was in the senior officer's room, he could not destroy that map. Perhaps he could go to the toilet and flush it down the lavatory? It would only take a second.

The other weak part of his story was how he had entered the airfield. If anyone made an inspection of the perimeter fence, they would discover how he had broken in. They would be looking for the wirecutters. He would take them to the bike. They would not be there. Jemima had taken them. He could say that they had been stolen.

He needed to have more time to prepare his answers.

Erich was escorted to his cell. He was locked in and two soldiers were positioned outside the door. There was a barred window. And within ten minutes, he was stripped and searched. But, in that brief time, Erich had swallowed his map - piece by piece. He wished he had had some water to flush it down. But he chewed furiously to destroy the evidence. After he had been strip searched, he was given a cup of tea. That helped to destroy all evidence. There was nothing else in his pockets to interest them.

He sat back on the wooden board that would be his bed. He had not escaped - but he had survived. He had not blabbed. He had betrayed no one. He had only told them the truth. He now had time to prepare his story. He would be punished. But he could put up with any amount of suffering.

His fellow prisoners would admire his courage. But, from now on, in the eyes of the British authorities, he would be a marked man. For him, the war was most definitely over. But, at least, he had tried to escape. And, one day, he would see Jemima again - and thank her for all she had done. What a wonderful child she was!

7: The Gipsy Arrives

(Epilogue: August 1941)

Fifty-Five

Whilst I was in hospital, I was told that, back home, I had had a visitor.

"A gipsy came to see you. She knew you'd had a baby."

I smiled.

"Perhaps she'll bring us some good luck?"

John was hopeful.

"I crossed her palm with silver."

Jemima was also impressed.

"She had real gold earrings."

Perhaps I should have mentioned the gipsy woman before now.

It was not her first visit to Bidworth. Just a few days before war was declared - just before my story began - she arrived at the door.

In those days, gipsies were still fairly romantic figures, with dark brown faces, flashing eyes, red head-scarves and - as Jemima had said - real gold earrings.

This one was very true to type.

Having nothing better to do, I invited her in. She said she would like a cup of tea and offered me a reading. I asked her how much.

"A shilling," she said.

I thought the going rate was sixpence; but I didn't quibble. What was a shilling?

We sat down with our cups of tea and she looked at my hands.

"You're a clever woman," she said. "Plenty of brains. But inside... not quite so sure." She shook her head sadly as she looked at some of the lines on my palm. "There's someone in your family you're frightened of..."

I nodded.

"My uncle," I said.

"A very rich man," she said. "I see him talking. Very well dressed. White cuffs. I see him in court."

"He's a lawyer."

She sipped her tea and returned to my hands.

"Numbers," she said. "It's all numbers. Strings of numbers. I've never seen so many."

"I've been studying mathematics at university."

I'm not sure she understood what the word 'mathematics' meant. She continued to look puzzled.

"Now it's all turned to letters. Thousands of letters. Millions. But they don't mean anything. You're going to find them very frustrating..."

I looked at her blankly.

"... but they're very important. They could save your country."

I raised my eyebrows.

She looked deep into my eyes.

"If you receive an offer, you must accept. Don't hesitate. Accept. You mustn't say 'no'."

At that time, no one was offering me anything. Both John and I were in limbo. We hadn't applied for any jobs. I could understand the numbers - but not the millions of letters. I couldn't think what they could possibly be; but, clearly, the gipsy foresaw my work at Bletchley Park.

She looked at other lines on my hand.

"An unwanted child," she said. "Oh, yes. She will cause you a lot of trouble. Heartache. Worry. But she will be all right. You will not be expecting her - but she comes to you out of violence."

For the next two years, I assumed that this was a

reference to Jemima - a prediction amply fulfilled. But, eventually, I decided that she must be referring to the baby. It was perhaps as well that the gipsy woman had not been more explicit.

At the time, what I really wanted to hear about was John and whether he would return safely from Argentina, But I was determined not to give her any clues. I waited impatiently for her to mention him.

"You have a close friend?"

"Yes."

"Not your husband?"

"No."

"He is very far away."

She looked at me.

I nodded.

"He has a long journey in front of him. I see water. A lot of water."

"Will he come home safely?"

She paused - long enough to make me anxious. Very slowly, she said: "The journey is dangerous; but he should make it."

"He's in Argentina."

"He is concentrating very hard. I see him frowning. His mind is like an engine..."

"It's a chess championship," I said. "An international competition."

"That would explain it."

I looked at her hopefully.

"Do you see us getting married?"

The gipsy nodded.

"I see a marriage. It is cold. Not many guests. I see rings." Suddenly, she drew back. "Oh, that is bad! I see them being torn off your fingers!" She crossed herself. "That is terrible!" She breathed heavily - as if she was choking. "But you will get them back. And quite quickly."

At the time, I couldn't imagine what she was talking about; but it seemed that everything would turn out right.

I relaxed.

She looked up. "War is not far away. A very brutal war. It will touch you in many ways. There is violence. Bombs. Refugees. You will have the enemy in your house - here."

She touched the table. "But he is a good man. He is hurt. You will care for him." She laughed. "And he will be very important to someone close to you."

I asked: "Will we survive the war?"

"Yes," she said quietly. "But you will not live to a great age. You will have a lot of happiness. Happiness and tragedy in equal measure. And you will meet it with great courage."

"And my child?" I asked. "Will she survive?"

The gipsy smiled.

"Yes. She will live to a great age. She will be much admired. A great character. You will be very fortunate in your daughter."

I gave her an extra florin for being so forthcoming and also for telling me most of the good things I had wanted to hear. Whatever the tragedies she envisaged, so long as John came home safely, if we were married and survived the war... that was enough to be going on with.

When Jemima appeared on my doorstep so soon after the gipsy's visit, I assumed that she was the child the woman had been talking about. I was not planning to have any children of my own; so Jemima seemed to fit the bill. Once she was adopted, both John and I thought of her as our daughter.

But once I fell pregnant, I began to think that perhaps the gipsy's words would apply to my unborn child. It was for that reason that I did not seek to terminate my pregnancy when logic suggested I should.

I could not get those words out of my mind. 'Much admired...', 'a great character...', 'very fortunate...' If those words were true, it would be criminal to destroy the child's life.

As it lay in its small basket on the sitting room floor, it was difficult to know what the future held for the little soul. Dusty licked her face. Jemima made a great fuss of her. After all, she was her step-sister. One had to think about that.

When John picked her up in his arms, she seemed so tiny. I couldn't believe that he could feel any affection for her when she was another man's child. But I expect he loved her because she was mine.

I remained strangely detached. I didn't feel any sudden burst of maternal affection. I was curious. A spectator of all her twists and turns. I couldn't really associate her with me. She was a stranger - and yet she had to be fed and cared for. I felt inadequate. Motherhood was not my chosen vocation. And yet, I supposed, other people would force me into that role just as Mrs Williams had forced me to take in an unwanted evacuee.

That had worked. It had brought with it a lot of happiness and fun. Would this alien child - conceived in the violence of war, also prove an uncovenanted blessing? If the gipsy woman was to be believed, she would. But could her predictions be trusted? It would be a long time before we would know.

And now she had called at the house again. Something had told her that the child had been born. Perhaps she had more to tell me? And I had missed her.

I comforted myself with the thought that, having called twice, she would probably call again and give me another glimpse into the future. She had been right so far. But I longed to know more...

I turned to John.

"I feel like a cup of milky coffee."
He shook his head sadly.
"We've run out of milk. I'll have to go to the shop."
I laughed.
Some things never changed.